Where Wisteria

Falls

Chloe Openshaw

Dedicated to my two loves.

With a grateful heart, you can reach to the stars and beyond.

One

THE SUN BEGAN TO RISE OVER THE CUMBRIAN VILLAGE of Finchley, its delicate rays splashing in through eighty-three-year-old Elsie Lane's bedroom window. The warming sensation encouraged her weathered eye lids to open. She slipped her feet into a pair of well-worn slippers, and wrapped a floral, floor-length dressing gown round her body. She soaked her arthritic body in a scalding bath, and ate her predictable slice-and-a-half of granary toast. She poured herself a chilled tumbler of grapefruit juice, and attempted to complete the previous day's crossword. After opening all the windows to allow in the fresh, summer scents, she began the washing up. It was a standard start to what would become another extraordinary day at her lake house home, Wisteria.

A police helicopter swooped above a cocoon of blossoming trees. Its dark shadow stalked the sky before hovering over the secluded lake house nook. A storm of ripples emerged across the private lake and the waves broke the surface of the murky water. The constant drone of the engine disturbed any wildlife daring to hide below. The howl of the copter's engine also interrupted the Sunday symphony that could be heard from a nearby church. Behind the stained glass windows, the choir and accompanying congregation continued to enchant with their heavenly echoes, oblivious to the hullabaloo occurring outside.

Orchestrating the operation from her vantagepoint on land,

Police Sergeant Claire Swift pressed the button on her radio.

'Ready when you are,' she said.

She watched the search light on the vehicle's underbelly illuminate the gloomy lake cavity, along with the anchored police boat. Two search divers placed their oxygen masks over their mouths before falling backwards. Their bodies were sucked beneath the surface and disappeared in a blink. Swift's feet teetered at the edge of the lake, her impatience visible to all her superintendents.

'They're under,' she announced, raising her hand and checking her watch. 'Starting the clock.'

Let's not find a body. Not today, she thought. The bulky uniform concealed her skeleton of nerves, the same nerves that followed her to every potential crime scene. Her police training had taught her how to control the nerves, but all her years on the job had proven that the nerves would never leave. It was time to hand in your badge when the tingle of apprehension stopped rocking your boots, because it meant you no longer cared. Sergeant Claire Swift could be accused of many things, but lack of caring wasn't one of them.

The constant hum of the helicopter's rotors penetrated the shabby exterior of Elsie Lane's house, set back only a few metres from the lake, as she busied herself in the kitchen. The ageing foundations vibrated beneath her slippers whilst she carried on washing up. The cascading pressure ploughed through the core of the Victorian house like a hurricane, rattling the delicate crockery dancing on the draining board.

'What the—' she mumbled, her spectacles edging down her nose and her hand reaching out to catch a cup before it toppled over. Outside the kitchen window, caught up in the gust, a myriad of wisteria petals and garden foliage tumbled through the air, falling like a colourful summer downpour. Elsie's eyes glanced over her garden upon hearing the commotion, the chaotic view from her window causing her jaw to jitter.

An invading swarm of police officers swept over Wisteria

like a box of escaped locusts. Elsie's bow legs wavered beneath her weight, her hand moved to steady herself against the sink, preventing her slight stature from crashing to the floor.

'My God,' she mumbled. 'What in heaven's name?' Her internal organs churned at the sight of the police presence and fear stripped her of her all-natural blush, casting her a ghost. The shock caused a dart of pain to puncture her heart, stealing away a moment's breath.

There was a thud on the front door.

'Mrs Lane, are you home?' she heard Swift's familiar voice shout, followed by a barrage of banging from the door knocker. The clamour made Elsie flinch, the china cup cradled within her fingers falling to the ground, shattering to shards on the stone tiles. *She's back.* Elsie knew who was at the door without having to look. Sergeant Swift's voice sent pangs of pain to every nerve ending, causing a light-headedness to sabotage Elsie's composure.

'Mrs Lane, are you in there?' Swift shouted again, her fist now banging against the feeble, woodworm-ridden front door.

Elsie cowered behind the kitchen archway. All she was able to do was press her back against the wall for support, her dizzy head making the room swirl, as if she was trapped in the epicentre of a tornado.

'It's the police, Mrs Lane. Please open the door,' added Sergeant Swift, who was now standing on the porch with a sense of impatience, her foot unable to refrain from a constant cycle of tapping. Elsie caught sight of the officer's reflection on the front of the oven. Swift's eyes were scanning the kitchen, examining the spots where it might be possible for someone to hide themselves in the shadows. Elsie held her breath, closed her eyes and prayed not to be spotted. Swift took off her hat, her striking coral red hair falling in perfect ripples onto her shoulders.

Having been to Wisteria previously, Swift searched for clues to indicate that Elsie was home. Her distinctive olive and lemon anorak was hanging from a hook in the hallway; the smell of freshly brewed coffee was seeping through the many crevices underpinning the house, and the array of open, downstairs windows all served to give the game away.

Where are you, Mrs Lane? thought Swift.

'Stay calm,' mumbled Elsie. She wiped her shaking, arthritic hands down her pinafore, leaving behind a trail of soap bubbles, before taking a deep breath and stepping out from the safety of the kitchen. Standing in full sight of the officers, the speckles of light seeping into the house illuminated her worrisome expression. Had Elsie caught sight of herself in the mirror, she wouldn't have recognised her ghostly reflection. More wrinkles infested Elsie's face than she cared to count, each bearing testament to the hard life she had experienced.

'Hello, Mrs Lane. Can we come in?' asked Swift upon catching sight of Elsie's shadow. Skulking towards the front door, Elsie eased the net curtain aside, witnessing their concerned expressions. Their grimaces sent splinters down her spine.

'Mrs Lane, we need to speak with you,' repeated Swift in an attempt to drag Elsie's mind out of its temporary state of paralysis.

'We're searching the lake,' added the accompanying officer. Elsie's cataract eyes struggled to read the letter the officer had pressed against the glass. 'We have a warrant.' Even with the dainty, half-moon glasses perched on the end of her stunted nose, Elsie's scrambled mind couldn't decipher the blurry stream of words covering the page, nothing but flashing dots appearing before her strained eyes.

Elsie stood up straight. 'I'm not stupid. Any bloody idiot can see you're searching my lake,' she began. She realigned her glasses, gaining a better view of the officers' faces. Swift hadn't changed since the last time that Elsie had set eyes upon her. Her porcelain skin was still scattered with a splash of endearing, pale freckles. Her hair was its usual vibrant shade, and her lips were adorned with her signature, understated thin layer of cherry gloss. Swift oozed natural beauty. And, if someone were to hazard a guess at her profession, a police sergeant wouldn't be the most obvious guess.

'But what exactly, may I ask, are you searching my lake for, Sergeant Swift?' Elsie ignored the warrant and peered beyond, watching in the distance as more police careered up her driveway, cars crushing the stones beneath their wheels, skidding to an abrupt halt.

'There's been a pair of black-rimmed glasses handed in, Mrs Lane,' replied Swift, 'and they match the description you provided of your husband's. The glasses were found over at the far side of your lake.' Swift was pointing into the distance with her radio. Elsie didn't show any signs of reaction, her eyes remaining glued to the helicopter. Her heart fell to her feet. *Oh Henry, where are you?*

'You must stay inside, Mrs Lane. We'll come to speak with you once the search is complete,' concluded Swift. The two officers walked away and the police officer spoke into her radio. 'The house is locked down. We're good to go.' She placed her hat back on, scooping her hair effortlessly into a neat bun beneath, and took up a strategic position on the front lawn.

'Bale, Roper and Carter, take your teams and perform a search of the surrounding woods whilst we're here,' she instructed. 'Look for anything that's been disturbed or abandoned, no matter how insignificant. I want you to pick up anything, *anything,* which you think appears out of place. I don't know how long we've got, or when we'll be able to come back, so let's crack on. Is that understood?' Swift's team on the ground didn't need clarification. They knew the score, and they knew what Swift was after. New evidence.

Wisteria was so called because, during the late spring and early summer months, the exterior of the house became decorated with crawling wisteria trees, the delicate branches twisting around drainpipes and across windowsills, providing the house with a second skin. Down by the lake, hidden amongst decade-old trees and shrubbery, numerous garden arches also displayed the same crawling wisteria, the lake itself often hidden by a scattering of summer lilac leaves.

Nestled on a palatial piece of land, the house was settled on the outskirts of a village called Finchley, in Cumbria. Acres and acres of private woods acted as a shield for the lake house, and, with no public footpaths intersecting the area, it remained guarded from onlookers. Much of the land at Wisteria hadn't been disturbed for decades; not even Elsie and her family had ventured much further than the woods that hugged the immediate perimeter of lake. Wisteria was a nature lover's dream, with acres of unspoiled woodlands and an array of nesting wildlife for company, the site was beautiful and, despite many favourable financial offers having been made in the past, it was not for sale.

Swift waited for her radio to signal, watching her team disperse quicker than ants. The homemade porridge decorated with a healthy dollop of marmalade that she'd eaten for breakfast lay heavy, a barrage of nerves infesting her stomach. Being back at Wisteria stirred Swift's buried emotions. Spine-tingling chills circulated through to her core, and, despite her calm façade, she felt terrified. Given the nugget of evidence obtained, and subsequent means of entry, Swift had pounced on Wisteria in order to search for pensioner Henry Lane, who had been reported missing by a concerned family member. The Lane family had a notoriously complicated history and the disappearance of Henry was not the only occurrence to plague the name. Swift found her mind drifting towards the other missing Lane, the granddaughter, Lucy, the missing person Swift had long since craved to find.

Lucy Catherine Lane had vanished from Wisteria without trace six years previous. Her grandparents had been looking after her that day, and yet they'd both been unable to explain what had happened to their four-year-old granddaughter. It appeared that the little girl had simply vanished into thin air. But Swift didn't believe in disappearing acts, magic or illusions. She believed in facts, and evidence.

Was today set to be the day that Claire Swift would solve one of the few unsolved cases that'd haunted her impressive career? The missing person case of Lucy Lane, an identical twin. If today, June 3rd, 1988, *was* to be the day, then Swift wasn't prepared.

She needed time to brace herself for a breakthrough on Lucy's case, because Lucy wasn't just another missing person. Lucy was someone Claire had been searching for six years. Lucy was a girl that Claire would never be able to forget, an unforgettable face. Lucy was the girl that gave Claire endless nightmares and haunted her thoughts on sleepless nights. Lucy was the little girl that, no matter where Claire went, she was always searching for her familiar face. Lucy was the missing girl that Claire was responsible for finding and had, thus far, failed to do so.

The pair of glasses that had been handed in to the police weren't really enough to warrant a full-scale search of the lake. Swift knew that, and so did those around her, though nobody dared challenge her decision. And, had Elsie been physically able to inspect the warrant in detail, then perhaps she would have identified the underhand tactics. But Swift chanced her arm, and happened to strike it lucky. She had come to know Elsie over the years, and she knew that the elderly lady's eyesight was failing, the mucky, yellow fog created by her cataract a real giveaway. Swift took every opportunity she could get to gain entry to the elusive lake house grounds at Wisteria. Today's ambush was an opportunity not to be missed.

Elsie's hand released the curtain and her back slumped against the door, her lungs filling with oxygen in an attempt to banish the threatening dam of tears building behind her eyes.

'Bloody busybodies,' she muttered whilst walking back into the kitchen. 'Rotten sods,' she snapped, her shaking hand begrudgingly grabbing the brush before sweeping up the broken china that lay strewn across the floor. She paused at the kitchen window and watched Swift's every move like a sniper. If there was to be any breaking news, then Swift would be the first to know.

Elsie looked out across her lake. *They're not going to find Henry down there, are they?* she thought, biting her bottom lip, whilst additional frown lines scattered her weathered face like creases in linen. She told herself that, had Henry been in the lake, she'd have heard the splash, or witnessed his discarded clothes. But what if he'd fallen in the lake during the night, when she was in a deep sleep? What if he'd fallen in, fully clothed, leaving behind no signs of entry? And what if he hadn't fallen in at all, but jumped? The more Elsie pondered, the harder she bit her lip, a form of subconscious self-punishment. Elsie admired her wedding ring. In her mind, she knew she should have kept a closer eye on her husband, that was her role, after all. She should have locked the doors and hidden the keys so he couldn't easily wander off without her. *This is all my fault.*

Sergeant Swift remained in situ on the bank, her right foot tapping. She methodically scanned the lake, trying to see that missing clue, the missing piece to the puzzle. Her instincts told her that today, June 3rd, 1988, was going to be the day that she was destined to make a breakthrough and uncover something substantial at Wisteria. But Swift didn't know what that *something* would be. She just prayed that it wouldn't be a child's body.

Two

Upstairs, Mary Elizabeth Lane heard the clatter of smashing china, but it was the sight of something darting past her window that caused her to jump. She climbed up onto her toybox and peered out from one of the many windows overlooking the lake from her snug attic hideaway. The officers who stood below continued to talk, their voices travelling up through her window, and she caught sight of their unmistakable uniforms.

They're here again.

Her gaze diverted, catching sight of the helicopter above, her eyes following its repetitive circle. Fear flooded Mary's body, making her stomach queasy. She stretched to open her bedroom window wider, leaning out and catching snippets of the conversation below. The deafening sound of the helicopter flooded into her ears. Her hair swirled, the wind ripping through her auburn ribbons. Her eyes squinted when leaves and dust spun up in a whirlwind, threatening an ambush.

Jumping down from the toybox, Mary grabbed a tissue. Whenever the police visited, it usually resulted in her needing a tissue; experience had taught her as much. She covered her ears with her hands, regaining her position in front of the window. Her eyes welled, tracing the repetitive flightpath, additional tears trickling down her cheeks.

'Listen up, everyone,' she heard a woman's voice call out from the garden below. 'We're not leaving until we are *confident,* and I mean *confident,* that every inch of this entire lake has been combed. We don't want to be coming back again.' Silencing the police officer's words, Mary closed her bedroom window with a bang and snaked her way through the internal intricacies of her grandma's house.

She paused at the bottom of the stairs.

'What they looking for *this* time, Grandma?' she asked, looking through the archway to the kitchen where her grandma was sitting at the table. 'Are they—' She paused, taking in a deep breath. 'Are they looking for Lucy or Grandad?' Her eyes dropped to the floor, not really wanting to hear her grandmother's reply, or witness any kind of tell-tale look that may have automatically appeared on Elsie's face. A moment of silence followed before Elsie dared to speak.

'They're looking for Grandad, Mary,' she announced whilst picking up a tattered copy of the *Radio Times* that was resting on the table, her fingers flicking through the pages in an attempt to conceal her shaking hands. 'But they're wasting everyone's time.' Mary walked into the kitchen, a look of despair spreading across her face.

'Somebody took a pair of glasses that they found at the lake and handed them in to the police,' said Elsie. 'Now they think that they belong to your grandad – which, of course, they *will* do because, as both you and I know, Mary, Grandad must've lost *hundreds* of pairs of glasses over the years whilst he's been out there walking round the lake.' Her arthritic fingers struggled to turn the magazine pages. 'Wisteria is a cemetery for lost spectacles,' she added, casting aside the magazine and plunging her trembling hands into her pinafore pocket. 'And all your missing bouncy balls.'

Mary crossed her arms with conviction.

'I'm *ten* now, Grandma. You don't need to treat me like a baby. I know Grandad is missing. And I know that Lucy is still missing. And I haven't played with bouncy balls for *years*.' Mary cast her gaze out past the kitchen net curtains. 'Should I go out and tell them?' she asked, her eyes watching the policemen dispersing round the perimeter of the lake, their black jackets dotting the greenery like sprinkles of poppyseed. 'Should I go and tell them that they *are* Grandad's glasses, but that he's definitely not at home because we've already looked everywhere?' She wiped away a stray tear that'd escaped, recalling how she'd already helped her parents search the entire house.

'No, Mary,' said Elsie. 'The police *always* think they know best, and they'll insist on looking anyway, so let's leave them be. Your mum and dad will be here soon, so shall we make a fresh batch of blackberry jam? I bet they'll like some for their morning toast tomorrow.' She stood and walked over to the window. She cast her stare out over the myriad of lilac wisteria trees that surrounded her lake, discreetly looking over the top of her glasses, the helicopter swirling in the air like an eagle ready to pounce on its prey.

'Okay, Grandma,' Mary replied with an exaggerated sigh. 'I guess the only place we didn't look for Grandad was *in* the lake,' she continued, her fingers fiddling to turn on the radio, the music attempting to drown out the noise. 'What you doing, Grandma?' she asked with a puzzled expression, watching Elsie rummage through all the cupboards.

'I just need to find the big pan. Have you seen it?'

'It'll be in the cupboard under the sink, Grandma.'

Elsie became flustered. She knew where it'd be. She told herself that, given a few more seconds, she would have remembered where the pan was kept.

'Silly me, of course it will,' she replied, attempting a light-hearted, *everything is okay* kind of laugh. 'Right, let's make some jam,' she said whilst wrapping an oversized pinafore around Mary's waist and tumbling a pile of plump blackberries into a saucepan.

'Just a silly mistake, Elsie, you're not losing your marbles,' she mumbled beneath her breath so that Mary couldn't hear. It wasn't unusual for Elsie to talk to herself; it had become a habit over the years.

Standing on a stool, Mary stirred the concoction, pretending to concentrate, but really her eyes remained focused on the search. She watched the boat bobbing about on the water, waiting for the divers to emerge from the abyss. She traced the direction as the officers on land dispersed and disappeared into the woods, their black uniforms soon camouflaged by the thick foliage.

'Will they have a look for Lucy again whilst they're searching the woods, Grandma?' Elsie froze upon hearing the question, her brain attempting to find an appropriate string of words to formulate a suitable reply.

Where are you, Lucy? Come home. I miss you.

Despite the fact that Mary's identical twin sister had been missing for six years, Mary still spoke to her sister. She would sometimes pretend that Lucy was sitting right next to her, and talk to her like she'd never vanished. She would sometimes even pretend to hold her hand, and imagined what it would feel like to be able to see her sister again.

Elsie remained silent and Mary continued to wait for a reply, and the longer it took to come, the more she realised she already knew the answer. Elsie put her arm around her granddaughter and pressing her warm lips against her cheek before whispering: 'I don't know, Mary.' Unlike Mary, Elsie couldn't watch what was going on outside anymore, and so busied herself and switched on the kettle.

The surface of the lake exploded as a diver emerged, causing Mary to gasp. She pressed her hand over her mouth.

She waited and watched the water for what felt like a lifetime.

'We've got something,' she heard a voice bellow, a head bobbing above the water, the diver removing his mask and giving a thumb's up signal to Sergeant Swift. Mary saw the radio fall from her hand.

Swift's frame wavered despite the lack of wind, and she took in a deep, invisible breath to steady herself. All the surrounding officers froze in unison; it was like they were playing a game of musical statues, and the music had paused. For a moment, the world surrounding Wisteria stopped. Every single person that was congregated around the lake became frozen in time. No voices could be heard. Nobody moved or flinched. Nobody dared to speak. And Sergeant Swift's foot stopped tapping.

In the diver's hand was a black bag.

Mary stopped stirring the jam. 'I'm scared,' she said, the unattended, molten liquid spilling over the cooker and on to the floor. Mary's eyes refused to blink, despite the intense stinging. 'What is it?' she mouthed again, her eyes watching the haul being pulled out of the lake.

Her mind frantically processed all the mean-spirited jibes she'd seen in the papers about her grandparents. 'The Lake House Horrors', one paper had reported a few days after Lucy had disappeared. 'Guilty Grandparents', reported the *Finchley Observer*. Mary had also overheard a conversation between two ladies in a supermarket after Lucy had vanished, and she'd never forgotten the exact string of words. *'They're guilty. They know what happened to their granddaughter, they just don't want to confess.'*

'There's more,' Mary heard another officer announce through a speaker, his words travelling in through the open kitchen window, breaking the silence. A second search diver's head bobbed up, followed by another bin liner. Mary's heart galloped whilst she watched the objects being pulled into the waiting dinghy.

Elsie hadn't heard the announcement above the radio, her back now facing the window, her mind preoccupied with finding suitable jam jars.

Mary failed to notice the jam pouring down the side of the pan, steam erupting from what now resembled a cauldron.

'Grandma, have *you* hidden anything in the lake?' Mary asked. Elsie's body remained concealed behind a wall cupboard door, her mouth mumbling in frustration at something or other. Mary dropped her wooden spoon, taking hold of her grandad's binoculars that he kept in the cupboard beneath the kitchen sink, placing them against her eyes.

'What is it?' she whispered, standing back on her stool and scanning the boat. Officers inspected the contents, their hands rummaging inside the sodden black bags. One of the divers took hold of a skull, cradling it delicately in the palm of his hands, before raising it from the boat's cavity, ready for Swift and the other officers to witness.

Lucy? Grandad?

A gasp exploded from Mary's body. She took a silent, deep swallow, forcing her saliva past the lump lodged in her throat. Her frame stiffened at the sight of the skull. Tears tumbled down her pale face and her body was held hostage, paralysed in a state of shock.

It can't be them. Please don't let it be them. Lucy? Grandad? I'm scared, where are you?

Mary could barely see past the storm of tears mounting in her eyes. She was grateful for the tears; at least they obscured the image of the skull. She felt scared to look over her shoulder, fearful of her grandma. Instead, she wanted to open the kitchen window and jump.

The floor creaked. Elsie was approaching from behind.

'Grandma, I'm scared,' said Mary, turning slowly and witnessing Elsie's approach.

'How are we doing over here?' asked Elsie with a whimsical tone, totally unaware of the emotional turmoil her granddaughter was suffering. Mary jumped when Elsie touched her shoulders, causing her to drop the binoculars.

'Oh, my goodness, what's happened?' asked Elsie with a shriek, finally noticing the sea of jam that now covered the floor. 'It's everywhere!' Elsie's temper erupted. 'I leave you for one minute, and look what's happened!'. Elsie frantically grabbed the steaming pan from the stove and tossed it into the sink of water, spatters of blackberry juice dotting her face like poisoned freckles, a whoosh of steam exploding when hot met cold.

'Where are the sponges?' she barked, opening every cupboard

in an attempt to uncover the absent cleaning aids. Mary's platform wobbled, her shaking body dislodging the stool upon sight of the divers pulling out more bags. Her eyes widened upon sight of another, smaller skull. She watched the policeman working to clean away debris from the open jaw, removing weeds and dirt. Mary felt a wave of nausea flood her stomach, and all she could see was her sister.

Her footing became unsteady. She tumbled to the floor upon sight of the blackened eye sockets, her head banging against the tiles.

'They've found something,' she announced, looking round for her grandma, pressing her head to check if it was bleeding.

'Mary! Are you alright?' Elsie rushed over upon hearing the crash to find her granddaughter crumpled in a heap, lying motionless on the floor. Fear infested every bone in Mary's body, the rumours she'd heard about her grandparents rushing through her mind.

Please don't hurt me, thought Mary upon seeing the anger on her Grandma's face, her hands covering her head.

'They've found something in the lake,' she said, her eyes daring to look up at Elsie. 'Skulls. Two skulls.' Mary pushed herself into a corner, further away from her grandma. 'It's Grandad and Lucy, isn't it? The things people have said are right, aren't they?' Mary caught sight of a knife that'd fallen on the floor, her hand reaching to grab it.

'What?' replied Elsie. Elsie took hold of the binoculars and peered out over the lake. 'Oh, Mary, that's not Grandad or Lucy. It'll be the dogs,' she added. Elsie bent down and helped Mary to her feet, hugging her granddaughter whilst their bodies swayed in unison. 'All the pets we've ever had are buried in that lake. Grandad thought they'd be happier there,' she continued, parting their bodies so that she could wipe her granddaughter's tears.

'They didn't look like animal skulls,' questioned Mary, her stiffened body trying to arch away from Elsie.

'From a distance, an animal skull probably looks just like

any other skull – a bit scary,' Elsie began, bending down to look Mary in the eyes. 'I'll show you some pictures of animal skulls, and then some of human ones, and then you'll be able to see the difference. I think there's a book in the basement, an encyclopaedia that will show pictures.'

Mary thought for a moment, watching Elsie's expression. 'You promise it's just dogs, Grandma?'

'I promise they are,' said Elsie. 'I love you so much, Mary. Please, never believe those lies that people say. They don't know me, Mary. And they don't know your grandad. They're just spiteful rumours. I'd never hurt you, and I never hurt Lucy,' She pulled her granddaughter closer to her chest. Mary released the breath that'd been held captive within her lungs. She loved her grandparents so much, and wanted more than anything for all the mean-spirited rumours to be untrue. Mary had never given up on the hope that her sister would be found, proving to the world that her grandparents were innocent.

'Love you too, Grandma,' she said, reciprocating the affectionate embrace. 'I was scared. I saw the skulls and thought they'd found Grandad and Lucy in the lake. I didn't know what to do. I didn't know what to think.'

'Oh, Mary. I don't know where Lucy and Grandad are, but I *do* know that they're not in the lake.' Elsie's tears were becoming lodged in the crevices of her face. 'I'm sure they'll both be home soon; we just have to keep being patient.' She kissed Mary's hand, allowing her lips to linger. 'Now, let's get some tea ready, just in case they both come back tonight. What do you think we should have?' Elsie continued to ignore the swarm of activity outside.

'A plate piled with chips and tomato ketchup. That's my favourite, Grandma,' Mary replied, wiping her eyes before glancing back out of the window. 'I think they've finished,' she announced, watching the helicopter zoom off into the distance, taking with it the constant hum that continued to ring in her ears long after its departure.

'Good. Maybe *now* they'll focus their efforts elsewhere,'

muttered Elsie, shrugging her shoulders. A knock at the front door made Mary and Elsie both jump, their heads turning in unison.

'Mrs Lane, we've finished,' shouted Sergeant Swift through the front door. Elsie opened it ajar. 'We found these at the bottom of the lake, thought we should ask before returning them,' added Swift, holding out a white box. 'I'm very sorry we disturbed the remains. I do hope you understand that we had no choice.' Swift eased the door further ajar and placed the box on the floor next to Elsie's feet. Elsie's foot shifted the box aside so that she could slam the door.

'There will be no need for you to return my pets to their grave, thank you, Sergeant Swift. Maybe you'll use your time more effectively now, and go out and find my husband and granddaughter.' Elsie was shouting now. 'And don't *dare* return to Wisteria until you've done so, no matter what accusations those lying bastards feed to you,' she concluded, turning to walk away.

Mary remained at the door, her hands draped by her side. She needed someone to hold her hand, and tell her that everything would be alright. The police had just searched the lake for her grandad, and that wasn't normal in her eyes. It wasn't normal in anyone's eyes. When nobody came to her aid, she wanted to open the front door and run away. She didn't know where she would run to, and she didn't care. All she knew was that she wanted to escape from everyone and everything that made her sad. And being back at Wisteria for the summer holidays always made her unhappy.

She looked through the glass pane of the door and watched the police beginning to disappear, leaving Wisteria to wallow. She glanced over at the box beneath the coat stand, her hand hovering on the door handle before releasing. She walked over and slumped her body beside the box.

I'm glad you weren't in the lake, Lucy, but where are you? Mary's eyes looked around the deserted hallway searching for her sister. Even though Mary had already looked under the hallway table in her grandparents' house a hundred times, she looked again, just in case. Sometimes, she would move her hand through an empty space, thinking that Lucy might still be there, but invisible. Lucy wasn't hiding under the hallway table, but Mary still spoke to her like she was standing right next to her.

Do you know where Grandad is, Lucy? He's missing, too. Everyone's worried, just like they're still worried about you. I'm lonely without you, Lucy. Come home. Then we could run away together.

A rattling noise came from within the kitchen.

'Mary, do you know where my glasses are?' bellowed Elsie.

'Look in your pinny, Grandma,' Mary shouted. She looked up and watched to see if her grandma appeared.

'Got them,' replied Elsie.

'Grandma gets muddled, Lucy. Not as much as Grandad, but it happens,' said Mary in a soft voice, closing her eyes and picturing her sister. 'Mum and Dad are always too drunk to notice stuff like that, and I'm scared to tell them. I think they'd take Grandma away if they thought she's getting like Grandad, she wouldn't be able to look after herself here.' She pressed her head into her knees, suppressing the thought. 'Grandma is all I have left.'

Mary opened her eyes, hoping to see her sister. 'Please come home, Lucy.'

The sound of a car travelling up the drive made Mary jump, the front door swinging open before she could move.

'Well, we tried.' Mary recognised her dad's voice. 'We've searched everywhere we could bloody well think of, but we can't find him anywhere. He could be sodding miles away by now.' He and his wife, Martha, walked in through the front door. Hank threw his keys on the side table, failing to notice Mary huddled beneath the thick collection of coats, the top half of her body camouflaged.

'We went to the hospitals and showed his photo to anyone who bothered looking, but still nothing,' added Martha, flinging her coat over the end of the banister before messing with her hair in front of the mirror, admiring her windswept waves. She stumbled through to the kitchen, the smell of alcohol lingering in her wake.

'What's been going on?' asked Hank, taking stock of the kitchen in disarray. Elsie failed to turn around.

'The police searched the lake for your dad, but obviously they didn't find him, and now they've left,' she replied in a matter-of-fact tone.

'What?' snapped Hank.

'Oh. You meant in here?' said Elsie, when she saw all the spilt jam. 'We've been making a fresh batch of jam and had a little accident, that's why there's so much mess.'

'I can't believe they've searched here *again*,' shouted Hank, his fist leaving an indentation in the plasterboard wall. 'This is all your bloody fault. None of this would've ever happened had you just looked after him like you were supposed to do.' Hank stormed out of the room, barging past Martha who was standing in the archway to the kitchen. Hank's feet banged against the stairs, like a stampede was passing.

A few moments of silence passed before Mary dared to speak, appearing from beneath the coats, her hand still placed over the box of skulls and animal skeletons.

'Can we get a dog, Mum?'

Martha jumped.

'Mary, you gave me a fright! I didn't see you down there. Whatever are you doing?' Martha replied, tripping over her feet and falling haphazardly. Sitting on the bottom of the stairs, she struggled with her shoes to get them off her feet, before flinging one across the floor towards Mary.

'You said *ages* ago that we could, but whenever I ask, you say it's not a good time,' added Mary. 'So, what do you think?'

'What do I think about what, Mary?' huffed Martha, her balance wavering.

'About getting a dog? It could be my new friend to play with.'

'It's not the right time, Mary. How many times do I have to

say it?' Martha tossed her other shoe towards the coat rack. 'Put them away for me.' She stumbled to her feet and disappeared into the lounge, leaving Mary alone in the hallway.

The house succumbed to silence, and Mary hated nothing more than silence. Silence scared her, even more than the shouting. It was the apprehension of what was to come that felt so terrifying. At least if people were shouting you didn't have to dread anything, because it was already happening.

She ran upstairs to her bedroom. Scurrying beneath her bed, she grabbed a box that had been pushed right to the back, where it couldn't easily be seen. She pulled it out and opened the lid, taking out one of her favourite cuddly toys. It was a bear that she'd had as a baby called Mr Twitch. Mary thought that she was a bit too old now to be playing with such a baby toy, but holding ragged Mr Twitch made her feel safe, and comforted. She would talk to Mr Twitch when she felt lonely, and took hold of it once her parents had tucked her in at night. In Mary's eyes, she only played with the bear when nobody was looking, so it didn't really matter if it was a baby toy or not. And nobody would ever find out about her secret box because she always made sure that it was hidden away. For years, her parents had remained unawares of Mary's secret box, and its contents.

Along with Mr Twitch, Mary had also placed one of her sister's old cuddly toys in the box too. It hadn't been Lucy's favourite, that one had gone missing years ago and was a doll called Penelope Pickles. But the soft toy Mary had chosen to hide came a close second, and Lucy had played with it regularly. Mary had taken Lucy's cuddly toy off her sister's bed years ago, hiding it away. She prayed that her mum wouldn't notice the missing item, knowing that Martha would be furious that she had touched something belonging to Lucy. Luckily, the missing item went unnoticed.

Mary also had a photo of her and Lucy sat on the sofa together back at home. The picture had finger prints on the front, and the corners were a bit tatty from being held with such frequency, but to Mary, those things didn't matter. She would take a look at the photo on those days that she felt fearful that she was forgetting what Lucy looked like. Really, all Mary needed to do was look in the mirror, and she would see Lucy staring back.

'Since Lucy went missing, all they do is fight, and ignore me. It's like I'm not even here. Like I don't exist,' she said, talking to Mr Twitch. Mary shrugged her shoulders, shaking away her hidden sadness, the truthful words leaving scars in her mouth. 'All they care about is Lucy, drinking, and now finding Grandad.' She pressed the bear to her face.

'I wish I would go missing too, then they might notice me again,' she whispered before walking over towards her window. Her long strands of tatty hair lay strewn across her face, her vision blurred, tears smearing her gawky glasses. But Mary wasn't alone. She was being watched.

With an overwhelming sense of relief now that the police had vacated the area, a resident close to Wisteria released the breath they'd been holding. Having peered through the net curtains overlooking the main road, double checking every last officer had gone, the neighbour resumed their stakeout position. Through the lens of a telescope, a pair of wide-open eyes watched the attic windows of the lake house like a sniper. The person admired Mary as she stood with Mr Twitch alone at her bedroom window, their shaking fingers working to focus the lens and get a better view. He was able to capture the way that Mary's tears fell from her cheeks, the way her hair draped from her shoulders, plus the look of despair that was scattered across her face. The eyes behind the lens didn't blink, his lips mouthing the words *not long now, Mary.*

Three

PERRY GOLIFER SAT HUDDLED IN THE CORNER OF THE Black Friar. Beneath the dim lighting of the quaint pub, his carefully-crafted disguise worked to conceal his appearance. He wore an oversized pair of fake, gold-rimmed glasses, a black office suit and a stuck-on moustache. He had taken the time to dye his brown hair a shade of strawberry blond, the side parting held in place by gel. His completed ensemble did a good job of masking his well-known features – so far, nobody had recognised him. The *Guardian* newspaper resting on the table also acted as a prop, as did the untouched glass of warm, flat beer. The social consumption of alcohol was not the driving force behind Perry Golifer's visit to his local watering hole, and every bad bone in his body braced itself in anticipation for what was to come.

The door opened with a creak.

A gust of cool, crisp air blasted its way through the intimate bar, the pages of Perry's newspaper fluttering with the breeze. He immediately looked towards the source of the disturbance. *Is this them?* Working hard not to alter his external, calm demeanour, Perry maintained his poker-like expression, his eyes watching above his glasses. Hank and Martha Lane entered, making their way to the bar.

I knew they'd come.

A smug sense of satisfaction became visible beneath his disguise. He dipped his head the second Martha glanced round, her eyes searching for a suitable, vacant table.

'What can I get you?' Perry heard the landlord ask Hank. The handful of other patrons paused their monotone conversations, causing an awkward silence to linger over the bar.

'A large glass of wine, a double shot of tequila, and a bottle of beer, please,' replied Hank, rooting in his pocket for his wallet.

'You're not really going to serve them are you, Dougie?' Perry heard the man who was seated at the far end of the bar ask the landlord. 'Thought this place prided itself on keeping good company.' The other customers jumped on the bandwagon, adding muffled noises of support in the periphery.

'This is my pub, Alf,' replied Dougie. 'As always, I'll choose who to serve.'

Alf shook his head, his disappointment drowning amid a glut of beer. Alf looked like part of the furniture; his backside perched on a tall bar stool, a cigarette hanging out of his mouth.

'You're the only one in this town that'll give them the time of day after what they did.'

'And what have we done, exactly?' snapped Hank.

'Leave it. It's not worth it,' whispered Martha, cowering behind her husband. Martha wanted to reach behind the bar, grab her drink, and take it away to savour elsewhere. The insults weren't her problem. The bickering that was delaying her from having a drink was the problem.

'If you have something else to say, then come on, out with it,' challenged Hank, the lunchtime beers he had enjoyed now fuelling his bad temper. He slammed his money on the bar.

'There'll be no fighting in here, gentlemen. If you can't act civil, I'll ask you both to leave,' intervened Dougie, at which point both men fell into silence.

Perry observed the tension at the bar from afar, his erratic heartbeat intensifying the moment Martha and Hank sat at the table right next to him. Martha's familiar perfume drifted amongst the ribbons of yellow smoke. Perry attempted to steady his nerves, inhaling deeply.

Martha grabbed the glass the moment Hank's hand set it down on the table.

'God, I really need this,' she said to Hank. The liquid trickled down her throat, satisfying her underlying craving that, no matter how much she drank, was never quenched.

With his gaze fixed on Martha, out of the corner of his eye Perry watched the contents of her glass disappear down her throat. He turned the page of his newspaper and slipped his hand inside his jacket pocket, pulling out a ready-sharpened pencil.

'They don't deserve you' were the words he scribbled, right below a tattered photo of Mary. He turned the page, covering his inscription just before Hank brushed past his table.

'I knew it'd kick off, but I don't care. It's their problem, not ours,' said Hank, his tumbler of tequila soon draining.

'But they're all watching us, I know they are. I can feel them,' replied Martha, trying to avoid making eye contact with anybody. 'Should we just go?'

Perry's internal anger suddenly appeared on his face, his crimson cheeks flushing beneath his glasses. *I'll get angry if you leave now.*

'Unless you want to carry on hiding empty bottles in our suitcase,' replied Hank, 'or in the boot of the car, or in the lake, or anywhere else that we can think of, I suggest we stay.'

'You make us sound like we're some sort of bloody alcoholics,' Martha said bitterly. 'There's nothing wrong with us liking a drink during what's meant to be our summer holiday. After what we've been through, it's hardly a bloody surprise I need a stiff drink or two.'

Hank raised his eyes at Martha's empty glass before standing. 'I don't have a problem, but you do. You just won't admit it.'

Perry watched Hank make his way back to the bar, ordering a tequila refill and a bottle of red wine. He raised his head, turning to his left. *Just as I remember.* His extended stare threatened to uncover his identity the longer he dared to scrutinise every inch of Martha's dishevelled appearance. His excitement and frustration were becoming visible, his shaking hands hiding beneath the table. *You don't deserve to have another daughter. They don't deserve you, Mary.*

'More drinks,' announced Hank, putting another round on the table, forcing Perry to turn away.

'If we have these, we won't get back in time to say goodnight before she goes to bed,' replied Martha, staring at the bottle of wine, her maternal instincts at war with the deep-rooted craving and the need she felt to unscrew the cap and drink. 'And we did promise Mary we wouldn't be late.' Upon hearing the name Mary, Perry's pupils widened. *She's all alone. And, where are they? Getting drunk in the pub.* Perry's mounting anger caused his teeth to grind.

'We'll put her to bed tomorrow,' replied Hank, taking hold of his drink, savouring his third glass of liquor like he hadn't drunk a drop in days. 'In any case, she spends so much time in her room listening to music that I bet she won't even notice if we're not back in time to say goodnight.'

Perry fumbled with the pencil in his hand, writing on his newspaper again. This time the lead scrawled. 'Stupid Bastard' and 'You'll Pay'.

'She always craves more attention when the anniversary of Lucy's disappearance is approaching, we know she does,' said Martha. 'She's already asked me what will happen at Crest Cove.'

Perry's heartbeat pounded when her heard the name Lucy. He continued to scribe in the newspaper, 'Crest Cove. Confirmed.'

'Those guys are talking shit about us again. I just heard my name, I'm sure I did,' Perry heard Hank mumble. The men at the bar were now staring across the room, one speaking so that everyone could hear. Dougie the landlord had nipped down to the cellar to change a barrel.

'Police were at the lake again today. I heard the copter circling,' began Alf, after downing another bottle of Dutch courage. 'For hours it was up there. They've got a bloody nerve turning up in here like there's nothing wrong. Arrest the lot of them and question them until they can do nothing but blurt out the truth.

Then they'll be begging for forgiveness.' Alf took his final swig, emptying his bottle. 'Then we'll see who wants to share a beer with them at the bar.'

Perry watched Hank necking the remainder of his drink before slamming his empty glass down on the table.

'I've had enough of this bullshit.' Hank stumbled towards the bar, his feet unable to navigate a straight line. 'Got something to say, then say it to my face!' Perry looked on from his corner nook, witnessing as Hank took a stand right in front of Alf's face.

'I said, you've a bloody nerve turning up here, acting like nothing's wrong,' Alf repeated, casually puffing on his cigarette. 'You've already lost one daughter by leaving her with those crazy bastards you call parents, and now you're doing it again. You should be at home, with your daughter, not coming in here where you're not wanted.' Alf slammed his own bottle on the bar. 'Or have you forgotten your daughter is missing?'

Hank took a prolonged, deep breath. Rage built behind his temples, waiting in the wings to explode. 'It's no fuckin' business of yours what I do, or where I go,' he spat. 'So why don't you keep your mouth shut, eh?' He turned to walk away, shaking his head.

'Coward,' muttered Alf beneath his breath.

'What did you say?' Hank paused, turning his head.

'You heard me. You're nothing but a bloody coward. You don't have the balls to admit that your daughter wouldn't have gone missing had you taken better care of her.'

Hank paced towards where Alf was sitting, stopping close enough to smell his stagnant breath.

Unperturbed, Alf continued. 'This charade you display each summer is growing tired. If you really cared for Lucy, you wouldn't be in here, drinking like a pathetic pisshead. You'd be out there still looking for her, or sat at home waiting for the phone to ring. You should be going over every detail, no matter how many times you've done it before, just in case you missed something. If you were innocent, you wouldn't stop; you'd never stop looking. That's what any other innocent parent would do. They should take your Mary into care, where at least she'd be safe—'

In one swift swipe, Hank grabbed Alf by the throat, lifting him off his stool and pinning him against the wall.

'Don't *ever* mention either of my daughters' names again.' Hank pressed tighter until his hands ached. Alf's face was filling with blood, turning plum. 'Or else I'll ram my fist so far down your throat that I'll be able to rip out every inch of your intestines. Do… you… understand?'

Alf forced his head to move up and down, and the forced nod was enough for Hank to release from his strangulating grip. Alf's body crumbled to the floor, his hands clutching his throat as he gulped in the stagnant, smoke-filled pub air. Rushing to his aid, other locals assisted Alf back to his feet, the outline of Hank's wedding ring had left its mark on the man's neck.

'Come on, we're going,' Hank turned to Martha, stumbling into Perry's table and causing his glass to spill. 'Sorry, mate.' Hank's hand grabbed the newspaper and packet of Benson & Hedges cigarettes that had fallen to the floor. Perry snatched the paper back, looking down to see if his photo of Mary had fallen free.

'Just an accident,' mumbled Perry in a deeper than usual voice, keeping his head bowed to avoid eye contact. Martha stood to assist, putting Perry's disguise further to the test.

'I'm so sorry, forgive my husband's clumsiness. Let us buy you another drink,' she insisted, trying to dry the table with a tattered tissue, resting her hand on Perry's arm as a sign of apology.

'I was just leaving,' replied Perry, hastily standing from his seat and vanishing with an awkward sense of urgency out the door.

'Come on, let's go too,' instructed Hank. 'I never liked this shithole, anyway.'

Outside, Perry remained hidden, waiting for the couple to reappear. Slumped in the driver's seat of his car with his head just visible above the steering wheel, he watched as they emerged from the pub, letting the door slam behind them. With his arm round her waist, Hank guided Martha across the tarmac, a bottle of beer still in his hand. He swigged the contents and tossed the bottle back in the direction of the pub.

'Bloody idiot's now going to drive home,' muttered Perry, his hand easing the key into the ignition. 'When he smashes their bodies head-on into a tree, she'll be all alone. No sister. No parents. Just some crazy grandparents who don't know their own names.'

Perry watched Hank's car reverse before it tore out onto the main road. Eager to keep up with the drunken driver, he pressed his foot against the accelerator. With his anger still bubbling, Hank seemed undeterred by the tailgating car.

'The fool can't even keep to his side of the road,' said Perry, watching Hank's vehicle swerving, struggling to navigate the winding main road.

Perry struggled to keep pace with the car along the main road before it took a sudden right-hand turn, veering onto a private lane. Hank drove onto the remote road that would eventually snake all the way through the woods and up to Wisteria.

'What's the bastard doing now?' Perry thought to himself as Hank made a sudden stop in front of the obscured house that was located only a few metres up the private track, just off from the main road. The dirty sign outside the house read Ivy Dean. Stopping his own car on the main road, Perry watched as Hank, illuminated by the single lamp post, hauled an empty bottle towards the secluded property. The sound of shattering glass echoed the length of the lane.

'Shit, my window!' This time it was Perry's face to turn plum. His fist scrunched into a ball just as Hank's car sped off up the dead-end lane towards Wisteria, dust and debris settling in the car's wake.

He reached over for the newspaper, opening it in the centre. The photo of Mary fell onto his lap. 'You'll soon be better off without them,' he said, his fingers tracing the features of Mary's face, features he could recall with precision from memory. 'They don't deserve you, Mary, and they didn't deserve Lucy. They don't look after you. But I will.' Perry pressed the photo against his chest, then slipped it back into the newspaper folds.

BACK IN HER attic bedroom at Wisteria, hidden beneath swathes of duvet and submerged by middle-of-the-night gloom, Mary slept alone. After hours of waiting for her parents to come home, Mary had eventually fallen asleep, permitting a night terror to rage its way through her susceptible mind, leaving behind emotional scars that would never heal. In her reoccurring nightmare, the crunching of leaves disturbed the eerie, midnight silence engulfing Wisteria. Footsteps approached the isolated house and a man looked up towards Mary's bedroom window, a premature smirk of satisfaction hidden beneath a black cap. The intruder eased the front door open with practiced precision, releasing the door knob with patience so that it didn't make a sound. Uninterested by the car keys or valuables that scattered the length of the hallway, the man climbed the stairs in order to reach his intended destination. Mary's head flipped from one side to another on her pillow the more her nightmare unfolded. Her arms fought with the duvet and her restless legs broke free from the disturbed covers, goosepimples scattering her exposed skin.

The intruder's impatience caused his feet to stumble and the uneven floorboards to creak, but the disturbance wasn't loud enough to wake the sleeping family. Soon enough, the man's shaking hand caressed Mary's door handle, easing the wood from the frame. It only took a few extended strides and he'd reached his target. He covered Mary's mouth, her eyes opening wide as he lifted her out of bed. He could see the white parts of her eyes through the darkness, a frightful look flooding her eyes. He carried the child out into the still of the night, disappearing into the backdrop. By the time her parents arose in the morning, Mary's bed was cold, the sun had risen above the trees and all traces of the abduction had vanished with the night.

This time, it was all just a nightmare.

Four

THE DATE IN QUESTION WAS JULY 17TH, 1982.

The location was Wisteria; a lake house located in Finchley, Cumbria, owned by Elsie and Henry Lane. A dusting of wispy clouds had decorated the sky like summer snowflakes the day that four-year-old Lucy Lane had gone missing from her grandparents' house during her family's annual summer visit.

That morning, a usual muster of sparrows fluttered amid the trees, causing a downpour of delicate, lilac petals. Before midday had broken, the chirpy postman had already pushed a collection of circulars through the rusting lake house letterbox. The Finchley post office had opened its doors bang on nine o'clock, and the ladies in the corner shop opposite had drank their usual two cups of milky, weak tea. Mrs Davenport, from 63 Barons Nook, had been to the park and picked up all the litter that had been discarded overnight, and Mr Archie Brookes, local councillor, had perused his daily schedule. He didn't think much was going on in his constituency that day, but he would soon be mistaken.

The day had started without hiccup.

When Mary and her twin sister Lucy had first stirred that morning, Martha had gotten out of bed and dressed them both in their favourite summer outfits. With the sun already in the sky, the weather outside appeared warm and inviting. So that they didn't wake the rest of the house, Martha took the girls outside to play whilst she sat sipping a steaming cup of strong coffee on the porch. Once Martha's coffee had performed its much-needed caffeine kick, she occupied the girls on the new swing beneath the early morning sun that splashed over the front garden. After half an hour of constant 'Push me harder, Mummy. Harder. Harder!', Martha's weary arms surrendered. So, she took out her camera and took some photos of the girls before their dresses became dirty.

Martha rarely missed an opportunity to take pictures of her girls; to date, her identical twin daughters were her finest accomplishment in life. Lucy, who was wearing a lilac, knee-length dress, matching socks and a matching bow in her hair, smiled effortlessly for the camera. The silver '*Lucy*' bracelet on her right hand shining each time the sun caught the metal. Her head was arched back and her legs aloft, her body swinging through the air. The smile on her face told only one story; that she was winning at life. Mary was dressed in an identical dress, sock, bow and shoe combination, only hers were all yellow. She was wearing a matching bracelet, the name '*Mary*' engraved into the silver.

After Hank had decided to drag his body out of bed, and had got himself washed and changed, the entire family sat and ate breakfast together. As a treat, they all enjoyed pancakes with honey and slices of fried, buttery banana. Had they known that it was destined to be the very last time that they would be eating breakfast as a family they would have savoured the moment. Hank wouldn't have ignored everyone by reading the sports section in the newspaper. Martha wouldn't have been preoccupied by painting her nails a vibrant shade of pink. Elsie would have tidied up the breakfast table, making sure that the milk was put back in the fridge, and Mary and Lucy wouldn't have fought over who got to eat the last pancake; Mary would have offered it to Lucy.

Hindsight wasn't on the menu that morning, so the family continued in their usual manner, oblivious to what was set to happen in only an hour's time.

After breakfast, it was time for Martha and Hank to leave for their planned day trip together.

'Mary, Lucy,' shouted Hank while grabbing his wallet, assuming the girls were upstairs in their bedroom playing. 'Mummy and Daddy are going now. But we'll be back soon, and we might bring something back if you both behave yourselves for Grandma and Grandad.' But his daughters had already strategically stationed themselves on the porch, hoping that their human barrier would prevent their parents from leaving them behind.

Their plan failed.

Martha skipped down the stairs, catching sight of the girls sitting cross-legged on the porch.

'Be good, girls,' she instructed before taking a quick glance in the mirror and applying a second layer of lipstick. She sauntered out through the open front door, passing both of her daughters without much remark, despite the fact that they were now crying loudly in unison.

'Come on, Hank, let's not waste any more time. It's not often we get a day out by ourselves, and the girls are getting upset,' she had said, tucking in her skirt under her thigh before slamming the car door. 'We'll be back before you know it, girls, and I'll give you both a cuddle as soon as I get home. I promise.' Martha blew kisses to the girls from the car, trying not to feel too guilty about savouring some time alone with her husband.

Elsie appeared in the hallway. 'Thanks again for this, Mum,' said Hank, his feet dodging the girls in an attempt to get out of the house without them grabbing onto his limbs. He got in the car and, without looking back, started the ignition and began to drive away. The knackered banger soon disappeared, the twins remaining abandoned on the porch, sobbing hysterically the way four-year-olds can on demand.

'Mummy, Mummy,' Lucy had cried, her arms naively outstretched, assuming her mum would get out of the car and run back to pick her up, offering the kind of maternal love that money couldn't buy. But Martha didn't turn around, and she wasn't thinking about how upsetting it was seeing her twins crying on the porch. She was already thinking about what shade of lipstick she was going to treat herself to, and how much money she could persuade Hank to part with, wanting to make the most of a rare day of shopping without the twins.

Once Elsie had managed to usher the girls inside, and only minutes after Hank and Martha had vacated the house, a catastrophic milk spillage rumbled the already fraught house. Mary had leant over to grab the cereal box in an attempt to help tidy things away, but by accident her arm had nudged the milk bottle, sending it tumbling to the floor. The sound of smashing glass induced more tears from both girls, their eyes red and faces blotchy from sobbing.

'Now, now, then. There's no need to cry over spilt milk, is there?' Elsie attempted to console, feeling fraught herself.

'It just means that we can't have those secret milkshakes we'd planned on making,' she said, her pinafore saturated. Elsie swept up all the glass and mopped over the sea of milk, trying to keep calm despite the constant crying paining her ears.

'You *promised* milkshakes, Grandma. Chocolate ones,' moaned Mary.

Whatever Mary wanted, then it was a pretty good assumption that so would Lucy, and vice versa.

'I want milkshake too, Grandma.' Lucy had slumped herself on the kitchen floor amid a stray pool of milk. She was holding her favourite doll, Penelope Pickles, and looking up at Elsie. 'I want Mummy. Is she home soon?'

All this had happened only moments after their parents had left the house, the dust on the driveway still settling after the car tyres had sped over the gravel.

Elsie ran her hands through her grey, tight curls. 'Right then. If shakes will bring smiles back to those little faces of yours, then I'll quickly nip to the shop and buy more milk. Mary, I'm leaving you in charge, okay? You're a whole three and a half minutes older than your sister, so, until I get back, or your grandad wakes up, you're the boss.' She grabbed a handful of change, tipping it into her soggy apron pocket.

'Can we not come too, Grandma?' Lucy had asked.

'I'll only be a few minutes, and by the time you get your shoes on, I'll be half way there.' Elsie dashed out the door. 'I'll be back in a jiffy, girls, and remember, don't go outside, don't make too much noise and wake up Grandad, and don't fall out with each other.' Feeling flustered and in a rush, before leaving she had forgotten to give the girls a quick kiss, or a hug. She had also forgotten to lock the front door. She'd forgotten to check that she'd turned the hob off after making the breakfast pancakes, and she'd decided not to wake Henry, knowing that he'd be unable to calm the storm alone.

'Okay, Grandma,' replied Mary, who forgot the instructions before Elsie had even made it to the main road.

Somewhat annoyed at being left, Mary snatched Penelope Pickles from out of her sister's hands, something she tended to do just to tease her sister. Mary headed straight outside to play on the swing. leaving Lucy crying on the kitchen floor, and her grandad upstairs in bed. She begrudged the fact that she had to look after her sister, like being three and a half minutes older made any difference. As stubborn as a stalemate, Mary did the opposite of what her grandma had instructed, and played on the swing outside, happy that she'd got to it first this time, and that she didn't have to watch her sister having all the fun.

Thanks to painful hips, and a multitude of bones riddled with arthritis, a good hour, if not longer, had passed before Elsie returned. Not the 'back in a jiffy' she had promised. The swing on the front lawn was empty when she hobbled up the driveway, her face grimacing with each additional stride, her worn joints grinding bone on bone. As soon as she walked through the door, she had intended on making milkshakes, just to keep the girls quiet for five minutes, before making a cuppa and easing her aching body into the lounge recliner.

Elsie entered through the front door, dumping the milk on the counter top.

Oddly, not a sound could be heard.

'Henry? Where are you?' she looked around the kitchen and lounge for clues. 'Where are the girls? Mary? Lucy?' she shouted. 'Where are you all?' She scurried upstairs.

Elsie searched in each of the upstairs rooms upon finding the ground floor deserted, her hand forcing the doors wide open. All the rooms were empty, and no noise could be heard in the loft. Forgetting about her painful hips, she shuffled back down the stairs and scanned the ground floor once again. The house was strangely silent. Whenever the girls stayed over during the holidays, there was rarely a moment when the house fell quiet; in fact, it was never silent. You could always hear the sound of laughing, or crying, or arguing, or playing, or any other ambiguous noises that, although weren't immediately identifiable, served to reassure that all was well.

Henry's chair in the lounge was empty. There were no toys strewn across the carpet. The television wasn't on. The floor beneath the coat rack still hosted a collection of shoes. The breakfast table was still cluttered with condiments. The floorboards in the attic weren't creaking beneath the shifting weight as Mary and Lucy imitated being ballerinas, the pair often falling to their feet during a failed pirouette, their bodies making a banging so hard that it could be heard downstairs in the kitchen. Lucy was no longer on the kitchen floor. And Mary was no longer sitting at the table waiting for her chocolate milkshake.

Henry must've woken up and taken the girls outside, thought Elsie.

Stepping outside, she allowed her eyes to scan the landscape in front of the house. The girls and their grandfather were nowhere to be seen, and Elsie's insides began a sickening cycle of churning. She took a deep breath in an attempt to calm herself and paused on the porch, straining her ears for signs of life. She could hear the trees rustling, and the sound of splashing each time a duck landed on the lake. But there were still no voices or sounds of children playing, only the occasional sounds made by nature.

Elsie took in a breath and tried to convince herself that

everything would be alright. The three of them were surely just playing down near the lake somewhere out of sight. Or, maybe they were all feeding the ducks – or, better still, picking a sprig of surprise summer flowers for her from the woods. That's what Henry, Mary and Lucy were doing, wasn't it? Picking flowers.

Finally, Elsie spotted movement in the distance.

'Oh, thank God,' she exclaimed, running as best as she could down towards the shabby jetty that was located at the far side of the lake. As she got closer, she could see Mary sitting with her legs dangling into the water, throwing stones into the lake.

'Mary, come away from the water at once,' screamed Elsie, scurrying down the wooden walkway. 'Where's Lucy? Where's Grandad?'

'I don't know. Do you like my rocket, Grandma? I've been all the way to the moon,' Mary replied, casting her hands into the air like she was pretending to be a rocket. Elsie grabbed her hand and began walking her back to the house.

'Where's your sister?' said Elsie in a raised voice, scaring Mary and making her cry. 'I'm sorry, I didn't mean to shout. We just need to find your sister.' Elsie stopped to give Mary a hug. 'Do you know where Lucy is, Mary?' she asked, bending down, looking deep into her granddaughter's eyes and hoping that the answer would magically materialise. 'Has she been playing with you?'

Mary looked blank in response to the long string of questions fired at her. Like Mary had already said, she'd been to the moon. She didn't know where Lucy was.

'What about Grandad, Mary? Do you know where he is?'

Mary looked up, feeling excited that she knew the answer to this particular question. 'Still asleep,' she replied, gazing up at the sky. If only Mary had recalled the sporadic shouting, explaining to her Grandma that she had felt scared, and that's why she had gone to the moon.

Elsie continued walking Mary back towards the house, ignoring the sinking feeling festering in her stomach. The pair marched upstairs.

'Stay here, Mary,' Elsie insisted, placing Mary on her bed. She closed the door and locked it, preventing Mary from witnessing something that her young eyes may never be able to forget. Elsie's screams haunted every inch of the house, the high-pitched tones permeating the wood, searching for a way to escape. Mary placed her hands over her ears, frightened by her grandma's constant screams.

There was still no sign of Lucy, or Henry.

Elsie had been back from the shops for only ten minutes, but it had felt like hours; a lifetime's sentence.

Flustered, Elsie wasn't sure what to do. She loitered on the porch, her head in a whirlwind. She thought about calling the police. She thought about screaming for somebody to help. She thought about going back in time and doing things differently. The one thing she couldn't do was to call Martha and Hank because she didn't know where they'd gone. And the longer she stood there on the porch, the more she started to question herself. *Did they take Lucy with them? Maybe Lucy had snuck into the car when I wasn't looking? Maybe they came back for her because she was so upset, and left a note and I just haven't seen it?* She went inside and searched the kitchen for a note of explanation.

Elsie knew deep down in her gut that Lucy hadn't gone out with her parents, and there was no note offering an alternative account. There was nothing, just silence.

'Lucy, where are you?'

The downstairs bathroom door stood ajar. It was the only room Elsie hadn't yet searched. She pushed the door open with her foot, only to discover Henry slumped in the bath. He was fully dressed, and spatters of blood dotted his filthy hands and clothes. A knife lay on the floor along with Lucy's tiny lilac socks.

Elsie screamed, just like they do in horror films. It was the kind of scream that could pierce eardrums, smash glass, or break windows. It was a haunting scream that would stay with her forever.

'Oh my God. Henry, what's happened? Are you alright? Where are you hurt?' She helped her husband out of the bath,

Henry's shaking body unsteady as his feet took his weight. 'Is this the only place you're cut?' she asked, finding a single nick on his right hand. She covered it with a towel and inspected the rest of his body. 'What's happened, Henry? Where's Lucy? Why are you so dirty?' Shrouded in a sense of confusion, Henry attempted to explain.

'I heard a man's voice. He was shouting,' he blurted in an erratic stream, his eyes looking up to the ceiling, scanning the area to check whether anyone was listening in to his conversation. 'He was coming to take Lucy away.'

Elsie grabbed his muddy hands, squeezing his palms. 'Which man, my darling?' she asked, trying to encourage Henry to recall exactly what had happened. 'What did he look like? Was it Perry Golifer, Henry? Tell me, was he the man that came? Did *he* take Lucy?' Her impatience drove her actions, her hands now shaking Henry's fragile body, trying to force the information out.

But Henry wasn't able to respond. Despite his best efforts, he couldn't answer what had become the million-pound question. Where was Lucy? His tangled thoughts became more confused with each additional question Elsie asked, making it impossible to drag any elements of lucidity from within his muddled mind.

Elsie tried again, just like she would come to do many times over the years that followed.

'Henry, please, look at me. Look me in the eyes. The bad man has gone now, and you're safe. But where's Lucy?' she asked, her body crumpling to the floor, hysterical.

Henry turned to face his wife, finally looking at her, Elsie's hopes momentarily rising.

'Gladys? Is it really you?' he asked. Elsie cried harder at the utter hopelessness, her husband mistaking her for his childhood sweetheart. The blood on Elsie's hands smeared further across her face the more she wiped her eyes. She looked like the victim of a brutal attack, fatally injured and left to die.

'Oh, Henry. Where's Lucy? I beg of you, just tell me where she is,' she sobbed. Henry remained silent. Unbeknown to them both, a continual stream of delusional thoughts were drowning his mind, a mind that was riddled with disease. If only his condition had been recognised and understood earlier. If only Elsie hadn't ignored the warning signs, burying her head in the sand, too scared of what medical professionals may diagnose.

She left him on the floor and ran back outside. She searched the woods, looking for areas that had been disturbed. She felt sure that all the mud on his hands must've meant that he'd been playing with the girls in the woods, and that that's where she'd find Lucy. But, after searching as far as her crumbling hips would carry her, and as best as her cataract eyes could see, Elsie failed to find anything. Not even a leaf looked out of place. But Wisteria was so big that it would take an army of people a number of days to comb through every inch of land.

She abandoned that search and went back to the house.

Acting purely on panic and not knowing what else to do, Elsie hid the knife and Lucy's lilac socks. She stuffed them into a washing sack before squashing them into the back of the old tumble dryer that was in the cluttered basement. Henry had attempted to fix the knackered machine years ago, and the back panel had remained loose ever since. With the bloody evidence hidden, and the tumble dryer pushed back against the wall like it had never been moved, she then set about washing down the tub and bathroom floor, ensuring every speck of blood was removed. Stripping off her clothes, and standing only in her undergarments, Elsie washed her face and hands, putting her soiled clothes in the washing machine. She looked in the mirror to check that all the blood had gone.

She then washed Henry's hands so that no blood could be seen, and noticed that his wedding band was missing from his finger. She scoured the room, searching for the ring, but couldn't find it anywhere. Henry hadn't even noticed that it had come off, let alone know where it was. With time running out, she stopped looking and instead combed Henry's hair before putting his clothes in the washing machine with hers, setting the dial to a quick wash cycle. Whilst Mary was still locked in her bedroom, Elsie gave Henry specific instructions, sitting him on a chair and whispering.

She grabbed hold of his face and held it close to hers. 'Listen to me, Henry,' she began. 'Are you sure you didn't see anybody take Lucy away? Are you sure you don't know where she is?' Henry replied with a meek nod.

'If you want to help me find Lucy, then you mustn't say anything about the voice you heard, not unless you know who it was that took her away,' said Elsie. 'Just tell the police, and everybody else that asks, that you were asleep, okay? You were asleep when Lucy went missing. And that you didn't hear anything, or see anyone. If you tell them about being in the bathroom with a knife, they will send you to jail, Henry, and then you and me will never be able to find Lucy. Do you understand?' Henry nodded his head, but that didn't guarantee that he had understood. With Henry, there were no guarantees anymore. The expression on her husband's face terrified Elsie, spurring on the churning of her internal organs. Henry's face told a silent story, a story that, thus far, had no conclusion.

Hours after she had arrived home with the milk, Elsie's shaking hand picked up the phone and made the call to the police. But by this point, it was too late. Lucy was gone, and so was the only evidence pertaining to her disappearance. Although unable to do much until a child had been missing for over twenty-four hours, Sergeant Claire Swift and an accompanying officer did arrive at Wisteria. They searched the house and immediate vicinity, and asked all the relevant questions, but it wasn't until the following day that the vast amount of land surrounding Wisteria was finally searched by a handful of local officers. The most obvious thought running through everyone's mind was that Lucy had fallen into the lake and drowned, but police divers searched the entire lake and found nothing.

Elsie watched the search being conducted from the house, holding her breath, not knowing what they might find. She knew

Henry wouldn't have done anything to hurt their granddaughter; it wasn't in his nature, and he loved his granddaughters more than life itself. But the image of the bloody knife stalked Elsie like the shadow of death. Regardless, the police failed to uncover anything. Not a single lead was found in the surrounding area. It felt bittersweet to Elsie at the time; on the one hand, she was devastated that Lucy hadn't been found safe and well, but, on the other hand, she felt relieved that the little girl hadn't been found dead in the lake, or with knife wounds scattering her body. Further extensive police searches of the house and lake found no evidence of any wrongdoing, only a host of reminders that a child was no longer at home.

Throughout Henry's questioning, Elsie had held her breath once again, praying that her instructions had managed to sink into his muddled brain. And it worked. He didn't say anything to contradict his wife's tale, and his story of events never wavered. He had taken what his wife had said as gospel, wholeheartedly believing that his lies would somehow protect his lost granddaughter.

The official story that Elsie fed to the police, plus Hank and Martha, was that Henry had been asleep upstairs when she left to nip to the shop. And that he was still asleep when she returned, not knowing about anything that had happened in her absence. The entire family knew that Henry was a heavy sleeper, and so it only served to strengthen a story that was based on lies. It had always been the running joke that Henry would have been able to sleep through a disaster – and, on this occasion, it was thought that he actually had.

Mary hadn't seen her grandad in the bathroom. So, when she was questioned, she backed up the story that her grandad was in bed asleep, just like her grandma had said. She didn't remember hearing Henry's shouting; her grandma's screams were the only sound she could recall. And, after sensitive questioning, Mary's story became confused, a tale that centred around her going to the moon in a rocket. The police couldn't rely on her statement;

she was just a child that had only recently turned four. Her account amounted to nothing. She didn't know where her sister was, and she hadn't seen anyone at the house. That was the extent of her statement.

During the days, weeks, months and years that followed that frightful morning on July 17th, 1982, Elsie went over and over in her mind whether lying to the police had been the right thing to do. She thought about little else, sending herself crazy. Whilst she slept, images of Lucy flooded her mind and, for a moment, it felt like she'd never gone missing. She could see her grandchild sat in the kitchen smiling, she could hear her voice and smell the sweet scent of her hair. But then, come morning, when she had no choice but to wake up, Elsie had to relive the nightmare all over again.

On some days, Elsie would pick up the phone, ready to call the police and confess everything, but she would always throw down the receiver just before anyone answered. On other days, when she really thought she'd made the wrong decision, she went to the basement and got out the knife and socks, ready to take to the police. And, on one occasion, she made it as far as the bus stop on the main road, the police station coming into view. But then she thought about Henry back at home, and what would happen to him, and so she turned back.

In Elsie's mind, it always came back to the fact that Henry didn't know what had happened that day, and that was all that mattered. Had she left the bloody knife and socks in situ, he wouldn't have been able to explain how or why they'd got there, and the police would have assumed he was guilty. With the evidence put before them, a jury would have found Henry guilty; there would have been too much stacked against him.

The search for Lucy only lasted a number of weeks before the police had no choice but to scale back their efforts and use their resources on other cases. Martha, Hank and Mary also had no choice but to return home, leaving Lucy behind. They had to get on with life, as harsh and as brutal as it felt. Hank needed to return to work, a mounting pile of bills still requiring payment. Mary had to start school, and Martha had to try and maintain her façade that everything was alright.

Once alone at Wisteria, when there were no listening ears or prying eyes, Elsie questioned Henry time and time again, putting him on trial herself. Sometimes, he would state that he'd been asleep in his bedroom the entire time she had been out, and that he had heard nothing, and saw nothing. And, on other occasions, he'd said he'd heard a man's voice shouting, threatening to take Lucy away. But that's all he knew. He didn't know who the man was. He didn't know what he looked like. But, most of all, he didn't know what had happened to Lucy, or where she had gone. Those parts of the puzzle had become lost in his mind.

You see, that was the main problem, and the second secret Elsie was keeping from the world, a secret she could no longer pretend wasn't real. Henry had started to suffer from symptoms linked to the onset of Alzheimer's before Lucy's disappearance. His condition was undiagnosed, having not attended a doctor's surgery in over two decades, and nobody knew about his erratic behaviour, except for Elsie. At the time, even she didn't know exactly what was wrong with him, and put his occasional odd behaviour down to old age and a bad case of acting senile. Up until that point, Elsie hadn't considered Henry to be a threat to himself or anyone else. He and Elsie lived a largely secluded life away from others so there was no need for outside intervention. But Elsie now knew that something more sinister was occurring in the depths of her husband's brain, she just hadn't wanted to admit it, up until the day that Lucy had vanished.

No chocolate milkshakes were ever prepared at Wisteria the day that Lucy vanished; or any day thereafter. In the days and weeks following the disappearance of Lucy Lane, the police gathered intelligence on each person considered to be a prime suspect. Photos of Lucy's own grandparents, along with Hank and Martha, were displayed on the police station wall. A mug shot of Wisteria's closest neighbour, Perry Golifer, was the final prime suspect to be named in the case. The police retrieved Perry's old police file and combed its contents, the Ivy Dean loner having already been questioned some years earlier in relation to the case of another missing child.

But six years on without any kind of breakthrough, had the police made an oversight when it came to identifying the prime suspects? Mary Lane, now ten, often experienced a sickening feeling in the pit of her stomach, a feeling that haunted her shadow. Thoughts of *what if* plagued Mary's mind. What if she had been responsible for her sister's disappearance. Had she and Lucy both been playing near the lake that morning, and following a play fight, had Mary accidentally knocked her sister into the water? What if the police search hadn't been thorough, the deep, dark crevices of the vast lake concealing the small body? Or had Mary locked her sister in a secret hideaway that only they knew about? The girls were always hiding from their parents, causing momentary pangs of panic to infest their parent's hearts.

What if the girls had been bickering over a toy, causing Mary to display the hidden anger she usually managed to control? Did Mary take her frustrations out on Lucy, causing her sister to run away, and never return? Mary had heard stories and seen photos where she and Lucy were both in floods of tears having been arguing with one another over something silly. The fact remained that Mary was one of the last people to see her sister before she vanished. Was four-year-old Mary Elizabeth Lane responsible for the disappearance of Lucy?

Buried deep within the depths of Mary's memory, the truth lay dormant, waiting to be revealed.

Five

EVEN THE EARLY MORNING SUN SEEPING THROUGH THE disintegrating curtains in Martha's bedroom couldn't inject colour back into her ghostly, gaunt features. The sun shone directly over her face, and yet her eyes didn't flinch. Her body lay motionless. Her hand draped over the edge of the bed and an empty bottle of gin lay on the floor where she'd dropped it after passing out. The gentle flutter of fresh air drifting in through the open window scattered loose strands of hair across her face, the tickling sensation also failing to induce any kind of involuntary reaction. Martha Lane lay lifeless next to her husband. She wasn't dead – but, at a glance, it looked like she was.

A constant, obnoxious noise resonated from downstairs, awaking Hank at least two hours earlier than he would've liked. Lying fully clothed on top of the duvet, he looked over at his wife; one of her arms was sprawled across the bed, her hair dishevelled. She, too, was lying fully dressed in rumpled clothes worn the previous evening. Hank stirred, his legs nudging Martha in the process and his hand knocking into hers, and yet still she didn't wake. An array of empty bottles cluttered the floor, creating a collection worthy of a winery. The only bottle in the room with dregs in was the one hiding in the side pocket of Martha's handbag. An alcoholic never liked to run dry.

Hank parted his parched lips. Despite the quantity of fluid that he'd consumed in the past twelve hours, his mouth felt like it hadn't been hydrated for hours.

'You awake?' he asked, glancing over at his wife once his eyes adjusted to the light. With still no sign of movement, he prodded Martha's ribs. 'Wake up.' Momentarily forgetting all about his hangover, Hank's heart plummeted at the sight of his wife's motionless body. 'Martha?' he whispered, positioning his ear over her gaping mouth, at which point her eyes opened wide.

'Bloody hell, I thought you were dead! You look like shit.'

'Your breath is enough to wake the bloody dead,' she replied, pushing Hank away and rolling over. Martha wasn't a morning person, usually too consumed by a crippling hangover. And she wasn't particularly an evening person, either; an angry drunk, always too pissed to be polite. Anytime between dawn and dusk also wasn't a great time for Martha, because all she cared about was how long it would be until her next drink. Martha's irritability was the worst on her list of terrible traits, a list that would take longer to read than the phone book.

Martha wasn't an ideal mother figure. But, then again, nobody was ever vetted before having children of their own, Martha included. In her defence, she hadn't always been so pathetic; it was just for the past six years or so. Nor had she always been an alcoholic. Believe it or not, she had once prided herself on being the best turned-out mum on the nursery run. Whilst Hank worked full time as a teacher, Martha was a stay-at-home wife, and played the role with military perfection.

She'd had ample time in which to present herself as a model parent, and that's exactly what she had achieved after the birth of her twin daughters. Despite raising twin girls and having little time to herself, Martha made it look like she had all the time in the world. Her sense of fashion made the playground resemble a fashion parade, and many of the mums at the time had wished that they had her slim physique. She maintained an immaculate hairstyle, visiting the salon weekly to ensure there wasn't a split end in sight. She wore perfectly-applied makeup every day, even on those mornings when the girls tested her patience. Other mums would turn up to nursey looking like they'd lost a battle with a hairdryer or blusher brush, and yet Martha was pristine. Apparently, 'Marvellous Martha', as she had been known for a time, could do no wrong. If only those people could see her now. How the tables had turned.

Hank staggered out of bed and got dressed. He caught a glimpse of himself in a mirror after putting his heavy rimmed glasses on. There were more frown lines scattered over his face than what he remembered, and his skin looked washed out. With his thinning hair and side parting, he was a younger version of his dad. His thoughts turned to Henry, and he felt like crying. He walked down the stairs, leaving his wife to fester alone.

'What's that bloody noise?' he barked. 'Turn it the fuck off!' he insisted, looking at Elsie, who continued to hoover the lounge with meticulous detail. 'I said, turn it off.' Hank ripped the cord from the socket, throwing it to the floor.

'I can't hear myself think,' he shouted. 'My head's about to explode and you're hoovering the entire bloody house when there isn't a speck of dirt to be seen.'

Elsie turned, her face furious.

'If I didn't wake you up, it'd be another day wasted, wouldn't it?' she said. 'You could be out there, looking for your father. But instead, you're just wasting your time sleeping.' Elsie dropped the hoover and stormed off into the kitchen. Hank followed at a marching pace.

'You're too bloody busy,' continued Elsie. 'Your dad's missing and all you're doing is drinking yourself to death. You need help, Hank. The pair of you need help. You've got Mary to think about. You're in denial if you think there's nothing wrong.'

'You're a fine one to talk about denial,' snapped Hank. 'You kept Dad's problem hidden. If you'd told me sooner, maybe we could've got him some help. But it's too late now, isn't it? Looks like he's lost his whole bloody bag of marbles now, and he can't even find his way home.'

After the tragic day that his granddaughter had gone missing,

Henry Lane's Alzheimer's gradually worsened. Elsie managed to hide the truth from Hank and Martha for years, only seeing them for a few weeks each summer. But last July, during their annual visit, everything changed. Henry had an outburst whilst everyone was there, and there was no more hiding. Whilst enjoying a family evening meal, Henry suddenly became suspicious of Hank, accusing him of spying. It was the first time that Hank and Martha had witnessed his upsetting behaviour.

Elsie had then confessed. She had been backed into a corner and was no longer able to blame Henry's bizarre behaviour on having drunk too much cider the night before. She explained how he'd been acting of late, but didn't tell them how long it had been going on for, downplaying the situation and saying that it had only been occurring this past twelve months or so.

But in reality, Elsie had been a witness to Henry's odd behaviour for years. It all started just a few months after Lucy vanished.

'I won't let you take her away,' Elsie had overheard Henry shouting one morning whilst she was watering the bedding plants in the garden. She watched Henry jumping out of his seat and running over towards the kitchen. She thought at first that the commotion was coming from the television, but when she watched Henry grabbing a knife, she was scared that they were actually being robbed, and that Henry was in danger. She dropped her watering can and dashed to his aid. Henry was terrified when Elsie appeared through the back door.

'I've got a knife,' he said, holding a butchering blade. Henry took hold of her, believing her to be Lucy. He wrapped his arms round her body, holding the knife out in front. His arms held onto his wife so tight, that Elsie's skin became badly bruised, looking like she'd received a beating.

'Can you hear him, Lucy?' Henry asked, sweeping the blade through the air. Elsie tried to calm the confusion raging through his mind.

'Lucy isn't here, Henry. Lucy's gone. Remember? It's me, Elsie,' she said, trying to wriggle free. 'Who can you hear, Henry? Who is coming to take Lucy?' she continued, turning to try and take hold of the knife.

'Shush! They're coming inside,' Henry replied, thinking he'd heard footsteps approaching the porch, holding out the knife and thrashing it through the air like a machete. Henry dragged Elsie upstairs. 'Come on, Lucy, we'll be safer up here.'

Elsie looked back, witnessing her quiet, empty house. A sickening feeling stirred in her stomach, the very same feeling she had experienced the day that Lucy had vanished. She pictured the knife she had found in the bathroom, the knife she had hidden in the basement. She pictured Lucy's socks, and Henry's bloody hands. For the first time in her whole life, she felt scared of her own husband. She didn't recognise him, the frightful look on his face stealing his true identity. He didn't sound like his normal self, and his aggressive behaviour was something she had never experienced before. She begged for him to let her go, now fearful for her life. Henry made Elsie hide underneath Lucy's bed, pushing her down and pressing her head against the floor.

'Let me go, please, you're hurting me.' Henry didn't hear her pleads, and didn't release his grip.

As the pair remained prisoners, hiding under the bed, Elsie began to play along with what she would later realise was some sort of hallucination.

'That was close,' she said, after many long minutes of hiding. 'I think they've gone. We're safe now, Henry.' She took hold of her husband's hand, squeezing so that he could feel the pressure and differentiate fiction from reality. Henry's demeanour began to change and his frantic behaviour stopped. His breathing slowed to a regular pace, his hand released the knife, and he let go of Elsie's body.

'What shall we have for lunch?' Henry asked, like nothing had happened. 'I feel like a corned beef sandwich.' Henry then walked down stairs and sat back in his chair, continuing to watch the television programme that was still playing in the background. Elsie examined her body, the delicate skin around her abdomen sore to the touch, blood pooling beneath her fragile skin. Her hands were shaking. She got out from under the bed and peered down the stairs, seeing that Henry was sat back in the lounge, laughing along to the television. Cautiously, she followed him downstairs, standing by his side. And, just like she had attempted to do from day one, Elsie tried to find out what had happened the day that Lucy went missing, knowing that Henry had just relived a similar moment.

'Henry, when the man came last time to take Lucy, what did he look like? Where did Lucy go to hide?' she asked. The same response always followed, no matter how many times over the years she'd asked.

'I was in bed. I didn't see anything. I didn't hear anything.'

But just like Mary, deep down in the darkest parts of Henry's diseased memory, the truth was there.

Six

I N THE KITCHEN, THE ARGUMENT BETWEEN ELSIE AND HANK stepped up a gear. Elsie slammed her cup down.

'Your father hasn't lost his mind, Hank. His mind is still there, and, no matter what, he's still your dad.'

Hank bit back. 'Martha and I have been running around like clueless bloody clowns for the past few days looking for him, so don't act like I don't care, because I do.' Elsie remained silent, the pair at loggerheads at the kitchen table.

Hank was the first to break the tension. 'I promise I want to help, Mum. As soon as you told us that Dad was missing, we got in the car and travelled straight up. I didn't even question missing the last few days of term. Work doesn't matter. Family comes first. So, let's go through things again. I need you to tell me *everything*. Every single detail from the few days leading up to Dad's disappearance. Even if you think it's not important, tell me anyway. Humour me.' Frustration caused him to be heavy-handed with a brimming mug of coffee, banging it on the table.

'You're so bloody angry,' Elsie replied. 'No wonder poor Mary always looks so scared. I'm not sure I've seen her smile since she arrived.' Her face crumpled as she turned to get some more milk out of the fridge. 'She's just a child, Hank, and yet she looks like she's carrying the weight of the world on her shoulders.'

'Is it any wonder I'm so bloody angry?' Hank snapped, his voice rising. 'I'm still trying to cope with the loss of Lucy, and so are Mary and Martha. We all are, and I'm doing my best to keep this family together. The way I act, and the way Mary acts, is normal given what we've been through, wouldn't you agree?' Hank didn't pause for breath, or allow Elsie to reply. 'And now I have the added pressure of trying to find Dad. And, on top of all that, it appears that everyone up here still seems to be of the opinion that *I'm* some sort of monster who is responsible for Lucy's disappearance. The police swarm us like flies on shit and yet you don't care.' In his anger, he grabbed a jar of jam and flung it against a cupboard, the sound of glass shattering on the tiles striking close to Elsie's head.

A figure appeared in the kitchen. 'Don't you *ever* say that we've lost her,' snapped Martha, directing a spiteful stare towards Hank. 'We're not coping with a *loss*. Nobody has told us that Lucy is dead, have they? Or have I somehow missed that part? She hasn't gone forever. She's just missing. She's been taken from us and now, after six years of searching, you're just giving up on her, aren't you? You're making it seem like she's gone forever and that there's no hope. Without hope, Hank, we have nothing. Don't you understand that?' she continued, her slippers crunching over the broken glass littering the floor. 'If you're telling me there's no hope, then I may as well just lie down now and beg to die.'

Hank sat still; his head hung low.

'I'm sorry. To both of you,' he said after an extended, awkward silence. 'Mum, I don't mean to be so aggressive,' he apologised, getting up and putting his arm round Elsie, placing a kiss on her head. 'And I'm sorry for saying what I did,' he continued, going over and hugging Martha, pressing his face into her shoulder. 'I haven't given up on her,' he whispered into her ear. 'I'll never give up on finding Lucy, I promise.'

Pulling a chair next to Elsie, Hank sat back at the table.

'Mum, I know it's hard, but I do need to know everything. I need to know what was going through Dad's mind. What he was thinking, how he was behaving and what he was talking about. Anything you remember could help us to find out where he's gone.' Hank took hold of his mum's bruise-ridden hand. 'We haven't got much time. All of Dad's things are still in the cupboard, and he hasn't taken any clothes or money,' he said, handing his mum a tissue. Elsie looked up.

'I'd left him downstairs watching the TV the night before, as usual,' she replied. 'But when I woke up in the morning, his side of the bed wasn't rumpled.' Elsie blew her nose and wiped her eyes. 'He was nowhere to be seen, Hank. There was nothing out of place. There was nothing unusual. The house was just empty, and quiet.'

'What about the days leading up to it?'

'I've already told you,' replied Elsie. 'Your dad had been doing alright these past few weeks. He'd been going through a good spell, no major episodes to speak of.' She paused to wipe her eyes again. 'He'd been going on about Golifer, something about spotting him over by the far side of the lake. But most days your dad would think someone was here, it was nothing unusual. I've never seen anyone come near here in months – years, even. Only the postman and milkman.'

'You live hidden away. You don't have any friends, and only Perry Golifer as a neighbour,' said Hank. 'That's why nobody comes here, Mum.' He walked over to the window and looked up at the sky, searching the clouds for answers. Searching for a miracle.

'Me and your dad have lived in Finchley for over fifty years,' said Elsie, 'and people thought we were strange from the very first day we arrived. They didn't give us a chance. So why would I want to make friends?' Elsie looked at Martha, then back at Hank. 'And they've always blamed me and your dad for what happened to Lucy, like *we* were responsible. Do you know how that feels?' Martha raised her eyebrows, taking an exaggerated intake of breath and clearing her throat.

'Do you have something to say, Martha?' Elsie snapped.

'Well, you and Henry *were* in part responsible, weren't you?' said Martha. 'I mean, *you* were meant to be taking care of Lucy that day. We left her with you, thinking that she'd be safe, and yet she went missing. You left my children unsupervised, knowing that Henry was in bed asleep, and nobody could vouch for your story, only you.'

'After all these years, I can't believe we're still having this same bloody discussion,' barked Elsie. 'You're as bad as them out there. You know what happened. You shouldn't need people to vouch for *my* story. I'm your mother-in-law. I'm family. Henry was upstairs asleep and I nipped out for milk. That's it. I left my money on the shop counter because nobody was there and I wanted to get back home quickly. And when I got back, Henry was still upstairs asleep and Lucy was gone. Mary was outside playing. I didn't see anybody because there was nobody around. It was early. My only mistake that day was going out for milk. I was trying my best to make the girls stop crying after you'd both gone and left them balling their eyes out!'

Elsie protested her innocence in such a manner that one couldn't help but question whether she was telling the truth.

Martha muttered something beneath her breath.

'Pardon?'

'It's a little strange that nobody – *nobody*, not one single person – saw you that morning,' said Martha. You hardly blend into a crowd, Elsie, looking the way you do, always wearing your pinafore and slippers, even when out in public. Every single time I go up that main street, I see a car, or a pedestrian, or a bus, or a cyclist. Not once in the past six years have I driven up that road and not seen anybody. And yet, you were on foot, and were out for over an hour, and you didn't see a single soul, and nobody saw you.'

'Finchley is a small place, you know that,' said Elsie. 'It's not like I was walking in town without being seen by anyone. Most people round here are over sixty. They're not up at the crack of dawn to get to work. Somebody will have seen me that morning, they just didn't want to come forward.'

Martha's eyebrows raised.

'Just say what you have to say, Martha.'

'Your story can't help but raise concerns, that's all I'm saying,' said Martha. 'You were the last adult to see Lucy, and yet you don't know what happened to her. And Henry slept through everything, apparently, and doesn't remember hearing anything unusual. Utter craziness.'

Elsie's blood boiled. 'Don't you dare insinuate that Henry and I are crazy, because we're not! Neither of us would ever have hurt Lucy. You know that better than anyone.' Elsie was just getting started. 'And, whilst we all seem to be speaking our minds, then so will I.' She pointed her finger with more conviction than a barrister sentencing someone to life without parole. 'Had you not left them that day, crying their eyes out because they didn't want their mummy to go, then Lucy would never have vanished. Just admit it. So, why don't you try pointing the finger at yourself?'

Martha's face reddened. 'Don't you think I go over and over in my mind every single detail of that day, thinking, wishing and praying that I'd done things differently?' she snapped. 'I don't sleep at night. Instead, I punish myself for not having chosen to stay at the house and have a picnic. Or wishing that the car had broken down so we couldn't have gone anywhere. Or wishing that it'd rained so that we wouldn't have wanted to go for a day trip at all.' She flung her arms in the air in frustration. 'I already hate myself, Elsie, so there's really no need to try and make me feel guilty.'

The room fell quiet as Martha sat back down, resting her head on the table and shielding herself with her arms. 'But I naïvely assumed that I could trust my own mother-in-law with my daughters. How wrong I was.' She shook her head, refusing to look at Elsie. It was a case of déjà vu, repeating the same arguments.

Elsie stood up and banged things on the counter top, storming around the kitchen. 'You must trust me. You must know, deep down, that I would never have done anything to hurt Lucy. Otherwise, you wouldn't still leave Mary with me, would you?

And thank goodness you do. She's better off with me, anyway. You never used to be like this, Martha, always angry and drunk. You're throwing everything away because you can't control your bloody addiction.'

Martha lifted her head. 'I'm no different to anyone else by choosing to have a couple of glasses of wine to help me sleep and unwind,' she replied. 'And regardless of what I believe, I have no bloody choice but to leave Mary with you, because Hank insists on it. If it were up to me, I'd never again leave her alone with you.' Martha's hands were shaking and dark bags hung below her eyes. She smelt of stale alcohol, and her bones were beginning to protrude. Her cheekbones more pronounced than ever, and her face appeared gaunt. She looked like an alcoholic.

Hank held out his hands, acting as peacemaker. 'Come on, you two,' he intervened. 'I really can't take any more fighting between ourselves.' Martha and Elsie obeyed his request for a ceasefire.

'None of this is helping,' he continued. 'None of us are to blame. Nobody in this room woke up that morning wishing for Lucy to go missing, did we?' Hank turned to his mum. 'You shut yourself away from the world, and so people are suspicious and wonder what you have to hide. If they don't get answers, Mum, then they will make up their own stories, whether they're true or not.'

'People in this bloody village can believe all they want,' said Elsie. 'And the same goes for the police, and the same goes for you!' She looked at Martha. 'I still remember the way that the police looked at me, wanting to know why I couldn't give them better answers, or tell them exactly where Lucy was.'

Elsie looked through to the hallway at one of Lucy's photos. 'Don't you think I still feel guilty? I live with the guilt every single day. I'd do anything to get Lucy back, you know I would. Even after all these years, I think about her every minute of every day. I go over each detail like it happened only moments ago, just in case I missed something.'

She began to cry. 'All everybody round here is interested in is making out like me and Henry could be capable of causing harm to Lucy. The person they should be pointing the finger at is Golifer. You know it, the police know it, and yet they do nothing.'

At the time of Lucy's disappearance, Perry Golifer was living in his Ivy Dean property only a stone's throw away from Elsie and Henry Lane's lake house. Their two properties nestled on the periphery of the village. Six years on, and he still lived hidden away in the same house. From the attic window at Wisteria, you could see over to Perry's house through the dividing trees and, on a clear day, if you looked with binoculars, you'd be able to see right into his back garden. Perry had been spotted lurking in the village the same day that Lucy had disappeared, an unusual sighting for a man who kept himself hidden behind the gates of his ivy-covered property. Nobody knew much about him, or wanted to take the time to get to know him, his reputation shunning him from society.

'They questioned Golifer about Lucy, Mum, we all know that,' said Hank. 'They didn't have any evidence. That's not the police's fault. They couldn't arrest him without a reason.'

Aged in his late thirties at the time of Lucy's disappearance, whenever seen in the village, a tatty cigarette usually hung from the corner of Golifer's mouth, and he typically dressed top to toe in denim. His charcoal hair and patchy stubble accentuated his scruffy appearance. He looked like a stereotypical "bad guy", the kind you might see in the movies.

'Don't defend him, Hank,' snapped Martha, shaking her head. 'Elsie's right. It wasn't just us who thought he could have had something to do with it. Others did, too, yet they let him go despite his record.'

Perry Golifer was the prime suspect in an investigation only a few years prior to Lucy's disappearance, when a young girl called Katie Banks had gone missing on her way home from the local Finchley Catholic Primary School. Golifer had been spotted loitering by the school on a number of days leading up to the disappearance of Katie, but he was never found to be guilty of her murder.

'They only bloody questioned him on his whereabouts the day our Lucy went missing, that stupid Officer Swift confessed as much,' said Martha. 'But that's all they did. They didn't get a warrant and search his house, did they?'

'Let's not start this again,' shouted Hank, frustration infiltrating his words. 'We're just wasting time by talking about him. We need to find Dad, and all we're doing is bloody bickering.' He looked at Elsie. 'Mum, Martha and I have searched the whole of Finchley, and nobody has seen Dad. Some people couldn't even recall the last time they'd spotted him in the village,' he said, holding his head in his hands. 'So, today, why don't we call some hospitals further afield to see if anyone's found him?' Hank shrugged his shoulders, turning back to face Elsie. 'The police seem too busy investigating us to focus their search anywhere else, so it's up to us, isn't it?' he said, grabbing the phone book. 'Another day of aimlessly wandering round Finchley will drive me utterly insane.'

'Why don't we knock on Golifer's door?' asked Elsie. 'Ask if he's seen Dad? He's my only neighbour, and maybe he saw which way he went? He could have been in his garden and just happened to notice the direction Henry was heading.' Her statement struck like a bullet.

Martha bolted out of her seat. 'You must be bloody joking. I'm not asking that bastard for any favours. Absolutely not. How could you even suggest such a thing, Elsie? Have you not heard anything we've just said? Have you suddenly forgotten the past? You're out of your bloody mind.'

'If the police *really* thought he'd taken Lucy, then they'd have got a warrant and stormed their way in,' said Elsie. 'A long time has passed, Martha, and now we need his help to find Henry. He might just let us take a look in his garden, check that Henry isn't sheltering behind any of those bushes, or in his shed. And, if he lets us in now, then it's doubtful he ever had anything to hide, right?'

'What makes you think he's just going to open the door to us?' said Martha.

'If Dad was hiding over in his garden, we'd know about it, Mum,' added Hank. 'Golifer would kick him out in a bloody second, and Dad would recognise his surroundings. Finchley is a tiny village; even if confused, I'm sure he'd find his way home from just over there. He'd be able to see the bloody lake in the distance.'

'We're all worried about Henry, Elsie,' said Martha. 'But knocking on Perry Golifer's door isn't going to bring him home. We need to search further afield. Like Hank says, if Henry was close to home, he'd find his way back.'

In Elsie's mind, they were right, Finchley was a small village. The centre was made up of only a handful of shops, and therefore offered a limited supply of secluded nooks in which he would have been able to hide, or remain hidden for any substantial length of time. The small number of shops and businesses were nestled in a horseshoe shape around the sea front, and they created a quaint, cobbled square and focal point for passers-by.

The only noteworthy attraction credited to Finchley was a disued lighthouse set not too far offshore. The red and white building stood vibrant, especially when the sun rose, warming the colourful, iconic stripes. There was a modest church, plus a couple of pubs, all of which were located only a few metres away from the centre.

But even though Finchley was a small village with few and far between places to hide, that is exactly what Henry lane was doing. He was hiding.

Seven

UNBEKNOWN TO HANK, MARTHA AND ELSIE, MARY HAD been listening in on their entire conversation. She had stationed herself on the landing when she'd heard the hoover and banging of her parents' bedroom door. Her hands held the banister rails, her head squeezing through the gap, just like a cartoon animation of a prisoner locked behind bars. Mary could hear every word being spoken. It wasn't like she was secretly listening in on a private conversation – the raised voices would've been audible from the front lawn.

Indentation marks appeared on her skin the longer she lingered, the sharp edges of the wood cutting into her cheeks. At the point at which it was insinuated that both her sister and grandad could be over at Perry Golifer's house, she began to cry. She could see his house from her bedroom window; if they were both over there, then she wanted to go and bring them home, even if her parents didn't think it was a good idea.

Mary ran back to her bedroom, slamming the door in an attempt to drown out the shouting before it could follow her inside. But she could still hear the argument, her mum's voice becoming irate. Martha often tended to sound irate when speaking about Lucy. Mary hid herself under her duvet and covered her ears. Beneath the duvet felt like her safe place to hide, a place where the world didn't feel so scary.

Could Lucy and Grandad really be hiding over there in that creepy looking house? she thought, the words jamming in her brain. She stood up and walked to the window, gazing out towards Perry's house. She squinted, trying to make out any movement behind his windows. Mary had heard her family arguing about Perry many times over the years- maybe he had been the one who had taken her sister away.

'Grandad, can you hear me?' she whispered, taking a few seconds to listen for a reply. 'Shout really loud if you can hear me. I'm over here,' she said, waving through the window, watching for a response. 'Lucy, can *you* hear me? Please come home. I'm lonely without you.'

She moved away deflated, and instead looked underneath the bed again, just in case Lucy happened to be there, but she wasn't. She looked in the wardrobe, behind all the clothes, but Lucy wasn't there either. She pulled up the lid on the toy box, which was full of nothing but junk. Pangs of guilt bubbled within Mary's insides, the *what if* haunting her once again. Mary wasn't surprised at not finding her sister, but the disappointment felt just as bad as the first time she'd looked. The desperation to learn that she wasn't to blame for her sister's disappearance led Mary to continually search for Lucy. She also felt a longing to be able to trust her grandparents, knowing that they weren't to blame either.

Mary reached underneath her bed, grabbing her hidden box.

'I've kept my box hidden from Mum and Dad,' she said before pausing, listening to make sure nobody was climbing the stairs. 'Mum would be *so* cross if she knew I had something of yours that she doesn't know about. She thinks she knows everything. But she doesn't. We always had secrets, me and you, didn't we? And we still do.' Mary looked at the box, her fingers hovering over the squiggles her sister had drawn in red felt tip pen. 'Do you hear how loud Mum shouts, Lucy, whenever I touch something of yours? *How would you like it if I touched your toys when you weren't here? Lucy will be back soon, and then you can play with the toys together.*' Mary mimicked her mum's voice. 'But I know you wouldn't mind me touching your stuff, Lucy, because we always shared everything, didn't we?'

Mary's whole body visibly shrunk when she exhaled. She opened the box and took out the photo of her and Lucy.

'I'm not even allowed to sleep in our bedroom at home anymore. I'm in the small room now, that's my new bedroom. It's dead tiny and there's no room to play. But I don't dare grumble because Mum would shout, and she shouts enough already.' Mary reached out her hand and closed her eyes. She imagined her sister's warm touch against hers. 'Mum thinks she's the only one that misses you, Lucy. But you're my twin sister, so I miss you more than anyone.'

Mary could still hear muffled bits of the conversation from below, plus the sound of someone climbing the stairs, opening and closing doors. She opened her door so a tiny crack appeared, and listened in.

'I can't find it anywhere, Hank. Dad must've been wearing it,' shouted Elsie, who was continuing to rummage through Henry's chest of drawers, flinging clothes onto the bed in a constant stream. Martha and Hank appeared at the top of the stairs, so Mary eased her door closed, pressing her ear against the wood.

'It's important that we know what Dad is wearing, Mum,' said Hank. 'So look again, make sure it isn't here.'

'If it is the Merlot-coloured jumper, Elsie, I don't remember seeing it since we arrived,' said Martha.

Mary hated it when her mum mentioned alcohol in a conversation, pretending like she didn't have a problem. Why couldn't her mum just say the red-coloured jumper like normal people would? What was more upsetting, however, was the fact that Mary even knew what Merlot was. Not only did she know what it was, but she knew how it tasted.

During a Saturday morning not too long ago, when her parents were still in bed and hungover, Mary had gone into the kitchen at just gone ten o'clock, wanting to fix herself some breakfast. Her stomach had been rumbling so much that she felt faint. With not a drop of milk in the fridge, Mary had pulled over a chair and used it to reach up to the top shelf, taking hold of the carton of cranberry juice. She didn't particularly care for cranberry, it was a bit tart, but on this occasion, it was a better option than nothing. After pouring herself a glass and taking a sizeable gulp, she spat out what hadn't yet managed to escape down her gullet, spraying the liquid out like a hosepipe. The cranberry juice had been replaced with red wine, later identified as a Bargain Booze special called Oyster Bay Merlot. 'A classic New Zealand wine with a fruity flavour', a wine that paired well with a rare roast beef, coq au vin or lamb chops. But not well suited for a child's breakfast beverage. Since that occasion, every time Mary made herself a drink, she gave it a whiff first, just to make sure. She wasn't a fan of Merlot. Cranberry juice tasted better.

Mary knew exactly which of her Grandad's jumper they were all talking about. It was his favourite red jumper that he kept in his shed and often wore whilst pottering about outside. It had a tiny fish stitched over the chest, and he always wore it, regardless of whether it was spring, summer, autumn or winter. Grandad Lane didn't seem to shift with the seasons; his red jumper was suitable for all occasions, the type of clothing that kept you warm in winter, yet cool in summer. Mary thought she'd seen the jumper somewhere since her arrival at Wisteria, or perhaps it was just wishful thinking on her part. If she'd seen the jumper, then maybe that would mean that her grandad wasn't missing after all; maybe he was just avoiding having to speak with everyone, or get caught up in the middle of endless arguments. Mary wouldn't be cross with him if that was the case. She just wished that he'd taken her to hide with him.

Mary walked back across her room and stood in front of the window, looking out, stretching up so that she could see. The sun manoeuvred itself slowly from behind a cloud and shone directly into her room, her eyes catching sight of something moving. She pressed her face to the window, and looked towards the house across the woods. She leapt back at the sight of a figure in Perry's garden, cowering behind her curtains. Not that anyone could have seen her, not unless they were specifically looking, like she was.

Is it Grandad? she thought, recalling the conversation she'd just heard in the kitchen about the possibility of Henry hiding in Perry's bushes or garden shed. She grabbed the binoculars she kept on her windowsill, typically used for watching the ducks landing on the lake. She climbed onto the toy box to get a better view, crouching on her knees to keep the majority of her body hidden. The person Mary had seen wasn't Henry. Life just wasn't like that in Mary's world.

'It's Perry,' she gasped, cigarette smoke wafting through the air, the trail of fumes becoming faint as the smoke was carried away by the breeze. Perry Golifer's baseball cap bobbed above the fence. He was rummaging in his garden, the tatty cap on his head worn in the unorthodox way, twisted backwards.

'Do you have my sister and grandad?' she whispered.

Shielding her eyes from the sun with cupped hands, Mary pressed her forehead against the window.

'What's he doing? What's that?' she gasped. Mary could see something clenched in Perry's hand. A scarf? Or maybe a blanket? Or maybe it could've been a carrier bag. It was pretty hard to tell from such a distance what it was that Perry was holding.

Mary pressed her head closer to the window and grabbed the binoculars, straining her eyes so that she could follow Perry's every move whilst he roamed the garden. She stood still, trying to prevent her hands from shaking, her warm breath spreading itself over the window. Perry's clenched fist filled the lenses of her binoculars once he came into focus, and for the first time she was able to see what he as clutching. Gripped between his fingers was fabric, unmistakable deep red fabric.

Grandad's jumper?

Mary told herself to take a breath, her erratic breathing was causing her head to feel like it was spinning. Her mouth felt dry and her hands began to shake, the binocular string dangling from her fingers. She didn't know for sure that Perry was holding her Grandad's red jumper -lots of people could own a red jumper of some sort. Before she blurted out the discovery to her family,

Mary needed to be sure what Perry was holding and, from such a distance, she couldn't be certain.

The sound of a police siren in the distance caused Perry to stand still in his garden. Mary didn't take her eyes off him, his body remaining crouched, moving only when the siren faded seconds later. A sudden movement from him caused Mary to drop her binoculars, her body stooping below the windowsill. Her face was flushed, her heart pumping erratically. A sudden recollection made Mary's body judder, her memory now recalling where she had seen her grandad's jumper. Crawling across the floor, Mary placed her box back under the bed before darting downstairs and out past the kitchen.

'I'm just going out to play for a bit. I'll be back soon,' she shouted. Her mum, dad and Elsie were still bickering in the kitchen about where to look for Henry.

Mary careered out the door, not waiting for a reply, allowing the door to bang on its hinges. Upon reaching her grandad's shed, the weathered building that was nestled just at the side of the lake, she paused for breath.

'It must be in here somewhere,' she said, opening the door just like she had done a few days previous, the bottom scraping along the ground. The door eased ajar, just like it had done each time the girls had taken to crouching in the garden hideaway as young children. The sun's glare seeped into the crevice, casting light over the dingy interior. Mary loved rooting around in the shed. She never knew what she was going to find – old toys of hers and Lucy's, things that had belonged to her dad when he was younger, or even things from her parents' wedding day, like her mum's bouquet, petals from which had been preserved by being pressed into a book. The tatty shed was like a Tardis.

She searched further back, rummaging through the stacked boxes and piles of junk.

'It's gone,' she announced, clattering stuff out the way to reveal her sister's old bike. The pink shopping basket usually attached to the handlebars was missing, as was the red jumper which she now recalled seeing inside the basket the day she arrived at Wisteria. She had been sat in the shed, right next to the bike, and had eaten a packet of crisps. She'd purposefully left the empty packet in the basket so that her parents wouldn't know she'd taken them. Wrenching the door wide open and searching on the floor, Mary looked everywhere for her Grandad's jumper and the other missing things. The jumper had to be there somewhere; she'd seen it only days prior. But despite her efforts to find it, the jumper had now gone.

In her rush, she failed to see the spyhole that'd been created in the wall, the view from which led straight up to Mary's attic bedroom.

Eight

THE ABANDONED ALLOTMENTS OF WILLOW WOODS basked in the early morning sun, the light rising over the low-lying Cumbrian hills. Only the intermittent sound of the chirping of wrens could be heard when alarm clocks brushed past the hour of 4.00 am. The majority of Finchley residents hadn't yet stirred, or were not even close to commencing their day. But Elsie Lane had already awoken and had put on her olive and lemon anorak. Like an unwanted mouse, she scurried in secret through the house. She eased the front door open, being careful to avoid making any noise. She didn't want to wake the rest of the house; they would question why she was up at such an early hour, and she wouldn't be able to tell them the truth.

Elsie plodded round to the side of the house until she reached the basement door. She struggled to pull the tumble dryer away from the wall, but forced a gap just big enough for her hand to fit through. She knelt on the stone floor, her knees aching upon the unyielding surface whilst her arm stretched behind. The back of the dryer pulled away with ease, her hand feeling for the washing bag she'd hidden the day that Lucy vanished.

She rummaged, trying to locate the bag, but she felt nothing but pipes. *Where is it?* The longer it took her to find, the more Elsie became paranoid that someone was watching her. But then, after a few more seconds, her hand found something loose and she pulled the bag free. She rolled over onto her thigh, and held the items close to her chest. *Thank goodness.* She didn't need to look in the bag; she knew exactly what was inside. She'd thought about little else for the previous six years.

With the bag hidden beneath her coat, and the house still sleeping, Elsie meandered her way up the deserted stretch of road. The fact that she was wearing slippers wasn't an accident, or a sign that she was becoming a bit loopy; Elsie had always worn slippers on the rare occasions she chose to venture beyond the perimeter of her property. It never bothered her that people sniggered; it gave them something to talk about other than the weather. Her slippers were comfy, that was all.

Her head was stooped, threatening to topple the crimson hat uncharacteristically perched over her curls. There was still an early morning chill clinging to the air, but Elsie didn't notice; she was too preoccupied to take notice of the world around her. Drops of dew clung to leaf tips, and her feet made a fresh track through the scattering of blossom petals on the pavement. The walk seemed to take an age, and an unnerving level of apprehension filled her bones. The road seemed never-ending and, with each step, she questioned her plan. But it was too late now for second thoughts; her destination was in sight. She urged herself to take a few more paces, then she'd be out of sight and able to breathe easier.

The dilapidated gate containing the allotment grounds creaked open. Elsie's handprint remained visible on the wood amid a pool of early-morning moisture that had not yet evaporated. The barren patch of untended land at Willow Woods hadn't altered in years, the local community having failed to make use of the space despite the initial interest. When the allotments first opened their gates over ten years ago, there was an influx of people bidding for a patch of the land; it was as if the ten rods plot that you would be allocated was going to be more valuable than gold bullion. Which, of course, it wasn't. Even if the terrible British summers happened to be kind, and you were able to harvest some potatoes, a few scraggy carrots, a waterlogged courgette or a bunch of unripe tomatoes, the income you could make from selling the produce at market would barely cover the cost of the initial packets of seeds. And, if you were hoping to feed a family off the plot, then someone, if not everyone, would be left hungry at meal times.

Despite owning acres of land, Henry Lane had purchased a plot at the communal allotment site. He loved the excitement and prospect of growing nothing more than what amounted to an odd tomato and misshapen potato. He wasn't looking to make money. And he wasn't looking to feed himself and his wife. He just wanted to have a go, not that Elsie shared his initial enthusiasm.

'The trees shade all the land round our lake and woods,' he'd said in defence when Elsie questioned why on Earth he felt the need to purchase the allotment. 'And people on the television say that gardening is good for you; a bit of exercise will do me good.'

Only Elsie knew about Henry's allotment patch. It was not that they intentionally kept it a secret from the rest of the family, but it had just never come up in conversation. And no sooner was the project launched than the whole thing failed in spectacular style. After too many terrible consecutive winters, followed by too many terrible summers, the land became infertile and it was impossible to grow anything other than weeds, let alone fruit and vegetables. The allotments became abandoned and nothing more than council wasteland.

Wading through the long grass, Elsie searched for familiarity, any points of reference. She recalled having sat on a bench, which was nowhere to be seen. She also recalled that Henry's plot of land had been situated near a path that led out onto another field. However, looking around, she couldn't see any trace of a path, or entrance to another field. Time, of course, had moved on since her last visit during late autumn/early winter by her reckoning, when the leaves were bare. And, now that it was summer, of course the landscape took on a different identity. It was now July and the trees were in bloom, offering no olive branch. It was like Elsie was stepping into Willow Woods for the very first time.

Her feet were drenched in dew. The cool moisture soaked through her slippers and penetrated her skin.

'Where is it?' Elsie mumbled, a look of confusion taking residency. Having walked the perimeter twice, she began to rethink her plan and, in her mind, debated alternative locations for where she could hide the contents of her bag.

But then came a breakthrough.

'Here we are,' she said, pausing at the far side of Willow Woods. The sight of an upturned green bucket caught her attention, the rusty bucket lying abandoned amongst an ambush of thorny weeds. 'I knew it,' she said, taking hold of the very bucket that she'd sometimes used as a seat when the illusive bench was occupied.

The once well-maintained area began to breathe a sense of comforting familiarity the more Elsie scrutinised the now neglected, modest patch of land. All the canes Henry had initially planted were still visible, albeit broken up, lying scattered over the ground. A flood of emotions threatened to topple Elsie's façade. She could picture Henry kneeling on the grass, using his hoe to turn the soil. The look of satisfaction that had swept across his face once he had completed his patch was still fresh in her mind. She could picture the plot like nothing had changed, like time had stood still. She could hear Henry debating with himself about how and where was best to plant which seeds. Elsie looked around, the voice and image so vivid, but Henry wasn't there.

She wiped her eyes. 'Where are you, Henry?' she whispered. Images of her husband haunted the allotment no matter where she cast her glance. Her tears fell harder on realising that, not only was Henry no longer here, tending to his allotment at Willow Woods, but he wasn't back at home, either. In her mind, she couldn't picture where he was, or who he was with, or even if he was safe.

Elsie lowered her body to the floor, her aching joints resting on the soft ground. She bowed her head for a moment, as if praying.

'I need you, Henry. I can't manage on my own. I don't know how to live without you here by my side.' Elsie's mouth produced plumes of white mist, her warm breath escaping into the fresh, new dawn. 'I need to talk to you,' she continued. 'There's so much I need your help with.' She looked up to the sky, the morning haze starting to disperse, bringing into view the promise of a striking summer's day.

'Hank and Martha are here, Henry. They've brought Mary, too. I'm worried about them. They're not coping, and I don't know what to do. I don't know what I *can* do.' Elsie's emotions erupted. The dark fears she usually kept inside were finally being granted the opportunity to be released. The dam had been broken, and a barrage of guilt and pain flowed like a torrent.

She clasped her hands together, an offering of self-comfort. 'And I'm worried.' She took a deep breath before continuing with her moment of private confession. 'Things I remember happening to you, all those years ago, are happening to me. I know they are.' Elsie shook her head. 'It's happening and there's nothing I can do to stop it.'

She blew her nose and took a deep breath. 'I'm having to write silly notes so I don't forget where I've put things. I remember where they are eventually, but it takes me so long. And I sometimes struggle to find the right word, like it just isn't there anymore. Mary's starting to notice, I know she is, which is making me fluster. I shouldn't be alone with her. What if I leave the cooker on? Or what if I'm busy doing something and she wanders off? Hank and Martha are too busy to notice. They're in a mess, Henry. Drinking too much. They're a wreck, the pair of them.'

There was no priest that morning to offer advice or support. Her confessions simply drifted away, becoming lost forever.

She took a trowel out of her anorak and began to dig into the soft, moist earth.

'I'm scared that if I don't hide these now, I might forget,' she whispered. 'And eventually someone will find them, I know they will. And then there'd be more questions, and we still don't know the answers, do we? So, what's the point in showing anyone now? It'd only bring it all back. It'd cause more upset, and it's not going to bring Lucy home, is it? It'll be safe here, I know it will.' Frantically digging out a small patch of earth, she turned to check her surroundings every few seconds.

The dark shadow of paranoia set in.

The sound of a car tearing down the lane caused Elsie to pause and hold her breath. She thought someone had seen her and that the police were on her trail. Or that Hank had heard her leave and he'd followed her, wanting to know what she was up to. The driver of the car was just a bakery worker heading off to work. Once the car whizzed past and the sound of its engine faded into the distance, she continued digging. Mud stained her knees and her clothes were soon covered in dirt. After over ten minutes of burrowing, Elsie's hands tired. She became careless and accidentally nicked herself with the trowel on her left hand. The pierced skin produced drops of blood.

'Ouch,' she scowled, shaking her hand to alleviate the pain. The blood dripped onto the ground and merged with the wet grass.

She wrapped the wounded hand with a handkerchief, stemming the flow. The hidden carrier bag beneath her coat fell to the ground, the contents tipping out. The pair of lilac socks and the knife lay on the ground. The socks were so tiny, like they could have fitted a doll. Lucy's feet at the time could only have been a child's size seven. And, even though six years had passed since the socks had been seen, they were undoubtably Lucy's. Elsie permitted herself a moment, her hands taking hold of the socks, pressing them to her face, her nose drinking in any lingering scent of Lucy. The material felt soft against her skin, and for a moment, it felt like Lucy had never disappeared. The socks still showed traces of blood and, if inspected, contained fragments of her DNA. Elsie looked round before stuffing the evidence back into the bag, only nature bearing witness.

She heard a man's voice shouting, 'Rascal? Where are you?' The sound of footsteps became increasingly louder in the distance. Elsie placed the carrier bag into the freshly dug hole, scooping mud back over with her hands in a frantic fashion. With only half of the hole covered, Elsie heard a noise coming from behind.

'Go away,' she shooed upon sight of a white, excited Spaniel, its tail wagging profusely. The Spaniel's legs bounded over until its paws were covered in mud, its nose sniffing Elsie and the disturbed land. 'Shoo!' she insisted, pushing Rascal away, encouraging him to run. In true Spaniel style, Rascal assumed that Elsie was part of a big game. And so, he refused to go as instructed, and instead barked.

'Rascal?' Elsie heard the man's voice shout again. But this time the voice was louder, the man now only metres away at the other side of the dividing trees. Rascal scarpered, soon uninterested by Elsie's standoffish approach, and chased after his next adventure in the adjoining field.

'There you are,' announced his owner when Rascal appeared next to him in the next field, circling his feet. 'Come on, I think that's enough for now.'

Elsie remained still. She listened until the sound of the early morning dog walker vanished.

She drove her hands back into the dirt. 'Nearly done,' she said, her hands covered with soil. The carrier bag was soon buried and the ground re-filled. Stones, grass and loose foliage were placed over the top of the site to disguise the recent disturbance. 'No one will find them there,' she added, towering over the small patch of land that now concealed the secret she'd kept for so long. She lowered her head at that poignant moment. Her actions meant that she would never now hand the evidence into the police. It felt like she was burying more than just some socks and a knife.

It felt like she was burying Lucy's memory.

Even if she didn't want to admit it, and believed in her motives, Elsie was as guilty as anyone.

She turned her back on the patch of allotment, leaving behind the specs of blood her cataract eyes had failed to spot and disguise. Her hands were smeared with a concoction of blood and dirt. Her slippers felt heavy with saturation and her footprints embedded themselves into the moist ground with each step she took, navigating her way to the exit.

Once through the gate, Elsie saw that the main road had increased in traffic and commuter activity. Early risers were already partway through their journey to the office. The milkman had started to make his rounds, and the other ambiguous noises that were created when a once sleeping village had started to stir echoed through the trees that lined both sides of the road.

Elsie felt vulnerable; a stationary target. And she was right. She looked a state. The mud on her clothes, the slippers on her feet, and her peculiar choice of headwear all worked to cast her as an outsider. Most of the people out and about in the village at such an early hour each day recognised their fellow commuters. The same cars travelled in the same direction, along the same stretch of road, at the same time every single day. The same cyclist navigated her daily commute to the hospital where she worked as an anaesthesiologist; she, too, recognised most of the cars that passed her. The village worked like clockwork, and Elsie didn't fit into this standard, morning portrait.

She remained on the pavement, resembling a deer caught in a car's headlights. A stream of cars sped past her, the drivers' subconscious minds registering the discrepancy to their daily commute; but each one failed to stop to check whether the odd-looking lady was alright. The majority of the passers-by didn't think twice about the vulnerable, elderly lady wearing nothing on her feet but her slippers. But once at work and settled into his comfortable office chair, Steven Knicks picked up the phone and called the police, reporting the peculiar woman he had passed.

Back on the road, in the distance, Elsie caught sight of the church steeple, its pinnacle scraping the sky. The building grabbed her attention and caused her to become distracted, and she crossed the road without looking.

The door to the church was closed, the grounds quiet, and no signs of life could be seen. The vicarage in the distance also stood still, its inhabitants not yet partaking in the dawning of the new day. Elsie placed her hand on the church door handle just as a police siren sounded in the distance, its piercing noise becoming louder upon approach. Elsie's heart drummed. Her hand pressed all the way down on the handle, the door releasing just as the police car tore up the road. She disappeared inside, shutting the door behind her. God was on her side, his doors open, permitting her a temporary refuge.

The police siren screeched and was still audible in spite of Elsie's best effort to block out the sound with the towering church door. Elsie's back was pressed against it, her lungs trying to regain control of her breathing. The car sounded like it had paused in the near vicinity, the sirens finally stopping, but replaced by the sound of a car door banging closed.

Inside the church, Elsie walked towards the alter and paused, her head tilting upwards. Beams of sunlight reflected through the windows, illuminating the cavity with iridescent rays representing each shade of the rainbow. Her hands shook inside her apron pocket, the cut seeping blood through the saturated handkerchief.

'Please, come home, Henry,' she said to the heavens, her head arched and eyes closed. Whilst kneeling at the altar, she failed to hear the developments outside.

Sergeant Swift was scribbling in her notepad the statement provided by Steven Knicks, whose testimony stated that he'd witnessed a lady who appeared injured with blood on her hands. Steven had said that the lady looked afraid and confused.

After putting a message out to local officers on duty in the area, Swift scanned the street in both directions, looking for any clues as to which way the lady may have travelled. There were no dropped items littering the pavement. There was no noticeable damage to the church or sign of a disturbance. There were no traces of blood. There was no wounded victim. There wasn't much of anything. Annoyed by the potentially overzealous member of the public who could have jumped to the wrong assumption, Swift sighed. She'd missed her breakfast, all for a wild goose chase.

Now that she was here, Swift decided to check the church

grounds, the only building in close proximity to the sighting. That way, when she got back to the station, she could say that she'd looked with a good degree of thoroughness for the potential victim. Her heavy, black boots strode up the paved path that navigated the church circumference. The intricate steeple stretched above the treetops, the crucifix pinnacle sparkling in the sun. The church door was closed. There was no sound of a congregation coming from inside, obviously because it was way too early. She was surprised when the heavy wooden door eased open.

'Hello? Is there anyone in here?'

Nobody answered.

Despite there being no artificial lighting, the church interior was sufficiently illuminated by the sun beaming in through the windows. Swift bypassed the stone entrance and ascended the carpeted aisle. The lines of pews either side were neatly arranged with hymn books and donation envelopes. Her eyes scanned each deserted row in turn, her mind preoccupied with thoughts of what she was going to have for her now late breakfast. The call had come in before she'd even had a chance to put the kettle on, and Swift needed to consume sizeable amounts of caffeine to kick start her body before a shift. Coffee was her Achilles' heel.

The steps up to the alter were arranged with knee rests, one of which looked out of place, indentations in the padding from the last pair of knees. She didn't really think anything of it, and so stepped down to the right and paused alongside the antique confessional booth.

Elsie remained hidden inside. She could hear Swift only feet away, and she could smell her perfume. The purple curtain separated their two bodies. Elsie held her breath and prayed. She thought about revealing herself. Maybe this was a sign from God? An opportune moment had presented itself in which she could confess all her sins. Elsie opened her eyes and held out her hand to open the curtain.

Just then, a gust forced open the church door. It banged

against the wall, making Swift jump.

'Shit,' she announced, immediately feeling terrible for swearing in such a sacred place. 'I'll just leave now,' she said, looking up to the alter like she was speaking directly with God, apologising for her foul-mouthed language. She walked back down the aisle, too busy hurrying to notice the faint, wet patches caused by Elsie's slippers. She closed the wooden door behind her.

Outside, Swift paced round the side of the building, the full-length stained-glass window coming into view, its colours lighting her face. The surrounding cemetery seemed undisturbed, with no visible signs of recent activity or potential further witnesses to this apparent sighting of an injured lady. Lowering her head, Swift now focused her attention and searched for traces of blood that could have dripped from the alleged victim. The colourful carpet of summer petals scattering the ground camouflaged any potential evidence.

Some of the ancient gravestones located at the back of the church challenged Swift's height the nearer she approached. The impressive, broad works of stone were showing their age, the names now illegible on their weathered façades. Swift peered behind the rows of gravestones, inspecting for irregularities or signs of disturbance. There were plenty of graveyard gargoyles, their perturbing, angry-looking eyes bearing witness to all cemetery activity. They'd seen Elsie walk into the church. They knew she was hiding in the confessional booth. They knew that Steven Knicks had been correct in his statement.

Swift pressed the button on her shoulder radio.

'No signs of anything here. I'm heading back to the station. Put the kettle on and order us some breakfast. I'm starved.'

Nine

HUDDLED IN THE FOETAL POSITION, WEARING A KNITTED cardigan, Henry Lane remained hidden in an abandoned outbuilding. Scrunched into the far corner with his back pressed against a dirty wall, years' worth of dust scattered over his body, dislodged debris clinging to his clothes. His positioning in the building was strategic. The corner crevice provided him with a perfect vantagepoint, enabling him to witness anyone attempting to enter through the only entrance. In Henry's mind, his hideaway was surrounded. The voices in his mind were out looking for him, ready to take him away. And, as long as he didn't move, he would be safe. If only his confused brain would allow him to realise that there was no need to hide. There were no bad people on the hunt or lookout. There were no men trying to locate his whereabouts, and the building wasn't surrounded.

The shelter wasn't equipped with electricity or heating. It was, in essence, just a crumbling building that had once been used as a cow shed in the early 1900s. But Henry wasn't after any of life's luxuries, or even necessities; all he wanted to do was remain incognito. And, thus far, his mission to achieve anonymity had been successful.

After a few days of sleeping rough, Henry's eyelids grew increasingly heavy. His body had only rested for a few hours since he'd wandered away from Wisteria a few nights previous. Having fallen asleep in his chair back at home, a nightmare had woken him up, but when he opened his eyes, the night terror transpired to be real. He could hear people outside, footsteps traipsing through the woods, getting closer to his house. In Henry's mind, he needed to escape before they found him. Henry hadn't known where he was going, and hadn't taken anything with him. All he wanted to do was escape the voices. But, no matter how far he ran, and no matter in which direction he scarpered, the voices remained his shadow.

The disused cow shed was located in a field next to the local park. The area didn't have any appealing play equipment that attracted children and families during warm weekends. In fact, the single, rusting slide and broken swing couldn't even qualify as a park. There were broken bottles scattered amongst the grass, more litter than a recycling tip, and there were recent signs of rat droppings amongst the rubbish. Dog walkers were the main visitors to the area, the wide expanse of grass allowing their pets to be let off the lead a safe distance away from the main road. The farmer who owned both fields had retired and no longer maintained the land. The cow shed was out of sight from the main road and, actually, most people didn't even know that the shed existed. So, as hiding places went, the rundown cattle coop was a safe choice.

For now, Henry's whereabouts wasn't under threat of being exposed.

ACROSS THE FIELDS, and less than a mile away from the cow shed, the Lane family awoke to another day.

'I don't know how Mum lives like this,' huffed Hank, looking at the crammed kitchen cupboards, tins threatening to topple as soon as the door was released. 'Drives me utterly *insane*,' he said, walking over to inspect all the out-of-date food that was growing mould in the fridge. 'It's bloody disgusting.'

Mary looked up at her dad from the table, anticipating that his temper was about to explode. Mary had become an expert at predicting what her parents would do next, and prided herself whenever her prediction materialised. Her secret game gave her something to think about other than just the arguments. The arguments made her head and ears hurt and, without knowing which one of her grandma's pots of pills could take the pain away, she decided to suffer in silence, as always.

Unbeknown to Mary, any of the pills would've taken away her pain, indefinitely. She could, of course, have just asked her mum for something to ease the pain, but she then ran the risk of being given one of Martha's made-up concoctions. Mary had fallen foul to this trap once before when complaining of stomach ache. Martha had proceeded to give her a drink consisting of boiled liquorice, vinegar and lemons, which naturally had only made Mary vomit. Recalling the vomiting incident ever since, Mary always decided to suffer in silence whenever something was hurting – which, on balance, was a good decision. All the traumatising events that Mary had experienced thus far in her life had caused her to act and think much older than her years, and she had become quite self-sufficient for a ten-year-old. On the days when her mum wasn't able to look after herself, let alone Mary, she would prepare herself food, brush her teeth twice per day, and make sure she looked smart for school, pressing out any creases or scratching off any mud soiling her uniform. Someone looking at Mary for the first time would never guess the turmoil occurring inside. Despite the crumbling family life occurring around her, Mary did her best to ensure she looked and acted like a regular girl.

Back in the kitchen, Martha busied herself with making some coffee. 'We're only here for the holidays, and all that out of date food hasn't done them any harm so far, has it? Your mum's in better health than you and I.' Not that being in better health than Martha was anything to boast about, her being a fully-fledged alcoholic.

'Well, that's debatable, isn't it?' snapped Hank, emptying a whole bottle of curdled milk, the lumps clogging the plughole.

'We can't stop coming back, Hank,' Martha snapped back.

'We can't give up. We can't just stop looking for her now. The year we don't come would mean that it's over. This year could be the year we're destined to find her. We just don't know, do we?' She looked out of the kitchen window, imagining how Lucy once lay on the grass as a baby, attempting her first crawl in a light pink onesie.

'I'm not saying we'll stop coming,' replied Hank. 'All I'm saying is it isn't easy.'

'Easy?' shouted Martha. 'Exactly which aspect of your daughter going missing is *supposed* to be easy?'

Mary dipped her head and gave herself an invisible pat on the back for guessing the predicted argument.

I knew the row would start.

Each year, when the family returned to Finchley, the arguments between her parents increased in frequency. Martha and Hank fought when they were back home in Whitney, but daily life acted to dilute the underlying tension. Hank would be teaching during the week, and the never-ending pile of marking kept him busy during the evenings. That only left the weekends for her parents to tolerate each other. However, during their annual, summer stay at Wisteria, there was nowhere to hide.

Being back in Finchley always brought back the pain of losing Lucy; and yet, despite this, Martha insisted on returning. Each year when they returned to Wisteria, she somehow expected to find Lucy still sitting on the porch, crying, exactly where she'd left her, as if time hadn't moved on. And, each year, when the car pulled up to the house, Martha would close her eyes until the car came to a complete stop, at which point she would open her eyes and expect to see her daughter. The holiday always started on a disappointing note when Lucy obviously wasn't there.

'You're putting words in my mouth, as bloody usual,' Hank said. 'All I'm saying is that if Mum would just learn to take better care of the place, it'd be easier on all of us whilst we're staying here.'

Hank *hated* staying at his childhood home. It was not that

he'd had a bad childhood – quite the contrary. Wisteria had been Hank's own, private playground, and he'd been the envy of his entire class all the way through secondary school. What child wouldn't want their own lake and woods to play in? And, back then, Elsie and Henry weren't quite so eccentric. Admittedly, they didn't fit the mould of most other parents, but they didn't stand out too much, either. But, over the years, everything changed.

'And it's not just about Lucy this year, is it?' Hank continued. 'We need to try and find my dad, and make sure Mum's okay.' He caught sight of the local paper resting on the kitchen worktop, a picture of his dad accompanied by the word 'Missing'.

'He's not well, Martha,' he said. 'We know that, in his current state, he's not going to last longer than a few more nights if he's sleeping rough, which we're assuming he is.' He held the paper up close, staring at his dad's heavy, black-rimmed glasses, hoping that, somehow, they'd provide a clue as to his whereabouts. Hank cast the paper aside when the answer didn't appear, and spread jam liberally across his toast, the moisture saturating the bread until it was soggy. Elsie walked into the kitchen. A bandage was wrapped around her left hand.

Her timing wasn't great, or her choice of words.

'Save some for your dad, he'll be home soon,' she said, watching Hank apply another layer of blackberry jam in an attempt to cover his cremated slice of toast. Hank's fist slammed on the table, rattling the vase of flowers that created a centrepiece.

'You've said that every day for the past six years about Lucy, and where's she, eh?' he shouted. 'Still bloody missing. And now you've managed to go and lose Dad, too. It's no bloody wonder that the police surround us like flies round dogshit. I'm surprised they don't just lock us all up.' Elsie didn't react verbally, but her tut and shake of the head sufficed.

Mary glanced up from her bowl of Sugar Puffs. She managed to look over to her mum without moving her head, the sound of the mushy cereal gulping down her throat, breaking the awkwardness. She thought about mentioning the jumper of

Grandad's that she thought she might have spotted in Perry's garden, but feared the shouting that would follow, and so chose to remain quiet, telling herself that it probably wasn't his anyway.

Please stop arguing.

Bickering at breakfast didn't bode well for the day ahead, Mary had learnt as much over the years. After an early morning argument, her parents tended to spend the whole day acting frosty with one another, each refusing to apologise. Mary remained caught in the middle, often acting as peacemaker, all at the delicate age of ten. If Mary could survive the struggles of her childhood, she was going to go far in life.

'Before Dad can eat any of your bloody jam, we need to find him first,' continued Hank, 'and I honestly don't know what else to do. I don't know where else to look. We've spent the past few days searching this entire area, but nobody's seen him.'

'Grandma, what's happened to your hand?' asked Mary.

'Oh, nothing. I just nicked it when I was doing a bit of gardening,' Elsie replied, placing her hand into her pocket. Mary had never seen her grandma gardening.

'I know,' suggested Mary. 'Why don't we visit some old people's homes? There's Audley Lodge which isn't far away, is it? Grandad *always* said that the food smelled nice whenever we passed it.'

'Great idea, Mary,' replied Hank, slamming the fridge door. 'Maybe your grandad thought he'd be better off there than staying another minute in this bloody mad house. And who could blame him?' He glared at Elsie. 'We'll leave in ten minutes.'

Hank stormed off up the stairs, banging the bathroom door so hard that all the picture frames hanging in the hall wobbled on their fixings. One photo fell off and smashed upon impact, shards of glass scattering like a dropped bag of marbles. Elsie continued to do the washing up like nothing had happened, wincing as the hot, soapy water seeped into her open wound.

'Quick. Get the dustpan and brush, Mary,' insisted Martha, slamming her coffee down. She scurried into the hallway, waiting for Mary. 'We need to tidy up before your dad sees all this mess. He'll get cross again.'

Martha picked up the exposed photo that'd fallen to the floor. She gazed at it for a moment.

'That was Lucy's favourite lilac dress, and she loved that hair bow. She was wearing that exact outfit the day we lost her,' she said, sitting amongst the shards of glass, turning to stroke Mary's cheek when she came and crouched alongside. 'Look, can you see her doll Penelope Pickles is still in her hand, she never let that doll go. And can you see her bracelet shining in the sun?' asked Martha, admiring the gift she had bought for both of her daughters on their fourth birthday. 'I got your names engraved on them. You both loved those bracelets so much, and I can still remember how happy Lucy's face looked when she unwrapped it.'

Mary looked down, pretending to study the photo she'd seen a million times before. Mary had always felt uneasy about her own appearance, knowing that her face reminded Martha of Lucy. Sometimes, Mary would go the extreme measures of trying to hide her features, pulling her long hair across her cheeks, or pretending she was looking at something in a different direction, just so that her mum didn't have to look at her face. If she could have worn a mask, Mary would have grabbed the disguise with both hands.

Whilst sitting next to her mum on the floor, Mary offered some of the wisdom now resting on her shoulders.

'Grandad could be out looking for Lucy, Mum. Maybe he's known all this time where she is, but because he gets muddled, he's only just remembered. So, if we find Grandad, maybe we'll find Lucy, too?' In a rare display of permitted affection, Mary sat on Martha's knee, burying her head into her mum's messy mop of brown, curly hair.

'I remind you of Lucy, don't I, Mum? That's why you always try to make me look different in these stupid clothes.' She looked down at the brown corduroy dungarees she loathed, that made her look like a tomboy. 'I want to change my hair, and my clothes. I don't want to remind you of Lucy, but I don't want to look like this, either.'

Martha jumped up, causing Mary to fall from her knee, her hands landing amongst the broken bits of glass.

'We've spoken about this,' she replied, towering over Mary, her hands placed on her hips. 'When we're here, in Finchley, people mistake you for Lucy. It's really upsetting for me, can't you understand that? I don't ask for much from you, Mary.' Her mother began fixing the bulky jumper that had slipped off her shoulder, her petit frame and protruding bones becoming visible beneath. 'So, I expect you to do this one thing for me.'

'But I'm not allowed to pick what I wear at home either,' Mary replied. 'It's not just when we're here, is it? People laugh at me because I look so stupid. I don't want to remind you of Lucy, but I *hate* being picked on.'

Martha struck Mary across the face before running upstairs, ashamed of her action but unable to offer an apology.

Mary continued to sit amongst the glass, her cheek throbbing, the sting awakening every nerve in her face. Mary took hold of the photo of Lucy, the exact same picture the police had used to publicise her sister's disappearance. The entire world had seen the photo of Lucy sitting on the swing wearing her lilac dress. At the time of her disappearance, the photo was paraded everywhere – in newspapers, in shops, on the news and on the cover of magazines.

Mary inspected the photo in her hand. 'I was once pretty like you, Lucy,' she whispered, admiring Lucy's frilly, lilac dress and jelly shoes, wishing that she could wear something so quintessentially girly. Lucy's immaculately-combed hair rested with ease on her shoulders, her fringe framing her face and the lilac bow completing the perfect look.

'It's not fair, Lucy,' she whispered. 'Mum doesn't like me anymore, not without you here. I wish I'd gone missing, too, then I wouldn't have to look like this.' Dropping the photo, she took hold of her scraggly, long hair, the split, brown strands stretching the length of her back in uneven, tatty lengths.

'And, if we'd both gone missing, then I wouldn't have to wear these stupid, ugly glasses,' she continued, taking off her frames, seeing perfectly well without the ghastly, square spectacles which Mary didn't *need* to wear unless she was watching television. Martha insisted on the glasses being worn at all times, and didn't care that Mary's eyes might suffer in the long run as a result. All Martha cared about was that the glasses altered her daughter's appearance. The spectacles transformed her facial features just enough so that, when looking at her, Martha didn't immediately think of Lucy.

Mary picked up the photo again, wiping away her tears. 'No matter how hard Mum tries to change me, I'll always remind her of you.'

'Who you talking to, Mary?' shouted Elsie from the kitchen.

'No one, Grandma,' Mary replied, watching to see if Elsie appeared. 'Just come home, Lucy,' she whispered after a few seconds, looking at the photo. 'Then I can take off these stupid glasses and we can play together, just like we used to.'

'Who you talking to, Mary?' asked Hank this time, his feet trundling down the stairs. 'What have you done now?' he snapped, his arms flinging through the air with exasperation. 'You better clean it all up,' he insisted, stepping over his daughter, who was still slumped on the floor amid the sea of glass. His foot knocked her shoulder, but he didn't apologise; he never did these days. 'What have I told you about being more careful? You should know better than to make such a mess.'

It's not my mess, it's yours.

'And put your glasses on before Mum comes down,' he added. 'She'll be cross as hell if she sees you without them on. And we're leaving soon, so hurry up.' Hank walked into the lounge, switched on the TV and slumped himself into his favourite recliner.

Mary looked at the photo of Lucy, thinking to herself *I wish I could disappear.*

It was almost like someone had heard her wish.

Ten

THE LANES' FAMILY CAR WAS A RUSTY BROWN, BATTERED Maxi. It had an obnoxious leather interior that wreaked havoc in the scorching summer months if you were brave enough to sit on the molten lava seats with bare skin. Today was one of those fiery days. Mary and her family drove to the first residential home located only a few miles down the road from Wisteria. When Mary caught sight of Audley Lodge - an ugly, grey building more suited to demolition - she couldn't imagine her grandad wanting to stay there, or anybody else in their right mind. Mary thought to herself that her grandma's burnt toast covered in gelatine-heavy, congealed jam had to be better than anything this place would serve up.

'It looks horrible, and it really stinks,' she said, a breeze drifting in through her open window and bringing with it the stifling scent of fresh manure. 'Grandad won't be here, will he?' she asked, scrunching up her nose and trying to block out the pungent stench.

'Probably not,' replied Hank, scanning the decrepit building. 'But we may as well check now that we're here. Stay put, you two, there's no point us all going in. I'll just leave them a photo.' Hank slammed the car door and walked up to the building, leaving Mary alone in the car with her mum.

'I hope we find Grandad soon,' she said. 'I'd hate to be the girl in school whose grandad *and* sister are missing. People will think I'm weird.' She looked out the window. 'We're not weird, are we, Mum?'

Martha turned to face Mary from her passenger seat.

'We're not weird, Mary. We're just different to everybody else.'

But I don't want to be different to everyone else. How is that better?

Martha placed her hand on the half-empty bottle of gin concealed within her handbag, her cravings gnawing away at every last bit of willpower she possessed.

'Oh, look. Dad's forgotten the photo. I'll just take it inside,' she said upon noticing the photo on the dashboard, her hands fumbling with impatience on the handle.

'Lock the door, Mary, and don't open it for anyone. I'll only be a minute,' Martha concluded, slamming the door before running over to the main entrance, doing her best to remain upright in her ocean-blue high heels.

Mary gazed across the street, propping her chin up with her hand in boredom.

I hate the summer holidays.

While gazing out of the window, Mary caught sight of a man striding up the street, walking beneath the cherry trees that lined the pavement of the main road.

Is it him?

She slouched in her seat, trying to hide whilst still peering out of the window. She watched as the man turned his head and bent down, pretending to tie his shoe whilst actually checking his surroundings.

It's him, isn't it?

Perry Golifer turned back and continued to scurry down the street. He wasn't tying his shoe lace; he was watching Mary.

Mary looked back at the building. 'Come on, where are you?' she said, urging her parents to appear whilst she looked up, trying to keep sight of Perry, his shadow vanishing into the distance. 'He's getting away.' Mary opened the car door and she stepped out. The pungent smell of manure hit her in the face, and her feet danced on the spot due to the rocketing levels of anxiety railroading her body.

'What should I do?' she mumbled before dashing across the road, just catching a glimpse of Perry who was now turning the corner, heading into the heart of Finchley village.

Where's Mum?

Mary ran down the lane, holding onto her backpack. *What am I doing?* Her gentle jog developed into a run, her head turning back every few seconds, hoping to see her parents in pursuit. The pavement remained deserted, the road covered in darkness by the arching woods running parallel. Mary snaked the same corner that Perry had taken. Unbeknown to her, Perry had clocked Mary sitting in the family car, and knew that she was alone.

'Where did he go?' she said to herself upon reaching the village square. Perry was nowhere to be seen. A small gathering of people pottered in and out of shops, whilst a few others sat outside the café, reading a paper and sipping on what smelled like very strong coffee, the type her parents always had in the morning to counteract the previous night's excessive consumption of alcohol.

'I've lost him,' she said, wandering across the square. She walked past each shopfront and peered in through the windows. She paused at the sweet shop, gazing up at the assortment of glass jars, all brimming with boiled sweets of every shape, size and colour.

'I love chocolate limes,' said a voice from behind, the smell of stale cigarette smoke tailgating the words. 'Which are your favourites, Mary?'

Perry stood uncomfortably close to Mary, his shadow visible in the reflection of the shop window. Her eyes opened wide when she saw his reflection; a washed-out denim jacket, blue cap and a packet of Benson and Hedges poking out of his jacket pocket. She released a tiny gasp of breath when he crouched. Her skin shivered, sensing the warmth of his breath on her neck.

'How do you know my name?' she asked, her voice barely audible. Mary remained still, facing the shop, her body frozen whilst a scream fell lifeless in her lungs.

'This is a pretty small village, Mary, and I've lived here a long time,' Perry replied, whispering into her ear, his breath flickering through her fine hair. 'I think I must know everyone's name by now.'

Mary's internal organs tumbled. Her cheeks flushed, as if she was wearing some of her mum's rose petal blusher. She turned around, pulling away until she backed against the shop window. She caught sight of something sticking out of his side pocket.

'Do you like comics?' Perry asked, following her gaze. 'These ones are the best, they have all the good jokes in the back, and stickers in the front. Do you want to have a look?' He checked his surroundings, looking to see if any of the passers-by had clocked the conversation, or if the shop assistants had noticed the goings on. For now, nobody in the square was any the wiser. Mary shook her head, looking over her shoulders for her parents.

Where are they?

'I'm sorry, Mary. You don't even know who I am, do you?'

I do know who you are.

'My name is Perry. I live near your grandma's house.' Perry took hold of Mary's hand. 'It's nice to meet you.' To Mary, shaking Perry's hand felt odd. Knowing what her parents thought about him, she thought that his hand would feel cold, his skin rough, and that he'd have dirt under his nails – maybe scars covering his skin. To her surprise, Perry's hand felt, and looked, completely normal.

'I do know who you are. You're the man that people think took my sister.' She immediately regretted making the brave accusation. Perry continued to grip her hand, wrapping his fingers around hers, prolonging the formal introduction and opportunity to touch.

'People say nasty things all the time, but it doesn't mean they're true, Mary.' In an attempt to manipulate, Perry displayed a perfected look of pity, his shoulders shrugging. 'I bet people say horrible things about you too, don't they? But it doesn't mean they're true.'

Come on, Mum, where are you?

'For example, I bet that your mum and dad say that you don't help them enough, or that you answer them back. But I bet they're wrong, aren't they?' Mary felt uneasy, looking past Perry and over his shoulder, checking again to see if they had appeared.

They probably haven't even noticed I've gone.

'Are you with someone, Mary?' he asked, following her gaze.

'My parents,' she replied after an extended pause. 'They're looking for my Grandad, he's missing.'

Perry worked his charm, producing his best sympathetic tone of voice.

'I'm sorry to hear that, Mary.'

Perry displayed a convincing act, an act that would fool even the most worldly-wise ten-year-old. He placed his hand on her shoulder, squeezing to offer sympathy to her situation. She shook her shoulder, encouraging his hand to move.

'Why do people think you took my sister?' Mary looked up and waited for an answer to her accusation.

'Dunno,' Perry replied, showing his palms in an exasperated manner and diverting his stare. 'I guess because I live the closest to where your sister went missing. The police think I should have heard something, or that I should have seen something. But I didn't. Maybe if I had, I could have helped to keep her safe.' He noticed a lady paying for her items in the shop, ready to leave. 'I feel bad that I didn't see anything, Mary, but it wasn't my fault. I didn't do anything wrong. I just couldn't help them find her.' Perry's nervous fingers fumbled behind his back, excitement building the longer he got to speak with Mary.

'I read in the papers that you were with your sister the day she disappeared,' he continued, watching the customer exiting the shop, walking away without any acknowledgement. The lady was too preoccupied with checking that the shop assistant had given her the correct change. 'So, you of all people will know that I wasn't there at your grandma's house the day that your sister went missing, and so I couldn't have taken Lucy.'

'I was only four.' Mary was quick to defend. 'I don't remember that far back,' she added. Mary tried not to show the nerves that were sabotaging every sensation in her body.

'I did hear screams that day. They were really loud,' confessed Perry.

'If you heard screams, why didn't you go and help?'

'I always heard screams coming from your grandparents' house,' said Perry. 'And so, one day I did go over and check that everything was okay. I was worried. And I saw that both you and your sister were playing in the paddling pool on the front lawn, splashing each other with cold water, screaming with excitement. The screams I heard that day were just the same as the ones I heard the day that Lucy went missing. I just assumed you were both playing.'

Mary had seen dozens of photos of her and Lucy on the lawn at Wisteria, playing in the paddling pool. His words had jogged a forgotten memory, taking Mary by surprise that she could remember so far back.

I remember playing in Grandma's paddling pool, but I don't remember the screams.

With the piercing screams a forgotten memory, Mary thought back to everything she'd heard spoken about the day her sister went missing, and concluded that she'd never heard anyone mention that there were screams the day that Lucy vanished. Surely, she'd have remembered such a specific detail, having heard the tale so many times over the years? Mary's mind worked on overdrive, wondering if the screams that Perry had heard had come from Lucy, or from herself? Had anyone other than Perry heard the screams? There were new questions which she didn't know the answer to, but maybe her parents would.

'Let's sit on the bench for a bit,' Perry suggested, interrupting Mary's train of thought. 'You can have some of my chocolate limes. I bet they're your favourite.' He walked a few paces around the corner, sitting on the bench that was out of sight from the main pedestrian traffic. He hoped that his laissez-faire approach would encourage Mary to follow.

How does he know that limes are my favourite?

Mary stood alone, watching him walking away, wondering if she should run back to the car, or stay and talk. She could see that the square was dotted with only a couple of people now, both engrossed with reading the paper. There was still no sign of her parents.

'Did the police talk to you about my sister?' she asked, taking a seat at the very far end of the bench, as far away from Perry as she could get.

'I think everyone in the entire village was questioned, Mary. We all wanted to help. I even offered to form part of the search party because I know the area so well.'

I didn't know that, either.

'It was such a terrible day and I remember it like it happened yesterday,' Perry continued. He began making sniffling noises and wiping his eye, making sure Mary had noticed his display of emotions.

To me, it feels like Lucy has been missing forever.

'If you've always lived in Finchley, and you know everyone, then you'll know my grandad. He's called Henry.'

'I do know your grandad, but not very well.'

'Have you seen him? Like I said, he's gone missing.' Mary asked, kicking the stones with her feet and swinging her legs.

Perry shuffled a bit closer along the bench. 'I haven't seen your grandad in a long time.' He took out some sweets from his pocket. 'Would you like one?' With a rumbling stomach, Mary nodded.

'Thanks. I'm not allowed these at home. Mum says they'll rot my teeth.'

'She's probably right. But it can be our little secret. What do you think?'

Mary nodded again, reciprocating Perry's smile.

'Before he went missing, my grandad said that he saw you near his lake. Nobody believes him, though,' she said. 'Did you go near the lake?'

'I don't like fishing, or swimming,' Perry replied. 'And I can't remember the last time I was at your grandparents' lake. Must've been years ago.'

Mary had her suspicions that he was lying, and Perry noticed a change of expression on her face.

'Actually, I forgot,' he said. 'Your grandad did once lend me one of his garden rakes, and I returned it not too long ago. I'd forgotten I had it. I knocked on the door but nobody was home, so I put it back in the shed.'

'Did you borrow anything else?'

Perry looked uneasy for the first time, thinking about the bunch of items he'd taken only days earlier, amongst which were Lucy's basket and Henry's jumper. Until he got what he really wanted, Perry was always eager to obtain new items for his collection. Whenever Mary returned to Wisteria, Perry knew that there would be things for the taking. The day after she'd arrived at the lake house, Perry had been secretly rummaging in the shed at Wisteria. He had spotted an empty crisp packet and juice carton in an old bike basket, and crumbs from where Mary had been careless when eating her secret snack.

In the basket, there was also a handful of marbles that Mary had been playing with, plus a hair band entwined with loose strands of her hair. Perry knew that all the items were Mary's, and he could almost imagine her sat huddled in the shed, alone. He wanted her belongings, any that he could lay his hand to, and so he snapped the basket off the bike and took the lot away. Once back at home, he wasn't bothered about the basket or jumper, and threw those behind the shed in his own garden, but the other items were put in their rightful place.

'No, Mary. I didn't borrow anything else.' Perry didn't think that anyone would have noticed the missing bicycle basket with the tatty red jumper stuffed inside. It had been positioned right at the back of the shed with clutter piled all around. But Mary was observant, and in his excitement, Perry was getting careless.

'An old bicycle basket is missing from the shed. Did you see it when you went in? It's an old one of Lucy's.'

'I don't think so,' he was quick to reply, before changing the subject.

'I'm glad your mum and dad aren't here,' he commented. 'It can't be nice for you when they go out drinking all the time. My parents used to drink, and it made them shout and argue all the time.' His ploy to change the topic worked perfectly.

'How do you know my parents drink a lot?'

'There aren't many secrets in Finchley, Mary. Everyone knows everyone else's business.' Perry handed her another lime, a smile breaking across her face when he gave her a couple, his clumsy hand purposefully grazing her skin.

'They always shout,' she mumbled. 'And argue.' Mary looked up, still waiting for her mum to come running, screaming with concern. The two people reading the paper had moved on; only Mary and Perry remained.

'Shall we be friends, Mary?' asked Perry. 'We're neighbours after all, and it'd be nice for us to be pals whilst you're visiting for the summer.' He reached out to touch her hand. Mary looked down; the weight of his hand on hers felt uncomfortable. Her facial expression conveyed her feeling of apprehension.

'I bet I'm more fun to hang out with than your parents. We can eat chocolate limes and read comics.' Perry's attempt at persuasion continued. 'And, at my house, I have cool games that we could play. I bet there are no games at your grandparents' place.'

The only game at her grandparents' house was chess, and there was nothing Mary hated more than a boring game of chess. It was a game that she didn't even understand, let alone enjoy. She remained silent, still feeling uneasy, the warmth of Perry's hand penetrating, making her skin clammy.

'Think about it. You know where I live,' he said, moving his hand. 'But if you do want to be friends and come over, it's probably best we don't tell your parents. It'd give them something else to shout at you about, wouldn't it? Our new friendship can just be our secret. What do you think?'

'I best get going. My mum will start to worry.' Mary stood. 'Thanks for the limes,' she shouted before picking up her pace. Mary knew instantly that she didn't want to be his friend, she didn't need to think about it. Perry was old, he smelt horrible and even if he didn't turn out to be the bad person she'd heard people describe him as, in her eyes, he kind of looked like someone who did bad things. But as she walked away, the thought did cross her mind that maybe if she just pretended to be his friend, that it would be easier for her to snoop round his garden and have a look for Lucy or her Grandad. At least then she'd know for sure.

Perry watched her run away and made sure she was out of sight before taking out the photo he always carried on his person. The photo was ripped on one side and a young girl with brown hair and a sweet smile beamed out at him. The other half of the photograph, the side that depicted an identical young girl wearing lilac, was kept safe on his wall at home.

Eleven

MARTHA WAS RUNNING DOWN THE MAIN ROAD. HER blue high heels had been cast aside. She looked like a crazy woman who'd managed to escape from a psychiatric institution. She was barefoot and crying, waving her arms through the air and screaming a tangle of illegible sentences.

'Where've you been?' she shouted, witnessing Mary walking towards Audley Lodge. Martha grabbed hold of Mary's arms and shook her body. Drivers from passing cars rubbernecked at the scene. 'Do you know how worried we've been? I've been going out of my bloody mind for the past five minutes,' she yelled, hugging her daughter and holding on to her body. 'I didn't know where you were.'

Mary pulled away, hating the stench of alcohol, her stomach churning at the all-too-familiar vulgar smell.

Hank ran up to them. 'Where've you been? You've had your mum and me going out of our bloody minds. We've searched that place from top to toe thinking that you'd followed us inside. Even the staff have been looking. What were you doing out here?' He signalled back to the group of staff waiting on the pavement that everything was okay, and they disappeared back inside.

'I saw Perry Golifer.' The colour in Martha's face drained in a second. 'And I thought I should follow him for you.'

'You did what?' yelled Martha, rage firing through her blood, awakening every nerve ending in her body. 'How bloody stupid of you! Do you not know how dangerous he is?' Martha pushed her daughter away in frustration, the little girl's feet tripping, her body falling to the ground. Placing her hands on her hips, Martha paced around Mary as she sat helpless on the floor.

'I just don't bloody believe it.'

Mary glanced back up the road, watching to see if Perry appeared.

'You think he took Lucy,' said Mary, pulling herself up. 'That's why we come back here every year, isn't it? It's not just so that we can see Grandma and Grandad, is it?' As her eyelashes blinked, a swath of tears released.

'Yes, I think he took Lucy. And yes, that's why we come here every year. And if I tell you to stay away from him, then that's *exactly* what you will do. *Do you understand?*' Martha grabbed Mary's face, pulling it close to hers until their noses touched.

'You're hurting me.'

'All right, Martha,' said Hank, pulling Mary free from his wife's grip. 'She knows what she did was wrong, don't you, Mary?'

'I wanted to follow him for you,' said Mary. 'I was trying to help. I was trying to find Lucy and see if he'd seen Grandad, so I spoke to him, just like Grandma had suggested. I was trying to make you happy.' Martha's eyes opened wide, threatening to explode from their sockets, her face reddening with rage.

'You *spoke* to him? Tell me you're joking. Tell me you're bloody joking?' Mary didn't dare speak, but ducked instead, trying to avoid her mum's arms each time they were flung through the air.

'He said he didn't take Lucy. And he hasn't seen Grandad.'

Martha's hands covered her face, her body crouching down to the floor.

'Oh, God. I can't believe you actually spoke to that bastard.' Hank took hold of Martha, brushing back her hair so he could look into her eyes.

'Just breathe, Martha,' he urged, watching his wife's state of hysteria heighten.

'Anything could have happened to her,' she whispered. 'And I was too busy having a drink.'

'Just sit there a minute and calm down,' Hank said, placing his wife on the curb whilst he walked over to Mary, who was now leaning against the car.

'What else did Perry say, Mary?' he asked in a calm tone. Mary became mute, her fear stealing her words, so she shrugged.

'Dunno. Just stuff.'

'Did he touch you? Did he hurt you? Tell me, Mary. I need to know.' Hank scanned the road in both directions. 'Where is that sonofabitch? I'm going over there. I'll have this out with him.' Martha's head flung up.

'If you go over there and barge into his house, he'll be straight on to the police,' she snapped. 'Then they'll arrest you, and then what? I've already lost a daughter, and now my father-in-law. Do you think I could cope with losing my husband too? Do you?' Her voice was scaring Mary.

'I can't just sit back and let him do this,' said Hank, shaking his head. 'Bloody bastard.'

'Don't you think I'm desperate to march over there, too?' Martha added. 'But I don't want to ruin a chance of ever finding my daughter alive. He knows something, Hank, I know he does, and we've only got one chance to make him tell us. If we piss him off, then who knows what'll happen? He could disappear, and then what? Our only hope of getting Lucy back would be gone.' She glanced over at Mary upon realising her choice of words. Mary's delicate heart skipped a beat, her mind processing the frightening words.

Mary's body threatened to topple. *Is Lucy dead? Is she never coming back?* In Mary's mind, her sister was out there somewhere, just not at home. Although the sickening feeling she often experienced told her so, she never wanted to believe that Lucy was dead. Someone had simply taken her, right? And she would come home, one day.

'Why don't you go and sit in the car, Mary?' suggested Martha, not even looking over. Following orders, Mary sat in the back seat, leaving the window open a crack so that she could still hear her parents' voices.

'That sonofabitch has crossed the line, Martha,' said Hank. 'He had a bloody nerve speaking to Mary like that, you said it yourself.' His anger brewed at a steady rate, reaching near boiling point. 'Why would he need to speak with her? I want to bloody strangle him.' His hands trembled, his anger spilling into his face and eyeballs, the whites of his eyes infiltrated with splashes of red.

'If we barge in now, he'll have the police down on us before we even get past the front door, and then we're screwed, aren't we?' Martha replied. Black bags under her eyes were catching escaped tears.

'And the police would be on his side. We'd be the ones in the wrong by breaking in,' she continued. 'And if we go by the book and go to the police first, tell them what he's done, he wouldn't let them in even if they asked for a quick chat, I know he wouldn't. And do you know why he wouldn't? Because he has something to hide, that's why. The police know it. We know it. And yet we're sodding powerless, either way.'

'But he's getting away with what he's just done, Martha, and we're bloody well letting him!'

Martha didn't hear the word *just*, and bit. 'And what has he done? Murdered our daughter?' barked Martha. 'That's what you mean, isn't it?' She stood up. 'You bastard!' She swiped Hank across the face. 'I'll leave you and find her by myself if you ever speak like she's dead again.' Hank didn't try to explain what he had actually meant, he knew his wife wouldn't hear his words, not yet anyway.

In the car, Mary covered her ears. *Make it stop. Please, make it stop.* The words 'murdered our daughter' lodged in her brain. Mary knew what murder meant; she'd seen her grandad watching programmes on television about such terrifying crimes. She didn't want her sister to have been murdered; that'd mean that she was never coming home.

Martha's black mascara left blotchy smudge marks down her pale face. 'I'm going to go and call the police from inside, tell them what's happened. Maybe they'll be able to do something, anything. You stay with Mary, I won't be long.' Martha walked back into the care home and Hank went over to the car, opening

Mary's door and crouching down.

'Please, don't get upset,' he said to Mary. 'Your mum and I are just angry, and when adults get angry, they say things that they *really* don't mean,' he explained, taking hold of Mary's hand. 'I need you to tell me again *exactly* what Perry Golifer said. It's *really* important.'

Mary thought through the whole conversation.

'I asked him if he was the one who took Lucy. He said no,' she began in a calm, slow voice. 'I asked him if he'd seen Grandad. He said no.' Mary fidgeted with her hair, contemplating telling her dad that Perry had heard screams the day that Lucy went missing. She thought about the secret Perry had insisted she keep, the one about them possibly being friends. And, with her dad staring at her through seething eyes, she decided that she'd already caused enough trouble, and she didn't want to cause any more.

'That's it, Dad. That's all he said,' Mary lied, shrugging her shoulders, too scared to tell him the whole truth, knowing full well that her dad would explode. Hank erupted anyway, standing up and banging his fist into the bonnet, followed by a series of kicks against the front tyre, all of which caused him more injury than it did to the car.

Mary closed the car door, scared by watching her dad. Her finger pressed down on the lock before he reached her door. He circled the car like a hungry shar. It was when Hank got this angry that he sometimes lashed out, Mary and Martha often getting caught in the crossfire. In the past, Mary had always given her dad the benefit of the doubt whenever he had hit her. She told herself that he had done it by accident, like he hadn't noticed her and she had just been in the way. She knew she was kidding herself. When Hank struck, he did so with precision, and never missed.

Hank himself used alcohol as an excuse for his aggression. When he sobered up, often the next day, he became riddled with guilt once he'd managed to recall what he'd done, or when he caught sight of one of the bruises he'd caused to his wife or daughter. He'd try and play Mr Nice Guy, attempting to make it up to them, but, more often than not, the damage had already been done. Hank wasn't an alcoholic like his wife, but he would become frequently drunk, and he became a different person when under the influence. Mary always forgave him, as most daughters would, until the next time.

Martha returned and got in the car, her face looking like thunder.

'Bloody useless bastards,' she seethed. 'I asked to be put through to Sergeant Swift, thinking she'd help us knowing the background. She just said that what happened hasn't provided them with any new evidence in Lucy's case, and therefore they have no grounds to go to his house. All he did was talk to Mary, and in the eyes of the law he did nothing wrong.' Martha opened her handbag, taking a swig from her nearly empty bottle of gin. 'That's better,' she mumbled before draining every last drop into her mouth and tossing the bottle onto the floor.

The car shook when Hank threw himself back into the driver's seat, turning to look at Mary. She cowered away as far as she could, trying to stay out of reach of his arm.

'If you ever do anything as stupid as that again, Mary, you'll be sorry.'

She waited for a strike, but this time it didn't come. All she had done was try to help, didn't they understand that? Everything Mary ever did was to try and make things better; to make her parents happy. Nothing she did was ever good enough.

'I won't speak to him again, I promise,' lied Mary. Unsatisfied by Perry's response to her questions, and in the back of her mind still thinking she'd seen him with her grandad's jumper, she had every intention of somehow finding out if he'd stolen the things from the shed. And if that meant talking to him again, then so be it.

Spying from behind Audley Lodge, Perry watched as the Lane's car began to drive away, his heartbeat still pounding after his interaction with Mary. For so many years he had imagined what it would feel like to talk to her, to touch her body and smell her skin. And now that he had, he wanted more. He was getting closer. He could just feel it in his bones.

Twelve

Sunday shifts at Finchley police station were notorious for being an easy ride.

A doddle of a day.

Very little criminal activity occurred in the sleepy village at the best of times, but Sundays were the quietest day of the entire week, the station operating on skeleton staff. There was always ample time for a brew and biscuits on Sundays, plus an opportunity to catch up on the pile of paperwork that got left during the week.

Sergeant Claire Swift approached the station a little before eight in the morning on her second Sunday shift of the month. The staffing rota was calculated so that each senior member of the team only had to work one Sunday per month, but Swift needed the money that came with doing a bit of overtime. She'd booked, but not yet paid for, her upcoming two-week holiday. A fortnight in Tahiti was just what she needed. Time to unwind, rest and forget about the pressures that came with being a police sergeant. Now she just needed to pay for it.

She had never been married, apart from to her job, and never thought twice about holidaying alone. Her female colleagues thought she was barmy, travelling alone, eating alone, sitting in a bar alone. For Swift, however, sitting on the beach by herself whilst holding a book in one hand and a sangria in the other would do her nicely. She wasn't interested in meeting a man, and she wasn't interested in sightseeing. All Claire wanted to do on her summer holiday was sit by the sea and sip on a never-ending supply of cocktails.

The rusty chain on her knackered push bike clunked when she attempted to change gear going up the slight incline at Langley Lane, her legs already tired after pedalling the twenty-mile door-to-door trek. The front wheel of her bike had just passed through the station gate when she heard one of the office phones ringing.

Unusual.

The ghastly frown lines that Claire loathed appeared all across her forehead, leaving their mark even when her scrunched skin relaxed. Along with the pension and private healthcare plan that she paid into, Swift also suggested that the force should offer reduced prices on spa treatments like facials, every one of her wrinkles the direct result of her job. Her boss refused the idea and mocked her, naturally. He happened to be a young-ish guy with flawless skin.

On a Sunday, the phone didn't usually ring until at least ten o'clock, and even then it was typically Tom's Teatime Treats, the café down the road, making sure they'd got the correct breakfast order before the delivery boy set off with the box of warm bacon butties. White, floury baps laced with butter and ketchup and filled with crispy bacon was the station's standing weekly order. Culinary perfection in the crew's eyes.

Swift looked up at the station. 'They'll ring back if it's important,' she muttered, disembarking from her bike, her bottom suffering from a serious bout of saddle sore. With her head also delicate after a few too many vodkas the previous evening, Claire trundled in with her bag and helmet under her arm.

She was the first to arrive. Typical. That meant she had to brew up.

The four desks in the open-plan main office remained scattered with piles of paperwork, half-empty mugs of tea and brimming bins. The cleaner wouldn't be in until the following morning; even then, she refused to wash up dirty cups and cutlery. That wasn't part of the cleaning contract. Besides, Maggie dared anyone to refer to her as a 'cleaner'; she was an Office Improvement Assistant. In her eyes, her title made all the difference because, although it still meant she spent her days tidying up after messy people, it looked much better on her curriculum vitae.

With her backpack still on her back, Claire threw her helmet on her desk and her cycle jacket over the coat rack just as the phone rang again.

Claire assumed the call would be regarding an unattended car, or parking dispute. The norm.

'Bloody hell, this best be good,' she said, her hand reaching down to pick up the phone on her desk, a red flashing light indicating a message had already been left on the answering machine. Within only a few seconds of lifting the receiver, the voice on the other end caused Swift to swing around so that her body was facing the main wall. With the phone still pressed against her ear, her stomach tightened, and the additional churning sensation wasn't because of the previous night's drinking binge.

The wall that Swift was staring at was completely covered with evidence relating to the cases of two missing children: Katie Banks and Lucy Lane. The left-hand side of the wall was dedicated to Katie's case. She had been the first child to ever go missing from Finchley village, disappearing two years before Lucy, in 1980. Similarities existed between the two cases: both girls were of similar age at the time of their disappearance, both girls shared the same ethnicity, both were pretty. However, perhaps most striking of all, both girls had disappeared during the month of July, but two years apart.

Katie Banks had never been found. Perry Golifer had been the prime suspect in the case, and his house had been searched. Despite several rounds of questioning, he was never brought to trial due to a lack of evidence. The case was no longer being actively investigated. Swift hadn't been the Officer in Charge (OIC) in the case of Katie Banks, but she was the OIC on the Lucy Lane investigation.

On the right-hand side of the wall, an A3-sized picture of Lucy acted as the central point in the complex collage. Surrounding the central photo of Lucy was a gallery of suspects. Not mugshots per se, but shots of possible suspects' mugs. Images of Elsie, Henry, Hank, Martha and Perry Golifer all circled the little girl with the broad, beaming smile, lilac dress and accompanying accessories.

Along with photos taken from the crime scene at Wisteria on the day that Lucy had vanished, there were numerous photos of singular pieces of potential evidence. Photos of her bedroom and all her possessions, photos of the lake, plus photos of her bedroom back at home in Whitney. There were also dozens of newspaper articles scattered on the wall, along with an array of other paraphernalia that all comprised the body of evidence the police had obtained in the six years since the case had first been opened. Not that any of the evidence had done any good thus far. Lucy was still missing. The police didn't even know if Lucy had been abducted, or if she'd been murdered, or if she'd run away. Despite the wall of evidence, the police actually knew very little.

The missing person case of Lucy Lane was no longer classed as active. Limited resources had forced the police to stop investigating after only twelve months. If new information was presented, and warranted sufficient reason, then the case could be reopened, of course. But, until then, the police were no longer carrying out relevant investigations. If the police continued to look for every person reported missing, then they wouldn't have time to investigate anything else. That was just a fact that the families of missing people didn't want to hear.

With all that being said, not a single officer in Finchley could bring themselves to take down the evidence. And Sergeant Claire Swift would certainly have had something to say had anyone been stupid enough to archive the evidence. In the police world, taking down evidence when a case had not been solved signified defeat, and that they were giving up. In the minds of all the longstanding staff at Finchley station, plus those who had retired, the case of Lucy Lane was the one that they would never forget, or give up on.

Nobody gave up on a missing child.

It was just an unwritten rule.

With the phone receiver pressed to her ear, Swift's eyes gravitated directly towards the main photo of Lucy. She could recall each and every detail on the picture, having looked at it most days for the past six years. Swift had memorised the way that Lucy's lilac dress hovered in the wind, and the way the lilac bow kept her neat hairstyle in position. She loved the way her tiny bracelet shone as the sun caught the metal, her name just about visible if you looked close enough. Even though she didn't have children of her own, Swift knew that Lucy's smile told its own story. No narration was required. Lucy's smile told the story of a toddler having a brilliant time playing on a swing. The smile said *push me harder* to whoever it was who was stood behind her, lunging her through the air. After all, what could be better than playing on a swing during the long summer months when you were only four years old?

Without looking, Swift knew that, in the picture, Lucy was wearing matching lilac socks with frills at the top, her feet sitting snug in a pair of jelly sandals. Lucy was holding a doll in her hand, Penelope Pickles, her favourite toy that she couldn't sleep without. Swift also knew, without looking, that there were two birds in the background of the photo, the sparrows soaring through the sky on what looked like a scorching summer's day. In the photo, there was only a dusting of cloud confetti overhead, and Lucy's smile told everyone that she was happy. This last picture ever taken of Lucy Lane had become ingrained on Claire Swift's memory over the years. She had wanted to somehow place herself in the photo, and yell at Martha, who had taken the photo, not to let Lucy out of her sight, even for a second. *Keep hold of her. Watch her every move.* The same levels of frustration mounted inside Swift upon looking at the photo, realising her inability to alter what had happened, and thus far, her inability to find Lucy. The image would never be erased, and nor would she ever want it to be. At least, not until Lucy was found, alive she hoped, and the memory could then be replaced with happier ones.

Swift often imagined how Lucy would look now, an important process in the fight to uncover her whereabouts. She needed to acknowledge that time had moved on, and so would have Lucy's appearance. In her mind, Lucy at age ten would have longer hair without a bow. She'd wear it in a long fishtail plait running down her back. Instead of the lilac dress, she'd be sporting a bright pink shell suit, because that's what Swift saw all the kids in the park wearing. Lucy would also be wearing trainers, and might have a sparkly silver bag hooked over her shoulder. The one thing that hadn't changed in Swift's mind was Lucy's smile. It was still beaming, and still showed that Lucy was happy in life.

'I'll be right there. Don't touch anything. Don't let anyone else in. Just give me five minutes.' She threw the receiver down and bolted out the door.

Swift mounted her bike, foregoing the mandated helmet, and set off immediately, peddling down the lane, her backside raised off the seat in an attempt to avoid unnecessary discomfort. The streets were pretty quiet - it was a Sunday morning after all. There wasn't any pollution in the air from the morning rush hour to clog her lungs, and there weren't any buses impatiently overtaking. Swift didn't notice any of these anomalies to her usual cycling experience, her mind being focused elsewhere.

The church came into view in the distance.

Nearly there, just keep pedalling.

On the previous occasions when there had been possible snippets of new evidence uncovered relating to Lucy's case, the same thoughts always rushed through Swift's mind. Will this be the day that Lucy is found? Will she be alive? Who'll tell her parents? How will they react? Who has she been with all this time? Will we have enough evidence to prosecute the sonofabitch that took her? Will Lucy look like she's been mistreated? What will be her first words?

Swift's feet pedalled through the pain barrier in an attempt to reach her destination. Her mind was already racing.

Is it a coincidence that I was there only days ago? Did I miss something?

Swift saw cars beginning to line the street in the distance, some jostling for the few remaining spaces that were closest to the entrance. The Sunday service was due to commence in a little over half an hour. Dumping the bike against the wall, Swift made her way to the entrance. She was greeted by the priest, his arms crossed behind his back whilst he waited on the steps.

Swift pulled out her gloves. 'Morning. I'm Sergeant Swift. We spoke on the phone.'

The pair walked into the church, closing the door behind them. 'Has anyone else entered apart from yourself?' she asked upon her approach to the altar, the priest struggling to keep pace.

He shook his head. 'No. Just myself.'

'Where is it?'

He held out his hand, indicating to the left. 'I found it just here.' Resting between two candles in the middle of the altar was the missing person picture of Lucy, the corners crumpled and the vibrant colour faded, but the same picture nonetheless.

Swift pulled on her gloves. 'Have you touched it at all?'

The priest shook his head. 'No. It was in that exact place when I came across it.'

Swift picked up the poster by the corner, noticing on the back were the written words 'Please pray for her.' Swift held the photo up to the light.

'That looks like it's been written recently. The words don't look faded, like the photo.'

'I'm sorry, what did you say?' asked the priest. Swift's internal thought process hadn't meant to be heard, but she had a habit of thinking aloud, much to the dismay of colleagues when on duty at a scene.

Why pray for her? Are you telling us she's dead? Have her circumstances suddenly changed? Where is she, you bastards?

Luckily this time, Swift's blasphemy went unheard.

She placed the picture in an evidence bag and sealed it. 'Am

I okay to walk around?' she asked, looking over at the other side of the altar, wanting to gain a different perspective, but unsure of whether she was allowed.

'Please do.'

Swift saw no footprints, no damage, and no other obvious signs of a disturbance in the vicinity. It was like the photo had just magically appeared, or been carefully placed.

'I was actually here just the other day,' said Swift, 'after a report came through of a sighting of a vulnerable adult. I was surprised to find the door unlocked at such an early hour. Is that standard practice?'

'This is God's house,' replied the priest, 'and his doors are always open, at least in summer. We have to be more cautious in winter. One year we found a homeless man asleep beneath one of the pews. He'd been there a few days. Some residents of this village treat this church as their second home, and we're open whenever they need us.' Swift raised her eyebrows.

'So, you wouldn't be able to tell me if any new faces have entered the church in the past few days? Or if any of those who form part of your regular congregation have not been themselves, or seemed upset or anxious in any way?'

'I'm afraid not, Officer Swift.'

It's Sergeant, actually.

'Where's the other item you mentioned?' she asked. The priest extended his arm, indicating for Swift to lead the way.

'It's in the confessional booth, just over there.' Having never attended church, or indeed confessional, Swift seemed unsure of the imposing wooden structure, the two compartment curtains closed.

'Please, can you show me?'

The priest drew back one of the curtains. Lying on the floor, next to the step that allows penitents to kneel, was a handheld trowel, blood splattered on the handle.

'Can I go inside?' Swift asked, wanting to ensure that any religious customs she remained ignorant of were respected. The priest nodded. She knelt and inspected the booth, the small space dimly lit with only the latticed opening allowing any means of incoming light. She took out her torch, shining in all crevices, ensuring nothing went unnoticed.

No signs of a struggle. No blood anywhere else. Was it left intentionally? Was it the same person who left the photo? Surely, it has to be one and the same person, doesn't it? Is someone trying to provide us with new clues? Is someone teasing us? Is someone merely relishing in the fact that we still haven't found her? And why now? What's the significance? The anniversary of Lucy's disappearance is approaching, maybe that's the motive? To Swift, none of it made much sense. It wasn't like an item of clothing had been found that could've been Lucy's. There hadn't been a recent photo left, evidencing that she was still alive. There was no ransom demand. The items didn't make sense.

The anniversary of Lucy's disappearance was only days away, and it was always a solemn time for Sergeant Swift. The anniversary was a reminder of her failings - the case that got away. This specific time of year always brought a resurgence in publicity, which led to an influx of new calls and possible sightings. The public were just as desperate to find Lucy as she was. But, no matter how good-natured their intentions, in the past six years all the new calls received concerning Lucy had each, in turn, led to dead ends.

During police training, it was drilled into cadets that you should never get emotionally involved during an investigation; it would only serve to hinder judgement, and cloud an officer's ability to think and reason logically. But all the police officers who were part of the Finchley force were emotional about the case of Lucy Lane, including Swift. And, no matter how random the new evidence was, she let her hopes climb.

The door flung open; the congregation eager to enter.

'Keep them out, please,' Swift barked, shocked by the sudden violation of what she considered her potential crime scene. 'I'll only be a few more minutes.'

The priest ushered the members of the congregation out of the church. Closing the door, he left Swift alone. She took out a camera from her backpack and started to take photos of the trowel before bagging it up. *What does it mean? Think Claire, think.*

She walked back towards the alter. She thought about the knee rest that had looked out of place the other day, kicking herself and thinking that the person could have been in such close proximity to her. She took a glance back down the aisle towards the door, ensuring she was alone, before kneeling and lowering her head, just as Elsie had done days earlier before leaving the photo of Lucy, her own desperate cry for help.

'I'm not asking for a miracle, but I am asking for help. Please, bring her home,' Swift prayed, her eyes remaining closed for a couple of seconds, the image of Lucy Lane on the swing running through her mind on repeat. 'I'll never ask for anything again.' Swift wasn't religious, and never had been, but at that moment she found herself vulnerable, and needing help.

The case of Lucy Lane was no longer closed. It had just been officially reopened.

Thirteen

A FINCHLEY PAPERBOY PAUSED WITH REGULAR CAUTION outside Ivy Dean. Charlie held onto the gate's metal railings whilst peering through into the creepy hollow. Would he be feeling brave enough to actually walk up the path and push the paper through the letterbox? That was debatable. It hadn't happened so far in Charlie's short paperboy career. Charlie's mum had said she'd put an extra fiver into his wages if he threw the paper over the gate, rather than venture into what she believed was a lion's den. Unbeknown to his mum, Charlie's friends had offered to give him twenty quid if he went up to the door and knocked, before pushing the paper through.

All the curtains were closed at Perry's house. The house remained eerily silent and still – like the sleeping Rottweiler you wouldn't want to wake. There were no visible lights on, so any inhabitants were likely to still be in bed, right? Overcome with bravery, the brash paperboy dismounted his bike and pressed his hand on the gate. An unexpected sound erupted, like a gunshot, causing a flurry of blackbirds to sweep through the towering cluster of trees in the garden.

Perry looked on from the attic, his finger releasing the trigger on his pellet gun, a smile of satisfaction emerging when he watched Charlie's startled reaction. Charlie tossed the newspaper over the railings before scrambling with his pedals, cycling towards Wisteria as fast as he could. Today wasn't going to be the day that Perry's paper would be hand delivered. Maybe tomorrow Charlie would collect his extra twenty quid.

Behind the curtains, Perry moved away from the window, sufficiently satisfied, at least for now. But it wouldn't last – his sense of satisfaction never did. Scaring away the paperboy was part of the ritual process that Perry completed every day, seven days a week. Ensuring that Charlie didn't go near the front door was the first ritual. Perry wasn't so concerned with the milk lady, the postman or the random leaflet droppers, because they all simply delivered their respective goods and left. They didn't seem interested in lingering on the porch, or listening for any sounds that might have been coming from inside. They didn't try to look past the curtains concealing the lounge window to see what was lurking behind.

The adult delivery people knew better than to linger at Perry's – and, to be honest, if anything was going on, they didn't want to be the ones to uncover it. The last thing anybody in Finchley wanted to do was be on Perry's property for longer than was required. Everyone had heard the rumours. They'd read the papers, and they all feared Perry Golifer.

The second ritual of the day that Perry performed was to scour the papers for any new articles to add to his collection. He'd spread the papers over his bed, flicking through each page, his eyes well trained to spot certain words, certain pictures. A good day for Perry was when there was something new reported. He would read the article over and over, until memorised, before cutting it out with meticulous precision and adding it to his wall.

The next ritual he completed was to ensure his shrine was intact, and that any pieces of paper that were coming loose were reattached. Perry would spend hours admiring his collection of photos on the wall. He ran his hands across some of his personal favourites, looking at them like he'd never seen them before. His prolific collection contained photos of all sizes; some of the pictures were taken recently, whilst others dated back a number of years. Perry preferred the newest additions to his private collection, the ones taken only days ago, where the ink was still tacky round the edges. Despite the vast collection, there was always room for more.

Out of all the photos that were scattered across his wall, the wall directly behind the headboard of his double bed, there was one common theme running throughout, linking all the pictures together. And that was the consistency of the subject matter. If only Hank had followed his gut and stormed his way into Perry's property. If only the raft of delivery people took as much interest as Charlie the paperboy, then maybe the collection would have been discovered.

The final ritual that Perry performed was to check his camera – clean the lens, test that the batteries were working, and ensure there were enough exposures left on the roll. There was nothing quite so disappointing than seeing the perfect shot, only to run into technical issues – or, worse, run out of film. The image could be lost forever, and the opportunity may never arise again. Taken aback by the Lane family arriving at Wisteria a couple of days earlier than he expected, Perry wasn't as prepared as he would have liked to be.

The Lane family always arrived in Finchley on the Saturday after the schools had broken up for the summer holidays. For the past six years, the family had run like clockwork. But not this year. This summer, they had thrown Perry a curveball by arriving in Cumbria a whole three days early, on the Thursday. Perry didn't like change, or surprises for that matter. His life was regimented. His house was regimented. And anyone entering his world, or already part of his life, would become regimented too, like it or not.

There were no such intricate morning rituals at Wisteria, but there were certain habits that were rarely broken during the holidays; the first one being Mary fetching the newspaper from the letterbox. Charlie had no qualms about pushing the paper through Elsie's letterbox, and, when the box rattled, Hank could be guaranteed to shout seconds later. And today he performed right on queue.

'Mary, fetch the paper.'

She always obeyed, otherwise he'd simply shout again, and that was just annoying.

'We're all having a ride up to Cape Rise today,' he added. 'We love it up there, and so does Grandad Henry. If he was physically able, I know he'd try to go back there.' Mary placed the newspaper on the kitchen table. 'And I'm sick of just sitting here waiting for the phone to ring.'

'That's a great idea,' said Martha, her hands trembling as she made herself a black coffee. 'I don't know why we didn't think of going there before. It'll do us all good to get out for the day. A change of scenery.' She paused. 'Why are there so many bloody sticky notes everywhere?' she asked, noticing Elsie's reminders for the very first time with sober eyes. 'She must do it to help your dad, do you think?' Hank paid little attention; he was too busy studying a map, navigating the best journey for their planned trip. Neither of them had witnessed the times when Elsie questioned her own memory, and the sticky notes were just one anomaly in a house full of peculiarity.

'Can I stay here? I'm not feeling very well,' asked Mary, still wearing her pyjamas. 'I've got bad tummy ache. I promise I'll be good.' The ink from the newspaper always seemed to rub off onto her hands, no matter how she tried to hold it. She would then rub her hand down her pyjamas, a grey streak running the length of her left leg. 'I want to go back to bed. You'll stay with me, won't you, Grandma?'

Elsie appeared in the kitchen. She had failed to hear her granddaughter's question, cotton buds still wedged into her ear canals to avoid any unwanted draught. Elsie walked straight over to the fridge and placed a piece of paper under the magnet of the Isle of White, the words 'February 27th' scribbled almost illegibly.

'What's that, Mum?' asked Hank, noticing the paper. Elsie felt agitated.

'Just your Dad's birthday. I don't want to forget it despite the fact he's not here,' she snapped. 'I don't have a diary anymore.' Elsie walked back out of the room.

'I was only asking.' Hank raised his eyebrows, brushing off the typically odd behaviour.

'So, can I, Dad? Can I stay with Grandma?'

'No way,' mouthed Martha across the table to Hank, subtly shaking her head.

'Mary, go upstairs and get back into bed if you're not well,' he instructed, watching Mary leave the room and listening to her footsteps climbing the stairs.

'I know what happened yesterday was awful,' Hank continued when she was out of earshot, 'but it wasn't Mum's fault, was it? Mary was out with us. We know she'll be safe here, and if she's not feeling very well, she'll only spoil our day, won't she?' He stroked his wife's cheek. 'Mum knows not to leave the house. And Mary's old enough now to be left. She isn't a baby anymore, Martha. At some point, she'll want to venture out just with her friends, and we won't be able to keep her locked away forever. And if Mum does anything more unusual than normal, we'll tell Mary to call 999!' He laughed, kissing Martha on the lips and winking to lighten the atmosphere. 'Now, let's get going.'

FROM HER OPEN attic window, Mary heard the car's tyres crunch over the cobbled drive, the sound fading as the car snaked the path. She jumped out of bed, throwing back the blanket her mum had wrapped her up in, and got dressed. She then ran over to the window, watching to make sure her parents had gone, and hadn't forgotten anything. Martha and Hank were already making their way out of the village, planning their day, which now centred around which pubs they were going to frequent.

Scrambling on to the floor, she pulled her turquois backpack out from where she'd hidden it beneath her bed, checking that she'd packed her torch, her grandad's penknife, plus an emergency packet of crisps and carton of juice. Mary's plan for the day was to search for her grandad, and as always, keep searching for Lucy. She didn't think her Grandad would be far away. He loved being at home, and loathed the prospect of venturing beyond the woods. He had to be close by, he just had to be. By looking in every corner of Wisteria, plus the surrounding woods, Mary felt sure she would find him. Wisteria was bigger than most normal houses, so maybe Grandad was still at home, hiding somewhere where nobody had looked. In Mary's mind, anything was possible, and anything was better than spending a whole day trapped between her parents.

Wisteria was a grand house. It may have been in need of some internal maintenance, and a good pruning on the outside to bring its former façade back to its original glory, but the character hadn't been lost. Original doors, high ceilings, fireplaces in many of the rooms, and various secret nooks all added to the mystery and character of Wisteria. The house was spread over four floors – from the attic all the way down to a basement. Each room was decorated in its own unique fashion, and some rooms had barely been used in years.

Elsie and Henry tended to use only a handful of the rooms – after all, for fifty weeks out of the year, there were only the two of them in occupancy. On a few occasions of late, right before he went missing, Henry had managed to become lost in his own house. He would accidentally enter through a wrong door and, the room being so unfamiliar, he wouldn't know where he was.

The size of the house had seemed appealing to Mary and Lucy when they were toddlers. When they played hide-and-seek, it meant that the game could last for a good half-hour, if not longer. And the room that they always forgot to look in was the pokey vestibule at the rear of the property. It was a neglected hovel that served no real purpose, other than being a great place to house clutter and critters.

Mary crept down her attic stairs and paused. She didn't know why, but searching the house felt intimidating. She couldn't hear her grandma pottering about downstairs, though she was sure that she would be around, somewhere. She started her search with what she considered to be safe rooms, those in which she'd already been in since her arrival – Elsie's bedroom, her parents' bedroom, and the bathroom. Henry wasn't in any.

The next door to search behind upstairs was another bedroom. Mary hadn't known whose it was, or if anyone had ever slept in it, but she did know that the bed had a valance, probably the same one she'd hidden under as a child. The door felt heavy to open, and it smelt peculiar inside. Musty. Her feet teetered inside, only a few paces. She crouched on the floor, but didn't see anyone or anything hiding under the bed, her hands and knees becoming covered with decades' worth of dust. There were some empty spirit bottles that Martha had attempted to hide, and failed.

Mary stepped a few more paces into the room.

The double wardrobe was locked, the dark, mahogany wood covered with a fine layer of filth that transferred to Mary's hands when she pulled on the handles. There were fingerprints already edged into the dust, which she failed to noticed. She looked around for the brass key that she recalled from years ago, puzzled as to why it wasn't rested in the lock like it usually was. There were some ornaments resting on the dresser, garish statues and figurines, none of which Mary cared for, the solemn faces making her feel jittery. There was a collection of vases on the window sill, among which Mary spotted the wardrobe key. Creeping across the room, she took hold of it then walked back to the wardrobe.

'Grandad? Lucy? Are you in here?' she whispered. Standing in front of the doors, Mary twisted the key, pulling at the handles. She didn't recall either her or her sister hiding in the wardrobe in the past, but it was big enough to hide a person inside, if not two. Her mouth felt dry and her eyes blinked in time with the tick of a clock. And, with one quick pull, the doors swung open in unison. A load of coats and towels spilled out onto the floor, the sudden movement causing her to release a scream. The house wasn't known to be haunted; however, to Mary, it sometimes felt like it was. She stuffed all the items back in, locked the door and left, the creepy eyes of the figurines following her movement.

The last room upstairs had been her grandad's office, though he never really did much work in it, other than polish his collection of rare sovereign coins. The space wasn't much bigger than a box room, and the oak table and tall, leather-backed chair situated before the window occupied much of the space. The chair used to be one of Lucy's favourite places to hide because, from the door, you couldn't see her body sheltering in the chair's deep cavity unless you swivelled it round. Mary would often open the door, think that Lucy wasn't there, then close the door and leave again. And all the while, Lucy would be sitting on her grandad's chair, giggling with her hand over her mouth.

Mary stood outside the room and pressed her ear against the door, listening for familiarity; her sister's giggles, or her grandad's laboured breathing. Placing her hand on the brass knob, Mary twisted the handle, releasing the hinges and pushing the door open. The room felt cold, gloomy and undisturbed. A fine sprinkling of dust scattered the room like dirty snow. The chair was facing the window; however, despite being taller now, Mary still couldn't see over the high back.

'Lucy, are you in here?'

The dust irritated her nose the further she entered, and the once familiar smell of her grandad's furniture polish no longer clung to the air.

'Grandad?' Mary placed her hand on the chair, and spun it round.

'Argh!' she screamed, when the door behind her slammed shut, the breeze swooping through the house forcing the wood back into its frame.

The chair was vacant. Lucy wasn't there, and neither was Henry. However, although there were no immediate visible signs that the pair had ever been in the room, a closer inspection would have found traces of both. Some strands of Lucy's brown hair were embedded into the carpet, some from the day she vanished. There were marks on the table, residue from Lucy's tears. There was a tissue on the floor, resting beneath the radiator, the exact one Henry had used to wipe his granddaughter's eyes the day she had gone missing. There were also millions of flecks of Henry's skin, the fine dusting taking residency amongst the dust particles.

Henry and Lucy were all around; you just had to look close enough.

Mary made her way downstairs. She paused on the bottom step and looked around, her heart beating. She walked in slow motion, one foot at a time, peering into the lounge, then the kitchen, then the cupboard under the stairs. Still no signs of Lucy or Henry. After checking the dining room, the only person she came across was Elsie, who was cleaning the window in the redundant vestibule. Odd. Elsie wasn't au fait with a duster, or chamois leather.

'Grandma, my tummy feels much better now,' said Mary. 'Can I go out in the garden and play? I think the fresh air would do me good.'

When she was back at home, Mary's parents always fobbed her off with the notion that the fresh air would do her some good, no matter what it was she was complaining of. It wouldn't be unfathomable to assume that, had Mary gone to her parents with a broken leg, they would have sent her outside for some fresh air. Their garden at home was secure, and offered no means of escape, or easy entry for intruders. In her parents' eyes, when at home, Mary could be seen but not heard in the garden, perfect for when they were arguing, or drinking.

'I promise not to go near the lake,' she said to Elsie in her most persuasive voice.

'That was a quick recovery,' said Elsie. 'Did you not want a nice day out with your mum and dad?'

'Not really. I didn't want to hear more arguing.'

Fair point, thought Elsie. 'Well, alright then. But only on the condition that you stay where I can see you,' she replied, shuffling into the lounge and getting comfortable in her reclining chair, her knitting needles and cup of tea on the side table. 'Cleaning one window is quite enough for today, so I'm going to be sitting here doing some knitting.' She pushed back so that her feet were raised. 'Ah, that's better. Now remember, stay where I can see you, otherwise there'll be big trouble.'

Elsie had been doing a whole raft of random chores to keep herself occupied since Henry had gone missing, like knitting for the first time in years, baking cakes, and stocking up on homemade condiments. She had also taken to cleaning windows, most of which had antique dirt decorating the interior and exterior glass. Elsie had always been of the impression that a sparkling house represented a wasted life. However, in the past few days she had wanted to keep busy, fearing she'd end up going out of her mind with worry, an example of which had been evidenced just that morning.

Elsie got out of bed and had started running Henry his morning bath, something she'd done every day for most of her married life. For someone who didn't particularly like swimming, Henry had certainly spent enough time soaking in the tub over the decades. It was only when she went back in the bedroom to tell him that it was ready that she remembered he wasn't there. The sheets on his side of the bed still showed no sign of him resting there, remaining cold, neat and unused. Elsie sat on Henry's side of the bed, resting her feet in his slippers, questioning over and over, *Where are you, Henry?*

On average, Mary knew that it only took her grandma about ten minutes to doze off once she got comfortable in her recliner, and so she bided her time and played just in front of the lounge window, as instructed.

'It shouldn't be long now, then I'm going,' she whispered after another five minutes. Mary looked through the window for a fourth time and saw her grandma's eyes closed. Elsie's head had drooped to one side and her glasses were falling off the end of her nose, her mouth ajar, saliva seeping onto the cushion.

If only Elsie had awoken from her nap by the inconveniences that usually drag her out of sleep, like the urgency to use the bathroom or the uncomfortable feeling of her false teeth resting on her gums. She would have awoken to see the framed view of her summer garden. It may have taken a few moments to notice, but sooner or later Elsie would have noticed that the crucial thing missing from her window was her innocent granddaughter, who had been playing on the lawn. Unfortunately, neither Elsie's bladder nor sore gums could disturb her sleep. She was out for the count, and Mary was gone.

Fourteen

THE EXTENDED DRIVEWAY OF WISTERIA STRETCHED ALL the way to the main road. The path snaked through a dense canopy of trees which formed an imposing, dark tunnel that, if navigating alone, even in the daytime, felt haunted. Despite the early-morning July sun scattering its radiant golden droplets over Wisteria, this source of natural light failed to reach Mary, who was walking alone through the tunnel. She turned on her torch, her body becoming engulfed by the hungry forest. The thick umbrella of foliage ate up every drop of light before the rays had a chance to reach the path below, creating a constant feeling of night-time gloom.

Her feet stopped. The surrounding woods swallowed her frame. Noises emerged from within the seclusion of the forest's embrace, its Chinese whispers spreading like the plague. Mary looked up at Perry's house in the distance, the trees providing a protective barrier, only the attic window visible.

Is someone watching me? she thought.

Mary's torch flicked from one direction to another, her eyes scanning in a 360-degree circle, her body spinning. Suffering beneath a dizzy and muddled state of unease, she ran, deciding not to bother searching the woods, not today. But she'd only moved a few paces when her feet paused upon hearing the sound of children's voices, her heart pounding so hard within her chest that it physically ached. The whispers travelled through the trees, the wind causing the sound to change direction, making it hard to know where the voices were coming from.

'Right. Who's going in?' Mary heard a male voice ask.

She remained hidden behind an enormous tree trunk that nestled just before Perry Golifer's property. She spied on the four children that were huddled just by the side of Ivy Dean, hidden by the cluster of bushes, and out of sight from the main road. The boy who'd asked the initial question had gelled spiky hair, his jaw clenching and unclenching as he chewed on what Mary presumed to be a flavoured piece of gum.

'You're all too scared, aren't you?' asked the lad with the gum. 'How will we ever know the truth unless we go in?'

'It's too risky, Josh,' the only girl summoned up the courage to reply. 'It's dangerous. I think we should go to the park instead.'

'You're all just wimps,' replied Josh, flapping his arms in frustration. The group of kids were older than Mary, maybe in their mid-teens. The notorious house of Perry Golifer always attracted bored kids during the summer holidays, over the years each child hearing their own version of haunted tales about what when on behind the curtains at Ivy Dean. Mary didn't recognise the kids, but then she didn't know many people in Finchley. To her, everyone around here was a stranger.

'I'll go in,' she announced. Mary moved her body out from behind the tree so she stood in full view. All the kids looked. Josh walked over, circling her body, his eyes inspecting her from head-to-toe like she was some sort of rare, exotic breed.

'And who are *you*?' he asked, standing right in front of Mary, pressing his nose so close that it almost touched hers. Josh had bad breath; she wondered if that's why he was chewing strawberry-flavoured gum.

'I'm staying with my grandma. She lives back there. My name's Mary.' She extended her arm, pointing towards Wisteria.

'What? The looney lake lady is *your* grandma?' said Josh. 'The weirdo woman who lives in her basement?' Mary remained quiet, ignoring the cruel insults. 'Trust me when I say that *you* of all people don't want to be going in there. Everyone knows that it was Perry Golifer who took your sister, and probably killed her in that very house.' Josh's unwavering expression scared Mary. It scared his accompanying friends, too. 'We've heard screams coming from inside, haven't we?' The kids nodded, their sounds of agreement drowned out by the squawking black birds perched on the chimney.

Josh continued. 'My dad is mates with the postman that delivers here. When he's been doing his morning rounds, he's heard screams, loud screams, coming from inside.' Mary tried to listen for the supposed noises. She couldn't hear any screams.

'Your sister's in there right now,' said Josh. 'He'll be giving her water, to keep her alive, just so that he can carry on tormenting her. That's what he does. He killed Katie Banks and buried her body, probably right over there in his own back garden. Did you know that, Mary?'

Mary fought back her tears. She listened again for any screams, a car exhaust blowing in the distance making them all jump.

'There's no way you can go in. You get scared by a bloody car,' he mocked. His voice dropped to a whisper. 'And if you *do* go in, you'll never come out. After all, you're next on his list, the next in line to be taken. A child killer never just strikes a few times, you know. He keeps going until he's got a whole collection of dead children.' Josh stared into Mary's eyes. Mary forced back her tears, her expression hard as stone.

'I'm not scared,' she replied. 'That bastard should be the one who's scared.' Mary's choice of language took herself by surprise, and Josh. She heard her parents use bad language all the time, but had never been brave enough to use it herself, until now.

'He's got a shed in his back garden where he keeps his chosen children,' said Josh. 'He hangs them from the roof by their necks, their bodies dangle there until maggots have eaten all their flesh, and only a skeleton is left on the floor.' Josh made quite the narrator.

Mary plunged her arms forwards. 'You're a bloody idiot,' she spat, shoving Josh, his body falling to the ground. 'My sister's alive, and I'll prove it to you,' she said, standing over him, her foot pressed on his chest, preventing him from moving. 'Just tell me what to do,' she said, moving her foot and allowing him to stand. He got to his feet and ran his hand through his hair and brushed dust off his clothes, Danny Zuko style.

'That's more like it, Mary,' he said, indicating with his hand for everyone to gather. 'We wait until he leaves in his car. We've been stalking the house for weeks. At this time every day, he leaves and doesn't come back for at least fifteen minutes.'

Josh was right. Perry did always leave at the same time because it formed part of his daily ritual. He would make a trip to the pokey corner shop a couple of miles down the road to purchase his usual packet of cigarettes.

'So that's when you'll go in,' continued Josh. 'It'll give you just enough time to run in through the gates and through to his back garden, and to check the shed.' Mary listened to the plan. Her entire body trembled. She hid her shaking hands behind her back, hoping the others wouldn't notice. Her outburst of courage already felt like a mistake. In her mind, pretending to be friends with Perry in order to search the garden felt like a better idea, but it was too late now.

'You need to wear this,' instructed Josh, pulling out an oversized T-shirt and balaclava. 'Just in case. If he comes back early, you don't want him to recognise you, otherwise... that's it.'

That's what? thought Mary, but she didn't dare ask, despite having a good idea what Josh meant.

Mary put on the T-shirt and pulled the balaclava over her head, only her eyes remaining visible. It was a bit big, but she didn't care. It covered her glasses and long hair, and would hide any tears that she could feel were about to escape.

'We'll keep watch out here. If he comes back early, we'll let you know on this,' Josh instructed, thrusting a walkie-talkie into Mary's hand. 'When you open the shed and see the bodies, scream, and then we'll call the police and get help.'

Mary thought through the plan, imagining opening the door and seeing her sister's remains in a pile on the floor, her recognisable lilac bow scattered amongst the dusty skeleton. The thought made her wretch, her throat swallowing back anything that threatened an embarrassing ambush. Although the others couldn't see it, her skin was deathly white beneath the balaclava. The material soaked up a few stray tears before they had time to escape.

'And if I find nothing but a load of old junk, then what?' she asked, trying to get rid of the haunting images sabotaging her mind. 'Maybe he's not the one who took my sister, or Katie Banks, after all.'

'Shush,' said one of the other boys. They all looked round upon hearing a door slam. 'He's leaving, and bang on time.' Perry got in his car and drove off, the group ducking so that they remained hidden.

'Go. Now,' ordered Josh. 'You've only got fifteen minutes to get in and get out,' he added whilst pushing Mary on the back, urging her to walk towards the house. Mary's feet crept forward with reluctance. With her heart cradled in her mouth, she cast a glance up and down the main road.

He's definitely gone, hasn't he?

She stared at the building upon entering the grounds of Ivy Dean through the towering, black gates. The front of the house remained hidden by unkempt ivy, its green foliage covering the house like a second skin. The bay windows were filthy, a fine layer of muck covering the glass, and the curtains were closed. The front door was set back into a brick porch. Mary noticed a pair of tatty trainers cast aside on the doormat and a rusty sign to the side stating *Keep Out*.

Mary walked round the side of the house, keeping her tread light as though she was walking over eggshells. Her heart was thumping with such force it threatened to escape from its caged prison. Her blood rushed at double-speed through her veins, which felt as though they could rupture and spill.

'Are you there yet?' bellowed Josh's voice through the walkie-talkie. The unexpected noise made Mary jump, the bulky device dropping from her hand and clattering to the floor. She bent down, her hands aimlessly scrambling to pick it up, her eyes remaining glued to the gates, watching for Perry's return.

Mary's finger pressed the button. 'I'm in the garden.' Her eyes scanned the enclosed area. She held the radio to her mouth, steadying her trembling hand and gripping the transmitter tight so she didn't drop it again. 'It looks normal. A messy garden with loads of rubbish and other stuff.'

'Keep going. You've not got much time,' insisted Josh. 'Can you see the shed?' Mary looked to her left, catching sight of the brown, weathered shed at the far side, the roof infested with overgrown trees and moss. She released her finger from the transmit button, silencing Josh.

'Grandad? Can you hear me?' she whispered. 'It's me, Mary.' She listened for a reply, or any sound that indicated someone could have been lurking. 'Grandad? Are you here?' If there was a time for Henry to appear, it was now.

'I said, can you see the shed?' shouted Josh again, his loud voice travelling over the fence.

'Yeah, I see it. There's something nailed to the door.' Mary took a big swallow. 'And there's a hammer, and a spade, and some rubbish bags at the side of it,' she added in one breath. Her eyes darted from one thing to another, panic railroading her words and actions.

'What's nailed to the door?' Josh asked. 'Go over and get a better look.'

I'm too scared.

Mary caught sight of a red jumper lying on the floor behind the shed, the one she'd thought she'd spotted from her attic window. The dirty sleeve was just visible, the material plucked and worn. Taking a few steps closer, she bent down to get a better look, the tiny fish that was stitched on the front coming into view, her sisters bike basket lying abandoned at the side. *I knew it.* She jumped as the sleeve moved in the wind, holding her breath in expectation for her grandad to appear, but he didn't.

'Grandad, can you hear me?' There was no further movement, and Mary's heart sank at the disappointment. She didn't really understand why Perry had taken the broken bike basket out of her grandparent's shed, or why he had her grandad's red jumper, but she wanted to find out.

'Are you still there?' Josh's voice bellowed, his words breaking the silence engulfing the garden. 'You're not moving fast enough. He'll be back soon. Just open the door and tell me what you see!' Mary stood.

'The thing nailed to the door is a picture of a clown,' she said in the walkie-talkie. The laughing clown face looked scary, not a friendly clown like the type that would show up at a child's birthday party holding balloons and a top hat full of tricks.

'And there's a rusty lock,' she added.

Mary pulled on the padlock. *Please don't open*, she thought, her hand pushing on the door whilst her mind once again produced the image of her sister's skeleton.

'I can't get in.'

'Grab something and whack it,' shouted Josh. Mary grabbed a brick off the floor and cast her arm back, the brick feeling heavy in her palm. She closed her eyes before catapulting the brick against the lock.

'Are you in?' Josh asked, the crashing noise echoing over the dividing fence, a mass of crows fluttering away in unison. Mary opened her eyes.

'No.'

'Then bloody well belt it again!'

Mary picked up another brick and stood closer. She lunged the rock against the door and the broken, rusty lock fell to the ground.

She'd done it. She was in.

The door automatically eased open and the hinge creaked. A small gap appeared.

'Quick, Mary. Get out, he's back!' shouted Josh.

Mary dropped her radio in the long grass by the side of the shed, as she swung her head around to look back at the house.

'Run. He's coming.'

Mary bent down to find the walkie-talkie. Through the crack of the open shed door, she thought she caught sight of something, but the dark interior was obscuring her view.

'Lucy?' she whimpered, immediately thinking about what Josh had warned. She reached out and touched the hair that spread across the floor. As she pulled at the soft strands, she could sense the weight of the body it was attached to. The sound of car tyres crunching over the driveway rang in her ears like a siren. Panicking, she closed her eyes before yanking hard on the mess of hair she gripped in her hands. The face of a doll moved itself into Mary's view, its hair entwined around her fingers. Terrified after a short glance at the porcelain skin, she stood up and scrambled into the bushes at the side of the shed, her body fully submerged in the heart of the spikey foliage. The sound of footsteps now travelled towards her hideout. She moved quickly to stuff the doll under her clothes, its hair still knotted in her fingers.

'Mary. He's coming. Get out of there,' the walkie-talkie announced unapologetically, the device lying abandoned in the grass. 'He's gonna get you.'

Maybe Josh had a conscience after all, but just not quite enough to go in and help the girl whom he'd placed in danger. Instead, he ran in the opposite direction.

Mary peered out from the bush, catching sight of the radio resting within the blades of grass, the red light flashing like a beacon, indicating that another message was about to be transmitted. Just as she got up, a figure appeared from the side of the house whilst muffled, crackly words were spoken through the walkie-talkie, the sound breaking up as the device lost range.

Mary squatted back down in the bush. She watched through the foliage as Perry's black boots halted by the patio doors, the sound of him puffing on a cigarette made her ears prickle, the smoky fumes poisoning the air. Her eyes followed the shadow of his body to the shed, her heart pumping. She placed her hand over her mouth, not trusting that her fright wouldn't escape.

'What the bloody hell?' Mary heard Perry swear. She watched him lean down, picking up the broken lock and examining it in his palm.

Please don't see me. Please leave me alone.

'Where are you, you bloody bastards?' he announced. He picked up a spade and thrashed it through the dense bushes. 'I'll find you. There's nowhere to hide. If you're in here, I've got you now.'

Perry had become used to people breaking into his property; it had happened a handful of times over the years. Some mornings, he would wake up to find insults spray painted over his car, or across his windows. The paint was always red, and clear for everyone passing to read. His tyres had also been slashed in the past, and he'd had a brick thrown through his window. No amount of terrorising would force Perry Golifer to move from his ivy-covered house. He liked his home, and all the contents that he'd collected over the years. To Perry, his possessions were priceless, and moving would only threaten to destroy all that mattered to him, and all that he was still yearning to take.

Mary ducked, her hands now covering her head for protection, the spade crashing into the shrubbery.

'Are you out?' Mary heard Josh's voice beckon through the walkie-talkie, diverting Perry's attention just before he'd had chance to expose her hunching in the bushes. Perry searched for the origin of the sound with the spade still clenched in his hand. Mary watched as he took hold of the radio, the red light flashing, indicating it was about to transmit a message.

'Where are you?' The sound of Josh's voice stole Mary's breath, her eyes refusing to blink. The garden fell silent. Mary felt light-headed as a number of painful seconds passed with her holding the air in her lungs captive, depriving herself of oxygen.

'Don't you mean, where are *you*?' replied Perry, his finger pressing down hard on the transmission button. 'Which little bastard am I speaking to?' The break in silence permitted Mary to gasp for breath. A united bellow of screams erupted, followed by a collection of footsteps disappearing further into the distance, the echoes fading until silence remained.

Perry stood still, casting his head in the direction of the kerfuffle, tossing the radio aside.

'Bloody nuisance kids,' he mumbled, kicking the shed door wide open. Perry entered, his body submerging in a temporary darkness.

Mary knew it was her opportunity to escape, and so threw herself out from her hiding place in an attempt to make a run for it. Landing awkward, she struggled to stand, her ankle buckling beneath her weight. Looking down, she saw her legs were tangled in weeds, thorns attacking her shins and causing a trickle of blood to seep down into her socks. With her heart in her mouth, she scrambled in an attempt to free herself, but her ankle gave way, toppling her frame to the floor, her head taking the brunt of the impact as she lay motionless on the grass. Despite her foggy vision and the sharp pains now radiating across her scalp, she willed her eyes to cast their gaze towards the shed, certain that she could hear the faint echoes of a girl screaming. Her eyes closed beneath the throbbing pain, her heart sank, and the last three words she could muster were, 'Somebody, help me.'

Fifteen

THE SIGHT OF THE FLASHING RADIO ENCOURAGED MARY'S limbs to react. Her surroundings rushed back into view and her head swelled as she realised where she was. She could still hear Perry rummaging around in his shed, and willed every muscle in her body to take action. Moving as quickly as her lethargy would allow, she stumbled to hide herself round the side of the house, pressing her back against the wall once out of sight from the garden, gasping for breath.

'Who's there?' Perry's voice cut into the air. Mary scrambled past the car, through the gates and out onto the main road, her head throbbing as a trickle of blood wept from her wound. She paused for more breath. Josh and the others were nowhere to be seen, the tunnel of trees leading back up to her grandma's house appearing even darker than before.

Keep running.

She crossed the road without checking for approaching traffic, and catapulted her body over the wall, landing in the public-access woods. She couldn't speak. She couldn't scream. She could barely breathe. Her head was throbbing and, in her periphery, she could hear the sounds of footsteps.

Just keep running.

Like a startled animal, Mary ran through the deserted, dense woods, scrambling over branches as quickly as she possibly could. The faint sound of cars travelling down the road echoed in her ears, the hum of a passing vehicle carrying with it a cough.

Don't stop, Mary, keep on running.

She wasn't running back to Wisteria. Mary may have only been ten, but she wasn't stupid. Far from it. She didn't want Perry to know it had been her in his garden; not a chance. She knew she needed to out-run him.

'There's nowhere to hide,' she heard his voice holler, the faint sound of his body jumping over the wall kicked her system into overdrive. She didn't turn to look, she just kept on running. The sound of his boots crunching over the foliage in pursuit acted as a fuel, her legs now moving faster than they ever had before, despite her throbbing ankle. 'I'll find you. Nobody breaks into my house and gets away with it. Nobody.'

Out of breath, Mary paused and rested her back against a hefty trunk, fear forcing her eyes closed beneath the balaclava. She strained her ears to listen. Beneath her disguise, her warm breath made her face hot and clammy. Her cheeks felt flushed and her head was still throbbing where she had fallen.

'I'm getting closer, aren't I?' he said softly, his boots leaving indentations in the foliage, his eyes scanning the forest, following the trail of disturbed leaves. 'I can smell you,' he said, Mary's delicate scent leaving a dangerous, invisible trail.

Should I run?

Mary's eyes shot open. Her feet became nailed to the ground in fear. She felt the doll stuffed down her jumper, making sure she hadn't dropped it, leaving a visible trail to her location. She wrapped her arms around her shaking body in an attempt to keep it still. She could hear a noise. Her eyes darted from one side to another.

'Why don't you come out and we can talk? Maybe we could be friends?' suggested Perry, still scanning the woods, his internal organs churning with excitement at the prospect of catching a new victim. The thrill of the chase made his palms line with sweat; his mouth became dry and his impatience mounted. Above the sound of his laboured breathing, he heard the snap of a branch in the distance, his head turning to see Mary's hidden body.

'There you are,' he whispered, a smirk appearing on his face. He checked his surroundings, there was nobody else around. Perfect. Perry approached Mary's concealed body, his carefully placed feet trying to avoid making any noise, though his growing impatience threatened to alert Mary to his approach. He paused and held his breath, before taking a glance over his shoulder, the surrounding area still perfectly deserted. He could hear Mary's erratic breathing coming from behind the tree, one side of her shaking body now visible with only a few paces separating them.

'It's a girl,' he mouthed upon spotting Mary's trainers. With his heart in his mouth, his pupils dilated with anticipation. His anger at the intrusion of his property was replaced by excitement. He took a final step closer, his focused eyes failing to see the outstretched bramble, the thorny obstacle wrapping round his foot and wrenching, causing him to fall. Mary jumped at the thud of Perry's body crashing to the floor and released a scream when she turned to witness his outstretched arm reaching for her. She made a dash, Perry's fingers clutching at her trousers before losing grip as she ran.

'I'll get you,' he shouted, attempting to free his leg whilst keeping his eyes fixed on Mary. He watched as she ran, her eyes looking back at her attacker through her balaclava. Their stares locked for a second, the moment of eye contact encouraging Perry to wrench at his leg in order to free himself. Mary turned back, the barrage of trees before her appearing unfamiliar with no clear escape. She paused, her body standing still but her head spinning in every direction, urging familiarity to appear and a way out to emerge. She wanted to take off her balaclava so she could see clearer, her face burning up with panic and sweat.

'Help,' she screamed before running once again, her cry for help panicking Perry.

His gaze was momentarily pulled away from Mary whilst he ripped his leg free, the thorns producing blood, and a second later when he looked back, she had disappeared from his line of sight. Unbeknownst to him, her petite frame had also been dragged to the ground as her feet were taken hostage by rogue foliage. She heard a light thud and realised her glasses had fallen from her face.

Where are they? Mary fretted. She frantically searched the ground for her spectacles, the sight of Perry standing in the distance instilling panic. She didn't want to leave them behind, if Perry saw them, she felt sure that he would know it was her that'd broken into his property. Her hands fumbled over the ground, her fingers feeling for the glasses. Mud covered her hands and her palms were littered with scrapes and scratches. The balaclava became lopsided, obscuring her line of sight and in the distance, the sound of someone running echoed through the trees. She stopped rummaging and held her breath. Tears penetrated the material of the balaclava and she looked round to check where Perry was, catching sight of him running towards her. Without moving her head, her hands felt around for her glasses once again, the tips of her fingers finally stumbling over the long stem of the frame before her hand grabbed.

'Got them,' she whispered, clutching the glasses and continuing to run. Her heart leapt at the sight of a wall not too far in the distance, the sound of cars confirming it led back to a main road. She scrambled towards it, willing her legs to keep moving despite the fallen branches that were strewn across the ground, threatening to send her tumbling once again. Upon reaching the wall, her legs scrambled up, her foot desperately trying to find something which would hoist her body. She looked over her shoulder, terrified when Perry had vanished.

'Where is he?' she cried, her legs still scrambling yet failing to secure themselves up the wall.

Having freed his leg, Perry trailed, concealing himself behind the trees. He watched Mary as she desperately tried to escape, the wall proving too mighty to climb, which he already anticipated would be the case. He smirked. He relished watching her struggle. He now knew for sure that it was a girl, long strands of hair dangling beneath the headwear.

'Help!' she shouted, her legs trying to scramble up what may as well have been a cliff face. She kicked her legs frantically whilst trying to hoist herself up with weary, trembling arms.

'What's your name?' asked Perry. Mary's legs stopped scrambling and her body slipped down. She froze. She reluctantly looked round. She watched Perry walk towards her, her back pressing into the wall.

'I've got you now,' he declared, grabbing hold of Mary's body and pressing her against the wall.

'Help!' she screamed from the depths of her lungs, her throat throbbing as it produced the high-pitched alarm. Perry removed her balaclava.

'Mary?' he announced, her face flinching as the material brushed over the graze above her eye. 'I didn't know it was you.' He released his grip and bent down. 'I haven't hurt you, have I?' A heightened sense of fear induced her kidneys to create an urgent need to urinate, causing additional panic. She shook her head.

'I'm not hurt,' she mumbled. 'You said I could come around, so I did,' she blurted, recalling his suggestion of being friends, hoping that her explanation would prevent him from hurting her. 'There were some kids messing about in your garden. I saw them run off.' Perry brushed down her clothes, removing the leaves and dirt covering her trousers. She flinched upon feeling his touch, terrified he would feel the stolen item beneath her clothes.

'I promise I won't hurt you,' he said, kneeling so that he was at the same height as her. 'I said I wanted to be your friend, remember?' Mary looked round, hoping to see someone approaching through the barren woods. 'I'm glad you decided to come over. Why are you wearing this? And why did you run away?' Perry looked at the balaclava on the floor.

'I didn't want anyone to see me going in, that's why I wore it,' explained Mary. 'I'd get into trouble with Mum and Dad if they found out.' She tried to control her breathing. 'And I got scared, you were shouting, so I thought I was in trouble for going in your garden when you weren't in. And so I ran.' She bit her bottom lip. Whilst hoping that he believed her tale, she crossed her legs, trying to prevent herself from having an accident. Perry moved her hair aside to take a look at the cut on her head. Her skin flinched. She felt sure that he'd be able to tell she was lying.

'I need to get back,' Mary continued. 'I didn't tell my grandma where I was going. She'll be worried.' Her body remained pressed against the wall, Perry preventing her from trying to move away when he touched her face. She didn't want him touching her, it felt wrong. Perry remained kneeling, just in front of Mary.

'It's good that you didn't tell your grandma, Mary. She doesn't like me very much. But that doesn't mean we can't still be friends, right?' he asked. 'Here, have some sweets. I always keep a packet in my pocket.' Perry held out his hand, nodding with encouragement for her to take some.

'Thanks,' she replied, the touch of her hand against his skin sending invisible shivers through his body.

'Who did you see in my garden, Mary?' he asked.

Think Mary, think.

'A boy, not sure who.' She shrugged her shoulders, hoping that there would be no more questions.

'And what was this boy saying to you?'

'Bad stuff.'

'What kind of bad stuff?' Perry's insides reeled at the thought of someone scuppering his efforts and progress. Mary looked over his shoulder, hoping that someone would finally be coming, and that she wouldn't have to answer. 'Mary, what kind of things was that boy saying?' Perry took hold of her hand and began stroking it, encouraging a reply.

'He said you keep weird stuff in your shed.' Mary watched his reaction as her words escaped. 'What's in your shed?' She immediately regretted asking her question.

Perry didn't hesitate. 'Garden stuff, like a lawnmower, hedge cutters, a few old buckets and some grass seed. I don't think that's weird, do you?' Mary shook her head. She could see his eyes, his pupils opening wide, almost enabling her to see her own reflection. She wanted to ask about her grandad's jumper, and why it was there, but she wasn't brave enough, she feared what he might do.

'Is that all there is in there? Just garden stuff?'

'Sure is. And if that boy comes over again, I'll take him round to my shed and show him inside. That'll make him stop spreading lies about me.' Mary watched as Perry causally slipped a sweet in his mouth, offering her another.

'Are you going to come over again?' he said. 'I'd like us to be friends.' Mary paused before answering.

'Maybe,' she shrugged, but the thought of even pretending to be Perry's friend made her body shiver beneath her clothes. The image of being alone with him in Ivy Dean scared her so much that a lump lodged itself in her throat. The thought of him touching her face or hand again made her skin crawl. In Mary's eyes, being friends with someone meant playing together, having tea at one another's house and having sleepovers. She had no intention of doing any of those things with Perry, and the longer she looked into his bloodshot eyes, the more she felt afraid. She tried her best not to let the deep, ingrained frown lines scattering his face make him look angry. She tried to push to the back of her mind all the terrible things she'd heard people say about him. She tried her best to not feel scared because something in her mind was stopping her from saying what she really thought before running away as fast as she could.

Mary wanted to know the truth, and that meant finding out if Perry Golifer had been the one who took her sister away. She didn't want to keep wondering if she or her grandparents had done something terrible to Lucy, either by accident or on purpose. And now that she had uncovered her own doubts about Perry Golifer, she wanted to know if he'd been the one who'd made her sister disappear. She knew she had to go back to his house, and so she made the first step to acting like his friend.

'I'm not sure when I'll be able to sneak out, but I'll try.' She felt the doll beneath her top. 'I best get going.' She then brushed past his shoulder and began to walk away. Perry's body shuddered at the brief moment of personal contact, resisting the urge to grab her, and run. In his mind, this wasn't how he'd envisaged taking her. This wasn't part of his plan. He didn't want anything to go wrong. He needed to be patient, not impulsive or careless. The anniversary event was fast approaching, and then he would strike.

'Okay, well, I hope you'll manage to come over to visit soon.' The moment she walked away, he kicked himself at not just taking the opportunity. He remained stooped in the woods. He grabbed a fallen tree branch and bent it until it snapped, his gaze following Mary until she was out of sight. He felt his arm where Mary had touched him, and he held the balaclava close to his face, inhaling the remnants of her scent.

Mary began to walk away and her pace soon developed into a run. She felt relief flood her body the further away from Perry she became, her legs not stopping until she reached the alleyway that led out toward the main road. She removed the t-shirt Josh had given her and stuffed it in a bush. She wiped her head with her sleeve, wincing as the wound stung. She felt the doll beneath her clothes and darted across the road, running all the way up the path leading to her grandma's house. She didn't stop until she'd reached the foot of the garden at Wisteria. Approaching the house with caution, she crept her way up to the lounge window and peered in. Her grandma's chair was empty.

Oh no.

'Did I or did I not make it clear, Mary Elizabeth Lane, that you were to play exactly where I could see you?' shouted Elsie, her figure appearing at the front door.

'I was just at the bottom of the lawn, Grandma,' said Mary. 'I wasn't far away, I promise. I told you where I was going, but you were asleep. You were snoring, so I didn't want to wake you.'

Elsie felt guilty that she'd fallen asleep, and had been caught in the act.

'Well, as long as you're alright,' she said. 'Let's not tell your mum and dad I fell asleep. I'm not sure they'd be very happy, and we don't want another argument, do we?'

'I promise I won't tell them, Grandma,' Mary replied. They both walked inside, Mary looking in the mirror, wiping her grazed head with her fingers.

'Have you hurt yourself?' quizzed Elsie, trying to touch Mary's head.

'It's nothing, Grandma. I fell off the broken swing again. Don't tell Dad I went on it, he'll be mad,' she lied, pulling away, 'especially when I'm meant to be feeling poorly.'

'Well. Go and get yourself cleaned up before they get home, and then our secrets will be safe.' Elsie winked at Mary.

'Thanks, Grandma,' she replied.

Mary went and sat on her bed. She opened her palm, revealing a cluster of sweets. She placed one in her mouth, savouring the sugary treat as it melted on her tongue. She pulled the doll out from under her clothes, witnessing properly for the first time what it was she had actually found on the floor in Perry's shed. Her face twisted at the sight, a number of deep frowns spreading across her face and creasing her skin. She threw the doll across the room. Her brown eyes released a torrent of tears, as though a sky filled with heavy clouds had just begun to ring them out. She pressed her back against the wall, folding her knees close to her chest. She didn't dare move. She didn't dare speak. It was as if someone terrifying was in her room; a ghost or ghoul.

'It can't be Lucy's,' she whispered eventually, too scared to look across the room. But Mary didn't need to look to get clarification. She knew what she'd found, without any element of doubt. The doll was in almost every picture featuring her sister, the photos showing Lucy holding the doll in her hand no matter what she happened to be doing. However, for a few moments, her naïve mind permitted her the luxury of remaining in denial, offering up other possibilities. Maybe the doll was now here, in her bedroom, because Lucy had come home?

'Lucy? Where are you?' she said. 'I need you. I want to talk to you. Please come out so that I can see you. Please, Lucy. I don't want to try and find you anymore.' Mary sat alone in her bedroom, a sense of sickness threatening an ambush. She bent down and checked under both their beds.

Lucy didn't appear.

'Penelope Pickles?' she then whimpered. Mary paced across the room. She bent down and picked up the doll, her whole body sinking. Her fingers dusted cobwebs off the red and blue checked dress, her dry lips blowing over the doll's face, removing the remaining dirt to reveal the true identity of the doll she remembered with such fondness.

'It can't be her. It can't be the same one,' she said, holding the doll with a delicate touch, a ghostly zephyr sweeping in through the open window. Mary checked under the beds again, then in the wardrobe, and then in the toy box. Lucy still wasn't there.

Clenching the doll, Mary dashed into her mum and dad's bedroom, closing the door behind her. She rummaged through her mum's half-emptied suitcase, failing to take stock of the numerous empty bottles. The photo album that her mum rarely let out of her sight lay hidden beneath a stained baby's comfort blanket. Mary took hold of the blanket and pressed it against her face, inhaling. The scent didn't smell familiar, yet provided the desired comfort. She gazed at the pattern adorning the material, her fingers tracing the embroidery etched into the material. She closed her eyes, and Lucy was right there by her side.

Mary looked up, once again hoping to see her sister standing in the room. She felt sure that Lucy was nearby, she could feel her – or, at least, she believed she felt something. Before Lucy went missing, wherever she went, so did her doll. Everyone knew that. Lucy and Penelope Pickles were inseparable.

Amongst a cast of assorted empty spirit bottles, Mary sat alone, her back pressed against the bed.

'If you can hear me, Lucy, please come and sit with me. I'm scared.' She took hold of the album resting on her lap, the pages brimming with nothing but photos of Lucy; from birth right up until the very day she went missing.

Mary's head shook before she'd even turned a page. *Please let me be wrong.*

Her fingers fumbled to open the album, revealing the first page of photos.

'Let me be wrong,' she said aloud, as if speaking it aloud would suddenly make her wish come true. All she could think about was the mean jibes that Josh had described, an image of her sister hanging from Perry's shed inducing such a deep sense of fear in her bones, that she closed her eyes and shook her head, trying to escape the haunting images.

After a few seconds, she dared to open her eyes and looked at the first photo of her sister. Tears fell fast down Mary's face. The doll remained clenched in her hand.

'Please don't let it be true,' she said again, turning to the next page and examining each photo in turn, praying to be mistaken. She knew that if the doll was Penelope Pickles, then it would most likely mean that Lucy was in the shed too.

On the fifth page, just as her hopes mounted, Mary spotted it. A doll with blonde, perfectly-combed hair lay next to her sister's smiling face, its blue and red checked dress clashing with Lucy's green pinafore. On the back of the photo it read 'Lucy and Penelope Pickles playing in the garden. Aged three and a half'. Mary thrust her hand into the air and catapulted the sweets she'd been holding across the room. They landed and shattered, scattering shards of boiled sugar across the floor.

Mary stood up and walked through to her bedroom. Her eyes didn't blink. Her facial expression didn't alter. Her breathing couldn't be seen nor heard. The skin across the knuckles on her right hand appeared white the more she gripped the doll dangling by her side. She locked her door, a deep-rooted feeling of fear now following her every move. She felt like she was being watched, and she wasn't mistaken. She felt vulnerable, like she herself could be the next child to vanish, and she wasn't mistaken.

Despite the fear for her own safety, in her mind, she was

saying the same words over and over – *he took Lucy, he took Lucy.* She paused in front of her bedroom window, her gaze looking out across to Ivy Dean. The sun shone in through her window causing a haunting shadow to appear. For a moment, it appeared that the twins, who were once inseparable, were finally reunited. Mary moved her head, shielding her eyes from the sun's glare. Upon witnessing the shadow, she held out her hand to stroke her shadow's hair, trying her hardest to pretend the figure was Lucy.

'Did he take you, Lucy?'

Sixteen

ENRY LANE DIDN'T KNOW THAT HE WAS DYING, BUT HE was. His internal organs were giving up the fight and failing to function sufficiently. His fragile heart, his weakened kidneys and his ailing liver were all on the brink of being unable to sustain life for any length of time. Henry was suffering. A look of defeat spread across his face like a disease. He knew he didn't feel very good, but he didn't know that this was how it felt to die.

Henry could feel his insides eating away at his own reserves, the scraps of food and water he'd scavenged from nearby bins unable to sustain his hefty frame. He felt dizzy and faint, his body failing to cope or function. The more his blood pressure plummeted, the harder it became to exist. He experienced a constant feeling of weakness in his joints and, at times, he was unable to move from his static position. Had he heard his name being called by those who were out searching for him in the near vicinity – the police, his family, and a handful of caring citizens – he wouldn't have been able to move in order to raise the alarm. The search party would have needed to break into the shed and uncover his body. But they didn't. They didn't know where to look for him. His secluded shed thus far remained unnoticed.

His vulnerable brain continued to concoct delusional thoughts, the voices in his mind storming louder than an army braced for battle on the frontline. Apart from the initial day when everyone had rallied to search the area, Henry hadn't actually heard a single sound coming from outside, because there was no one there.

The only person to pass his hideaway in the past twenty-four hours had been a lone dog walker. The man had been throwing a ball for his Border Terrier in the neglected park; and, on what was to be the dog walker's last throw, he'd flung the ball too far. The yellow, squeaky toy flew through the air and landed in the field where Henry was taking shelter. The gentleman and his dog had spent a good fifteen minutes looking for the ball, walking past the cow shed dozens of times, but failing to enter. And why would he have done? The building didn't look like it had been disturbed. There wasn't any external sign that it had been damaged, or broken into.

Henry had been asleep the whole time that the search for the ball was taking place, his body unable to fight against exhaustion. Had Henry heard the commotion, perhaps he would have tried to call out. Then again, perhaps he wouldn't. For now, though, Henry remained hidden in his bunker. But his clock was ticking.

ONLY A STONE's throw away from the cow shed, a trio of ducks flew past, their orchestrated manoeuvre ensuring they glided flawlessly over the lake at Wisteria before paddling, their beaks sifting to catch any lurking morsels.

Mary awoke. It'd been a couple of days since she'd found her sister's doll in Perry's shed. Penelope Pickles had spent every second stuffed beneath Mary's clothes. If only Penelope Pickles had been able to talk, and answer the only question running through Mary's mind: *Where's Lucy?*

Mary had barely left her attic bedroom in days, feeding her parents the lie that she wasn't feeling well. And although she did feel sick, her main motivation for hiding in her bedroom was to avoid any interaction with her parents. She didn't want them to somehow catch sight of Penelope Pickles, because then what? She didn't want them running over to Perry's to find her sister's bones crumpled in a heap on the shed floor, just like Josh had described. She thought the ordeal would be enough to kill her mum, and maybe it would. Mary didn't want to just have a dad, he wasn't very good at the girly stuff, not like her mum was. Life was hard enough to cope with without having her sister, without her mum too, Mary couldn't see how she would ever feel happy again.

Just the image of her sister's skeleton made Mary physically sick, causing her to dart to the bathroom every time she couldn't force away the terrifying image. The things Josh had said taunted her mind *your sister's in there right now. He'll be giving her water, to keep her alive, just so that he can carry on tormenting her.*

She just wanted to pretend that nothing had really happened, and that nothing bad was going to happen. In her bedroom she felt safe, like nobody could get her there. She just wanted to snuggle with Penelope Pickles. She felt safe with Penelope Pickles. It was as if Lucy was back by her side after all these years, and she didn't want to do anything that would take that wonderful feeling away. Mary closed her eyes and pictured Lucy holding her doll and, if she imagined hard enough, it was like Lucy was back in bed, and the sisters were lying side by side.

Help me. Somebody help.

Mary didn't know what to do, or who to turn to. She didn't feel like she could trust anybody. Her Grandma had been the one responsible for her sister the day she vanished, yet had no idea what happened. The police had failed to find any answers, and they were meant to be experts, and her parents were struggling to get through each day. The thought of telling her mum and dad anything terrified her, the slightest thing causing more shouting and arguments. At ten years old, Mary already understood that the only person she could trust was herself. If she really wanted to know if Perry Golifer had taken Lucy away on that July morning, then she would need to find out herself. And no matter how terrifying it would be, the thought of finding out that he was to blame, and not her or her grandparents, she felt would make it all worthwhile. She would know the truth, and in Mary's eyes, that was better than being forced to keep imagining what might have happened to her sister. But right now, right at this moment, Mary didn't feel brave enough to find out anything, the slightest sound of someone climbing the stairs made her wet herself.

Leave me alone, she would mumble until the noise vanished. She felt most vulnerable at night, terrified of the dark and what it might bring. The shadows in her bedroom making her believe that someone was in her room, ready to take her away. It had happened before to her sister; it could happen again.

And so she did what most children did when they felt scared; she hid beneath her duvet until the morning came, and with it, an increased sense of safety.

On this particular morning when Mary opened her eyes, the lack of noise in the house felt alarming; there was usually an argument to be heard, or the sound of her grandma clattering about in the kitchen. This morning, however, there was nothing but silence, so she crept out of bed and sunk her body into her muddy dungarees, stuffing Penelope Pickles down the front.

She opened her bedroom door and looked down onto the landing.

'Mum?' she whispered. There was no response. She bobbed her head into her parents' bedroom, but there was nobody there. 'Dad?'

Stepping tentatively down the stairs, she peered over the banister and down the deserted hallway. The scene could have been taken from a horror film, right before something terrible happens – which, inevitably, it always did. Without the sun beaming through any of the downstairs windows, and with all the lights turned off, the house felt intimidating. There was no smell of burnt toast. No whistling kettle. No noise from the TV. No raised voices. Only silence.

She called again. 'Mum?' Her voice echoed off the walls. The ground floor was deserted. Mary stood alone in the hallway, her bare feet feeling cold on the floorboards. She took out Penelope

Pickles from beneath her dungarees, holding the doll, her hand draped by her side.

Just before she had chance to call out again, the sound of laughter travelled in through an open window in the laundry room. Mary meandered down the hallway and out through the back door, the brightness outside forcing her eyes into a squint as the sun maneuvered itself away from the cluster of cumulus clouds. She hid Penelope Pickles back down her dungarees and walked round the side of the house towards the basement.

Although immediate relief flooded through Mary upon sight of her mum and grandma in the cluttered, dirt-infested basement, the feeling was short-lived.

'You've finally decided to get out of bed, have you?' said Martha, who continued to parade round the cluttered space wearing one of Elsie's ancient hats and holding an umbrella. 'I'm Gene Kelly from *Singin' in the Rain*,' she added, slurring her words.

Oh no. She's drunk, again, isn't she?

A scratched vinyl record played merrily in the background whilst Martha twirled, unsteady on her feet.

'What are you doing?' asked Mary, standing in the doorway. The basement at Wisteria resembled an Aladdin's Cave. The expanse of space buried at the bottom of the house was filled with more clutter than there were lampposts lining the streets of New York City. Terrified of throwing anything away, secret hoarders Elsie and Henry had accumulated over fifty years' worth of stuff. There were old electrical appliances without plugs, apparently just waiting to be fixed. There was a whole host of clothes, enough to fill a shop, waiting to come back into fashion. There were polka dot dresses from the thirties, tapered suites from the forties, and fashionable flares from the seventies, none of which stood a remote chance of fitting either one of them ever again.

'We're trying to find something that could give us a clue as to where Grandad has gone,' replied Elsie, who was kneeling amongst a sea of carboard boxes, all brimming with odds and sods of various shapes and sizes. 'You can come and help, if you like.' Just at that point, Martha took another twirl, but this time she tripped over her own feet and fell amongst a pile of dirty dusters.

Hank appeared in the doorway. 'Martha, for God's sake, pull yourself together will you,' he barked, witnessing the pathetic state of his wife. 'This can't go on.' He walked over to Martha, who's eyes were now closed, her intoxicated body permitting only the shallowest of breaths to be released, her bloodstream trying to absorb the vast amounts of alcohol ingested.

Hank looked to his left. 'Oh. Hi, Mary. I didn't notice you there. It's nice to finally see you out of bed. You've barely spoken or eaten for days. You feeling any better?'

Mary felt Penelope Pickles beneath her clothes, and was only able to shrug.

'What does this mean?' added Hank, imitating Mary's action. He was getting annoyed. 'I asked you a question, Mary. Are you feeling any better?'

This time, she shook her head. Had Hank been paying closer attention, he would've seen the slight bulge beneath Mary's clothes, and asked what it was. As such, he didn't.

'Well, I have something I think might make you feel better, or hopefully cheer you up,' he said. 'A big surprise.' He bent down and lifted Mary's chin with his hand. She flinched, mainly because she thought he'd spotted the doll.

'Did you hear me? I said we have a surprise for you.' he repeated. 'We've been planning it for a while, and this morning I went and brought him home.' Mary looked puzzled. *Him?*

'What is it?'

'Well, your mum and I have been talking and we think that the time is right.' Mary looked up. 'We think you're old enough to have a pet of your own now. How would you like that?'

'What? You mean a dog?' she replied, partaking in a conversation for the first time in days.

'Yep. A dog. If that's what you want?' Hank asked.

'I do, Dad. I really do.'

'The dog will need bones to chew whilst he stays here,' said Elsie from across the basement, a grimace spreading across her disgruntled face. 'Grandad will have a fit when he comes home and finds his slippers have been gnawed.'

'Dogs can't have bones, Mum,' said Hank. 'They're too dangerous.'

'Of course they can! Never brought any harm to my dogs,' Elsie replied, despite the fact that every dog she'd owned was now buried in the lake. 'Have you never heard the nursery rhyme *Give a Dog a Bone*?' Elsie began singing.

'That's just a stupid nursery rhyme,' snapped Hank, shaking his head. 'It doesn't tell you what happens when you give the dog a scrap bone, does it?'

'What happens?'

'Little fragments of bone get stuck in the dog's throat, and then you have to watch as it chokes to death.'

'Stop bickering,' interrupted Martha, pulling herself up, her head throbbing and spinning simultaneously. 'We can go and get the dog some chew sticks, but not before I have at least three cups of coffee.' Martha staggered out, tossing the umbrella on the floor. The record that had been playing in the background screeched to an abrupt conclusion.

'Can I really have one, Dad?' asked Mary.

'You've already got one. Go and look in the garden!' Hank replied, a rare smile spreading across his face.

'Really?' said Mary, looking out the window in disbelief.

'Come on, follow me,' he instructed, taking hold of Mary's hand and escorting her round to the side of the house, where they were met by a wooden dog kennel. 'He's in there. Go and have a peek. I collected him this morning.'

Mary let go of her dad's hand and walked closer.

'He's really friendly, Mary. His name is Einstein. He's a Labrador, just like the ones you've seen on TV.'

With immaculately groomed hair, pearly white teeth and brown, glossy eyes, the dog could've been taken straight from a TV studio.

Einstein was a real beauty. Pedigree perfection.

Mary bent down.

'Go on. Stroke him. He's all yours,' encouraged Hank. Mary looked at Einstein lying in his new home, his brown eyes looking up to greet Mary as she approached. She extended her hand cautiously. Einstein's black nose sniffed at her fingers, making her flinch.

'It's okay, Mary,' Hank reassured her. 'He's just getting to know you. He won't bite.' He, too, held out his hand before stroking Einstein's silky, cream fur. 'Einstein's here to make you happy. He'll play with you if you want him to.'

Hank and Martha had top trumped on this one, going some way to make up for the previous six years' worth of terrible surprises. Like the surprise of having no cake or candles on Mary's seventh birthday, or the year her Christmas presents were wrapped in tin foil because they didn't buy any wrapping paper. Or, the worst surprise of all, being the only child at school whose parents forgot, repeatedly, to come and collect her, leaving her sitting alone in school, wondering if they would turn up at all or if the caretaker would have to take her home again.

'I think he likes me already.' Einstein rolled over onto his back, urging Mary to tickle his belly.

'I told you, he's just a big softie, isn't he?' said Hank.

Einstein moved forwards out of his kennel and circled Mary before licking her face, his excitement dislodging her balance.

'I think you two will be the best of friends.'

'His tongue feels rough,' Mary laughed. Einstein danced with unapologetic buoyancy. 'Why's he called Einstein?'

'Because, apparently, he's really clever,' replied Hank. 'At least, that's what the woman told me when I paid. She was probably just trying to get a better price. Well, I think I can leave you two to play.' He stood up and walked back to the house.

Einstein's initial excitement calmed, enabling him and Mary to sit on the grass side by side, looking out towards the lake, the hazy summer sun shining over them.

'My name's Mary,' she began. Einstein rested his head on her lap like they'd always been companions. 'This is my grandma's home. We'll be staying here for a bit,' she explained, looking back towards the house, the pungent aroma of sizzling bacon wafting amidst the morning zephyr.

Einstein raised his head, his treacle-black nose sniffing with curiosity.

'I like you already,' Mary added. Einstein lowered his head and closed his eyes. 'I think you will make a great friend.'

Mary looked over towards Perry's house. 'Lucy used to be my best friend, but she's not here anymore. Lucy is my twin sister.' In the distance, mist rose from the lake, the sun performing its summer job to perfection, taking away any lingering chill and replacing it with rays of warmth.

'We stay at my grandma's house every summer, just to try and find her.' Mary pulled Penelope Pickles from beneath her clothes. 'This is Penelope Pickles. She was Lucy's doll. I found her over there.'

Mary pointed across to Ivy Dean.

'If I tell Dad what I found, he'll go and knock his door down.' A troublesome expression destroyed Mary's short-lived smile. 'Then they'll put Dad in jail for doing something bad, and it'll be all my fault. Mum will drink even more, enough to make her never wake up. Grandma will be put in an old people's home, and I'll be left on my own. Nobody will come and collect me from school. I'll be the girl without any family - I'm sure there's a name for children like that. I'd be given to someone else and they'd have to look after me.' Mary's head lowered. 'I don't know what to do. I'm so scared. I want to run away. I want everything to just be normal. I want Lucy back.' She pressed her face into the palms of her hands, halting her mumbled stream of words. Warm tears trickled down her pale skin, and Einstein licked her hands as soon as she lowered them.

She turned to check that nobody was watching her from the house. As usual, nobody was. 'I need to go back over there. I need to go and look for Lucy. He likes me. He'll let me in. But I'm scared. I'm scared to go over there again. I'm scared to open the door. I'm scared at what might be inside.' Mary imagined herself opening Perry Golifer's shed wide open, only this time instead of finding Penelope Pickles, she'd find a skull and pile of bones. The surface of her skin shivered, and it felt like something was crawling all over her. Her hands flicked her hair and scratched her trousers, trying to remove whatever it was she thought she could feel.

Mary pushed the harrowing image to the back of her mind. She did her very best not to think about the state she would inevitably find her sister in if she had been locked away in his shed all these years. Such a terrifying thought would have been enough to make her want to hide under her duvet and never reappear. She was just so thankful that she'd found something so precious that had belonged to her twin. Penelope Pickles provided Mary with a glimmer of hope, hope that maybe now, after all these years, she would finally uncover what had really happened to her sister.

Einstein raised his head, his ears pricking up. 'What can you hear?' said Mary.

'Are you two getting on well?' asked Hank, sneaking up on Mary from behind. Einstein jumped up and barked, acting as a brilliant distraction whilst Mary stuffed Penelope Pickles down her dungarees.

'Yes.'

'That's brilliant. I'm just nipping to the shop for a few bits and bobs with Grandma. Mum is inside eating breakfast.'

'Can I take Einstein for a walk?'

'You can walk him round the garden, but not near the lake,' Hank instructed. 'I'm not sure if Einstein can swim and we don't want any accidents.' He placed a delicate kiss on Mary's cheek before he went back to the car.

As soon as the vehicle was out of sight, Mary got up and walked towards the house. Peeking through the kitchen window, she watched as her mum searched frantically through the cupboards, her bacon sandwich sitting on the table, untouched.

Now that the house is empty and there's nobody to see her, she's looking for another drink.

Mary knew her mum all too well.

She watched as Martha scattered the contents of the kitchen haphazardly across the floor, searching for the spirits her body craved. Martha knew she would find some alcohol if she just looked hard enough. An experienced alcoholic always had a plethora of hiding places. Mary could've saved her mum some time and just told her to check the juice bottles on the top shelf in the fridge.

Martha's distraught demeanour made Mary turn away.

I bet that's where Dad's gone, to buy her some more. She shouts at him if he won't go.

She was right in her assumption. Elsie had tagged along so that she could choose Henry a new pack of mints, because, in her mind, that's exactly what he was going to need when or if he eventually came home.

Mary could no longer watch her mum. Witnessing Martha's pathetic state made Mary cry and there was nothing she could do to help. 'Come on, let's go. She's not going to be watching what I'm doing,' said Mary, looking down at Einstein, who was already standing faithfully by her side.

Mary was right again; Martha wasn't going to be paying attention to anything other than getting to the bottom of a bottle. It took her just under ten minutes, but Martha found the juice cartons on the top shelf in the fridge and, sure enough, she'd already filled them with vodka. Martha was always concerned about the whereabouts of her next alcoholic drink; it was a shame she wasn't equally concerned about the whereabouts of her daughter. It wasn't that she didn't care about Mary; like any other alcoholic, she just cared about alcohol more.

Seventeen

MARY AND EINSTEIN TRAIPSED THROUGH THE WOODS that separated her grandma's house from Perry's. The soil and leaves of the dense, dark woodlands crunched beneath her feet.

'You don't need to feel scared, Einstein. I'll look after you,' she said, her words offering reassurance to herself as much as to her new companion. Shadows danced in all directions, glimmers of sun breaking through the natural barrier, reflecting off trees to produce silhouettes. Every slight noise made her jump. The meekest of sounds made her head dart in all directions. She felt sure that there was somebody following her. To Mary, it felt like at any minute something terrible was about to happen, and the anticipation caused her little heart to gallop. At least it was daylight. The waking hours offered Mary some comfort, in her naïve mind bad people tended to do bad things during the night, when nobody could see. The world wasn't quite so scary in the morning. But all that was about to change.

'That's the house I told you about, right there.' Her feet paused a few metres away from Perry's towering garden fence. 'Everyone thinks the man who lives there took Lucy, and I think they might be right.' Mary stood still: a standing target in a predator's trap.

'Why would Penelope Pickles be in his shed and he not have Lucy in there too?' she said to herself. Remaining still, Mary could feel her face reddening under the heat of the sun, her thick dungarees making her legs prickly with heat. She stepped forward and stood on tiptoes, trying to see over the fence and into the front garden.

'His car isn't there. He must be out.'

Had Martha and Hank been any kind of reasonable parents, they would have taught Mary not to assume anything in life. Of course, just because a person's car wasn't parked on their driveway didn't automatically mean that the person wasn't home. The car could have been in the garage being repaired. It could have been that Perry had parked the car elsewhere to purposefully deceive. Or perhaps the dated car had broken down and been abandoned, which happened to be the case today.

Mary, with Einstein following, traced the fence round to the back of the property, the panels acting like a fortress. Most gardens had fences, that fact couldn't be disputed. But Perry's fence felt more like a wall, its purpose to keep people out – or maybe to keep people in, depending on who you asked. She looked around, searching for something to stand on so that she could see over.

Whilst distracted, she failed to hear the heavy breathing coming from just behind the fence. The warm particles of moisture trickled into the air like invisible dust. The breath had an underlying scent of something sweet, but from a distance, the smell wasn't potent enough to be identified by others in close proximity. Pity. Had Mary smelt the chocolate limes, she might have realised that Perry must've been near.

'I can see something,' she said, pressing the side of her face right up against the fence, peering through a hole with one eye. 'I can see into the garden,' she announced. Einstein rubbed himself against her legs, pausing at her feet. 'And the shed. There's a new lock on it. It's shiny and silver.' Mary looked down at Einstein. 'I need to check inside. I need to know the truth. I have to check that Lucy isn't in there.' The bond that Mary felt towards her sister, the sister she could barely recall apart from in photos, drove her actions, and pushed away her fears. Mary loved her sister so much, and understood the bond that existed between twins better than most. The separation had only served to strengthen how she felt, and until she found her sister, it felt like a part of her was missing.

Mary looked back through the hole. 'I need to try and climb over. I'm going to do it. I can do it, whilst he's not here' She stepped back, stuffed Penelope Pickles back beneath her clothes and searched her surroundings again for something to act as a means of elevation.

LURKING ON THE other side of the fence, with his face pressed against the wood, Perry perched on his knees. He'd been watching through one of the many spyholes he'd purposefully created over the years. The small holes weren't really noticeable, unless you were specifically looking. But when you did spot them, there were suddenly hundreds.

'Come closer, Mary,' he whispered, placing his hands on the fence, pushing his face right up against the hole, secretly spying.

He caught a waft of Mary's odour, her scent drifting through the air. Mary had washed her hands with lavender soap, and it was this scent that Perry could smell. His internal excitement sent shivers to every nerve in his body.

'I knew she'd come back. They always do.' The smirk of satisfaction plastered over his face upon admiring Mary was enough to send pains down every parent's spine.

'Keep on searching, Mary. There's no rush.' And, although he did bide his time, refusing to cave in to his impatience, Perry's desire was to pounce. That's what he *really* wanted to do. Its what he had wanted to do all along. 'She's lovely,' he mumbled. 'As pretty as her sister.' Perry Golifer had been infatuated with the twins from the very first day that he'd laid eyes upon them. He'd heard rumours that his neighbours had become grandparents to twins, and that the family would soon meet for the first time. He waited, patiently. He would sit up in his attic and watch out of the small window for any cars going up to Wisteria. After three days of spying, his patience paid off. The minute the brown Maxi pulled onto the private road, Perry dashed outside and made his way through the woods. Parting the trees with his hands, Perry watched Martha and Hank getting out of the car, each of them holding a bundle wrapped up in a pink blanket. He barely got to see the girls faces, but that didn't matter. He'd seen enough; the frilly pink bows wrapped around each twin indicating two girls. It was love at first sight. From that day on, he became their greatest fan, and their greatest threat.

Perry watched Mary kicking the undergrowth, her body moving out of view every time she diverted from his line of sight, before retuning seconds later.

But then all went quiet.

Perry panicked. He scrambled to another spyhole. 'Where is she?' He remained kneeling, hearing footsteps approaching on the other side of the fence.

His wicked eyes widened.

'I knew you'd be back,' he whispered upon hearing Mary's approaching footsteps on the other side of the fence. His face remained pressed against the hole. Refusing to blink, he waited patiently for his prey. He remained deathly still, huddled on the ground and eagerly awaiting his next glimpse of Mary. He didn't dare breathe; he willed his thumping heart to stop pounding for fear it would give him away. His hands pressed against the wood ensuring he was as close as possible. He could sense she was getting closer, her cantering breathing permeating the fence. Suddenly, his gaze through the hole was met with a pretty, brown eye.

'Aah!' she screamed. Mary fell back, her feet tripping over themselves, her body hitting the floor.

'Don't be scared,' Perry called out. 'It's just me. Perry. Sorry I gave you such a fright. I was just doing some gardening and I heard footsteps. I thought it was that nuisance boy coming back.'

He remained glued to the fence. 'Come and talk – if you want to, I mean.'

Perry watched Mary rising to her feet, leaves and twigs

impressed into the soft palms of her hands. She backed away some more, not taking her eyes off him. The only sensible thing for her to do was turn and run, but Perry wasn't going to make it so easy. He was a professional, after all; a professional who knew all the tricks of his sordid trade. And Mary was just a child, a scared, vulnerable child.

'Ah, there you are,' he said, spotting her through another hole in the fence. 'I'm glad you've come over again, Mary. Even better this time, because I'm home.'

Mary remained silent.

'My car is in the garage, so I was worried that you'd think that I was out.'

Mary opened her mouth. 'I did think you were out,' she muttered. Perry had managed to get her to speak, now all he had to do was reel her in. Easy. He'd been planning this for days, for months, for years.

'I'm glad you've come to see me.'

'I wasn't coming to see you. I'm just walking my new dog,' she replied in a muffled, stand-offish voice. Perry's eye disappeared from the hole. Mary edged back, feelings of terror guiding her away.

Where's he gone? Where is he? Mary's heart pumped beneath her clothes; her laboured breathing audible.

Perry's head appeared over the top of the fence, his feet balancing on a strategically placed chair.

'I'm up here, Mary,' he announced, appearing over the top of the fence. 'Well, it doesn't matter that you weren't coming to see me, does it? But now that you're here, you may as well come in.'

Mary felt her face flush, and she felt Penelope Pickles lurking beneath her clothes. The bravery she thought she could muster just wasn't there when the moment came, and she spoke without thought.

'I don't want to be your friend.' Her words exploded with the urgency of an erupting volcano. 'I've changed my mind.' Perry concealed his internal emotions and, instead, presented a fake, facial expression.

He was a true chameleon.

Hidden from view behind the fence, he scrunched his fist into a ball.

'That's a shame,' he replied. 'Why have you changed your mind? I thought we were getting along well? I even bought you loads of new sweets, and games for us to play together.'

Mary looked up, remaining silent, her voice unable to bypass the fear blocking her throat. Perry also fell silent. The sound of voices approached in the distance, a group of people meandering down the main road.

He pressed his finger to his lips, ordering silence.

Mary looked around. Her feet had become nailed to the ground, her body feeling unusually heavy, like she was sinking in mud.

Taking note of the fear on Mary's face and realising she wouldn't be so easily persuaded to follow him, Perry decided to play his trump card.

'Well, I guess if we're not going to be friends, I won't be able to help you find your sister,' he muttered, once the people in the distance had passed. He watched, waiting for the anticipated reaction. He knew this ploy would work – and, of course, it did. Mary took his bait.

'You told me you didn't know where Lucy was,' she replied. 'You said you hadn't seen her. You told the police you didn't know anything. Were you lying?' Mary's words forced their way past all the emotions tumbling through her heart. 'Do you know where she is?'

Mary watched Perry climbing the fence, his feet now balancing and his arms gripping on to the branches above, like he was some sort of trapeze artist.

'What're you doing?' Mary moved back.

Einstein displayed a bark of contempt, sensing his new owners fear, and Perry's abrupt actions.

'I'll just come and talk to you over that side, then we can see each other better,' he replied, dodging her question. Perry's whole body rested tentatively on top on the fence. This time, Einstein released a deep, angry bark, the noise ricocheting through every tree in the woods. He jumped up, trying to bite.

'If you jump down, I think he'll bite you.' Mary was now telling a lie of her own. She had no idea how Einstein would react in such a situation; she'd only known him for a few hours.

Perry remained perched on top of the fence, balancing with an occasional wobble.

Mary asked her question again, only this time it felt harder to get the words out. 'Do you know where Lucy is?' She wanted to cry. She could feel the emotion brimming beneath the surface. But somehow, she held it in.

Perry tried to smile at Einstein, attempting to win his affections.

'It's nice that your parents got you a dog.' Perry pulled out every trick in his arsenal. He peered into the distance. 'Where *are* your parents? I don't see them anywhere.' Perry had seen Hank and Elsie leave in the car. He'd been spying all morning, of course he'd seen them leaving. And, although he hadn't actually seen Martha getting plastered on the kitchen floor, he was able to hazard a good guess that that's what she'd be doing. He knew Martha almost as well as he knew Mary. Perry knew what Mary ate for breakfast. He knew what time she went to bed, and what time she got up. He knew which cartoon she liked, and which flavour of crisps were her favourite. He knew what type of shampoo she used, and what size clothes she wore. He knew which was her favourite teddy, and he knew all about the box she kept tucked away beneath her bed, Mr Twitch hidden within. Rummaging through bins told him a lot about Mary, as did watching her every move.

Perry acted relaxed, adopting a non-threatening stance by sitting on the fence and dangling his legs, his feet knocking against the wood. He grabbed some leaves off the tree and threw them into the air. He was acting like he was *one of them,* like he was just someone cool to hang about with, like a friend. And he was doing a convincing job. Mary continued to stand back, keeping a comfortable distance between herself and him.

Like a politician under fire, Perry still hadn't answered the question put forward. She asked again. 'Do you know where Lucy is?'

'Is Mum drinking again?' he deflected, steering the conversation in a direction he commanded. For Perry, it was about control and manipulation; his specialist subjects.

Mary shrugged. She didn't want to have to say the truth out loud, and who could blame her? She'd never admitted that her mum was an alcoholic, not to herself or to anyone else. It was embarrassing. Why couldn't her mum have just been a baker, or a nurse, or a doctor, or a dentist, or a florist? Why did *her* mum have to be an alcoholic?

Perry knew the answer to his question, which only served to enrage him. The thought of an alcoholic being able to look after a child didn't seem right to him. In his twisted mind, he believed that *he* would be a much better suitor for the job, which was the most ironic of all notions.

'If I was your friend, you wouldn't have to be on your own so much.'

Perry played the part of a true manipulator to perfection.

'You haven't answered my question,' replied Mary. 'Do you know where Lucy is? Can you help me find her?'

'No, I don't actually know where she is,' said Perry. 'But I can try and help you find her. We can look for her together. How does that sound? If we both start searching, I'm sure we'll find her.' He remained perched on the fence, looking down on Mary, his imposing frame dwarfing her petite stature.

'Lucy had a doll. She took it everywhere, she never let it go, not ever,' Mary announced without warning, a surge of bravery coming to the surface. 'If we find her doll, then we might find Lucy.'

Perry maintained his steely poker face.

'Have you seen a doll anywhere?' pressed Mary. 'It has a blue and red checked dress.'

He shook his head. 'No. I don't think I have.'

Quite the successful manipulator herself at her tender age, Mary caught Perry in a trap of her own.

'You're a liar. I found this in your shed.' Mary took hold of Penelope Pickles and held the doll high in the air.

The girl had courage.

'Do you have Lucy too?' she pressed. 'Tell me. I need to know. I'll run and tell the police if you don't.' She blurted the words in one breath, her tears streaming faster than her words. 'And they'll look in your shed, I know they will.'

Perry felt flustered. Unaware that the doll had been taken, he had been too concerned a few days earlier with checking that the other, more precious contents of his shed hadn't been touched. His demeanour shifted. His smile vanished. The glint in his eyes hinted that of another persona.

He dug his nails into his palms, releasing his frustration. 'I put Lucy's doll in my shed,' he began. His nails pierced the skin. He wanted the doll back. That doll, in his mind, was his. He'd worked hard to get it, so now he wanted it returned. It was one of his prized possessions. He'd risked everything when he took it, and now he wanted it back. 'And I'll explain how I got the doll, but you need to come inside first so that nobody can hear us.'

'Why do we need to go inside?' replied Mary, stuffing the doll up her top.

'People don't like me, Mary, apart from you, and some people want to get me into trouble. If they heard what I need to tell you about your sister's doll, I'm not sure what they'd do. All I want to do is help you find Lucy, and I think I can.'

He felt the odds shift back into his favour. Mary didn't take her eyes off him. Deep down, even though she didn't trust him, she felt desperate to believe that he could help. She wanted to believe that Lucy wasn't in his shed. She wanted to know that she hadn't pushed Lucy into the lake. She wanted to know that her Grandparents weren't to blame. She wanted to understand why he had her sister's doll. She had so many questions running through her mind, yet not a single answer.

Nobody else was willing to help her, and yet Perry Golifer was offering just that. She wanted to be brave enough to follow him into his house. but her mouth refused to agree, her brain overruling her heart.

'I best get going. Mum will be wondering where I am, and my dad will be back soon. He's only nipped to the shops. I'll try and come back soon.'

Mary turned and ran. But she'd be back, the offer presented to her was far too great to ignore. She was desperate, despite deep down knowing that she didn't wholly trust Perry, the risk was worth taking. He was willing to help and that would be enough to encourage her return.

'Bye, Mary,' Perry shouted. His fists ploughed through the air like a boxer psyching himself up for a big fight. His feet kicked the fence, causing the panels to splinter. Anger splashed over his face. He took out the crumpled photo of Mary from his pocket, scrunching it up in his hand. His metamorphosis from human to monster. If only Mary had turned around and witnessed his transformation, she would have seen his true colours and realised that he was never going to help her find Lucy.

Perry went inside and up to his bedroom. He took down a photo that was hanging on some rope above his chest of drawers, the ink still tacky, but dry enough to handle. There was an obvious space on the wall behind his bed, waiting to be filled. The new addition to his collection was a photo of Mary, taken only a few days ago when she was standing in her attic window. She was brushing her hair, still wearing her pyjamas. A rare photo. Even though it had been captured with the aid of a powerful lens, when taken from such a distance the new image of Mary hadn't developed as clearly as he would have liked. But Perry didn't really mind. There would be many more photo opportunities to follow, of that he felt certain. It was only a matter of time.

DURING HER FRANTIC run back home, Mary hoped that her mum would be going berserk back at the house upon her return, expecting to hear her shouting and screaming from the porch. Maybe a display of concern from her mum would encourage Mary to talk. At this very second, in the fragile state that Mary found herself, it really wouldn't have taken much coaxing. But when she emerged from the woods with Einstein, there was nobody there, and nobody was calling for her to come home. Her head dropped.

'I knew she wouldn't be waiting for me.'

Martha hadn't even noticed that Mary had been gone. By the time her daughter had returned, Martha had passed out on her bed.

Mary and Einstein climbed the stairs and went straight up to the attic, and she took to standing in her new favourite spot by the window, looking out across to Perry's. Unbeknown to Mary, Perry was looking straight back at her from his attic window, camera at the ready.

A noise resonated in her ears.

'Einstein. What're you doing?' she asked, turning around upon hearing the strange sound. She walked over to where the dog was lying at the foot of her bed, the sound of his teeth gnawing. Einstein looked up, his beady eyes watching a nuisance fly buzzing around his head. His jaws snapped, trying to bite the bug, before turning his attention back to his bone. Mary picked up the bone that was resting between his paws, saliva making the bone slippery.

Mary looked cross. 'I can't believe Grandma gave you this!' she said, looking at the bone now resting across her palm. 'Did she give it to you this morning when Dad brought you home?'

The stones on the driveway crunched in the distance, the noise failing to register in Mary's distracted ears.

'Dad will be so mad if he finds out you've had a bone.' The bedraggled piece of bone looked small in Mary's hand, and it was delicate, light to the touch.

Downstairs, Hank and Elsie had returned. Whilst Elsie unpacked the shopping bag, Hank looked round for Martha and Mary. He'd expected to see Mary still playing outside with Einstein, but beneath the warmth of the sunshine, the garden remained still. His socks muffled the sound of his footsteps, his stride climbing the stairs in seconds. Bobbing his head into the bedroom, he caught sight of his wife passed out on the bed. He lingered for a moment, watching to make sure her chest was moving, before heading up towards the attic.

He swung open Mary's bedroom door before she'd even heard his approach.

'Oh, there you are. We're home. What have you all been up to?' he asked, lingering in the doorway and catching sight of Mary and Einstein sat on the floor. Mary's face flushed; the bone clenched in the palm of her hand.

'Mum got drunk and fell asleep,' she replied in a matter of fact kind of way, like it wasn't anything unusual. 'And I took Einstein for a walk, just like I told you,' She was quick to reply, hoping he'd be satisfied and walk away. Hank never usually lingered in her bedroom. Had he admitted it to himself, Hank would have said that he hated the fact that all of Lucy's things were still just as she'd left them, and going into the bedroom was too hard, brought back too many memories. But he knew Martha wanted the room remaining just as it was, so it wasn't worth the argument.

'How are you and Einstein getting along?' he asked whilst patting his thigh, signalling for Einstein to approach. 'Come here, boy.' Einstein obeyed, allowing Hank to stroke behind his ears. Forgetting about Penelope Pickles in her pocket, Mary stood, the doll falling to the floor. The sound of the doll dropping made Hank divert his gaze, looking over towards Mary to see what'd fallen. Penelope Pickles lay exposed on the floor, the very doll that Hank had bought his daughter around the time of her second birthday. The very same doll that he'd tucked into Lucy's cot, and then placed in her bed as a toddler each evening as he'd kissed her goodnight. The same doll that he and Martha had had to pry away from Lucy during the night in order to wash and dry, before placing back besides their daughter before she'd awoken in the morning. The very same doll that had been missing since the day that Lucy Catherine Lane had vanished.

'I think I can hear Mum; hadn't you better check on her?' Mary was quick to divert, peering over Hank's shoulder like there was something amiss. Before Hank could set his eyes on Penelope Pickles, he turned his head towards the door, listening for his wife. Mary's foot pressed onto the doll, kicking her beneath the bed.

'I can't hear her?' he questioned. When Hank looked back round towards Mary, the doll had gone. If only the same sixth sense that twins so often share had extended to parents.

Eighteen

WHIMSICAL MUSIC ECHOED ITS WAY INTO FINCHLEY park. The familiar tune caused smiles to spread across every child's face as the ice cream van rolled into its stationary position. An elderly man sporting a white beard opened the side window to find a queue forming. Ripples of soft-scoop ice cream began to be handed out through the open window, parents paying over the odds just for a moment of peace.

'Can we have one, Mum?' asked Mary, watching in envy whilst people licked their lollies and ice creams, the tops of which were decorated with a heavy dusting of sherbet.

'I'm not standing in that bloody queue, we'd be there for hours,' muttered Hank. 'It's going to be hard enough just to find a place to sit.' Ever the grinch, Hank reluctantly rambled his way into the epicentre of the park pandemonium. It was a particularly sticky Saturday afternoon. The sun belted down scorching rays, causing pale faces to redden and ice creams to drip down the side of what were previously crispy cones.

'Why did you have to choose to come here?' said Hank. 'Of all places, Mary. On a hot day like today, it was always going to be packed.' He pushed his way through the crowd, searching for a spot to throw down his picnic blanket. 'Wouldn't a McDonald's have been easier?'

Mary's internal excitement drained. 'You said that if I came out of my bedroom, that we could go anywhere, all three of us.'

'Don't be sorry,' said Martha. 'Your dad needs to learn that, when you have young children, you go to the park on sunny days to eat ice cream. Isn't that right, Mary?'

Having been too scared to leave the grounds of Wisteria since finding Penelope Pickles, Mary thought that the crowded park would be a safe place to venture. She knew there would be lots of people, and she felt the safety in numbers. She also knew that a trip to the park would make her mum happy. Martha always appeared happiest when surrounded by children because it gave her hope that, maybe, just maybe, she'd spot Lucy. It also gave her an excuse to drink a glass of wine early, without it appearing abnormal. In Martha's opinion, wine was permitted on picnics, no matter what time of the day.

'Let's sit here,' suggested Mary, spotting a free patch of grass. 'It's not too far away from the climbing frames.' She took hold of the picnic blanket nestled under her dad's arm, whilst Martha began to unpack goodies from the cool box.

With a pork pie clenched in her hand, Mary's smile fell to the floor.

'What are they?' She watched in dismay as her mum pulled out a pile of posters. The picture of Lucy in the lilac dress on the swing had been blown up to cover a huge portion of the paper. At the top of the poster were the words 'Still Missing'.

Martha remained silent, despite Mary's reaction.

'We've had these printed ready for the anniversary, but I'm going to put some up whilst we're here,' she replied casually. Mary dropped to her knees on the ruffled picnic blanket, the pie falling from her hand.

'I thought this was meant to be fun?' she said, her hands flopping by her side. 'People will stare at us if we put up posters.' People in Finchley always stared at the Lane family, regardless of what they were doing. The family name was notorious, there was no escaping the Chinese whispers that followed their every move.

'Don't you want to find your sister?' snapped Hank, taking hold of some flyers.

'I do, but...'

But not right this second.

Mary's secret thought made her feel guilty. Of course she wanted to find Lucy, more than anything. But she also wanted to play on the slides and eat ice cream. She wanted to have just one day without feeling sad, that's all.

'If you're putting up posters, I'll go and play on the climbing frame. Is that okay?' she asked, watching all the kids having fun in the distance.

'Only if you don't go too far,' said Martha. 'And only for a few minutes. And only if I can see you.' She was beginning to stick Sellotape to the posters ready to attach to trees, fences, bins, lampposts and anything else she could find.

Mary ran over to the play area. For the first time in days, she wasn't looking over her shoulder, making sure that nobody was following her. She forgot about Perry Golifer. She forgot about Penelope Pickles. She forgot about Lucy. For the briefest of moments, she went back to being a carefree child thinking about nothing other than playing in the park. The feeling wouldn't last.

'Mum!' she shouted, from the top of the slide, struggling to see her parents amongst the crowd. 'Are you watching?' Mary looked from up high, a commotion breaking out in the distance, close to where her parents had been sitting.

Her heart fell to the floor. Her moment of excitement over. 'Oh no,' she mumbled.

She watched on in disbelief as her mum stood clutching a young girl wearing a vibrant purple dress, the kind of princess dressing-up costume you can buy in the supermarkets. The sound of high-pitched screams drowned out the ice cream van's music and caused all the children in the play area to look in the same direction.

Oh God. She thinks it's Lucy, doesn't she? From her vantagepoint, Mary knew it wasn't her sister. She wasn't sure how she knew, but she just knew. Her mum was mistaken.

An irate-looking woman wearing flip-flops ran over to Martha.

'Get off her!' she shouted. 'What the hell are you doing?' The woman tried to get Martha to release her daughter. 'This is my daughter, Heidi,' The woman repeated frantically.

'Lucy? Is it really you?' asked Martha hysterically. She dropped to her knees, tears streaming down her face. She scrutinised every inch of Heidi's face. Martha refused to let go, her trembling hands stroking the delicate features of the girl's face and hair.

'Get off my daughter!' shouted the woman again. 'Someone, please help me!' the lady screamed. Martha refused to release her grip.

'She's hurting my daughter!' screamed the lady.

A crowd gathered, the two women becoming more irate. Heidi was crying in the centre of the storm, before finally wriggling free and turning to hug her mum.

'Mummy,' she cried, burying her face in her mother's skirt, and wrapping her arms around her mother's thigh, clinging on with fright. 'I'm scared. Don't let her take me.'

Hank dropped the flyers that he was holding and ran. The posters got caught up in the breeze and tossed through the air, falling into the laps of the people scattered across the park. He took hold of his hysterical wife whilst looking at the girl, who was now crying in her mother's arms.

'Martha. It's not Lucy,' he said. 'She just looks a bit like her, doesn't she?' Hank took a second glance at Heidi, satisfying his own conscience and confirming that his wife was incorrect in her assumption. 'Her brown hair and dress are the same. But it's not her. It's not our Lucy. I promise.'

Martha jostled. 'Let me go!' she cried, struggling to free herself from Hank's restraint, her arms reaching out for Heidi. 'It is her. It's Lucy.' Hank grabbed his wife's arms and shook her.

'Martha, listen to me,' he insisted, looking into her eyes. 'This girl has a birthmark on her arm, see? Lucy didn't have that, did she?' Martha took a moment to reluctantly register her husband's comment before collapsing into his waiting arms. Hank was right, Lucy didn't have a large freckle or birthmark on her arm, but Heidi did. It was a tragic case of mistaken identity.

'I thought it was Lucy. I wanted it to be Lucy,' she cried, staring at Heidi, seeing nothing but her daughter's eyes staring back. 'Where is she? Where's *my* daughter?'

Heidi's mother ushered her daughter to safety and shouted for all to hear. 'You're bloody crazy. You should be locked up!'

Mary watched her mum from the top of the slide, her heart still on the floor.

'I'm glad she's not *my* mum,' said a boy who was standing at the bottom of the slide, Mary's feet plunging into the sand. 'She looks crazy.'

'I'm glad she's not my mum, either,' she replied before walking away, her head dipping to try and hide the embarrassment painted across her face. She didn't want anyone to see her, or know that the crazy lady was *her* mum.

'Leave us alone,' Mary heard her dad shout at the people gawking. 'There's nothing to see.'

Mary looked over at the deserted ice cream van in the distance, the old man losing all of his customers in the commotion. Knowing that she would be missing lunch, Mary could almost taste the raspberry sauce as she decided to walk over. With the only thought of ice cream in her mind, she let down her barriers and wandered off, and for one fateful moment, forgetting all about her fear of being watched.

ONLY METRES AWAY from Mary, Perry spied on her from behind a clump of trees that nestled in the play area. With practiced precision, he had successfullycamouflaged himself into the background. Nobody spotted his lurking shadow; an invisible predator. A crowded place didn't deter a human being like Perry Golifer, it actually had the opposite effect. Perry was drawn to the excitement, the risk that came hand in hand with a public place. The opportunity to speak to Mary in full view drove his wicked desires. A man like Perry Golifer didn't follow any kind of rule book; he was an anomaly in society; a misfit. Genetically, people like Perry Golifer had been programmed wrong. Somewhere along the way, something in his genetic makeup had become corrupt. His parents had been upstanding citizens, so they weren't to blame. His childhood was what most would have classed as 'normal', and he hadn't been exposed to anything other than the norm. But his dark side had always been there, right from conception. His twisted desires were just waiting to be fulfilled. Perry Golifer was a monster to the very core.

That morning, Perry had been watching Wisteria from the attic at Ivy Dean, and subsequently followed their car all the way to the park. Whilst watching Mary as she left the slide, he knew full well that she was debating what to do: go back over to her parents, or run and grab an ice cream. He could read her mind, or so he thought.

'Be patient,' he mumbled. His hands were shaking. His eyes were glued to Mary, watching her hair dance in the wind, her slight frame feeling the breeze. 'Bingo,' he whispered, watching Mary moving away from the crowd, turning her back on her parents.

'Keep walking,' he mouthed. He traced Mary's steps, and he himself walked towards the van, his heart pumping. He was soon within touching distance. Mary stopped, rummaging in her pocket and pulling out the handful of coins that her grandma had given her.

'Come on,' he mumbled in frustration, urging Mary to walk faster, his fingers dancing in his pockets, unable to stop fidgeting. 'Keep going.'

Satisfied she had enough money, Mary carried on walking. She kept looking back every now and then to see if the commotion had died down, the sea of people dividing her and her parents getting bigger, not smaller. She neared the van, losing sight of her mum altogether.

'Hello, Mary,' said Perry, taking his hands out of his pockets and tapping her on the shoulder. 'I'm so glad I've bumped into you again. I was just coming to get an ice cream myself.' The sound of Perry's voice made Mary feel faint, like she'd been injected with a high-octane dose of fear. The touch of his hand on her shoulder made her entire body tense, as if it had been electrocuted.

'Can I buy you one? There's a better place to buy ice cream if we walk just outside the park,' said Perry. He took hold of Mary's hand and the moment his sweaty skin touched hers, his internal excitement heightened. He began ushering her away from the van and towards the park exit before she'd had time to consent. Mary's legs felt heavy the further away she walked. All she felt able to do was follow his lead, the warmth from his skin penetrating hers. Her deepest fears were coming true, and the nightmare she'd lived for the past few days was now reality. Perry had been watching her, she was right in her suspicions. She was the next child on his list to be taken. She was surrounded by people, and yet nobody was running to her aid, nobody was yelling for him to let her go.

The pair wandered away from the crowds. The sight of Perry's dirty nails and yellow, stained skin made Mary's skin crawl. She looked around, spotting only a few people dotted on the periphery of the park. They continued to walk hand-in-hand, easily mistaken for father and daughter.

'I should get back to my mum, she doesn't know where I am,' Mary insisted. His grip suddenly tightened. 'You're hurting my hand.'

Perry bent down, inspecting her hand front and back. 'I'm sorry. I didn't realise.' His restraint loosened, but he didn't let go entirely. 'I want us to be friends, Mary. You said you'd come back to my house so that we could talk about how to find Lucy. And then, all three of us can be friends.' Dangling his golden bait again, he tried his best to persuade.

Mary remained silent.

'Can we be friends?' asked Perry.

'I should get going. My mum will start to worry.'

'Okay. But before you go, just tell me one thing. Have you told anyone?' Perry dipped his cap, keeping his head down, avoiding eye contact with any straggling passers-by.

Perry held his heart in his hands, eager to hear the answer to his question. 'I mean, did you tell your mum and dad that you've been talking to me? Or that you found Lucy's doll in my shed?'

Mary ignored the questions, her chest tightening beneath the strain of a scream so loud that, had her brain allowed it to be released, the entire park would be shocked into silence. He stroked Mary's hand, causing her body to flinch.

'You can tell me, I promise not to be cross,' he said. 'I just need to know if you kept our secret, then I'll know if I can trust you – I mean, with finding Lucy.'

Mary's face was frozen with fear. Her mind was muddled and she wanted to scream, but her scream wouldn't surface; it had been paralysed by the plume of terror soaring through her body.

She stood still, unable to move. Perry's impatience could be noted in his constant foot tapping, though Mary was unaware of it. He did his best to maintain his blasé façade, his underlying urge barely kept at bay. He wanted to grab her, of course he did, but he refrained. It wasn't the time. It wasn't the place. Not yet.

'I didn't tell anyone. I promise,' she finally replied, looking into Perry's bloodshot eyes for the first time, his pupils widening, inhaling her aroma. 'I did what you said. I haven't told anyone.'

He breathed a silent sigh of relief. He suspected the police would have been knocking down his door had she told them, but he needed the confirmation, he needed to know that he was still in control.

'Well, that is good to know,' he said, his warm breath dancing around Mary's ear as he leant in, her body remaining still. His lips touched her skin as he whispered. 'Does that mean we're friends and that we can find Lucy together?' Mary looked into his eyes, wiping away the tear that had managed to escape and was now trickling down her cheek. Her insides tumbled with panic and hesitation, all of which were sensed by Perry. He smiled and casually shrugged his shoulders, indicating that it was her choice and that he didn't really care either way. He turned, pretending that he was going to walk away, his mind urging Mary to speak, and his twisted motivations succeeded. Mary summoned all her courage and blurted out a question in an attempt to squash her remaining doubts.

'How can you help me find my sister?'

'Well, I think I know who took her,' he was quick to reply, dangling the mighty carrot. Mary's hopes shot beyond the spheres of the sky.

'Really?' He had her captivated, and he knew it.

'I've wanted to help find Lucy all this time, but nobody would listen to me,' said Perry. He lowered his head, his eyes scanning the ground, his heart all a-flutter, waiting for his carrot to be caught.

'Who do you think took her? Tell me,' Mary urged, standing with her hands by her side, remaining on guard. Perry looked up; a well-practised, polished grin plastered across his face.

'I'm not exactly sure of his name, but we can find him together,' he said. 'I know he still lives in Finchley, I see him at odd times out and about. I spotted him the very day that Lucy went missing. I was cleaning my windows in the attic and I saw this man walking up your grandparents' path. When I went out a bit later, I saw Lucy's doll lying on the floor outside my house. I knew it was Lucy's because I'd seen her with it before. She must've dropped it when the man I saw took her away.'

Perry thought back to that July morning in 1982, the day he'd planned on abducting both twins. Unbeknownst to her, Mary had scuppered his plans by separating herself from Lucy. After he'd been in the house searching for the girls, he then spotted Mary down by the lake and scurried over to where she was playing with the doll she had taken from her sister's hands. Just as he lifted Mary off the floor, Henry's shouting echoed down from the house, causing Perry to scramble into the woods, taking the doll with him but having to leave Mary on the jetty. His plot to take both girls had failed.

'I told the police that I had seen him near the house that morning,' he continued, 'but they let him go.' Perry's speech quickened, his enthusiasm clutching the golden opportunity with both hands. He looked round, making sure their encounter still hadn't been noticed. 'Mary, I saw this man with my own eyes. He was the only person to walk up the path to your grandparents' house that morning. I saw your grandma leaving, and then coming back with milk about an hour later. And the man I saw was the only person who went up to Wisteria in between. Nobody else could have gone anywhere near Lucy. That man took her, just like that.' Perry clicked his fingers in the air. 'And the screams I heard were probably from your grandad as he tried to stop the man from taking her. But he doesn't remember, does he?' Perry knew all about Henry's condition; it was amazing what you could uncover about a person from rooting through their bins.

Excitement rushed through Mary's veins the more lies he sadistically spun. A spark of hope igniting in her insides.

'Why didn't you give my sisters doll to the police, or tell my parents?' she asked.

'Your sister's doll is the only bit of evidence I have to prove that Lucy was taken. Your parents wouldn't have believed me.'

Perry went in for the kill.

'If you'll be my friend, we will find Lucy together, I know we will. With your help, I know we'll be able to bring her home. What do you think?'

Despite her fears, it was hard for Mary not to get her hopes up, and her mind tried to process all her thoughts.

Is he telling the truth? How else would he have her doll? How would he know Grandma went to get milk?

Mary thought about pretending to be his friend, just until they found Lucy. In the same moment, she pushed away her nerves and fears.

'If you help me find my sister, I'll be your friend.'

He smirked with satisfaction as Mary fell into his trap. She remained by his side, already thinking about the first thing she was going to tell Lucy when they found her, her bottom lip quivering with excitement.

When I see Lucy, I'm going to tell her that I love her. Then I'll give her Penelope Pickles.

'But you must promise not to tell anyone that we're friends,' said Perry, 'at least not until we've found Lucy. We wouldn't want to spoil our chances of bringing her home, would we?'

Still wound up in her fictitious vision of the future, Mary instantly replied. 'I promise.'

Perry kissed the back of her hand.

'How will we meet in secret?' continued Mary.

'Leave that to me, Mary,' said Perry. 'I'll come and get you, all you have to do is wait. Then we can start looking for Lucy.' Mary nodded in agreement.

'MARY! MARY!' Martha's hysterical screams silenced every conversation occurring in the entire park. Fear and panic flooded through Perry, and Mary witnessed his flushed face, his skin matching the colour of his blood-stained eyes. Mary glanced over to the far side of the park, and Perry released her hand.

'I'll come for you soon, Mary.'

Before she could reply, he moved swiftly and soon disappeared from sight, leaving her standing alone. The only evidence of his presence was the sweat that lingered on Mary's palm.

'MARY, WHERE ARE YOU?' she heard her mum shout once again. Mary ran towards the space where a crowd had congregated, weaving her way through the internal maze of bodies.

'I'm here, Mum,' she replied like nothing was wrong.

Martha's face turned puce. 'Where've you been?' she shouted, lifting Mary up and squeezing her body before putting her back down. 'What have I told you about wandering off? I couldn't see you. I didn't know where you were.'

Mary shifted the blame. 'I waved from the top of the slide. I shouted that I was going to get an ice cream. You mustn't have heard me,' she defended. 'I thought you said it was okay.'

'I didn't hear you, Mary. I didn't know where you'd gone. I thought someone had taken you,' cried Martha, shaking her daughter so much that her feet became unbalanced. The adrenaline soaring through Martha's body made her shake harder.

Hank put his arm around his wife. 'Let's just calm down,' he said. 'Mary knows she shouldn't have gone to get an ice cream on her own. But no one's hurt, and no harm was done.' Martha fell to her knees, her body swaying as she sobbed.

'I can't take it anymore,' she cried. 'Really, I can't take it.' Martha lay on the picnic blanket, tucking herself into the foetal position. 'I need a drink,' she repeated, lying motionless. 'Get me a bloody drink.'

'We need to get her home,' said Hank, packing up the bag. 'Grab hold of these whilst I carry your mum.' Hank scooped Martha off the floor and into his arms, her head resting against his shoulder. He carried her through the crowd of shameful onlookers. Mary looked at each face, holding on to the bottom of her dad's T-shirt, trying to hide.

'I think it's best we take her straight home, Mary,' he said. 'Sorry about the picnic. Another time, okay? We'll try again another day.'

When they reached their car, he placed Martha on the back seat, her eyes closed, the tears continuing to pour. Her body was craving alcohol and was now displaying classic withdrawal symptoms.

Mary didn't reply. Instead, she got in the back of the car and rested her mum's head on her lap, wiping away her own relentless stream of tears trickling down her pale cheek.

'This is all my fault, isn't it?'

'What's all your fault?' Hank asked, driving out onto the main road.

'I didn't want to be seen with you and Mum, so I did go off to the ice cream van without telling you,' she confessed, watching Perry disappearing in the distance. 'I lied when I said that I'd shouted that I was going to the ice cream van. I didn't ask. I just walked off.'

'Not to worry, Mary. Your mum was already upset, it wasn't

just because of what you did,' her dad explained. 'Mum was looking for Lucy and thought she'd seen her, but she was wrong.'

'I saw what happened,' she said, the car pulling away. Mary's eyes caught sight of Perry, the outline of his body becoming visible from behind a row of parked cars. He met Mary's gaze with a finger pressed to his lips. Mary acknowledged this silent demand with the slightest of smiles. In her next blink, he'd vanished.

Nineteen

MARTHA LANE COULDN'T SLEEP. HER PLAGUED MIND was tormented by images of Heidi, the girl from the park. Every time she dared to close her eyes, all she saw was the terrified expression on Heidi's face. The sounds made by Heidi's frantic mum were also still screeching through her ears, causing the beast of all headaches.

Her brain throbbed, banging incessantly against her skull, begging for release. She tossed one way, taking an age to find a comfortable position, before swinging her body over and trying to fall asleep on her other side. But the tormenting images followed. Her skin became clammy, as if she was coming down with a fever. Not long after midnight, she gave up on the hope of sleep and instead snuck out of bed. There was only one thing that could cure her insomnia. Hank failed to rouse, his scrunched-up, restless limbs taking advantage of the extra bed space.

Barefoot, and covered only by a long, lace night dress, Martha ventured outside, her white nightie whipping round her feet. The emergency bottle of vodka she'd stashed in a garden bucket a few days prior was nicely chilled by the time she pulled it out of the bushes. Under the light of the moon, she impatiently slumped herself on the lawn, tossing the bottle top aside before drinking enough to temporarily drown her sorrows. Once sufficiently immersed, and when the images of Heidi had been washed away, her body sunk into a deep state of oblivion. Her face remained flushed, and her skin became saturated by sweat, beads of moisture scattering her pale skin like goose bumps. The night-time critters didn't dare disturb the unusual visitor, Martha's blood not quite the delicacy the mosquitoes desired.

By morning, Martha's pores leaked liquor. She lay flat on the grass, having passed out with the empty bottle still clenched in her hand. Her limbs had barely moved all night, static in their original position. Luckily, Hank had been the first to wake. He spotted his wife's disturbing state from the lounge window once he drew the curtains back, naively assuming she had just gone downstairs to make a coffee. Quicker than a bolt of lightning, he dashed outside.

'Oh, God. Martha, wake up.' Scared to touch his wife's body, fearful she wouldn't move, Hank watched for her chest to give away any signs that she might be breathing. 'Oh, thank goodness.'

Martha was alive. At least, on this occasion she was.

He grabbed his wife's hand and, with his other, moved away the hair that was stuck to her cheek. Upon waking, Martha's blurred vision and slurred speech prompted Hank to break his wife's promise, and he made the call.

OVER THE PAST few summers, Martha had been a frequent visitor to Herons Hook, a rehabilitation facility located on the outskirts of Finchley. Vowing on her previous visit never to touch another drop, Martha had made Hank promise that, if she was ever to get in such a shocking state again, to just lock her in a room at home and, in her words, 'let me suffer in silence, or die'.

Martha did better on the wagon when back home in Whitney, where there wasn't the constant reminder of the place where she had lost Lucy. She did suffer bad days at home, like anyone else, but there weren't so many triggers that she had to sidestep just to stay sober. And then summer time would come around, and she became vulnerable all over again.

Over the years, Wisteria had become Martha's nemesis, the beast that she had to battle on an annual basis. Thus far, she'd lost the war. Hank wasn't an alcoholic, at least not yet. He was just a frequent, angry drunk, not that that was any better. But he did still have the ability to *choose* to have a drink – and, more often than not, he joined his wife in drowning their sorrows. If only they knew that an ocean's worth of alcohol couldn't drown their sorrows; nothing could.

'It's for the best,' he insisted, hauling Martha's broken body to the car.

She struggled and swore every step. 'I won't fucking go back there,' she spat, her weak body failing to make railroads against her husband's strength. 'I'd rather die.' Hank slammed the car door once Martha was trapped inside, locking it for good measure. Martha's shattered body flaked out on the back seat.

Martha loathed rehab more than she loathed the prospect of an empty bottle. She hated the decrepit building. She hated the other patients, all of whom, in her eyes, looked far more like an addict than her. She hated the way rehab made her *feel* like an alcoholic. She hated the smell of the facility; the stench of disinfectant numbing all other senses. She hated the staff, mainly because they refused to give in to her demands. She refused to eat the food. And she refused to partake in group sessions.

However, while an inpatient at Herons Hook, Martha was no longer able to pretend that she just liked the occasional glass or two, or three. In rehab, everybody had an addiction, whether they admitted it or not. There were hookers on heroin in one room and crack addicts climbing the walls in another. And, in the rest of the rooms, alcoholics could be seen scratching out their eyeballs, just as a means of distraction from the constant cravings eating away at their insides. Anything to prevent them from searching for just one more sip.

Herons Hook was no holiday.

THE CAR ROLLED down the hill towards the rehab building and Mary watched as the towering cast iron gates came into view. She hadn't wanted to go along for the ride, but her dad had insisted.

Mary had already decided that, when she was eighteen, she would insist on leaving home, and her parents would be powerless to stop her. She just had to make it through another eight years, or 2,920 days.

'It looks like a prison,' she said, holding her mum's limp hand in hers. Martha's skin felt cold to the touch despite the muggy heat of the day, threatening rain.

Hank tried to force a reassuring look onto his face. He wasn't a magician, so it didn't materialise.

'It's just an old building, Mary,' he said in an upbeat voice. The towering gates closed once the car entered, the metal clanging and locking into place. 'Mum is best off here. We know that, when things get too much, she's better off being surrounded by professionals. You know, experts that can help her get better.'

The intimidating Victorian building of Herons Hook Rehabilitation Facility was spread across two floors. The abandoned third floor was only frequented by the troubled spirits of previous patients, who roamed the halls unable to find an escape. The facility hadn't altered in decades and still retained the array of original windows, each decorated by an intricate, grey leaded design. Rickety chimneypots scattered the roof slates in a hotchpotch fashion, the disused fireplaces that once roared within the rooms below having not been lit in years. A dark, dense wall of woodlands served to keep the building encapsulated, shielding it from sight until you broke through the trees and entered the private grounds. To Finchley locals, Herons Hook had always been an unmentioned taboo; a place that attracted the wrong kind of people to the quaint, conservative area.

When Mary caught sight of the gates, a lump formed in her throat. The main entrance came into sight.

'Dad, why can't Mum just come home and rest at Grandma's?' she begged. 'I promise I'll play quietly. I promise not to wander off again.' As she spoke, two men wearing white uniforms approached the car and opened the passenger door once the car became stationary. Mary looked on in horror, recollections of her mum's previous visit rising to the surface.

'It feels like they're taking her,' she said. Mary began to cry.

Unwilling to release her mum's hand, the men in uniform assisted Martha out of the car and into an awaiting wheelchair, her head being guided back so that it rested on the padding. One of the members of staff bent down to speak to her.

'Hello again, Martha. Come on, let's get you inside, love,' he said, releasing Mary's hand from her mum's. 'I'll take her now, Mary, and thank you for looking after her during the journey here,' he continued. Martha's eyes opened, but her mouth remained closed. She uttered no words and made no reaction whilst she was being escorted into the facility.

'She'll be alright, Mary, I promise,' said Hank, putting his arm around his daughter, pulling her closer. 'Come on, let's go and make sure she gets settled.'

A vile smell walloped Mary in the face as soon as she entered through the main double doors, the stench even worse than what she recalled from her visit the previous summer. The corridor remained silent and deserted of all traces of life. Mary glanced around the empty, sterile shell. Shadows created by the snippets of sun breaking through the windows climbed her legs. She couldn't move, her limbs unwilling to escort her body any further into the hovel. Hank pulled harder on her hand, urging her feet to move.

'It'll be alright,' he said, continuing to tug, almost dragging her to the visitors' waiting area. 'Don't be scared.' They sat down and he rested his hand on Mary's lap, offering reassurance.

Mary's eyes scrutinised every inch of the room, waiting for her mum to be admitted, assessed and then settled into a bed. That was the procedure that was always followed at rehab. Mary was a seasoned pro; she knew what to expect, and when to expect it.

'But what are they doing to her now, Dad?' she asked, hearing her mum's cries, the screeches travelling down the hallway. It sounded like Martha was undergoing brain surgery, forgoing the aid of anaesthetic. Hank closed the waiting room door, shutting out the sound of his wife's screams.

'They're just getting her comfortable, and giving her some medicine,' he replied, kissing the back of Mary's hand. 'Have you not got any toys you can play with?' he asked, catching sight of her rucksack. The only things she'd brought was Einstein's bone and Penelope Pickles. Her two, little secrets.

Toys? I'm not a baby.

'I'm only three years off being a teenager, Dad. I don't need toys anymore.'

The waiting room door flung open. 'She's ready to see you now, Mr Lane,' announced the nurse. 'Do you want to follow me?'

Mary picked up her bag before following the nurse, holding her dad's hand as they navigated the corridor.

The nurse turned to look at Mary whilst walking with a brisk stride, her leather shoes squeaking on the wooden flooring.

'Now remember,' she said, 'Mum probably won't know that you're here. We just need to give her some time, okay?' The nurse paused outside a door located at the far end of the corridor. 'Just like last time, Mum will be tired and very sleepy,' she continued, 'but it's nothing to worry about. We're going to take good care of her.'

'You okay?' asked Hank, casting a watchful glance down to his daughter.

'I hate it when Mum doesn't talk, it feels like she isn't really here,' she replied, catching sight of Martha through a gap in the door. Her mum was lying motionless in bed. 'It's like she's dead. It scares me.' Mary cowered behind her dad.

'She'll be alright, Mary. Mum just needs to rest, that's all. I promise,' he reassured, taking hold of her hand and guiding her into the segregated room. He was lying, though, wasn't he? Martha didn't just need rest; she needed to be weaned off alcohol, a process that would be painful and disturbing – for everyone, not just her. There was no way to sugar-coat the truth, so Hank just lied instead. He found it easier that way.

Mary took a seat next to her mum's bed. Hank sat by the other side.

The isolation room walls were covered with a dull, grey

paint that was peeling in exactly the same places as the last time that Martha had been admitted into Herons Hook. Mary had memorised the room's décor, having spent so long at her mum's bedside the previous year. The same picture of a faded apple tree hung from the wall, and the bars covering the windows were still rusting. When she had asked previously, one of the nurses assured Mary that the bars were to keep people out, not to keep patients in. Mary hadn't believed her, and rightly so.

The once black and white laminated floor now appeared more of an off-grey colour, having been trampled over for the past twenty-something years without ever being replaced. The sink in the corner of the room still leaked, the constant drip of water irritating Mary the moment she heard the noise. The visitor's chair was also the same one Mary recalled, neither the peeling fabric nor wonky feet having been repaired.

I hate it here. It feels like a prison.

Mary was right. The place needed closing down, or an inspection at the very least to improve standards. However, being at an affordable price and within a short car journey of Wisteria, it was the best option for Martha in her current state. Like it or not, Martha was there to say.

Mary attempted to look out of the window, trying to shake off the feeling of being trapped, imprisoned.

Martha lay huddled beneath a pile of off-white bed sheets, her curly hair looking even more flyaway, her head drooped to one side, facing the window. The drip going into her arm fell at a steady pace, and the lingering nurse in top-to-toe white uniform felt her forehead.

'What's that?' asked Mary, watching the liquid seep into her mum's fragile wrist, the veins repeatedly punctured. Martha's arm looked like an overused pin cushion, dotted with holes where needles had been callously inserted.

'That's your mum's medicine, to help her feel better,' replied the nurse, ensuring Martha was tucked in properly. 'If you need me, you know where I am,' she concluded, closing the door and leaving the room.

Hank leant down and kissed Martha on the forehead. 'We're here, love,' he whispered, both he and Mary pulling their chairs closer now that the nurse wasn't in the way. Martha was no longer crying, but her vacant eyes were wide open, staring into the distance. Mary watched and waited for her mum to blink, but it never seemed to come.

'Dad, why aren't mum's eyes moving?' she asked after a few seconds. 'Does she know we're here?'

'Mum knows everything,' replied Hank. 'Even when you say you've brushed your teeth, but really you haven't, she knows. When you tell her that you have stomach ache, but really you don't want to go to school because you have a spelling test, she knows.' He attempted to lighten the mood with a little humour. The banter failed to impress, and Mary began to cry.

'The park wasn't a good idea, was it?' she said. 'This is all my fault, again.'

'The park was a great idea, Mary. We can still have some snacks right here if you like?' Hank suggested, looking round the room. 'The nibbles are still in the boot from yesterday.'

Mary scrunched her nose at the idea. The thought of sweaty cubes of cheese, stinking egg and cress sandwiches, and her grandma's warmed chicken liver pate made her want to vomit.

Hank took hold of her hand across the bed. 'Your mum misses Lucy, that's all, Mary. And sometimes she needs a break from all the sadness she feels. Mum just needs time to be able to sleep without worrying,' he said, taking hold of Mary's hand.

'I miss Lucy, too,' she said. 'And I want to find her and bring her home. Then Mum will be happy and she'll never have to come back here.'

Mary pulled her hand away. No matter how upset you felt, when you were ten it just wasn't okay to hold hands with your dad. It also annoyed her how he went from being nice one moment, to angry the next. She looked down at her arms and at the bruises that he'd created, and never wanted to hold his hand again. Mary never knew which way her dad's mood was going to go, making her constantly want to run away from him.

'How about I go and get the picnic?' he suggested, standing up. 'Then we can have snacks with Mum, just like you wanted.' Hank walked towards the door. 'I just need to have a quick talk with the nurses first, so keep Mum company for a few minutes, okay?' Hank waited for Mary to nod before he closed the door.

She pulled her chair even closer to the bed, resting her hand on her mum's pillow. Martha continued to stare out through the window, her body remaining motionless. Her mind had been forced into a silent state of slumber, enabling her body time to come to grips with the reality of what it felt like not to be induced with a daily abundance of wine, and vodka, and gin, and cider – or, if she was desperate, any cheap stuff the off-licence was selling for a pound per can.

'Hi, Mum,' Mary whispered, lowering her head so that her eyes were at the same level. 'Can you hear me?' Martha remained still, her eyes fixed. Mary stroked her mum's hair, the soft curls falling on to the pillow as she remained in a comatose state. 'Please say something, anything.'

Mary looked deep into her mum's eyes, their noses touching on the pillow, but Martha's subdued mind refused to cooperate. 'I'm scared, Mum. Please wake up.' Mary kissed her mum's lips, hoping that, like in the fairy tale story, a kiss would inject new life, waking up Sleeping Beauty. But Martha's cold lips didn't flinch. Her escaping breath was so shallow that Mary struggled to feel its warmth against her skin.

'What can I say that would make you wake up?' Mary thought of things that she knew ordinarily would provoke some response. 'If I swear, you can wake up and tell me off,' she suggested, looking round to ensure nobody was watching. 'Bastard.' The anticipated reaction failed to materialise. 'If you don't wake up, I'll go and get my hair cut, and you'll hate that.' Martha didn't react.

'I know what'll make you wake up,' Mary exclaimed, excited about the idea that'd popped into her head. Mary leant down to pick up her bag, opening the zip and plunging her hand in.

'I've brought someone to show you, Mum,' she said, pulling out Penelope Pickles and placing the doll right in front of Martha's line of vision. 'Look who I've found!' she said, making the doll dance on the bed, just like Lucy used to do *all the time,* much to everyone's annoyance. 'It's Penelope Pickles. Lucy's favourite doll,' she continued, hoping that the sight of the doll would act as a form of resuscitation. Mary lay Penelope Pickles on her mum's pillow. However, Martha didn't react, her shallow breathing barely audible, her lungs sucking in minimal amounts of oxygen. Mary tried something else.

'I have a secret,' she began, whispering into her mum's ear. 'I should've told you a few days ago, but I made a promise.' Mary stroked her mum's cheek as if she was a baby. 'But if it means you'll wake up, I'll tell you now.' Mary took a deep breath. 'I found Penelope Pickles in Perry Golifer's shed.' She waited, praying for a reaction, any sign of life to emerge. Martha remained in her cocoon. 'And that's not all. He said he knows who took Lucy,' Mary added, trying her best to break through her mum's steely exterior. Martha's unconscious state remained unbroken.

'Perry said that he saw someone, Mum, the day that Lucy went missing. A man. He thinks it was the man who took Lucy,' she said in one quick breath. 'Perry found Penelope Pickles lying on the floor in front of his house. Lucy must've dropped her, Mum, when she was taken away.' Mary waited for her mum to wake, jump out of bed and hug Mary for finding out such crucial information. But Martha didn't flinch, her eyes continued to stare out the window. If only she were able to hear. Her woes at Wisteria could all be over, just like that.

'If I promise to be his friend, he'll help me find the man, he'll help me find Lucy,' Mary explained. 'So, I'll do it, Mum. I'm going to pretend to be his friend. I'm scared, but it's okay. I'm ten now. I'm a big girl.' Her words failed to be heard.

'Isn't that brilliant news, Mum? When I bring Lucy home, you'll never be sad again, and we won't have to come back here.'

Mary tried to convince herself that the plan would work,

pushing away her underlying doubts and fears about Perry. 'He said not to tell you that we're looking for Lucy, at least not until we bring her home.'

Martha remained motionless; a mute.

Resigned to the reality that her mum wasn't going to wake, Mary followed her dad's instructions and continued to talk, keeping her mum company as best as she could.

'And, when Lucy does come home, we'll all be happy again, and maybe you'll let me wear some new clothes,' she said, looking down at her dowdy trousers. 'And I'd like to go out and play with my friends, too. I'm never allowed out anymore. I get bored on my own at home all the time.' She wiped her face with her sleeve and marvelled at the way her mum's eyes still didn't move. Mary took hold of Penelope Pickles and placed the doll back in her bag.

'I'll try my best to find Lucy, Mum, just for you. I promise I will,' she said, taking hold of Einstein's bone, pulling it out of her bag. Outside, Hank trundled through the main entrance with his arms full of picnic paraphernalia. He walked down the corridor towards his wife's room, the smell of rotten boiled egg following. Mary continued to talk to Martha, now about anything she could think of, anything to fill the silence.

'I have another secret, Mum,' said Mary. 'Grandma is giving Einstein bones, even though Dad told her not to. Look, I found this one in my bedroom.' She held the bone in her hand, placing it in front of Martha's face so that her mum could see it up close. 'I'm going to keep this a secret from Dad, otherwise he might take Einstein away, and he's my only friend.' Hank kicked the door open with his foot. The sudden loud intrusion into Mary's secret conversation with her mum caused her to jump. Startled, she fumbled with the bone in a desperate attempt to hide it before her dad saw. The bone fell to the floor.

'Mary?' said Hank, walking into the room, his vision blocked by the picnic boxes. Mary bent down, grabbing the bone and placing it back in her bag.

Hank approached the bed. 'Oh, you're there.'

'I was just showing Mum some of my things,' she replied, zipping up her bag. 'But she wasn't interested.'

'It's not that she isn't interested, Mary,' said Hank. 'Your mum is just asleep. Even though it looks like she's awake, her brain isn't. Does that make sense?' he asked, placing the picnic on the end of the bed. 'Now, you must be hungry, so let's have something to eat while Mum sleeps.' Mary had been hungry for days, but she hadn't wanted to get out of bed. Her stomach had become concave, her ribs threatening to poke through her skin.

'I need to go for a wee first,' she announced, getting up and glancing out of the glass pane of the door towards the long, main corridor. The passageway was eerily quiet.

'Will you be okay on your own, or shall I come with you?' said Hank.

'I'm ten. I can go by myself.' Mary shut the door and took a few steps down the corridor. She didn't feel alone, despite the empty hallway, and she kept glancing around, expecting someone to appear behind her. A gust of fresh air rushed in.

'Get hold of him!' she heard a man shout. The front doors of Herons Hook swung open and a flurry of people barged through.

'Let me go!' another man's voice shouted above the chaos. Mary watched the patient in question being escorted into the building, aggression seeping from his rigid body, a team of nurses struggling to restrain him.

'I'll bite your fuckin' hand off!' yelled the man, his body continuing to jostle. Mary cowered behind the deserted reception desk, conscious to remain out of sight. Three uniformed nurses grappled with the man, whose jaw continued to snap, his teeth attempting to bite, a good imitation of a crocodile.

'If you bite us, you'll go straight in the pit and miss evening meal,' one of the male nurses shouted. 'Do you understand?'

Still crouched on the floor, Mary moved around the side of the desk, watching the man flapping around like a fish on the end of a hook.

'Fuck the pit! Fuck evening meal. And fuck you, you bastards!'

the patient yelled while continuing to thrash his head.

The staff dragged the man around the corner, and Mary followed. She didn't want to, but she felt she needed to see what was happening. Her mum was staying here, so she needed to know what really went on, how they really helped people get better.

The room the nurses dragged the patient into was comprised only of a dental surgery-type chair, along with two surgical trays at either side, both laden with metal instruments. Mary pressed herself against the closed doors, standing on her tip-toes and arching her neck so that she could just see through the small, round panes of glass. The warmth of her breath formed a mist on the glass which momentarily obscured her view, but she remained glued to the window.

'It doesn't have to be so hard, Norman, just let us help you,' insisted a nurse, while others strapped down the patient's arms, tightening the restraints.

'You can't do this to me,' screamed the man. 'I don't want your fucking help. I don't want your poisons. Let me go!'

Mary watched on, the man's face turning purple as he struggled to free himself from the chair, the veins in his head bulging like blisters.

'This will just feel like a pinch, Norman, you know that,' said the nurse. 'We're not here to hurt you, remember? We're here to help.' Norman wasn't so convinced, and neither was Mary.

'That's poison! You're trying to kill me, aren't you, you bastards?!' he shouted, his eyes widening at the sight of the nurse holding a large needle, liquid slowing filling the tube.

'Get off me!' Norman continued to protest. His body lurched in the chair and Mary moved back from the door in anticipation of him breaking free and coming charging out of the room like a cannon. A scream louder than an exploding firework bellowed from inside the room as the nurse inserted the needle, the medication slowly entering the patient's bloodstream.

What are they doing to him?

Although she didn't want to watch, Mary couldn't make her

body move.

'Norman, you're making it more painful. Please, just keep still,' insisted the nurse, but the scream only intensified. Mary ducked to the floor, covering her ears with her hands and closing her eyes whilst praying for the torture to end, tears streaming down her cheeks.

Please, let it stop.

Silence finally fell throughout the corridor. After a few seconds, Mary stood up and peered back through the pane of glass, watching the needle being pulled out of Norman's neck. His body was finally still. Watching the nurses turning to leave the room in unison, Mary ran the length of the corridor, back to her dad.

'What's happened?' he asked upon seeing the wet patch on her crotch.

She looked down in embarrassment. 'I didn't make it in time. Sorry,' she replied, feeling the warm flood of pee dribbling down her leg.

'You're not a bloody baby, Mary. What's the matter with you?' barked Hank. No more Mr Nice Guy, he was back to being an angry father. He scraped his chair across the floor and stood. The anger on his face was enough to make Mary cower, pacing backwards until she felt the wall against her back.

'Sorry, I won't do it again,' Mary cried at the anticipation of another of her dad's lashes.

'Too bloody right you won't do it again,' he replied, grabbing her cheeks and pressing, directing the flow of tears as he squashed her face. 'You're an embarrassment. And I will *not* be humiliated like this. What if someone sees you? They'll think I haven't taught you right from wrong. They'll think I'm not a fit parent.' He released Mary's face and let her body fall to the floor. 'You can stink all day now. That'll teach you.' Mary pulled in her knees for comfort, wrapping her arms round her legs and burying her face.

I know I'm not a baby. I was just scared.

Hank walked back over to the bed and took up his position next to Martha. 'Get up, Mary, before the nurses come in.' Mary ignored his demand.

'I said, get off the bloody floor, now!'

Mary skulked over to the bed, standing behind Hank.

'Can we take Mum home? She's had enough rest, hasn't she?' she asked, turning around to look through to the corridor, watching the same nurses she'd just seen now approaching her mum's room.

'Sit down,' Hank replied, pulling up another chair next to his.

Mary remained standing. *I don't want to sit with you. Just tell me if Mum's coming home?*

Hank cast a disapproving look at Mary. 'She's staying here.'

Mary watched the nurses pausing at the reception desk.

'What can we do to make Mum come home now?' she asked, the sound of the nurses laughing travelled the length of the barren corridor. One of the nurses was carrying a metal tray covered with needles, just like the one that had been plunged into Norman's neck.

'Can you suddenly remember what happened to your sister? You where there weren't you? Can you bring Lucy home?' snapped Hank in reply. 'Because that's what you'd need to do for Mum to come home right now.'

Mary's breath was stolen by her dad's words. She had always suspected that her parents held her partly accountable for what had happened to Lucy. After all, she was there the day that Lucy had disappeared, and yet was unable to recall anything that would help return her sister to the safety of home. Before her dad could say another word to wound her already punctured heart, Mary turned and ran. With tears clouding her vision, she barged past the nurses, down the corridor and out of the main doors into the fresh air, leaving behind the sound of metal trays and needles crashing to the floor. Without taking a look back, she ran faster and only stopped when she was met with a locked gate at the end of the path.

There was no escape, not for Martha, and not for Mary.

Twenty

HY ISN'T HE COMING?
Mary lay awake. She didn't have a clock in her room, but the quietness of the road and the black sky told her it must've been the depths of the night. Her restless mind and body were unable to sleep. *Why hasn't he come for me yet?* was all she could think. She pressed her back against the corner, pulled her duvet up and waited for Perry. *He said he'd come for me, so why isn't he here?* Martha had now been an inpatient at Heron's Hook for three days. Mary hadn't been back to visit her mum, too frightened of bumping into Norman again, or witnessing the nurses inject her mum in the same way. Instead, she'd stayed at Wisteria with Elsie whilst Hank did the gruelling twice daily visits. But although Mary was scared of Herons Hook, and that's what she'd told Hank, she was really staying at Wisteria to wait for Perry. He said he'd come to get her, so she stayed at Wisteria and waited. It was now night three, and she was still waiting. But he hadn't forgotten, of course he hadn't, far from it, it was all part of his plan.

After Mary had heard her dad going to bed, she listened for footsteps coming up the drive. She'd left her window ajar purposefully so that she could hear anyone approaching the house. The breeze seeping in caused goosepimples to cover her skin, and every slight sound made her heart flutter with fear. *He'll come tonight; I know he will.*

Her eyelids were getting heavy, the lack of sleep was taking its toll. She got out of bed and walked over and watched from her bedroom window, trying to stay awake. Her eyes watched for flickers of light emerging from within the darkened woods. She stuck her head out of the window. *Where is he?* She could see that all of the lights over at Ivy Dean were off, the house pitch black. She looked across the room to her bedroom door, thinking she could hear someone climbing the stairs. *Is he here?* Holding her breath and blinking fast, she waited. But after a few seconds it all went quiet again. It wasn't him.

She looked out the window again, checking the front door. She wanted to see Perry coming, and be ready, rather than be taken by surprise. The thought of going somewhere, anywhere, alone with him petrified her. She tried to think of what she was going to say when he finally came, and what she would do, but it was so hard to imagine. And it would be so much worse if he came during the middle of the night when it was dark and creepy outside.

When Perry did finally come, the only thing Mary had decided was that she wouldn't hold his hand, even if she felt really scared. Instead, she would plunge her hands into her pockets, or sit on them should they go in his car. She didn't want to touch his hands, definitely not. Even though Perry was offering to help, Mary hadn't changed her mind about him; he still looked like a bad guy.

The wait felt excruciating. With each passing minute, her fear levels rose, making her debate if she was even brave enough to go through with the plan. She took hold of Penelope Pickles and thought about Lucy, and told herself over and over, *I can do this.* She thought about her mum in Herons Hook, and how desperate she was to bring her mum home. Thoughts of bringing her family back together encouraged Mary to push all of her fears aside, and brace herself for Perry's arrival. All the while, Perry sat watching her, just like he'd done the two nights previous. He'd snuck into the shed at Wisteria after the lights went out. Peering through one of the many spy holes he'd created, he watched Mary in the attic. *Almost time* he told himself. He watched Mary as she stood in the window. He knew she was waiting for him; his plan had worked. She had believed his story. She was waiting to go with him. It was the confirmation he needed. *Not long now, Mary.*

Mary finally fell asleep sometime close to 3 in the morning, her body still slumped in the corner of her room, Penelope Pickles still by her side. The bright morning sky shone onto her face, encouraging her eyes to open. Her heart sank, he hadn't been, again. She saw her sisters' doll, plus Lucy's empty bed across the room. And it was at that exact moment that it came to her. *I know what I need to do,* she said, talking to the doll, a smile beaming from her face. *I don't need to wait for him to help me bring Lucy home, I can do it all by myself.* Jumping out of bed and getting dressed, the details of her idea ran through her mind. *It's going to be perfect. She'll love it,* she said whilst creeping into Elsie's room. Mary eased the bedside table drawer open, taking out the bottle of sleeping pills she knew were kept at the back. Shaking the bottle to ensure it wasn't empty, Mary skipped down the stairs and made her way outside, walking round to the basement. She opened the door and placed Penelope Pickles in a bag she'd left there the day before. She then ran back inside.

She sat at the kitchen table, thinking through her plan. She couldn't eat breakfast; she wasn't at all hungry. There were toast crumbs and half a mug of cold coffee on the table, telling her that Hank hand already had his breakfast. She watched the stairs and waited for her dad to appear, which he would because he went visiting each morning after breakfast. The bathroom door slammed, followed by the sound of heavy feet descending the stairs.

'See you later, Mary, be good for Grandma.' With those eight short words delivered, he left without waiting for any kind of reply.

'Grandma, would you like a cup of tea?' she asked. Elsie was watching the news in the lounge whilst scanning the local paper, hoping that maybe today would be the day that Henry would be found.

'Yes please, Mary. Two sugars and a good splash of milk,' Elsie replied, oblivious to what Mary was plotting in the kitchen.

Mary took hold of the pill bottle, pressed down and unscrewed the top. She dropped two pills into her Grandma's cup, stirring to dissolve, exactly the way she'd watched Elsie do it in the past before bedtime. She then sat, pretending to watch cartoons. Struggling to stay awake, Elsie had put her tiredness down to the few tumblers of whiskey she'd drunk the night before. With Martha out of the house, Elsie felt free to have her nightcap, the only thing apart from pills which helped her to get any sleep. She didn't contemplate the notion that her own granddaughter was drugging her. Sure enough, after twenty minutes, Elsie was peacefully snoring, her body plummeting into a deep sleep, the sun warming her face as she lay stretched out on her favourite lounge recliner, Einstein curled up beside her feet, sleeping.

Mary scarpered in the same direction that her dad had fled, only she was on foot, and alone. She emerged on the main road, having run all the way from the house. She stopped on the pavement near Perry's house and cast her eyes over the building, failing to spot his shadow lurking behind the net curtain. His eyes widened with excitement. He pressed the shutter on his camera and snapped multiple close-ups of Mary.

'There she is. I knew she'd leave soon enough,' he whispered. A smirk spread across his face and smoke fired from both nostrils. A collection of cigarette butts lined the windowsill after a prolonged stakeout, flecks of ash dotting the woodwork and embedding into the tainted yellow net curtain.

Perry had followed Hank for the previous few days, and was fully aware of his whereabouts. Perry knew that Hank left the house around 10 o'clock, making the trip up to Herons Hook to visit Martha. Hank never returned until over an hour later. Perry also knew that Hank made the trip alone. Perry now knew for sure that Mary had been left behind, alone with her grandma at Wisteria.

A perfect opportunity to get a little closer.

He watched the little girl. A pair of binoculars rested in his hands, both sides warm where he'd been gripping them. He remained pressed against the window, watching her pace the pavement. Throwing the binoculars to the floor, he ran into the master bedroom, pulling back the curtain and looking up the main road.

'Is she going?'

Leaving his vantagepoint, Perry scurried down the stairs and, in a moment of panic, his feet stumbled, causing him to fall the final few steps. Unperturbed, he grabbed his keys and put on a pair of shoes, polished in anticipation of this moment. Once outside, he spied through the dense bushes, creeping up to the edge of his garden perimeter.

He stopped upon hearing a noise. Mary was still there, and now she was only an arm's length away. This wasn't the right time, Perry knew as much, but if he were to push his hands through the foliage, he'd be able to grab her from behind. But that's not what he wanted to do. He needed to be patient. He had it all planned in his mind. Mary's strawberry-scented shampoo drifted through the air whilst she danced nervously on the spot, the sweet aroma penetrating Perry's awaiting senses, his nostrils drinking in the scented air.

But his impatience got the better of him; even masters of their own trade sometimes fall foul. And so, Perry thrust his hands through the bush until they emerged on the other side, grabbing like a crab, but failing to catch. Thorns became implanted into his skin and he callously tugged his arms back through the mass of entwining branches, his skin breaking like tissue paper beneath the hawthorns. The sound of footsteps made him look out over his gate and on to the main road. His eyes followed Mary as she walked up the road heading towards Finchley village.

'Bitch,' he snarled. Opening his gate, Perry followed her up the road. He was prepared and dressed for such an occasion. He had ditched his usual ensemble and, instead, donned a disguise so that he wouldn't be recognised. His smart office suit and polished shoes tricked onlookers into thinking he was just another commuter forming part of the daily rat race. His fake moustache and glasses concealed his loathed, familiar features.

Having finally made up her mind that her plan was the right thing to do, her legs gained momentum the closer she got to her destination. The bell at Finchley's Fine Cuts hairdressers jingled when she eased the pink door open. *She's going to love it. I know she will. Just go inside,* she urged herself.

'Hello, my darling. Can we help you?' asked a lady who appeared, as if by magic, behind the counter. Although working as a hairdresser, the lady's hair in question seemed peculiar. It looked like a mass of curly, blonde wire, all piled up on the top of her head, all kept in place by a green scrunchie. If the lady was attempting to resemble a pineapple, she was succeeding.

The din coming from the collection of hairdryers drowned out her voice. Mary froze in the doorway and the lady continued to look at her, waiting for a reply to her question. Perry watched from across the road, leaning against a lamppost and grabbing a discarded newspaper out of the bin. He flicked through the pages, doing his best to blend into the background and not cause any suspicion - something which was easy to do when people were too busy trying to get to work on time.

'I'd like my hair cut,' replied Mary, finally, her voice barely audible above the racket.

'Are you with Mum or Dad?' asked the lady, a concerned look appearing on her face, her eyes looking beyond the door, watching for any lingering, accompanying adults. Perry held the paper aloft, dipping his head upon noticing the nuisance hairdresser peering across the road in his direction. If anyone was going to blow Perry's cover, it would be an over-observant hairdresser.

'Mum isn't well. She's been in a special hospital trying to get better,' recited Mary to the anticipated question, her practised answer was spoken with flawless ease. 'But she's hopefully coming home today and Dad has gone to visit. He gave me some money and told me to be as quick as I could.' She held out all the one-pound coins she'd raided from a jar she'd found in the basement. The receptionist scrutinised Mary's dishevelled appearance, searching her face for sincerity before accepting her story as authentic.

'Well, we better get started then, hadn't we?' replied Gwen, ushering Mary towards the back of the salon and wrapping her body up in a pink cloak before directing her to a chair propped up with extra padding. 'So, what are we going to do?' she asked, running her fingers through Mary's long, knotted strands, she soon found herself tangled. Mary avoided looking into the mirror and kept her head lowered. Mary never looked at her reflection any more, and hadn't done for years. She didn't like the thought of looking in the mirror and seeing Lucy staring back, it would make her miss her twin sister more.

'I want to surprise Mum,' she began, clearing her throat. 'And I think she'd like it if my hair looked pretty,' she explained, fiddling with the cloak ties. 'I think my mum would like it if my hair was shorter, so it stops about here.' Mary indicated by resting her hands on her shoulders. 'And I think she would like it if I had a fringe that comes down to here.' She placed her hands tentatively across her eyebrows.

Whilst still avoiding looking in the mirror, Mary mumbled her final request. 'And, if you could put this bow at the back, like this, I think it'd make Mum smile, a lot.' Mary delved her hand into her pocket, pulling out a lilac hair clip and placing it in exactly the same position that Lucy used to wear hers. 'Do you think you could do that?'

Gwen took hold of the clip and positioned it in the instructed place. 'Like this? I don't think that should be a problem,' she concluded, taking hold of some scissors and beginning to cut.

Mary's feet dangled from the hoisted chair. Her fingers fidgeted nervously beneath the cloak, waves of hair falling to the floor. She closed her eyes when the lady positioned her head straight, her face now directly in front of the mirror.

'Don't you want to look in the mirror?' asked Gwen, catching sight of Mary's face. 'Then you can see what's going on.'

'I'd like it to be a surprise for me, too,' she replied, her nose twitching, loose strands of hair tickling her skin. 'When I see Mum's reaction, then I'll look in the mirror, if that's okay?'

'In that case, why don't we do this?' suggested Gwen, turning Mary's chair around. 'Now you can't see any mirrors.'

Mary looked up. 'Thank you.' Casting her eyes around, she caught sight of a photo on the wall opposite; the picture of Lucy in a frame. Naturally, it was the one of Lucy on the swing, lilac dress and bow with Penelope Pickles in her hand. Mary's cheeks glowed. She stared at her sister's photo, unable to take her eyes off the exact hairstyle she'd just described to Gwen.

'That's a little girl that used to visit her grandma here in Finchley, every summer apparently,' said Gwen, following Mary's gaze. 'I never met Lucy, as I've only just moved to the village. But she looks so pretty in that dress, doesn't she?' Gwen's scissors froze mid-air whilst she admired the picture of Lucy. 'She went missing one sunny day, and has never been seen since. It's just so sad.' She sighed and continued to cut. 'Every day, when I come to work and see that picture, I pray that she'll be found, and that she can go back home to her family.'

I pray for that too, thought Mary.

'Your bow looks like that little girl's, doesn't it?'

Mary dipped her face, pushing her glasses back up her nose. She tried to conceal her face beneath her heavy new fringe as Gwen put the finishing touches to complete her new look, the lilac bow sitting in pride of place.

'We're nearly done,' said Gwen, standing at the side of Mary and looking in the mirror to ensure the bow was placed centrally. 'Now, are you sure you don't want to have a sneaky look in the mirror? I think you'll just *love* it,' she continued, admiring Mary's new hairstyle from every angle. Mary shook her head.

'I think Mum is going to be very pleased when she sees you,' whispered Gwen, bending down to remove Mary's cloak and shaking off all the loose strands, casting a confetti of hair through the air. Mary clattered all her coins on the counter ready to pay, whilst Gwen keyed numbers into the archaic till.

'Thank you very much,' she said, scooping up the money. 'I'm sorry, I didn't even ask your name?' she said. 'I always offer my young ladies and gents a lolly when they've had their hair cut. Would you like one?' Gwen held out the bowl of treats. Mary quickly took one and then made a dash through the door, leaving it reverberating on its hinges whilst she paced down the lane.

'Thank you,' she shouted back, the wind attempting to dislodge her new hairstyle, her legs galloping along the pavement.

Perry threw the paper into the bushes and followed. His idea to take Mary on the anniversary of Lucy's disappearance had gone by the wayside. He couldn't wait any longer. He'd waited years for this moment, and couldn't wait another day, not another minute longer. He wanted her now. It was time.

He traced Mary's steps, extending his stride as he neared. He was regularly forced to dip his head to avoid making eye contact with the odd passing pedestrian. He flicked his cigarette butt into a nearby drain just as Mary entered the driveway to Wisteria, her frame disappearing from sight.

Perry followed. *Perfect,* he thought as he approached the deserted patch of land.

He navigated the same stretch of woods, hiding whenever Mary's sixth sense caused her to stop and look round. Like a stalking black shadow, he refused to leave her side. Perturbed by what she could hear, but what she couldn't see, Mary began to run the rest of the way. Perry chased, his carelessness causing the sound of his footsteps to stretch far and wide.

'Where's she gone?' Wisteria came into view, the front garden empty. Perry ran across the driveway, the stones crunching beneath his feet. He scurried towards the porch and made an attempt to turn the doorknob, but the lock held it in place.

Inside, Elsie roused to the sound. However, before she could move to investigate, the sleeping pills reinstated their power and her eyelids were forced closed. A deep snore rattled in the back of her throat as her body lost control to the medication. She was definitely asleep.

Perry looked at his watch. The hour was almost up. Hank would be home soon, so he didn't have long.

'You just stay there,' he mumbled, spying through the lounge window, watching Elsie sleeping. He snuck round to the side of the house and crouched behind some bushes on the edge of the lawn, the crisp air becoming polluted by his smoke-infused breath. His impatience was growing, every echoing sound making his head gravitate in different directions.

'Where the bloody hell is she?' he mumbled, frantically searching every window for a sign of Mary's presence. A loud clattering noise suddenly rang out, making Perry's heart leap into his mouth. Fearing discovery, he was drawn out of his hideaway and began to snake across the lawn, making his way round to the back of the house. He paused at the dirty basement door window.

The single light struggled to break through the interior gloom. Inside, Perry watched Mary reaching behind the broken lawn mower. She rummaged around and fell backwards as she pulled out a box from the hidden space. *What's she doing?*

He placed his hand on the door handle, ready to press down, looking over his shoulder before he did so. But then he paused. A police car's siren blasted in the distance, the alarm causing him to remain frozen, holding his breath captive until the siren climaxed, then dispersed. *Are they coming for me?* was always his initial thought when hearing a police car. They weren't coming for him, not this time.

Perry watched. Mary was standing still, listening until the noise dissipated, the police car speeding past the entrance to Wisteria.

He continued to watch her fumble in the dark. He felt ready to open the door, but then Mary dropped her trousers and took off her T-shirt, her body shivering. Too startled to move, Perry watched, his mouth ajar.

Unaware that she was being watched, Mary eased herself into

a lilac, fancy dress costume that she'd persuaded her dad to buy her the day before, insisting that it'd make her happy whilst her mum was in hospital. Hank had reluctantly agreed to prevent Mary from nagging.

She flattened out the crumples with her hands before doing up the zip and reaching down for Penelope Pickles. Her imitation of Lucy was complete, her plan to bring her sister home coming together nicely. Perry's eyes became transfixed, locked on Mary. His brain tried to comprehend the vision he'd so often imagined in his mind, but which was now right before him, within touching distance. He admired Mary's transformed appearance. He watched whilst she spun on her toes like a ballerina, the dress skirt fanning.

She looks just like Lucy.

He knew, with precise detail, the way Lucy Lane looked in her lilac dress and, despite trying to spot differences, Perry couldn't find fault with the imitation. Seeing Mary without her spectacles meant he was able to admire her eyes without the clunky obstruction. In his mind, he was seeing both Mary and Lucy before him. And he wanted them both; he always had.

Perry heard a car coming up the driveway, followed by the sound of Einstein barking inside. He spied from the corner of the house.

'Fuck,' he snarled, his frustrations soon heightening. He watched Hank and Martha walk into the house, only a few feet away. *I'm too bloody late.* He darted into the woods, luck was on his side, he'd gone unnoticed.

Mary opened the basement door, the brightness of the sun startling her eyes, causing her to squint. He watched Mary tread carefully through the long blades of soft, vibrant grass, the lawn tickling her bare feet. She walked round to the front of the house holding the skirt of her dress, just like Lucy did when pretending to curtsey like a princess.

Mary was a standing target.

Take her, now, he urged himself.

Perry's adrenaline sent him forward, his legs weaving through the grass like a scorpion ready to sting. Suddenly, Hank's voice boomed from inside the house and Perry's instinct dictated he should turn and flee. He vanished into the woods, camouflaging quicker than a chameleon. Perry was getting careless, risking being caught. Although he'd been scared away this time, he'd return. He'd seen what he wanted, and he would be back to take her. It was only a matter of time.

Twenty-One

MARY PAUSED ON THE PORCH WITH PENELOPE PICKLES clenched in her right hand. She peered through the pane of glass, looking for her parents but seeing only Einstein in the hallway, his barks penetrating the door. She knew her parents were home; the car was on the drive and she'd heard her dad shouting. She searched inside for signs of her mum's return, wanting confirmation that she'd been released from Herons Hook.

Mary's dress fluttered round her legs, a gust sweeping it up, the material spreading like a fan as it danced in the breeze. The sweet, pungent aroma of Martha's perfume hung like an invisible cloud in the air, the subtle scent seeping up into Mary's nostrils and causing the butterflies in her stomach to infiltrate her whole body with excitement. She eased the door open. Einstein jumped up before running out onto the lawn.

Martha emerged from her bedroom and caught sight of Mary from the top of the stairs. 'Lucy?' she questioned immediately, the sight taking her breath away and causing her heart to perform an instant cycle of summersaults.

Mary hovered in the doorway, the lilac dress looking vibrant, the sun shining through the fine material, radiating up onto her facial features.

'Lucy?' Martha repeated, taking a step forward, her eyes still fixed on Mary, a look of disbelief sweeping across her face.

The shock drained Martha's face of all colour until only a ghost remained, hovering at the top of the stairs.

Mary waited for her mum's smile to appear. She waited for the explosion of excitement at seeing her dressed like Lucy. But, with the seconds passing, no smile was forthcoming. *Why isn't she smiling? Why does she look so sad? This was meant to make her happy.*

Mary didn't have time to correct her mum's mistaken identification. She watched in disbelief as Martha flung her body down the stairs, her feet gliding through the air, her right arm sliding down the banister, preventing her body from tumbling.

'Lucy, is it really you?' cried Martha again, her eyeballs bulging in their sockets. She knelt, gazing at Mary, searching every inch of her appearance. The sight of Penelope Pickles clenched in her daughter's hand was all the confirmation that Martha needed. 'Lucy?' she whispered, tentatively holding out her hand and taking hold of Mary's, touching it with such delicacy, scared that a heavy grip would break it, or make her disappear again. 'Oh, thank God.'

Mary shook her head. 'No, silly. It's me, Mary,' she replied after a few more agonising moments. Martha dropped Mary's hand like a hot coal. Her initial look of bewilderment vanished, replaced by a look of utter disappointment. Mary's tears began to roll, splashing against her trembling, naked feet.

'I wanted to look like Lucy, just for you.' Mary grabbed her dress with her left hand, lifting it to her face and wiping her eyes. 'Dad said if I brought Lucy home, you'd come out of hospital and wouldn't need to go back.'

A sense of devastation so indescribable stole years from Martha's face, and she urged her heart to stop beating in an attempt to escape the pain. Lines appeared across her face that would never fade. Grey hair had formed at the roots. The wafer-thin skin covering her hands now showed all the veins beneath, and her eyes lost their remaining glimmer; the remaining traces of hope.

Martha was speechless. Everything she had prayed for during

the previous six years had just been handed to her, only to be ripped away seconds later. Her disappointment was immeasurable. Martha was thinking that it had to be a joke, and the girls had managed to connive a plan to make Lucy's return home special. That's what all this was; just a silly joke.

But nobody was laughing.

'Lucy and me pretended to be one another *all* the time when we were little, just to trick you,' said Mary, 'and you thought it was funny, didn't you, Mum? It made you laugh.' However, her explanation didn't help. She watched her mum's expression crumbling in slow motion; and, no matter what she said to try and explain, her mum's collapse was inevitable.

Martha moved, finally. Her hands gravitated towards her head, her fingers sinking beneath her curly hair before she attempted to pull out clumps.

'How could you?' she erupted amid a prolonged screech, her hands trying to rip the dress off her daughter's frame, causing Mary to fall to the floor. Penelope Pickles was tossed across the floor and lay motionless beneath the coat rack.

'*How could you?*' Martha repeated, trying to shred the dress, tearing the cotton and severing the stitches. Martha stood still. 'Are you stupid?' She then began to stomp around the hallway, her rage brewing to a climax. 'How could you be so cruel?' She yelled so loud that Mary covered her ears. Lying on the floor, Mary curled herself into a ball beneath the swatches of ripped lilac fabric and prayed that she could go back in time, back to the moment before she made the decision to put on the dress, before she decided to march into town and have her hair cut. She knew now that she had been stupid. So stupid.

Martha grabbed a vase that was resting on a side table and hurled it to the floor. It landed to the side of Mary's head and smashed into pieces, shards of coloured glass scattering faster than a bag of dropped marbles.

'I thought it—'

'You thought what?' Martha interrupted. 'That it would make

things better? Well, it hasn't, has it?' She grabbed the side table and flipped it over, the noise reverberating down the hallway. 'I'll never get over this. *Never.*'

'I'm sorry,' said Mary, crying loudly. 'I was trying to make you happy. I wanted to make you smile. I wanted you to come home from hospital. I didn't want you staying there, it scares me…' Mary crawled away from her mum, but Martha grabbed the dress and tried to tear more fabric.

'Where did you get it from? Tell me,' she insisted, holding pieces of the dress in her hands, failing to hear her daughter's explanation.

'Dad bought it for me.'

Martha ripped the lilac bow out of Mary's hair. 'And this?' she shouted. Strands of auburn hair became severed from the roots. Mary screamed, her scalp delicate and bleeding.

Hank came crashing through the back door. 'Bloody hell, Martha, let her go.' Mary's scream continued. 'Martha, stop it!' he raged, grabbing his wife and dragging her away. Martha's legs continued to kick out. 'What are you doing?'

'Look at her, just look,' she cried. Martha was now sprawled out on the floor, her arms outstretched and her head rocking. 'Just look at her, Hank.' Mary continued to lie amongst the sea of glass splinters, her moist cheek resting on the cold floor, her lower limbs exposed.

'Mary, what have you done?' he asked, finally letting go of his wife before bending down, stroking Mary's short hair and looking at her tattered dress, vivid images of Lucy flashing through his mind. 'Why have you done this?'

'You said that Mum could come home if Lucy was here, so I wanted to look like her,' Mary cried. 'I wanted to look like Lucy instead of me. I wanted Mum to be happy.' She flung her arms round Hank, burying her face into his chest. 'I was pretending to be Lucy, just for Mum,' she sobbed, clinging onto her dad.

Hank turned to look at his wife as she rocked to and fro on the floor, her eyes refusing to blink. Martha mumbled Lucy's name over and over.

Elsie appeared at the back door. 'What's happened?' she asked, dashing over and bending down to see if Martha was hurt.

'It's alright, Mum, all just an accident,' Hank insisted. He scooped Mary into his arms, lifting her away from the glass and walked into the lounge, placing her on the sofa. He kissed her on the head. 'It'll be alright, Mary. Just stay there whilst I see to your mum.' He then walked back into the hallway, crouching on the floor next to Martha.

'I thought it was Lucy. I thought it was Lucy,' she repeated. 'She was right there, I saw her. I saw her with my own eyes. It wasn't someone else, it was her.' Her eyes were unblinking, her tears trickling in a steady flow. 'Tell me it was her. Please, just tell me it was her.'

Hank knew there were no words that would help. He knew that the two things that his wife needed were the two things he couldn't give her: Lucy, and a drink.

'Look at that,' Martha said, catching sight of Penelope Pickles peeking out amongst the shoes at the bottom of the coat rack. She stretched out and grabbed the doll before scrambling to her feet and running into the lounge.

'Where did you get this from?' she said, staring at Mary. 'Tell me. TELL ME, WHERE.' Her eyes were opened wide, the vein in her forehead bulging. 'It's Penelope Pickles, isn't it? Tell me I'm not seeing things. Tell me I'm not making it up. It's actually her, isn't it?' Martha rambled, getting more worked up with each word she spoke. She clung onto hope for a few more seconds. In her mind, it had to be Lucy, it just had to be. There was no other explanation. If Penelope Pickles was back, then so was Lucy, after all these years.

Hank followed her into the lounge. 'Martha, what are you going on about?' He then stared at the doll, his colour also draining. 'Is that Lucy's? Mary, where did you get it from?'

'I found it in Grandma's basement the other day,' Mary lied, too scared to tell the truth.

'This was your sister's. You do know that, don't you?' Hank

exclaimed, his hands shaking. He touched the doll whilst Martha cradled it; he also fearful it would somehow break if he touched it.

'I don't remember,' said Mary, still crying. 'I thought it must've been mine.'

'You should've told us about this the day you found it,' said Martha. 'Anything belonging to your sister is precious, don't you understand that?'

'I'm sorry.'

'Are you sure you found it in the basement? Think, Mary,' she demanded, stroking the doll's hair like it was real. Mary nodded, at which point Martha directed her anger at Elsie.

'Have you had this all along and not told us?' she shouted. 'You're hiding something, aren't you? I bloody well knew it. You know something, and yet you're not telling me. Where is she? What did you do to Lucy?

'I haven't done anything to her!' shouted Elsie.

'Then why do you have her doll? She always had it with her. She'd never let it go, not unless someone took it from her.'

Was it in the basement? thought Elsie, desperately trying to recall, but failing to locate the required memory.

'There's so much junk down there, Martha,' she replied finally. 'It's impossible to remember each and every item.'

'Junk?' screamed Martha. 'This isn't junk, you stupid woman!' At that point, Elsie walked away, storming out of the back door and letting it slam shut behind her.

'This isn't Mum's fault.' Martha didn't hear Hank's words.

'I'm sure – actually, I'm positive – that I haven't seen Penelope Pickles since the day Lucy went missing. Have you?' she asked Hank, while continuing to cry, holding the doll close to her chest as if it was Lucy herself.

'I don't think I have,' he replied. 'Martha, you need to calm down. I can't have you getting all in a state again.'

'You're asking me to calm down?' Martha shouted. 'What would you rather me do? Pretend like it doesn't mean anything?' she stared at him. 'I remember telling the police that Lucy would have had this exact doll with her the day she went missing. But I was wrong, wasn't I? I gave everybody the wrong information. The police could've been looking for a girl with a doll all this time, and they'd have been looking for the wrong girl.' Hysterical now, she began to shriek. 'Maybe all this time people have been reporting sightings of Lucy, but the police didn't think it was her because she wasn't carrying a doll? This could help find Lucy, don't you understand that?' She shoved the doll into Hank's face.

'Bloody hell, Martha,' he snapped, thrashing out and accidentally knocking the doll out of Martha's hand. She released another scream, the piercing sound hurting Mary's ears again.

'You bastard! Don't ever do that again.' Martha scrambled to pick up the doll, carefully brushing away the dust and making sure there was no damage. 'Don't you get it? Don't you realise how important this is?' Martha banged her fist against the wall, threatening to break her own knuckles. 'Nobody understands.' She fell to the floor, clenching the doll to her chest.

'Please, stop crying,' whispered Mary, the thought of her mum being taken back to Herons Hook made her feel sick.

'We should take Penelope Pickles to the police,' said Martha after a few seconds of silence. 'Maybe they can find something on the doll that could help us find Lucy? She never went anywhere without it. Maybe Lucy wasn't in the house after all? Maybe she was taken from the basement and the police were looking for clues in the wrong place all this time?' She continued to ramble, not hearing any other sounds apart from her own chaotic web of thoughts.

'We'll call Sergeant Swift, see what she thinks,' suggested Hank, just as Elsie returned, her arms laden with clothes that had been drying on the line.

'Elsie, think again,' said Martha, pouncing on her. 'Did Henry say anything, *anything* about Lucy playing in the basement that day? Mary, you were there, too. You were outside, weren't you? Do you remember seeing Lucy outside with you? Did she go into the basement?'

Elsie and Mary both remained silent, simultaneously shaking their heads. Mary wanted to tell her mum everything. She wanted to tell her about what Perry had said, about hearing her grandad shouting that day, about the man he saw and finding Penelope Pickles outside his house. She wanted to tell her mum that she had found the doll in Perry's shed. But she couldn't speak; the words imprisoned. It wasn't the right time. There would never be a right time.

'Bloody useless,' Martha muttered beneath her breath, shaking her head.

'Can I have Penelope Pickles back?' asked Mary tentatively. 'I promise I'll keep her safe for when Lucy comes home.' Martha pressed the treasured possession against her heart.

'Let her have it,' mouthed Hank, nodding his head with encouragement.

Martha wanted to run, and take the doll with her. She once again felt close to her missing daughter, closer than she'd felt since the day that Lucy vanished, and now that precious feeling was about to be taken away.

Hank encouraged her again, seeing Mary's pleading expression. 'Let her have it, Martha. She'll look after it.'

'When I've spoken to the police, they might want it,' replied Martha eventually, before handing Mary the doll. 'And, if they do, if it'll help find her, then I'll take it back.'

Mary reached out her arms. 'Okay.'

'Don't lose her. Promise me, you won't lose her.'

'I promise,' Mary replied.

Hank escorted his wife upstairs, laying her down on the bed and covering her with a blanket.

'Get me a drink,' said Martha. 'I'm begging you. Get me a fucking drink.' Hank ignored the request and closed the door, locking it behind him.

Martha, and her screams, became trapped inside the four walls that were now her prison. She was only a few days into her journey on the road to sobriety. She had been instructed to return to a stable environment, devoid of anything that could trigger her desire to want a drink. She'd been home fifteen minutes and already she was begging for the bottle.

At Finchley police station, Sergeant Swift took a phone call. She didn't wait until the conversation concluded, but instead indicated for someone to take her place. Without grabbing her purse or finishing her coffee, she flew out the door, faster than an arrow from a bow. The police siren on her car forewarned people of her approach. After only a few minutes, the car charged up the driveway to Wisteria, stopping right outside the front door.

Inside, hearing the noise, Hank frowned. *What now?*

Sergeant Swift got out and paced towards the porch.

'Mr Lane?' she shouted. 'Are you home?' With no immediate answer, she peered through the door, listening for a reply.

Hank dashed downstairs. 'I'm coming,' he shouted in reply to the incessant knocking. Mary walked over and shielded herself behind her dad when he opened the door slightly, offering only a narrow gap.

'Can I come in?' asked Swift, peering round, trying to get a better look, seeing the glass on the floor. 'Is everything okay?'

'Yes, everything's fine,' said Hank. 'But this isn't really a great time. Is there a problem?' He could just about hear the sound of Martha's sobs travelling down the stairs, so he spoke louder. 'I need to clean up this glass before someone gets hurt.'

Swift strategically placed her foot in the gap before speaking. 'There's been a reported sighting,' she began, glancing down at Mary, who bobbed her head round. 'Someone claims to have seen your daughter, Lucy.' Mary manoeuvred herself so that she was standing in front of her dad. Swift bent down, now ignoring Hank.

'I think the person who reported the sighting will have spotted Mary, not Lucy,' he attempted to explain. 'Mary's just had her hair cut and was wearing a lilac bow in her hair, so she does look very much like how we all remember Lucy. That's what someone will have seen I suspect.'

'Hi, my name's Claire,' began Swift, still ignoring Hank. Swift looked Mary up and down, noting her dishevelled, torn dress and tear-stained face.

The sight of Mary knocked Swift off guard. She hadn't expected the sighting to carry any real validity; and yet, here was Lucy, standing right before her. The dress was the same, just like in the photo; the hair was the same, and the eyes. Those eyes… how could they belong to anyone else other than Lucy? Swift knew Lucy's face in meticulous detail and, to her trained eye, Lucy was now standing right before her. She then noticed Penelope Pickles in her hand, it had to be Lucy, there was no other explanation.

She swallowed so hard that it was audible. Had Lucy been found after all this time? Had she never been missing? Was this all just some kind of prank, or a family's wrongdoing and subsequent coverup? Was it April Fool's day and she'd forgotten? Swift thought she was dreaming. To satisfy her own mind, she spoke to Mary directly.

'Can you tell me your name?' The question lingered in the air, and it felt like a lifetime before the answer came. Swift braced herself. Maybe today was the day that Lucy would be found, and the case would be solved with the best outcome.

'My name is Mary Elizabeth Lane.' Swift's heart sank. She was so desperate for Lucy to be alive that, in those few seconds, she'd already convinced herself that it was Lucy, and that she'd been returned. Life was never that simple or straightforward, Swift knew as much.

'Hi, Mary. Is it alright if I ask you another question?'

Mary nodded.

'Are you alright?'

Mary gave the merest of nods.

'Are you hurt?'

Mary shook her head, although she could feel the beginnings of bruises spread all over her body from where her mum had grabbed and clawed at her.

'Your dress is very pretty,' said Swift. 'Did you choose it yourself?' Another nod of acknowledgement. 'And I like your hair. Where did you get it cut?'

Mary looked at her dad before answering, knowing he was going to be angry once the lady left.

'Finchley's Fine Cuts.'

'I go there, too,' said Swift. 'It's nice, isn't it?' Mary failed to reply.

'And who's this?' Swift indicated to Penelope Pickles. Mary looked at her dad, wanting him to answer. Hank knew how his next statement was going to sound in the eyes of the police; it was going to make him sound guilty.

'This is actually a doll that used to be Lucy's – still is Lucy's,' said Hank, indicating to the doll that Mary was holding. 'We were positive that Lucy had it with her the day she disappeared, but it turns out that it's been in the basement all this time.'

Swift looked at the doll, recognising it herself from the many photos covering the evidence wall back at the station. Lucy had it with her when she disappeared – or so the official report from her family documented.

'Could it help in the investigation in any way?' asked Hank. 'My wife's worried that Lucy could've been spotted, but that you wouldn't have thought it was her if she didn't have the doll.'

'Can I take a look?' Swift asked, looking at Mary and holding out her hand. She touched the doll, wanting to press it to her face to see if it smelt how she imagined it would.

'Strange that, after all these years, this just appears, wouldn't you agree?' Swift directed the question at Hank, who couldn't deny the facts. Swift looked up the stairs upon hearing the sound of crying. 'Is Mum home?' she asked, handing Mary back the doll.

Hank answered. 'She's upstairs, having a shower. Like I said, this isn't a great time. So, if there's nothing else, we're a bit busy.'

'I'm just going to talk to your dad for a minute, but thanks for the little chat, Mary,' said Swift, indicating with her head for Hank to join her outside.

'Can we go and take a look round the garden?' she asked, making her way round the side of the house without waiting for a reply, wanting to check the basement. 'You can see why someone would be mistaken, thinking they'd seen Lucy?'

Hank walked quickly to catch up with her. Swift paused and pulled out the missing person poster of Lucy from her inside pocket. Swift always carried the photo of Lucy on her person, just as Perry did. It made her feel that, in some way, she was always searching, and that she would never give up.

'Even without someone seeing Mary in the dress, she looks just like Lucy. Wouldn't you agree?' Swift's tone of voice changed. She didn't have to tread carefully with adults, they could take care of themselves. In her mind, there was no need to pussy-foot around, and so she didn't.

And she had no time for Hank, that much was obvious. Though she would never state as much officially, she blamed him and Martha for what happened to Lucy. Their daughter had been four years old at the time of her disappearance, just a child. They were her parents. They were responsible for Lucy's safety, and yet they failed to keep her safe. It may have been a harsh judgement, but everybody was entitled to their own opinion, even police officers. Swift had a niggling feeling that wouldn't go away when it came to Hank Lane, and her niggling feelings were usually right.

Hank mirrored Swift's air of antagonism. 'Mary hasn't done anything wrong,' he said. 'If she wants to have her hair cut and wear a dress, then she bloody well can. Wouldn't *you* agree? If people mistake her, then that's alright too. They're twins, after all. It's not Mary's fault. At least people are still looking for Lucy. That's a good thing, isn't it?'

Swift didn't care for people who swore at her; it showed a lack of respect in her eyes. 'It certainly is good that the public are still aware,' she replied. 'They rarely forget about a missing child, Mr Lane. They'll continue to help us until we find out what happened to your daughter. And, after all, that's what we all want, isn't it?'

Perry's empty cigarette packet cartwheeled in the breeze just behind where Hank and Swift were standing in the garden, the sound of the basement door banging around the corner.

'What was that?' Swift asked, looking towards the basement. 'You won't mind if I take a look, will you?' Swift didn't wait for an answer before she started to walk towards the side of the house.

'It must be Mum,' said Hank. 'She's been hanging up some washing.' He followed, catching sight of the door ajar.

'Mum?' he announced before walking in. 'Are you in here?' The bedraggled interior remained in darkness until Hank turned on the single bulb ceiling light, projecting harsh shadows against the walls. Swift walked past Hank, pacing into the centre of the room and unclipping a torch from her belt hook. The masses of clutter became illuminated beneath the bright glare as the torchlight scanned the room. She wasn't sure what she was looking for, but she'd know when she saw it.

'Do you have rats?' she asked, bending down on all fours, shining the light across the floor, her eyes scanning every nook, grabbing the opportunity with both hands.

'I don't think so. But I rarely come down here, so it's possible,' Hank replied. 'The noise would've just been the door banging, and there's clearly nobody in here. So, if you don't mind, I really do have things to do.' He stood in the doorway, indicating with his hand for Swift to exit. 'Unless there was something else that you're here for?'

Swift knew there were limits to what she could do. She had no other reason to enforce a thorough search, despite her wanting to turn the basement upside down. She felt like Hank was hiding something; he was far too eager to usher her away.

She followed his lead, taking one last look before he closed the basement door. 'If you find anything else of Lucy's that we didn't know about, let us know, immediately,' she said. 'I'll document that the doll is here, and update Lucy's search profile.' Once back out on the driveway, Swift saw Mary standing at the lounge window, her heart skipping again at what she thought was Lucy.

'If I need to analyse the doll, I'll be back.' Swift wanted to take the doll, but she also wanted an excuse to return. 'Mr Lane, I think it'd be helpful not only for us, but your family, too, if Mary didn't look so much like Lucy during your stay here in Finchley. It's distressing for everyone when hopes are needlessly raised. Don't you agree?'

'Thanks for coming,' Hank replied, walking in through the front door before slamming it closed, failing to say goodbye. He waited until Swift vanished down the drive, watching her through the front door window.

Once she'd gone, he ripped Mary out of the dress, leaving her standing in only her knickers and vest. She watched her dad as he stuffed the dress, the shoes and the bow into the outside bin, ready for collection in a few days' time. Still with a face like thunder, he stormed back inside and slammed the front door for a second time.

'Do anything like that again, and I swear you'll never leave this house,' he said. 'Now, get upstairs and don't come out until I say so.' Mary grabbed Penelope Pickles and ran, her cold body dashing up the stairs. She called Einstein, her only friend, and he followed.

Mary did just as her dad had said and stayed in her room for the rest of the day. She wasn't brought any meals, but ate the packet of crisps she had in her backpack, she wasn't really hungry anyway. Elsie had wanted to take something up, a little morsel, but she was too scared. Hank would've hit the roof if he'd found out she'd gone behind his back.

Whilst locked away, Mary heard shouting and screaming throughout most of the afternoon. The screeches were coming mainly from Martha, who also spent the entire day and night locked away in her room, begging and pleading for a drink. Some time close to midnight, her screams faded, her voice horse and her body finally permitting her some sleep. Mary took to her position in the corner of the room, once again hoping that Perry would come for her. He was now her only hope. She needed him to help her find Lucy. She didn't sleep for more than a few hours, her body now starved of sleep.

For a few hours, Wisteria fell silent.

With her bedroom window closed, Mary failed to hear the stones on the driveway crunching, her eyes having finally shut only moments earlier. Her ears had subconsciously been alerted to the noise outside, but her sleeping brain failed to be roused. The footsteps crept closer, only a few feet away from Mary's bedroom window above. From the attic at Ivy Dean, Perry had been watching Mary's bedroom all night, and knew that she must've been asleep because there had been no signs of her standing at the bedroom window.

Dressed in top to toe black, he made his way right up to Wisteria. He checked to see if there were any open windows downstairs, but Hank had been thorough in closing them before bed. Perry climbed the steps that led up to the front door, his feet lingering on the outside door mat. *Please be open* he thought to himself. He held out his hand and gripped the door handle, pressing slowly. It was locked. He pressed his face to the glass, his eyes peering inside and his warm breath leaving behind a trail of mist.

Muttering to himself, he backed away, snaking to the back of the house to try the back door, which was also locked. Perry wanted to take Mary. After seeing her dressed as Lucy, the desire was too much to resist. The well thought out plan in his mind told him to wait, to be patient, but his heart told him to take her, now.

Refusing to be beaten, Perry pushed his hand against every downstairs window just in case one was closed, but not shut fully or locked. He peered in through the kitchen window, the blind having not been drawn. The interior of the house still drowned in middle of the night darkness. His warm, clammy hand pressed against one of the small, narrow windows located at the top of the main window, his skin leaving behind an invisible hand print. The glass eased away from the frame. It was open. With a ponding heart, he looked up, assessing if he could somehow climb through, but the window was too small. He shone his torch in, illuminating the photos of Lucy on the wall. His hand pressed the window so that it closed, a little heavy handed due to frustration. Undefeated, he checked the perimeter once more for means of entry, his finger prints lining the exterior of the house like an invisible, second skin. Wisteria was locked down. Unless he was going to risk breaking in whilst the family were inside, he had no choice but to wait. He refused to go home emptyhanded though, so walked over to the bins.

Whilst the house continued to sleep, he opened the outside bin and delved his hand inside, not knowing that it was to be his lucky night after all. His hand felt the soft material against his skin, his fingers pulling free a piece of torn material. His heart raced upon sight of the lilac dress, the lace becoming visible beneath the dim light of his torch. He pressed it against his nose, inhaling as deep as his lungs could muster. He plunged his hand back in, this time grabbing hold of the hair accessory just as the bathroom light illuminated within the house. In the next second, Perry was gone.

When morning broke the following day, Mary disobeyed her dad's instructions. She snuck through the house, doing her best not to wake anybody. With bare feet, she eased the front door open and went out just in her pyjamas. The temperature outside was already warm, indicating it was going to be another hot and sticky day. The birds were chirping and the main road was quiet. She peered around, making sure nobody was looking. She grabbed hold of the bin lid and rummaged through the contents, wanting to rescue her new dress. 'Where is it?' She'd liked pretending to be Lucy, and planned on putting the dress in her secret box beneath her bed, where nobody would see it.

Taking a glance over her shoulders, Mary stood on her tiptoes, rummaging around inside the wheelie bin, her fingers sifting through the contents. With her heart racing, her skin glided over something soft to the touch, her fingers grabbing hold of a fist full of material. She pulled the item out and crouched on the ground, looking back at the house for a second time. Wiping her eyes on the back of her dirty hand, she flattened out the crumpled dress, the costume resembling a tatty, disused rag having been tugged apart by Martha and Hank. With a confused expression on her face, Mary shook the dress, expecting to uncover the matching bow. When nothing appeared, she dove her hands back into the bin, scouring the contents for the missing hair accessory. But it had already been taken.

Only a stone's throw away at Ivy Dean, Perry Golifer eased his bedroom door closed, his free hand delving into his pocket, his back resting against the door. Clenched in his hand was the missing bow, accompanied by torn fragments of the lilac dress. He placed them amongst his collection, a collection that was still incomplete.

Twenty-Two

ARY RAN BACK INSIDE AND UP TO HER BEDROOM. SHE put on the dress that she'd retrieved from the bin. Although ripped and crumpled, it still looked pretty when she had eased her body into the swathes of material. Once in the dress, she decided to finally take a look in the mirror. She wanted to see what everyone else saw. She didn't want to be afraid of her reflection. But, most importantly, she now wanted more than anything to see her sister.

Upon opening her door, she could hear that the house was quiet. *If Mum sees me, she'll be furious.* But taking the chance was worth the risk in Mary's eyes. She teetered along the landing with Einstein before vanishing into the bathroom and closing the door. She thought that nobody had roused, but she was wrong.

She stepped up on to the footstool. 'Be brave,' she said, holding Penelope Pickles in her hand, clenching the doll for support and comfort. She looked up at the oval mirror. Balancing on her tiptoes, the shock nearly knocked the breath out of her when she finally mustered the courage to open her eyes and take a look in the mirror. For the very first time, she now understood what everyone had been talking about all this time. Tiny droplets tumbled down her cheeks, and she moved closer to the glass to examine her face.

'Lucy?' she whispered before turning to look over her shoulder, expecting her sister to be standing behind her. 'Is it really you?'

Mary searched the empty bathroom before turning back to her reflection, reaching out towards the mirror to try and touch the face that looked so much like her sister's. Mary had had an idea of what her own face looked like before her transformation because, on odd occasions, she'd accidentally walked past a shop window and caught sight of her own reflection. Or she'd been in a changing room whilst her mum was trying on some new clothes, surrounded by mirrors and, no matter how hard she tried to avoid looking, she inadvertently caught a quick glimpse of herself.

Mary therefore knew that her hair had looked like scraggy rats' tails. She knew that her glasses were ugly, and that her clothes were better suited to a boy. So, when she looked in the mirror now, all she saw was Lucy, her pretty twin sister.

'I'm going to find you,' she announced, pressing her palm against the mirror, imagining touching her sister's hand. 'We'll be together again really soon, Lucy.' Mary trembled as she listened, making sure nobody was coming. Her tears fell harder, the warm, salty moisture seeping into the corner of her mouth as she spoke.

'I'm ready for Perry to come and get me, I'm ready to find you,' she mumbled, wiping her eyes on a towel. 'I'm not sure when he'll come, but I'll do anything to try and find you, Lucy. Life is horrible without you,' Mary continued, pressing her forehead against the mirror and closing her eyes. 'They don't care about me anymore, not since you went missing. They forget I'm here; I know they do. All they think about is you, and if they're not thinking about you, then they're drinking.'

Mary sobbed. Speaking with her sister again felt more wonderful than she could have ever imagined, even if it was make-believe. And, for a few precious seconds, Lucy felt real, like she was really in the bathroom.

'When I come looking for you, I'll keep shouting, Lucy. All you need to do is shout back if you hear me, okay?' She took a deep intake of breath. 'I miss you, Lucy.' Mary wiped her eyes and admired her sister's reflection for one last time. 'I love you, Lucy, and I'm sorry I didn't play with you as much as I should've.

But when we're back together, I'll play with you all the time, I promise I will.' Mary leant forward and kissed her reflection.

'Mary! Who are you talking to?' shouted Elsie.

Oh God.

'Just singing to myself, Grandma,' Mary replied, opening the door ajar and peering through the gap, hiding her body. 'I'll be down in a minute.'

DOWNSTAIRS, ELSIE HAD just started picking at a chicken carcass for sandwich meat. Having changed into her normal clothes, Mary entered the kitchen.

'Where's Mum and Dad?'

'They've just left to go and do some shopping; didn't you hear them leaving?' asked Elsie. 'They thought it would be a good idea for you all to go on a picnic again. Mum is feeling a bit better and so I'm making some sandwiches and they've gone for snacks and drinks.'

Although hungry after a day without food, Mary's heart sank. *Not another picnic.* She didn't believe that they were out buying food, that was a lie and Mary knew that. She suspected her mum was either buying some alcohol, or her dad had taken her back to Herons Hook. She wasn't quite sure which was the better option. At least the screaming had stopped.

'You're not giving Einstein bones, are you, Grandma?' she asked, watching Elsie place a bunch of scrap bones to one side before putting the rest of the carcass into the bin. Einstein looked on with hope in his eyes, licking his lips and wagging his tail, waiting for another tasty treat.

'No, but I did give him a few bones on his first day so that he wouldn't want to run away,' replied Elsie. 'No dog would ever leave a home if he knew that there might be fresh bones on offer. That's what I always did when we brought one of our new dogs home.' She placed the bones in a separate bag ready to take straight to the outside bins.

'I knew you'd given him a bone, Grandma, because he left

one in my bedroom,' said Mary. 'I've hidden it now so that Dad doesn't find out.'

'I bet he's been rooting through the bin outside for more. That's what all dogs do when they smell something nice. They go rummaging,' Elsie explained, washing her hands. 'I'll put all these in another bag to try and hide the smell, then maybe he won't go rooting.' She wrapped up the bones in another carrier bag before heading outside.

Elsie's ability to pretend like everything was alright was admirable, yet not a second passed during the day where she didn't think about Henry. Sometimes she prayed aloud, whilst other times she prayed to herself.

Where are you, my love? Come home soon. I miss you. I'm so worried, we all are. Please come home.

Elsie questioned her own sanity more and more as the days passed, especially with Mary finding Penelope Pickles in the basement. *I'm sure it wasn't there*, Elsie repeated over and over to herself. She also doubted herself over Henry's whereabouts. Had Henry told her where he was going all along, and she'd just forgotten? Had she written where he was going on a sticky note, and just not seen it, or perhaps it had fallen somewhere out of sight? As a result of this paranoia, Elsie had turned each room upside down looking for the illusive note that would lead to her husband's location. She looked behind the fridge and found nothing but crumbs, spiders and decades' worth of dust. She'd looked down the sides and back of the sofa and found nothing but bits of old food, dirty tissues and a pen. She'd looked in all the unusual places she tended to find odd things, like in the washing basket, in the biscuit tin, underneath the tea cosy, or underneath her bed.

The note was never found, and that's because it didn't exist. Elsie wasn't losing her mind. She was making herself believe that she was by reading too much into a forgetful memory. Elsie was paranoid and was living out a self-fulfilling prophecy. She thought she was losing her marbles, but she really wasn't. She was just getting on a bit it, and had an ageing memory as a result. Had she gone to the doctor's surgery, the GP would have confirmed her memory was fine with a few simple tests. Like Henry, Elsie suffered from a severe hatred of medical professionals, and so avoided them, to her detriment.

Having found nothing during her search, Elsie thought it possible that Henry could have just gone to visit an old friend. Or maybe he had decided to go on an impromptu holiday, alone? Had he nipped to the shop and just decided not to come back? Did he not love her anymore? That was a possibility. People fell out of love every day, even after fifty-something years of marriage. Maybe Henry had looked at his wife that morning and realised that he just didn't love her. Had he left Wisteria of his own accord, and was now living a life happily elsewhere, without her?

Mary followed Elsie outside, grabbing her backpack from the end of the banister and throwing it over her shoulder. 'I'm going to take Einstein for a walk, Grandma. I'll be back soon.'

'Don't go too far, Mary,' Elsie replied. 'Mum and Dad won't be long. Then we can have a picnic.'

THE SUN FELT warm, despite it only being just gone nine in the morning; an unusually warm English summer gracing the typically cool island. Mary and Einstein meandered deeper into the woods, seeking shade and sheltering from the sun's heat beneath the protection of the foliage umbrella.

Einstein ran off and began barking in the distance.

'What's up?' Mary asked, running to where he was now resting. She bent over and placed her hand on her knees, trying to catch her breath, 'What're you barking for?'

Einstein was sitting in what had quickly become his favourite patch in the whole woods: a spot beneath a huddle of three apple trees that Henry had planted when he and Elsie had first moved to Wisteria. For many years, the trees had struggled to take hold, showing little signs of life, fighting to capture enough light to sustain growth. But, over recent years, the mighty trunks and flora had flourished, now evidenced by a collection of juicy, ruby apples.

'Where've you got all these from?' she asked, bending down, looking at the small collection of scrappy, meatless bones. 'You've been rooting in the bins again, haven't you? Just like Grandma said.'

Mary sat down, scrunching up her face, the collection of bones scattering the once settled soil. Some of the bones were the size of a standard ruler, feeling weighty in her palm, whilst others were delicate, and smaller than her finger.

'We'll have to hide all these, otherwise you'll get in trouble.' Mary brushed away some of the soil covering the bones, aligning one with her pinkie. 'It's smaller than my finger, look,' she said, holding the bone up to her hand before placing it in her backpack, along with a few other ones. 'We'll have to hide these somewhere where Dad won't look, and where you won't be able to get them.'

Mary put the bones in her bag before standing, brushing off the mud covering her knees and throwing her bag over her shoulder.

'Come on,' she said to Einstein. 'I know where we can hide them, a place where Dad will never find them.' Mary began to run back towards the lake, the morning dew causing the pale, wisteria petals to stick to her trainers. 'It's not much further,' she said, waiting for Einstein to catch up, leaves and twigs becoming stuck to his fur, draping from his under girth. Her destination came into full view. 'Here we are.'

Henry's shed looked more like a collection of tatty pieces of wood held together by rusting nails.

'There must be something in here that we can use to hide them in,' she said, kicking open the rickety door before taking a look inside. She edged herself into the gloomy, cobweb-ridden interior, years' worth of muck sprinkling over her head after being disturbed by the unexpected movement. She searched through her grandad's things, wafting the air, the dirt tickling her nose, threatening to produce a plume of sneezes.

'I've found something,' she announced, grabbing hold of her

old plastic, waterproof swimming bag before backing out and turning to show Einstein. 'We'll use this.'

Mary walked over to the wooden dinghy lying beached and broken on the bank; it had remained unused for years. 'I have a plan,' she began, tossing the empty swimming bag into the boat. 'We just need something to cut this with.'

She inspected the rope that was attached to the dinghy, following it back and loosening it from the tree trunk to which it was secured. Henry was no knot-tying expert. And, although he had often enjoyed sporting a captain's hat, on the few occasions he had been captain, he had experienced a calamity of some sort. As such, Elsie had banned him from using the boat for anything other than a fancy garden ornament. It was a miracle that the boat was still seaworthy, having not been used in decades.

'Perfect!' Mary said, the last of the threads of rope untangling, releasing the boat and allowing her to push it towards the water. Once the dinghy reached the lake, she grabbed hold, the water encouraging it to drift away. She lined the dinghy up alongside the jetty before jumping in.

'Come on,' she encouraged, trying to get Einstein to jump in. She took a treat out from her pocket, which Einstein immediately leapt to grab, his heavy landing causing the boat to judder. Mary grabbed the one, shabby-looking oar, and plunged it through the water, her arms struggling beneath the weight.

'I think we'll hide the bones over there,' she announced, looking across the lake. She continued to paddle as best she could despite that fact that her hands were aching from holding the cumbersome oar.

She looked back towards the house, not realising how far away she'd already drifted. The surrounding collection of blooming wisteria acted to frame the lake, creating a picture suited to any watercolour painting.

'Here will do,' she said. Einstein settled, lying contentedly in the hull. Mary pulled tight on the drawstrings so that the bones couldn't escape.

She held the bag aloft. 'Perfect,' she said before dropping the plastic bag into the water. The bag disappeared, the surface of the water soon settling and the disturbance subsiding.

'They'll be safe down there, Einstein. Nobody will *ever* know you've had them.' Mary stroked the dog's soft, warm fur while he basked beneath the mid-morning sun. She put her backpack back over her shoulders. 'And even if the police come back and search the lake again, they'd just think they're from another of Grandma's pets.'

Mary stood up in the boat, attempting to turn around and row back. She noticed her grandma appearing on the lawn, stealing her attention, and balance.

Elsie looked out over the garden, searching for Mary, ready to ask her if she wanted salad cream or mayonnaise on her picnic sandwiches, holding a bottle of each in her hands.

'Mary!' she shouted, the sight of her granddaughter alone in the middle of the lake causing her legs to weaken. Mary, startled by the high-pitched scream, lost her balance altogether and tripped over her own legs. Her body arched backwards as she fell into the water.

The surface of the lake soon settled, and there was no sign of Mary.

Twenty-Three

ELSIE RAN TOWARDS THE LAKE AS FAST AS HER LEGS WOULD carry her. The distance between herself and the water's edge appeared to expand the more she struggled to run, her slippers coming off and her glasses falling onto the jetty. She threw herself into the water, the perishing temperature sending her organs into shock, the water attacking her body sharper than a million pinpricks. Her mouth spluttered and she tried to keep herself afloat, having not swum a length in nearly fifty years.

Elsie had never wanted the bloody dingy, but went along with Henry just to keep him quiet, like she did on so many occasions. Henry had a romantic notion that they could both use the boat and have picnic lunches during the long summer afternoons. During their maiden voyage, however, Henry had experienced severe cramp in his leg and, amid the commotion, one of the oars fell into the water. Elsie experienced a terrible bout of sea sickness, and both were stranded for hours until they managed to paddle to the jetty. She had vowed never again to go into the lake.

That vow had now been broken.

'Mary! Mary!' she shouted, unable to see her granddaughter. 'Where are you?'

Elsie continued to swim, her arms flapping through the water, trying to reach the boat. The weight of Mary's limbs dragged her further beneath the surface of the lake. She opened her eyes, but the darkness stole her sight. A vague noise registered in her ears, whilst her brain continued to be paralysed by the cold blast attacking its delicate core. Her entire body was swallowed by the drag, and each bone throbbed beneath the shock of the chilling temperature. The further she was sucked beneath, the more she thought about Lucy and her grandad.

She could see the faces of both her sister and her grandad. The images were clear, more vivid than ever before. It was as if they were right before her. She held out her arms to grab hold, ready to take them home, but, as she did, they both disappeared. She looked again through the muddy water, but their faces had gone.

The bleakness of the bottom of the lake hindered Mary's perception, her eyes searching for light, but seeing nothing. Her arms and legs thrashed in an attempt to try and locate the surface, swirling her body in a useless cycle. In the panic, her mouth opened, attempting to splutter for breath, her lungs running out of oxygen. Her mind became confused, near a state of irreparable starvation. In that moment, she could now hear her sister's voice, screaming at her. It sounded like Lucy was by her side, clear as day, urging her to fight. *Mary, swim.*

And so, that's what she did.

ABOVE WATER, ELSIE's frantic search continued. 'Oh, God, Mary! Mary!' she continued to scream, her clothes and apron hindering her efforts to wade through the water. Her ageing legs felt heavy, her arthritic limbs threatening to drag her body below. She scanned the surface in a spinning motion, now unsure of the exact location where Mary had entered, the boat having moved.

'Mary, where are you?' she shouted. Einstein barked, watching Elsie's approach, his agitation rocking the boat, threatening to capsize.

Mary's head suddenly exploded above the surface of the water, her mouth erupting like a volcano. Water sprayed out of her nostrils and she spluttered in an attempt to expel the water flooding her lungs.

'Help!' she shouted, her arms wrestling with the water, trying to keep her body afloat.

Elsie looked around and yelled. 'Mary, grab the boat!' All Elsie could do was watch Mary struggling to keep afloat, her arms reaching out in vain. 'It's behind you, Mary. Turn around!'

Mary scrambled through the water, the remaining ounce of strength surging through her blood unable to keep her body afloat, the additional weight of her backpack dragging her beneath the surface once again.

Elsie reached out, grabbing her granddaughter by the arm, and pulling. 'I'm here, Mary! I've got you.' She wrapped one arm round Mary's waist and dragged her to the dinghy.

Mary grabbed hold of the boat. 'I'm sorry, Grandma...' she said, pulling herself inside and lying breathless next to Einstein. Her eyes scanned the boat, looking for Lucy.

Where did she go? I heard her. I definitely heard her. I saw her face. It was Lucy, it definitely was.

Through floods of tears and whilst still coughing up water, Mary looked around for Lucy, convinced she would be there, waiting for her to appear. Her sister's voice had been so clear, so distinctive. The image that Mary saw of Lucy remained clear in her mind. Lucy wasn't wearing a lilac dress anymore; she was wearing a pink T-shirt and yellow shorts. Lucy's hair was now long, but she was holding Penelope Pickles in her hand. Lucy was smiling, and waving, the same smile that she'd always had.

The disappointment of Lucy not being in the boat felt overwhelming. Mary refused to believe it wasn't true. She'd seen her. She'd heard her. She'd almost been able to reach her hand. Mary closed her eyes and opened them again, just to double check. But there was still no sign of Lucy.

'Goodness me,' said Elsie, yanking herself out of the water and into the boat. She struggled to get herself into the dinghy, sitting up when finally succeeding, trying to catch her breath. She wrung out the ends of her dress, the water forming pools in the base of the boat. With sodden hair, no glasses and no makeup, Elsie had aged in the past five minutes, making her look well over a hundred.

'You could've drowned, Mary,' she said in a soft voice, shaking her head in bemusement. 'Don't you know how dangerous the water is?' Mary didn't reply. She pulled her body up, keeping her head lowered, shivering from the cold.

Mary didn't seem to care that she'd almost drowned. She felt like jumping back in, just so that she could see and hear her sister again. 'Sorry, Grandma. I was hiding some bones that Einstein had found in the bins. I wanted to hide them before Dad comes home.' She rubbed her eyes, realising that she'd lost her glasses.

'What if something had happened?' said Elsie. 'What would I have told your mum and dad, eh?' She moved to sit closer to Mary. 'You could have drowned. We could have lost you.'

'Sorry, Grandma, it won't happen again,' replied Mary, throwing her arms around Elsie, squeezing tight. The picturesque lake returned, suitable once again for any artist to capture the precious moment. 'Please don't tell Mum and Dad. They'll be so cross.' Mary started to cry, looking back into the water and holding onto her grandma.

Where are you, Lucy? Come back. Please, come back. Mary tried to remember every detail of her sister's face, worried that, after such a brief encounter, she'd forget what she looked like. She held on to the image of Lucy with long hair in her pink T-shirt and yellow shorts.

'If you *promise* never to go near the lake again, I won't tell them,' Elsie replied, kissing Mary's head, and cupping her face with her wet hands. 'Gosh. You're so pale, like you've seen a ghost. It'll be the shock, as well as the cold attacking your body.' She began rubbing Mary's arms and blowing into her hands. 'Let's get you inside to warm up.' Elsie looked around for the missing oar, which had also gone overboard. 'How on earth are we going to get back?'

'We can use our arms instead,' said Mary. She plunged her hands into the cold lake, scooping back the water, guiding the boat towards the jetty. Elsie followed suit, lying on her front and pushing her arms through the water.

Mary stopped and looked around. 'Grandma, I must've lost my glasses,' she said, realising the spectacles weren't in the boat. 'What am I going to do?' The thought of her mum finding out was causing her additional panic.

'We'll tell your mum you lost them in the woods whilst walking Einstein,' Elsie suggested, winking. The boat finally made it to the shore. 'Anyway, I have an old pair that you left here last summer that you can use.'

After a few minutes of paddling, the boat finally reached the edge of the lake.

'You run inside and get dry,' said Elsie, helping Mary out of the dinghy. 'Your mum and dad might be home any minute, and if they see you like this, then we'll both be in big trouble. I'll put the boat back where it belongs so they don't notice.'

They needn't have rushed. Martha and Hank hadn't gone to the supermarket; they'd stopped off for a drink at the Black Fryer, just when it had opened its doors at the stroke of eleven. They didn't return home until tea time, slurring some excuse about having thought of somewhere to look for Henry. Of course, they hadn't found him, because they hadn't been looking. They'd spent all afternoon getting drunk, Martha rationalising that it was alright because she'd been through a terrible experience the previous day. She just couldn't help herself; and, after a day spent listening to her screams, Hank gave in to her demands.

Upstairs in the attic, Mary wrapped her shivering body in a warm towel. Her teeth were still chattering, and her skin prickly. Elsie came up with a mug of hot chocolate, kissing Mary on the cheek.

'Are you sure you're okay?' she asked, sitting next to Mary on the bed.

'I'm fine, Grandma. Just a bit cold.'

'Well, this will help once its inside warming your cockles,' she replied, taking a sip from her own steaming mug. 'I'm going to go and have a lie down, just until your mum and dad come home. Come and get me if you need me.'

When Elsie left her bedroom, Mary changed into some dry clothes and took out the contents of her wet backpack. She placed Penelope Pickles on the window ledge to dry out.

With an image of Lucy still clear in her mind, Mary decided to open up her sister's chest of drawers. She rummaged through Lucy's belongings, things that Martha had ordered her never to touch. And she never had, until today, when she no longer cared what her mum said. Mary had caught her mum on several occasions sifting through Lucy's belongings. So, if it was okay for her, then it was okay for Mary.

Despite the passing of time, Mary felt sure she could smell her sister in the fabrics once the first drawer was pulled open. Some of the items hadn't been washed since Lucy had last worn them, and these were the clothes that Martha felt most precious about, because she, too, believed that she could still smell Lucy in the material. Some of the clothes had grass stains where Lucy had fallen whilst playing on the lawn, and other items, which had obviously been her favourites, were faded, having been washed and worn with such frequency.

Mary held a faded pink T-shirt against her body, recalling pictures from her mum's photo album of Lucy wearing it. It didn't fit Mary now, but she didn't care, and that didn't stop her from squeezing it over her head. Wearing her own pyjama shorts, Mary looked in the mirror; once again, she saw her sister looking back.

She closed her eyes and prayed for Lucy or her grandad to call out again, or wave and smile; this time, Mary would grab quicker, and never let them go. Or, better still, when Mary opened her eyes, Lucy and her grandad would have returned. Mary held her hands to her eyes and waited, kneeling in the middle of the room.

There was no voice, and there was no image of her sister. So, Mary waited some more. She could hear the birds; she could hear the trees knocking against the roof; she could hear Einstein breathing in the corner; and she could hear her grandma snoring downstairs. The only thing she couldn't hear was Lucy's voice. After ten minutes of waiting, Mary removed her hands from her face, her eyes squinting at the change in brightness. Once her eyes adjusted, she looked around the empty room, her shoulders falling heavier than an avalanche.

Still wearing Lucy's top, Mary got out her colouring book and pencils and spent the afternoon drawing pictures of her sister. Lying on her tummy, beneath the sun that was splashing in through the window, she brought her sister back to life on paper. Her fingers gripped the pencil and her hand began to sketch, enabling her to transfer the image she had seen so vividly in her mind and recreate it on paper.

Very soon, there were decorated pieces of paper covering the entire floor, enough to create her own private homage to Lucy. Mary's body reacted in exactly the same way as it had done years previous, when the pair had hidden from each other. Mary would know when she was getting closer to Lucy simply by the tingling sensation on her skin. The delicate hairs on her body stood on end. Her heart slowed. Her hands felt warm. And she didn't feel alone. She didn't feel lonely.

Whilst sat alone in the bedroom, Mary's body tingled; and, in a way, her sixth sense wasn't wrong. She spent the afternoon surrounded by her sketches, and what felt like her sister, right there in person, in their bedroom. She prayed that the fleeting feeling of closeness would never go away; but, inevitably, at some point, it would.

Twenty-Four

THE DREADED DAY HAD ARRIVED.

Martha hung her head out of the car passenger window. Hank forced the banger to charge like a bullet down the third lane of the motorway, the car's undercarriage vibrating in protest at the speed, close to breaking point. Martha closed her eyes and allowed the force of the wind to distort her features. The strength of the gust slapped her cheeks, and her nose and eyes seeped simultaneously. Despite the power of the wind against her skin, she remained oblivious to the brutal battering; her senses numbed by one too many nightcaps the previous evening.

Martha's demise had begun the moment she had witnessed Mary standing at the front door, dressed identical to Lucy. That, coupled with the fact that it was the anniversary of the day on which Lucy had gone missing, was too much for Martha to bear. And so, in an attempt to numb the pain, she jumped head-first off the wagon.

After vowing never to touch another drop only hours previous, and having emptied the house of all her secret alcohol stashes, at some time close to 1.30 am, and before even a drop of liquor had passed her lips, she had threatened to kill herself. That was unless Hank didn't go and buy at least three bottles of booze, one of which she specified had to be a bottle of gin. Maybe Martha's threat was just bravado. Or maybe she meant it. Who knew? However, in the moment, Hank couldn't be sure either way, and so he bowed down to her incessant demands and brought back enough alcohol to drown her sorrows, her soul and her sanity. It was, after all, a better outcome than suicide.

With her head still hanging out of the window, the frontal wind did little to induce life back into her sodden sails. Martha looked like she was clinging to life. She sported a pale and pasty complexion. Dark bags hung below her bloodshot eyes, a druggie's complexion. She felt exhausted, to the point of being unable to think logically. Her body felt disorientated, and the motion of the car wasn't helping.

MARY FELT MISERABLE, sitting slumped in the back of the car. 'Are we nearly there yet?' she moaned, having asked the same question only moments earlier.

Despite looking in the rear view mirror several times to snap at Mary, Hank had failed to spot Perry Golifer tailgating, his car always strategically shielded behind another vehicle.

It was Martha who snapped this time. 'Mary, if you ask that question one more bloody time, I swear I'll make your dad stop the car and you can walk the rest of the way. Do you understand?' She stuck her head back out of the window.

Mary watched her mum's head hanging in the air, embarrassed by the reaction of the people travelling on the inside lanes. *I'd rather walk than watch a lorry take your head off.* She looked down at her clothes, slumping further down in her seat.

'Why do I have to wear this dress? You screamed at me when I put my dress on as a surprise.'

'Because, Mary, there's going to be reporters, and lots of photos being taken today,' replied Hank, his foot continuing to apply pressure on the pedal. 'So just for a few hours, it's really important that you look exactly like your sister, so everybody will know what Lucy looks like now, if they happened to cross paths with her. Mum won't be cross today, because she knows it's you. It won't be a shock, or surprise.'

'But I always look like Lucy, we're identical.'

'I know that, Mary,' said Hank. 'But people will only remember Lucy the way she looked six years ago, when she was four. If they see you wearing that dress and bow, they'll have a more up-to-date image of how Lucy will look now, facially, six years on. Your face has changed and developed so much, and Lucy's will have done in just the same way. Do you understand?'

Mary tried to rip the dress that her mum had bought, the dowdy, lilac material making her skin shiver. It was more like a church dress than a pretty dress you'd want to wear to a party.

'And now that you've had your hair cut,' added Hank, 'it couldn't be more perfect.'

Perfect? What's perfect about any of this? thought Mary, looking out of the window again.

'Lucy won't be wearing a dress if somebody sees her now,' said Mary. 'She'll be wearing a pink T-shirt and yellow shorts, like most normal girls our age.'

'You don't know that, Mary,' snapped Martha, who had been listening to the conversation, ready to bite at anyone, and anything.

'It could be worse, Mary,' said Hank. 'I could be asking you to wear a shower cap on your head, like Grandma.' He looked again in the rear-view mirror, casting a glance at the spotty shower cap wedged on Elsie's head. 'I can't believe you've come out looking like that, Mum.'

'Your father will recognise me in an instant wearing this,' replied Elsie. 'And, you never know, he may just follow the crowd today and turn up with everyone else on the beach. I want to make sure he would recognise me.' She chuckled softly to herself. 'Your father had a great fear of being late for anything, it drove me mad. So, if I know him, I bet that all this time he's just been making his own way to the beach so that he wouldn't be the last one to arrive.'

THE SECLUDED, PICTURESQUE beach at Crest Cove was where the anniversary of Lucy Lane's disappearance was always marked by her grieving family. Only a few days before Lucy vanished, she'd been playing with her red butterfly kite at Crest Cove, running back and forth along the beach, barefooted with the sand scratching her skin. Lucy's neck must've ached because, for over half an hour, she had held her face to the sky, her smile following the kite's snaking flight path. Lucy's effortless smile was one in a million; Mary and Lucy were beauties, there was no doubt about it. They had the whole package; an inner beauty that couldn't be hidden or taken away, nor was it in need of enhancement. And they were identical; two for the price of one.

The white, sandy beach at Crest Cove was situated thirty minutes west of Wisteria, and off the beaten track. Its remote location and lack of nearby amenities meant that the beach wasn't frequented by the usual mob of summer tourists looking to have fun in the sun, which is why the Lane family loved the area. Crest Cove had always felt like their own private playground. If you admired the Cove from one of the winding side roads running parallel, you would just see endless ripples of turquoise ribbons appearing in the hazy distance. On humid, summer days when the sun was dazzling, you couldn't always decipher where the sky ended and the sea began. This ocean tranquillity at Crest Cove was only interrupted by splashes of white where the timid waves broke, and the sound of seagulls soaring the skies. Crest Cove backed on to an expanse of billowing, pale sand dunes. There was a modest car park, which had only ever been visited by the ice cream van on two occasions in all the years that the Lane family had been visiting.

Although the sun was breaking through the scattered collection of clouds, early morning mist hung low over the motorway. The Lane family made their getaway, a cool chill lingering around their bodies, the ancient car taking too long to warm. Twenty minutes in, and Hank finally released his foot from the throttle and left the motorway, entering onto the deserted back road that would lead to their destination. Perry Golifer was still tailgating. He wasn't about to miss a day at the beach. With his sun hat and camera at the ready, he knew exactly what day it was, what it signified, and what was going to happen.

'What've you got there?' asked Elsie, seeing Mary rooting in her backpack.

'Just stuff, Grandma,' she replied, her fingers fumbling with a stray bone that she'd found trapped at the bottom, which, despite her best efforts, wouldn't pull free. 'Do you think we'll find Lucy or Grandad today?' Mary gazed into the distance, looking down onto the beach when it came into view, the morning mist finally lifting to reveal the beautiful stretch of virgin sand.

'I hope so, Mary,' replied Hank, he too looking at the beach. 'With you looking like you do, and with all these photos we have of Grandad, someone is bound to have spotted one of them. Imagine if we find them both? Now, wouldn't that be a spectacular day?' He navigated the car down the winding track that led to the beach, and Martha finally dragged her head back inside, sufficiently sedated by nature.

'Do you remember the red butterfly kite that Lucy loved?' asked Mary, scanning the beach, wishing so desperately to magically spot her sister still playing on the sand, like time hadn't moved on. Mary hadn't been a fan of kite flying, and now regretted all the times her parents had told her that she hadn't wanted to join in with the fun.

Given the chance to do it all over again, Mary would fly a kite with her sister every single day, until her arms ached and she could no longer hold the string. Even if it was raining, hailing or snowing, as long as there was a sufficient breeze, Mary would choose to play alongside Lucy for a whole lifetime.

'I do, Mary,' Martha was quick to reply. 'We came here every summer, and all your sister wanted to do was fly that kite.'

Mary looked out of the car window, her dad pulling into the car park, a crowd of people gathering, each one holding a lilac balloon with a purple bow fastened to the string.

'There's a big crowd this year,' Mary was first to announce, scanning the faces already congregating on the beach.

Hank turned off the ignition. 'Brilliant. Just what we want. It means that people aren't forgetting about her.' He took a cautious look across at Martha, scared that even just his glance could shatter her exterior, her fragility evident for all to witness.

Mary held back the tears she could feel building. She felt the lilac bow in her hair, making sure it was positioned just how Lucy had once worn hers. *Is this right, Lucy?* she thought, wanting for everything to be perfect, and for her parents to be proud of the performance she was about to put on.

The exposed seafront encouraged the wind to roll in off the Atlantic. With no barriers to break its force, the gusts swooped around the family when they got out of the car. The strength of the wind dislodged Elsie's flimsy shower cap, the plastic hat cartwheeling through the air until out of sight over the dunes. Elsie was too preoccupied to bother about her lost headwear, trying to regain her dignity by holding down her skirt each time the wind attempted to flash her underwear.

'Are you sure you're up for this?' asked Hank, steadying his wife's unstable stance. 'You can always stay in the car.'

'What, and have people think that I didn't bother this year?' snapped Martha. 'Or that I, Lucy's own mother, have given up on her? If I have to drag myself down there on all fours, then that's what I'll bloody well do.' Hank wished he hadn't asked.

Martha leant against the car, her head spinning faster than a whirlwind. Her vision remained blurred and her temples ached every time she squinted to focus. This year, the occasion was a formality to endure, and one in which Hank would be taking the lead. If you compared the previous year's publicity photos taken of the family on July 17th, the decline in Martha's well-being had been publicly documented. In previous photos, there was more meat to her bones, unlike this year where her clothes simply hung from her frame. In photos taken in earlier years, Martha had life in her face, her appearance was immaculate, and she looked like someone desperate to find her daughter. Six years on, and she just looked desperate.

Hank took the helium balloons out of the boot before handing them out. 'Right, is everyone ready?' he asked, facing the beach and drawing a sharp intake of breath.

'It's a perfect day for kite flying,' said Mary, holding onto her lilac balloon and Einstein's lead, watching the balloon bobbing about in the breeze.

'You're right, it is,' Hank replied. He looked down onto the crowd, trying to force away his emotions. He, too, couldn't help but imagine Lucy playing on the beach.

'Mum, I need you to watch Mary. These lot are going to be all over Martha and me like flies,' he requested, watching each journalist get out their notepads and voice recorders. Elsie didn't reply, still trying to maintain her dignity, wishing she'd worn trousers, not that she owned any. She was a dress person – or, at a push, she could wear a knee-length skirt and blouse.

The chattering that could be heard from the crowd stopped, the assembly of people turning to look at the family. The Lane family looked out into the crowd and noticed some familiar faces looking back. The ones who had attended every year came over to hug Martha and shake Hank's hand, trying to hide their sadness and sympathy beneath a smile. With outstretched arms, one lady approached, eager to be one of the first to console.

'How are you?' the lady asked, wrapping her arms around Martha. Aware of the alcohol still draining from her body, Martha reluctantly pulled away from the embrace that, for just one moment, felt better than alcohol. The stranger's sympathy was the exact sedative that Martha required and, for just a few seconds, she felt no pain.

Mary stood back. *Please don't hug me,* she thought, witnessing another lady fast approaching in her direction.

'Mary? My goodness, haven't you grown?' the lady in question commented, walking over to where Mary was standing, bending down until reaching eye level. 'I knew you and your sister when you were just toddlers. You'd come into my shop and get a bag of penny sweets each,' she said, her shoulder-length, white hair moving in the wind. 'Even then, I couldn't tell you apart. Sometimes, to trick me, you'd pretend to be each other, and then I got *really* confused,' the lady continued, a smile infecting her face, the fond memory coming back to life.

I don't remember you, or your penny sweets.

'The easy way to tell us apart was by this mark, just here,' explained Mary, pointing to a mark on the back of her right hand. 'I cut my hand on some glass when I was little, and it left this scar. Lucy doesn't have a scar like mine, so it was easy to tell us apart,' she continued. 'And my mum would dress me in yellow clothes, and my sister in lilac. So that was another way to tell us apart.' She hoped the lady would now leave.

The lady made a final attempt to break down Mary's barrier. 'I love your dress, it's especially pretty.'

Mary looked down at the dress, the material dancing around her shivering legs. 'I'm wearing it for my mum. She says it's to help people see what Lucy will look like now, you know, in case they spot her anywhere.' Mary diverted her gaze and searched for her parents, who had already got caught up in the commotion.

'Well, you look lovely, and so does your dog,' said the lady. 'I don't recall you having a dog last year.'

Hank waved his arm, indicating for Mary to follow. 'Come on,' he mouthed, clearly cross upon witnessing Mary standing far away, while looking around for Elsie, who was nowhere to be seen.

'I best go.'

The journalists did their job at directing Martha and Hank into place, each wanting to be the first to ask a question. It was a jostling match for who would spin the best story the following morning, and sell the most papers. Hank waved at Mary again, urging her to join him.

With inner loathing, Martha and Hank took their positions, centre stage, right in front of the semicircle of reporters. Mary reluctantly stood behind her mum, shielding herself within the ripples of the fabric of her dress, feeling uneasy as she peered out towards the sea of unfamiliar faces that were staring directly at her. Einstein posed for the cameras, too, standing on guard by Mary's side. Elsie emerged from within the crowd, standing to the left of Hank. She'd been looking for Henry, but without success.

Dazed and startled, Hank placed a steadying arm around his wife, dreading a headline in the morning papers reading 'Pisshead Parent Passes Out' or 'Wasted Wife Collapses'.

He cleared his throat in preparation, like any well-prepared public speaker.

'Thank you for coming, everyone. It means a great deal to my family that you've all gathered here today.' He paused for a moment and looked down, taking a deep breath. The first sentence of his speech hadn't meant to sound like he was about to read out a eulogy, but it did nonetheless. 'As you all know, our daughter, Lucy, went missing on this exact day six years ago. She was just four years old.'

Hank took hold of a flyer and held it aloft. 'This is a photo that was taken of Lucy only hours before she vanished, before she was taken from us.' His trembling hand was visible for all to see. The barrage of emotions that he kept hidden beneath the surface threatened to release. He took a breath, held back his tears and continued with what he wanted to say. 'Lucy is our daughter. Before she was torn away from her family, she was a healthy, happy four-year-old little girl with everything to live for. Not a single day goes by where we don't think about her, wonder where she is, and if she's being looked after. The not knowing where is she is torturous, and I wouldn't wish it upon any parent.' Hank cast a glance at the photo clenched between his fingers. 'The day that Lucy was taken, was the day that our world fell apart, and until our little girl is returned, our lives will never be the same. For as long as I live, I will never give up searching for her.' Hank looked to the floor, drew in a prolonged breath, quickly wiped his eyes with the back of his hand, and looked directly into one of the journalist's cameras pointing directly at him. 'I would like to address the person, or the people, responsible for my daughter's disappearance,' Hank's voice wavered, his emotions threatening to sabotage his words. 'I just want you to know that I will never stop until I find my daughter. You should always feel the need to be watching over your shoulder because I won't give up. So, I beg of you, please let her come home, to us, her rightful family who love and miss her more than anybody could ever understand.' He then took hold of Mary's hand and encouraged her out from behind Martha's shadow, placing her centre stage, and in the spotlight. 'And this is Mary.'

Mary could feel the crowd scrutinising her appearance whilst she stood in the full glare of the limelight, being paraded like a circus act. Reporters snapped away and flashes of light flickered from the crowd, multiple photos being taken.

'This is how we'd expect Lucy to look today,' said Hank. 'Mary and Lucy are identical twins, so it gives you all a clear vision of what Lucy will look like today.' As soon as Hank released his grip, Mary retreated into her shell, shielding herself once again in Martha's shadow.

'My family and I think about Lucy every single day and feel in our hearts that, one day, she'll be brought back home, where she belongs,' Hank continued, trying to control the emotions that lingered just beneath the surface.

Mary felt guilty.

Whilst she listened to her father's speech, she realised that, on some days over the past six years, she actually hadn't thought about Lucy at all because she'd been too busy playing and having fun.

I don't think I thought about you the day I went to London Zoo with school. I was too excited to see the giraffes. And there was the day I went to Megan Russell's ninth birthday party. I don't think I thought about you that day, either, because we went bowling and then out for tea at McDonald's. I'm sorry, Lucy, for not thinking about you every day. But I will from now on, I promise.

'We ask that you, too, never stop thinking about our daughter,' Hank continued. 'Wherever you go, in this country or abroad, please keep a lookout for Lucy, and help us to bring her home.'

The moment had arrived; and, this year, Hank was dreading it more than all the years previous.

It was question time.

One reporter, who'd almost forced Hank down the beach and placed him into position, put his hand up and asked his question without waiting to be acknowledged.

'Mr Lane, I heard a rumour that you'd had an altercation with Perry Golifer in a local pub. Can you confirm if this is true and, if so, tell us what the fight was about?' Hank wanted to reach over and plant a punch right in the middle of the smug reporter's oversized forehead.

'I believe many people in the past have punched Perry Golifer. Unfortunately, I'm not one of them. Are there any other more *relevant* questions?'

A woman wearing a chiffon scarf with a beehive hairstyle raised her hand faster than a NASA rocket could take off. 'Mrs Lane, I believe you've recently been admitted to Herons Hook. Is that to treat a dependency on alcohol or drugs?'

Martha resembled a dear caught in dazzling headlights. She tried to hide her hands behind her back, concealing the shakes still coursing through her body, her addicted organs craving just one more drink.

'I don't see how that's relevant,' said Hank. 'We're here to publicise the disappearance of our daughter, not to endure a public interrogation regarding our personal lives. I wouldn't dream of asking you something so personal. Are there any other questions?' He scanned the crowd, trying to spot anyone with a sympathetic face. He pointed to a man holding a can of Coke rather than a notepad or camera.

'The police recently searched your parents' lake. What were they looking for?'

'Who knows?' replied Hank angrily.

Hank pointed to a man who'd had his arm raised the entire time. It was Chester Harrington, the Great White Shark in the Finchley journalist circle. Chester took no prisoners when it came to getting the story he wanted. He knew exactly what sold papers, and anything connected to the Lane family had always boosted his sales. Chester played the game to a tee when conducting interviews. He acted professional and polite initially, until he wasn't getting what he wanted, at which point he'd soon switch his method of attack.

'Yes, you at the back.' Hank urged him to speak.

'Where's your father today?' asked Chester. 'Doesn't he usually make the trip back to Crest Cove too?'

On hearing the question, Elsie scanned each face in turn again, hoping that she'd catch sight of her husband. Tears began to fall and she bowed her head when she realised that Henry still wasn't part of the annual congregation.

Hank braced himself. 'My father isn't well. He's confused and vulnerable. We believe he's somewhere in Finchley and has lost his bearings, struggling to find his way home. So, we're asking for everyone to remain on the lookout, and notify the police should you happen to see him.'

With his arm sill raised, Chester, fired another question. 'Just to clarify, there are now *two* members of your family missing?' he asked, raising his wiry eyebrows. 'A little concerning, wouldn't you agree, Mr Lane?' Chester had Hank by the neck. 'An outsider looking in would be pointing the finger at yourself, your wife and your mother, surely? So, I'll ask this question on their behalf, Mr Lane. Are you, your wife, or your mother responsible for both disappearances?' There were heckles from the crowd and other noises signalling support for the reporter's astute observations.

Trying to keep a brave face, Hank willed himself to say something in reply.

'I'll think we'll leave it there,' said Hank. 'Please take some posters and hand them out wherever you can, and thank you to everyone for coming. We appreciate your support.'

Martha signalled for Mary to walk through the crowd, taking hold of Einstein's lead and insisting her daughter parade herself whilst handing out leaflets.

Mary mingled. She felt the stares and pitying looks from every person she passed. They didn't talk to her; what was there to say? Towards the back of the crowd, she caught sight of a figure standing alone in the distance, holding a balloon.

Why's that person standing so far back?

Mary began to walk towards the figure, intrigued by the mystery supporter and desperate to escape all the gawking. Elsie was chatting to anyone that would listen about Henry, and Martha and Hank were commencing game two with the reporters, ensuring that they were going to print something that was relevant and based on facts.

'It's him, isn't it?' Mary whispered to herself, squinting whilst trying to make out the figure on the edge of the dunes. 'He's come for me.' Her body immediately began to shake. Her mouth went dry and her stomach churned with anticipation. She'd waited for what felt like weeks for Perry to come, and now that he had, she was terrified.

She looked back towards the beach, her parents surrounded by reporters, and so she continued towards him, dropping the flyers when she was close enough to confirm it was him. The flyers drifted through the air like dropped confetti. The string of her balloon was still entwined around her fingers, strangling the skin as it pulled. Perry hid his camera in his bag and made sure his pockets were zipped up, the wind threatening to scoop away anything that it managed to catch.

Perry had planned this exact moment, having failed the previous years. He'd worn his disguise in order to blend into the crowd, and waited for his opportunity to strike. Having already successfully won Mary's trust, the hardest part had been achieved. All he needed to do now was take her, and she'd be gone, forever. It was perfect, the ultimate abduction during a time when the world was supposedly watching. He'd be remembered in history as the ballsiest bastard in town.

'She's coming,' Perry mumbled to himself as he watched Mary approach, his eyes returning regularly to Martha and Hank to ensure their attention remained diverted by the press and the crowd. Perry crouched so his body was hidden from view behind the sand dune greenery, his hand beckoning Mary.

Come on, Mary, just a bit further. He reeled her in, the loose member of the pack becoming an easier target to be picked off. Isn't that how nature worked? If he succeeded, and Mary went missing the very same day that her sister had, only six years apart, the tabloid headlines would surely be a dead cert. There would be photos of Lucy and Mary wearing matching lilac dresses, accompanied by the caption 'Vanishing Violets' or 'Now They've Both Gone'.

Twenty-Five

PERRY COULDN'T QUITE BELIEVE HIS LUCK. 'HI, MARY,' he began. 'I told you I'd find another opportunity for us to be together. I've missed you since I last spoke to you. Have you had your hair cut?' He eased his way into the conversation, conscious not to spook her, or to cause a scene.

She nodded. 'I was trying to make myself look like Lucy.' Mary looked over her shoulder.

'Your hair looks perfect, and you do look just like how I remember Lucy.' He scrutinised every inch of her, the missing piece to his collection. His lilac balloon hovered just above his head.

'Have you come to get me so that we can start to look for Lucy?' Mary asked. Perry moved closer, remaining stooped. 'I've been waiting.'

'I have come to take you,' Perry replied. 'I thought I could drive you home, and on the way back we can think about what we should do first.' He looked down towards the beach, watching Martha and Hank speaking to one person after the other in the distance, the congregation forming some kind of human cocoon around them. Perry loved the excitement. He loved the fear of being caught. He loved getting one over on Mary's parents. His pleasure was heightened. This, for him, was what it was all about. The chase. The thrill.

'My parents would be cross if I went home with you instead

of them.' She looked back, unable to spot her mum and dad anywhere. Her apprehension at being near Perry grew, he looked scary, even more so than she'd remembered. She thought about how angry her parents would be if she left, but then thought about how happy they'd be if she returned with Lucy. She looked at Perry.

'You promise we'll try and find Lucy?'

He smiled broadly. 'I promise.' Perry reached out to touch Mary's hair, repositioning the bow that'd fallen a little lopsided in the wind before taking hold of her hand.

'Then I'll go with you,' she replied. To stop herself from feeling so scared, Mary pictured herself playing with Lucy the following summer and how different their family trip to Crest Cove would be. She'd be running on the beach and flying her kite alongside her sister. Her kite would be bumblebee shaped, and have black and yellow stripes, and she would buy Lucy a new butterfly kite out of her pocket money, a rainbow-coloured kite butterfly with tassels falling from the wings.

'Are we going to go now?' she asked, trying to like the feeling of Perry's rough skin, his yellow-stained fingers sending shocks down her spine. She didn't want to hold his hand, and she tried to wriggle it free, but his grip was strong, and unyielding. She trembled beneath her flimsy clothes, the cold wind scooping up the dress, exposing her legs and sending a sharp chill all the way up through her body, igniting the roots of her teeth and causing them to chatter. In certain situations, Mary looked much younger than her ten years. Standing alone in the lilac dress, holding hands with a stranger, she looked like a child once again, instead of the young lady she'd been forced to develop into prematurely.

'Yes, let's go.' Perry glanced around as he stood up, his hands starting to shake. Pulling Mary away, the pair walked hand-in-hand back towards the dunes and further away from the sea front. His heart threatened to rupture and he glanced over his other shoulder, not quite believing his luck that they'd remained unseen by anybody. *Is it really going to be this easy?* he thought. He willed his legs not to pick up the pace too much. The excitement of the situation was just as he'd anticipated. Mary was holding his hand and no one took a second glance. He thought about what he was going to do with her first, once out of sight from everybody. He'd thought about little else for the past six years. He visualised in his mind exactly what he wanted to do, becoming lost in his own world already.

'Are you cold too?' she asked, feeling his body trembling, the crowd of people on the beach just about still in sight.

'I'm excited, Mary, not cold.' He pulled her closer, guiding her away, his pace quickening involuntarily. Mary flinched, unsettled by the forceful tug Perry placed on her arm, and accidentally released her balloon from her grip as she tried to wriggle her hand free from his.

'My balloon!' she shouted, turning to watch it float towards the sea, the wind scooping it up like a feather being propelled through the air. Mary heard her mum screaming in the distance, Martha's voice travelling along the wind upon realising her daughter was nowhere to be seen. Mary's lilac balloon floated over the crowd and soon got swept out to sea.

Perry released his grip as brashly as he had grabbed her and, before Mary or anybody knew it, he'd gone; vanished.

Mary looked all around, not willing to let go of an opportunity to find Lucy. She traced his footprints in the sand, but they stopped at the point where a pebbled path began. He'd vanished. Mary's hair swept across her face and her eyes suddenly produced a stream of tears. She stood alone for a few more seconds before giving up, and turned to walk slowly back towards her parents, unable to hide from or ignore the shouting voices that were now getting closer.

Mary appeared at the top of the dunes, now in full view of the crowd 'Mary! What are you doing?' raged Hank, running over and gripping his daughter by both shoulders. Martha, Elsie and Einstein followed close behind. The journalists also gravitated towards the scene, zoom camera lenses at the ready. This was a moment not to be missed; journalism gold.

'I let go of my balloon by accident,' she said. 'I wanted to try and catch it because I knew you'd be mad with me.'

Hank's anger erupted across his face, and he became unaware of the strength of his grip on his daughter's arms, the cameras zooming in on the public display of aggression.

You're hurting me.

'You stupid girl.' Hank released his grip, leaving indentation marks on Mary's skin. He turned to face Elsie. 'I thought I told you to watch her? Why weren't you watching her, for God's sake?'

Elsie pointed her finger in her son's face. 'Don't you dare blame me! I've been looking for your dad. Blame yourselves for once. You're not bloody fit to be parents, either of you.'

The sound of cameras clicking indicated that a raft of pictures were being taken, the journalists not knowing where to point their lenses first. Chester Harrington took a photo of Mary standing crying on her own. He took multiple photos of the heated argument breaking out between Hank and Elsie. And he got a close-up of Martha, capturing on film the very moment that she finally collapsed, an empty vodka bottle falling from her handbag.

Chester Harrington had his morning headline sorted – 'Martha Lane: Lame Parent'.

Hank heard the sound of the clicking camera shutters, turning to witness the pack of reporters watching his family at their lowest point. They had, quite literally, reached the bottom of the barrel. He flung his arms out, indicating for them to move.

'There's nothing more to see! You can all go now.' He grabbed Martha off the floor and helped her to her feet, checking her eyes before giving her a drink of water. Martha brushed herself down, straightened out her hair and forced life back into her face.

'I'm alright. I just felt dizzy,' she reassured. Mary stood crying.

'Mum's just exhausted,' said Hank, going over and putting an arm around Mary before kneeling in the sand in front of her. She flinched at his touch. 'And I'm sorry I shouted, and grabbed too tight. I don't care that you lost your balloon. I care about you.' He continued to hug her, and not because the cameras were still pointed their way, but in a genuine attempt to apologise. 'Sometimes, I get so wrapped up in things that I forget you're still only ten, and just my baby girl.'

In that moment, Hank couldn't quite believe what had happened to his family in such a short space of time. He'd lost a daughter, his wife was an alcoholic, his remaining daughter was scared of him, and his father had gone missing. This wasn't his life. This wasn't how things were supposed to pan out. Once he'd got married and had children, wasn't he supposed to live happily ever after? Wasn't that how the story went?

'It was my fault, not Grandma's,' said Mary. 'Don't be mad at her, Dad.'

Hank went over to offer a hug to his mum. It wasn't an apology, but, for Elsie, it was as good as.

'Sorry for what I said,' Elsie mumbled, only sorry in part for her choice of words.

'I think we're all sorry today, Mum,' Hank replied. He gave a sigh of despair. 'Come on, let's get these balloons released.'

Standing by the edge of the water and holding their balloons, Hank, Martha and Elsie all bowed their heads, saying their annual silent prayer before letting go of the strings. The balloons floated up toward the summer sun, tumbling into the distance on the changing wind. Soon, the lilac specks were almost untraceable in the iridescent sky.

Perry looked on from a distance having emerged from his hiding spot, swearing and kicking in anger, all the while watching Hank hugging his daughter.

That should be me.

He wanted to run down to the beach and snatch Mary from Hank's arms, taking her away, never to be seen again. Instead, he walked away, vowing that next time he wouldn't fail.

Down on the beach, with Elsie and Einstein in tow, Hank walked in between Martha and Mary, putting his arms around both, guiding them back towards the car. He squeezed their shoulders, trying to let them know that everything would be alright, even if he didn't know himself how life was ever going to get better. Nobody spoke, and yet the family of three was united, if only for a few moments. Had someone taken a picture now, the photo would have told a different story. Mary embraced the moment of security she felt and treasured the moment of silence.

As soon as Martha got in the car, she closed her eyes and her body shut down. Exhaustion and alcohol had drained every last ounce of life until all she was able to do was sleep. Hank was also quiet, concentrating on driving. He couldn't help but imagine what the front pages of all the local papers were going to be splattered with – an image of him grabbing Mary, or his wife collapsed on the beach next to an empty bottle of vodka. Either scenario served to raise his blood pressure, and he just hoped that something spectacular had happened in Finchley overnight that would take the heat off them. Highly unlikely.

Mary looked over to Elsie, sadness saturating her eyes. 'Grandad wasn't on the beach, was he, Grandma?' Elsie took a deep breath and took hold of her granddaughter's hand.

'No, Mary, he wasn't,' replied Elsie. 'Maybe he's just decided to nip out to buy you some chocolate buttons, because he knows they're one of your favourites, and now he's forgotten his way home. He gets so muddled. But soon, he'll remember where he is, and he'll find his way home.' She wasn't sure she believed her own words, but it was better than telling Mary what she really thought; that Henry's body was lying in a ditch somewhere, waiting to be found.

Elsie leant her head back on the rest, her eyes closed as she spoke. 'You know, I'm sure Penelope Pickles wasn't in the basement. I've been going over and over it in my mind.' Mary turned to look at Elsie, her grandma's words making her pulse race. 'You see, I know I'm getting forgetful, just like Grandad, so I made myself a note of what things I had of Lucy's so I wouldn't forget, and Penelope Pickles wasn't on that list.' Elsie didn't even have to open her eyes for Mary to know that the comment was directed towards her; nobody else was listening.

Mary fidgeted with her bag. 'You're right, Grandma, Penelope Pickles wasn't in the basement. I found her in the attic. She was stuffed at the back of the airing cupboard with all the Christmas decorations. I know I shouldn't have rooted through Lucy's things, but I miss her, and wanted to play with her toys, just for once.'

Mary was shaping up to being quite a proficient liar.

Christmas hadn't been celebrated at Wisteria since the year before Lucy had vanished. In fact, very few holidays or special occasions had been celebrated in the six years since her disappearance. The permanent cloud that hung above the house scared away any inclination to celebrate, and the feeling couldn't be shaken, not even by a raft of multicoloured fairy lights and garish baubles.

'I didn't want to tell Mum and Dad that I found it,' she whispered. 'I knew it would make them sad, and it wasn't going to bring Lucy home.' Elsie remained poker-faced, refraining from showing how she felt about the news.

Mary tried to wrap her grandma round her finger. 'Grandma, if you promise not to tell them that I lied about where I found Penelope Pickles, I promise not to tell them that you're starting to get a bit forgetful.' Elsie's body jerked at Mary's offer of blackmail. 'I can help to keep your secret so that they don't notice.'

Mary leant over towards her grandma when the song on the radio finished, and a commercial selling second-hand cars began. 'When you can't remember something, I could whisper the answer in your ear.' Elsie's eyes were still closed, but she was listening. Mary added to the deal. 'I don't want Dad to take you to live at Audley Lodge. If he knew about your forgetfulness, he wouldn't let you stay at home without Grandad. And it smells horrible at Audley Lodge, Grandma, doesn't it?'

There was a pause while Mary summoned up the courage to ensure that her grandma would keep her secret, ending her deal with the fatal blow, the blow that would be sure to seal the deal.

She checked to make sure her dad could not overhear, but he remained oblivious to their conversation.

'I know that Grandad was shouting the day that Lucy went missing,' she said quietly. 'Grandad wasn't asleep the whole time.'

Elsie's breath was stolen from her. She was winded. She wondered how Mary could possibly know about the shouting. Had she suddenly been able to recall hearing her grandad? What if she told Hank and Martha? What then? And what else had she remembered? Elsie wasn't prepared to have Henry's name questioned, especially as he wasn't home to defend himself. And she didn't want to go back on trial herself. She thought about what to say, but Mary got in first.

'But it's alright, Grandma, I'm good at keeping secrets and I won't tell. Grandad won't be able to remember why he was shouting, will he? And you don't know, either, do you, because you must've still been at the shop? So, nobody needs to know, do they?'

Elsie opened her eyes. 'I won't say anything if you don't.'

Twenty-Six

A PATHOLOGIST WORKING THE NIGHT SHIFT OPENED HIS instrument kit. His array of blades and tools appeared shiny, sharp and, as yet, unused, as they were placed on the awaiting table. Before commencing with the first dissection of the shift, he switched on the radio, eager to listen to his favourite midnight segment of *Stevie's Seventies Smashers.* Performing an autopsy wasn't quite the same without a bit of Slade blaring in the background. Autopsy acoustics.

The cold, naked body lay exposed on the autopsy table, ready to be examined. However, there weren't just the two of them present in the sterile room that night. Acting as witnesses to the autopsy were a gathering of ghosts, each spirit having emerged from a previous corpse that'd been dissected on the very same table. The spirits watched over as another deceased was about to join their alliance. At least, that's how the pathologist rationalised, talking aloud whilst performing his work. In his mind, it was much better to admit that he talked to ghosts than to admit that he talked to himself. But as far as most people were concerned, neither scenario was particularly great.

With his rubber gloves pulled up to his elbows and protective eyewear in place, the pathologist was ready to begin. He always started by visually inspecting the body's appearance, noting every little imperfection the deceased had fought their whole lives to conceal. No longer could the ugly, hair-ridden wart on a sagging buttock be masked beneath clothes. The pockets of cellulite that had gone unnoticed for decades, thanks to the clever usage of spandex, were now laid bare, every tiny dimple displayed. During an autopsy, even a person's moment of drunken madness could be seen, all their tattoos finally permitted their time to shine, as were any elusive polythelia. Even the most caring, respectful of pathologists would testify that, when a person dies, they leave their dignity at the door.

As the pathologist took hold of the organ knife and inserted it into the sternum, the doors swung open. The pathologist looked up to witness his bald assistant standing at the door, a loaded gurney at his side.

'Another one for you, boss. Looks set to be a busy one tonight.'

The new body waited in line. It was a Caucasian male. Late 70s. Stocky build. No identification found on his person. The next in line was, thus far, a John Doe.

TWO UNIFORMED POLICE officers approached Wisteria. The grandfather clock in Elsie's hallway hadn't long since struck two in the morning, the two, deep chimes rattling through the floorboards.

Only Mary awoke.

'They're here again.' She peered out of her bedroom window upon hearing the knock at the front door. She had gained a sixth sense over the years; she knew a police officer's knock when she heard one – assertive, loud, and incessant.

Einstein followed her to the window, standing at her feet, his twitching ears tickling her legs. She held Penelope Pickles in her right hand, gripping so hard that her knuckles turned white. *Are they here because of Lucy?* She tried not to cry, but the sight of the officers sent splinters of fear coursing through her body. *Or are they here because of Grandad?* She knew it could only be for one or the other. Penelope Pickles became illuminated by the outside security light that automatically switched on when detecting movement. Mary eased the window open, listening in on the conversation below. *Please don't let it be Lucy. I'll find her soon. I promise I will. I just need a bit more time.*

Sergeant Swift shook her head. 'I hate this bit. Worst part of the bloody job.' Mary could hear Swift's familiar voice, her own hidden silhouette above going unnoticed. 'I'll do this one, I think you did the last.'

Swift's hand rattled against the door, interrupting the nocturnal humming that hung over the misty lake.

Swift cleared her throat. 'Mrs Lane, can we come in?'

From her vantagepoint, Mary heard Elsie emerging out on the landing. The loose floorboard right outside her grandma's bedroom had creaked consistently every day for the past two decades, and had never been fixed.

Swift attempted to rouse the house once again. 'Mrs Lane, it's the police.'

Mary, with Einstein following, crept down on her attic stairs, listening in the shadows, her grandma making her way to the front door. Mary squinted, covering her eyes until they adjusted to the brightness of the hallway light.

At the front porch, Swift attempted a welcoming gesture, raising her hand and smiling when Elsie pulled back the curtain covering the door. 'We have some news, Mrs Lane,' she announced. 'Can we come in?'

Hank appeared at the top of the stairs, wrapping his dressing gown around his body. He also squinted his eyes, attempting to see who had dared to knock at such a startling hour. His face drained of all traces of life upon catching sight of the yellow and black uniforms.

'God. Is it Lucy?'

Still sat hidden on her stairs, Mary heard her dad's comment. She pulled her knees close to her chest, clenching Penelope Pickles, the cold air attacking her loosely covered body.

Hank raced down the stairs. 'Mum, for goodness' sake, open the door,' he demanded.

Swift tried again. 'Mrs Lane, can we come in?' This time, Elsie reluctantly cooperated, the small gap permitting a surge of fresh, cool air to flood through, rustling her nightgown, the material dancing around her naked, weathered feet.

'We have some news,' repeated Swift. By the look on Elsie's face, she had gathered as much.

Mary tiptoed down onto the main landing, pausing just outside Elsie's bedroom door. She tried to see past the two officers, hoping that Lucy would be standing behind them, having finally been found. *Where is she? Where's Lucy?* Her tears ran down her face. She couldn't prevent it; whenever she thought about seeing her sister again, she cried.

She tucked Penelope Pickles beneath her pyjama top, along with her arms, giving herself a hidden hug in an attempt to keep warm. *Please don't make me cry*, she thought, looking down at Swift.

Hearing the floorboards creaking, Swift looked up. 'I think it's best if we talk in private,' she suggested, looking at Hank, then looking back up the stairs to where Mary was hiding.

Mary stood, pressing her back against the wall, fearful her dad was going to be cross because she was out of bed, spying. He charged up the stairs like a bull.

'Have they found Lucy?' she asked. Hank didn't reply, but instead scooped his daughter up into his arms, carrying her up the attic stairs and back into her bedroom with Einstein faithfully following. 'Have they, Dad?' Hank held his emotions in check, forcing a brave front.

He placed Mary on her bed. 'It's nothing to worry about. Now, let's get you back in bed.' He tucked her in and made sure the duvet came right up to her chin.

The police are here and it's the middle of the night. Of course it's something to worry about.

Mary held her breath when her dad leant in to give her a kiss, the horrible, stale smell of alcohol making her flinch.

'Go back to sleep.'

Mary rolled over to turn away from Hank. 'Come and tell

me when you know if they've found Lucy, or Granddad. I'll be awake.'

Hank brushed Mary's hair away from her face; she could feel the tremble in his hand. He remained silent, turning to walk away.

'Promise me you will?'

Hank paused in the doorway before replying. 'I promise, Mary. I'll come and tell you.'

SWIFT AND THE other female police officer were waiting at the bottom of the stairs for Hank to reappear. Elsie remained clinging to the front door.

'I think we should go and sit down,' Swift suggested when Hank returned. 'Is it this way, Mrs Lane?' Swift pointed into the lounge. She knew the way, but was trying not to be presumptuous.

Elsie banged the door closed. 'I don't need to sit down. For God's sake, just tell me what it is. You come knocking on my door in the middle of the night, and then expect me to jump through your bloody hoops.' Elsie refused to move, despite Swift's insistence on her taking a seat. The other police officer manoeuvred herself so that she was now standing by Elsie's side.

'Leave me alone. Why are you standing so close?'

Swift took a breath and then exhaled as she spoke. 'We've found a body, Mrs Lane.'

Elsie, although inevitably prepared for such news, wobbled on her feet, trying to digest Swift's words. She opened her mouth to ask a question, but no words materialised. It was as if she had lost the ability to speak. Elsie had to concentrate on just being able to breathe, the pain coursing through her vital organs, sabotaging her ability to survive the shock. In the silence, which seemed to last a lifetime, the most insignificant thought ran through her mind. *I can remove that note stuck to the fridge reminding me to buy him some spam.* Elsie hated spam and only bought it for Henry. *One less sticky note to worry about.*

Hank asked his question. 'Is it Lucy?' Swift subtly shook her head, prompting him to take hold of his mum's hands. He pushed his fingers through hers so that they were interlocking. 'Dad?' Swift's silence acted as confirmation.

Where was he? What's happened to him? Who found him? So many questions tore through Hank's mind that he didn't know what to ask first, or what he wanted to know first.

'How did he die?'

'We don't know anything yet. It's too early to say.'

'Mum, come on,' said Hank, taking Elsie's hand. 'Let's go and sit down.'

She pulled her hands away. 'I won't sit down until they say what they have to say.'

'All we know is that a body has been found, Elsie,' said Swift. 'Although it's still very early days, we do know that it's a Caucasian elderly male, matching the rough age and build of your husband, Henry. I'm so sorry.'

Poised and ready, the police officer standing beside Elsie reached out and grabbed her, preventing Elsie's fragile frame from falling. Hank helped to assist his mum into the lounge, easing her into a seat.

Swift knelt in front of Elsie. 'I know it's a shock, but it's important that you continue to breathe for me, Elsie.' Deprived of oxygen, Elsie's eyes whirled in their sockets, her brain threatening to induce a blackout. 'Breathe, Mrs Lane.' Without Henry in her life, Elsie didn't want to breathe. 'Breathe, Mrs Lane,' said Swift again. Elsie took a forced inhalation, her lungs filling with oxygen before filtering it throughout her body.

'So, there's still a chance that it might not be my Henry?' she asked. Swift could do nothing else but nod.

'There is a high probability that it is, Elsie. But, until we get a formal identification, we just don't know.'

UPSTAIRS, MARY SMACKED her hand over her mouth, suppressing her reaction to Swift's statement, listening intently through a crack in her door. Tears streamed down her face. All she could picture was her Grandad Henry.

If Grandad is never coming home, who will put out the rubbish bins for Grandma when we're not here? Mary knew that it had always been Henry's job to put out the bins on the main road, ready for collection day; they were too heavy for Grandma. *And who will play snakes and ladders with me now?* Over the past few years, every time Mary had visited her grandparents, all she had done was play board games with Henry, her grandma insisting it would help with his memory. And, whenever Henry did get muddled and was unsure of how to play, Mary helped without him noticing. *It was Grandad's turn to choose which game we played next. Now he won't get a chance to pick.*

Mary remained hidden behind her door.

I wonder where they found him? I wonder where his body is now? Will I be able to see him again? Will he look the same?

She heard her mum getting out of bed, a thud echoing when her bare feet hit the floor. Martha's bedroom door swung open.

'Shush,' whispered Mary, tickling Einstein's head, trying to mute any sound from escaping. Unaware of her daughter hidden in the shadows, Martha made her way downstairs and into the lounge.

'What's going on?' She looked at Hank, then froze when she noticed the seated officers. 'Is it Lucy?' She began to cry, panic setting in, her mind predicting the officers' next words. Before anyone had a chance to respond, Martha repeated her question. 'It's Lucy, isn't it? You've found her, haven't you? Just bloody well tell me.'

Hank raised his head. 'It's Dad. They've found a body.' Martha pressed both of her hands against her face, her eyes flooding with tears, warm droplets of moisture rolling down her cheeks every time she blinked. She walked into the lounge and sat beside Elsie, putting an arm round her frail mother-in-law.

'Oh, Elsie. I'm so sorry.'

Swift interjected. 'It's not been confirmed yet. The body just matches the gender, age and build of Henry, and we have no other missing males matching his profile in this area. So, we need you to come to the morgue and make a formal identification. I'm so sorry.' Swift aimed her statement at Hank.

Elsie looked up. 'I don't *want* you to be sorry,' she barked, her lungs taking a deep breath, properly acknowledging the officers for the first time. 'If you hadn't wasted so much precious time searching my lake, then maybe you'd have found him in time. This is all *your* fault!'

The room fell silent and the police officers looked at one another for inspiration on how best to reply.

'My husband needed you,' continued Elsie. 'He needed help. I needed help, and all you did was assume something sinister had happened to him here, in his own home. You let the poisoned minds of everyone in this village cloud your judgement, and instead of getting out there and looking for him, you investigated me. *I've* looked after Henry every second for I don't know how many years. Have you *any* idea what that involves? Have you?' She was shouting now, scrutinising Swift's flawless face. 'And yet I know, deep down, that *you* still think that *I* could have harmed him.'

Swift took off her hat and took hold of Elsie's hand. 'I'm so sorry, Mrs Lane. We followed every possible lead and did our best given the information and evidence provided. I understand this must be a *very* difficult time.'

Elsie released herself from the officer's grip and began to walk out of the room. 'I'll never forgive you for this. My husband is dead, and you could have prevented it.'

'What happens now?' asked Hank, composing himself when Elsie was out of sight.

'One of my colleagues will escort you to make a formal identification of the body,' said Swift. 'Then we can be sure, either way.'

'I'll go and get dressed,' he replied whilst standing. 'I should go alone. Will you stay with Mum and Mary?' Martha nodded before leaving the room.

Hank walked out of the room. 'Give me five minutes to get ready.'

Unable to resist the temptation, Swift wandered around the lounge, much to the amazement of her colleague, who remained still and waited. Not knowing what she was looking for, but looking regardless, Swift perused. She knew the sensitivity of the situation, but all she was really doing in her own eyes was waiting, impatiently.

She saw a side table next to the window, the top covered with photo frames of various sizes, each one displaying a picture of Lucy. Having studied Lucy's face so much over the years, Swift knew without question it was her, and not Mary. *It's like a shrine,* she thought, picking up one photo frame and taking a look at the back. She unclipped the clasps, curious to see if the photo had been captioned. The words 'Lucy, aged two' were written on the back in pencil.

Swift continued to wander around the room, her eager eyes digesting every detail, her feet stopping at the small waste paper bin at the side of the recliner. She put on a glove before picking out a crumpled piece of paper.

Things to take to the allotment.

House keys

Coat

Plastic bag

Trowel

Knife

Socks

Twenty-Seven

AFTER HANK LEFT WITH SERGEANT SWIFT, MARY HAD pretended to be asleep when her mum stumbled into her room, presumably attempting to check that she was in bed. And, without even having to move her head off the pillow, Mary knew that her mum had been drinking again; she knew all the tell-tale signs by now. When drunk, Martha would always remove any shoes or socks she happened to be wearing, even in winter. As a result, the sound of her bare feet hitting the floor as she stumbled around was one that was all too familiar with Mary. She never asked her mum why she felt the need to remove her footwear, the reason didn't matter.

Another tell-tale sign that her mum had been drinking was her constant mumbling. Martha rambled for hours and hours to herself, usually until she passed out. To the external world, it appeared as though she was talking to nobody; like she was addressing an empty room. But Martha knew otherwise. Her drunken stupors led her to the gates of Narnia, and through to a world where she could speak with Lucy. When Martha was well-oiled, the conversations between her and Lucy always felt so real, as though Lucy was really sitting with her, having a mother-daughter chat. Martha would talk to Lucy about where she was, what she was doing, how she felt, and how much she was loved. Sometimes, you could see Martha moving her hand and, in her mind, she was stroking Lucy's hair.

The only other way to tell that she was drinking, if there was no bottle in her hand, was by her smile. There once was a time when Martha Lane beamed with an unyielding radiance; the lady who looked like she'd won the jackpot. If her car broke down on a dreary Monday morning, then so what? If her nail broke after just being manicured, it didn't matter. If someone stole her purse and all her worldly possessions, who cared? Not Martha. Anything could have happened in her life, and yet she would still have been the happiest person in the room because she had a loving husband, and adorable twin girls - the family she'd always dreamt of. As far as Martha was concerned, she had everything.

But Martha's smile was stolen from her face on the morning of 17th July, 1982. Then, for a few precious, intoxicated hours, when in her drunken mind her family was reunited, her smile returned.

The bottle of gin wedged in Martha's hand threatened to spill, as she desperately tried, unsuccessfully, to walk in a straight line across Mary's bedroom.

'I love you, Mary,' was the slurred string of words Martha attempted to voice. Mary wanted to be able to hug her mum and talk about how scared she felt about her grandad, about the body that had been found. Instead, she lay still, pretending to sleep. *Go away. Leave me alone.*

Martha staggered downstairs. She emptied the cupboards and searched the fridge, gathering up all the alcohol she could find. She even unearthed Elsie's bottle of hidden whiskey, grabbing hold before taking an immediate swig. Mary watched from the landing, pressing her face through the spindles. She knew what her mum was doing, she'd seen it all before. It was no use trying to stop her. There was no plausible way to prevent Martha from drinking, not once she had set her hands on alcohol.

During one of her more brutal binges, Martha emptied bottle after bottle, adamant that she wanted to stay for as long as she could in her Narnia Nirvana. Mary just listened and waited for her mum to pass out, which she always did, sooner or later.

On this occasion, it took Martha less than forty-five minutes to consume the required amount of alcohol in order for her body to collapse.

When it finally went quiet, Mary went back to her bedroom, listening out for her dad's return. She heard the clock downstairs indicate that it was four in the morning, the clattering chimes failing to drag Martha out of her alcohol-induced coma.

Einstein jumped down off the bed and walked towards the window, growling and wagging his tail.

'What's wrong?' Mary asked. 'Is Dad back already?' She crept across the room to look outside, a small fleck of light catching her attention. The light shone through the darkness, heading towards the lake.

'It must be Perry. He's coming back for me, isn't he?' Mary fumbled in the dark for her clothes, putting on anything she could find before grabbing her torch and backpack. 'Let's go.' She eased the door open and crept down the stairs before pausing on the main landing, pressing her ear against her grandma's door, avoiding the creaky floorboard. She peered through the gap in the door, watching whilst Elsie lay on the bed. Mary could tell her grandma had been crying, the bed was scattered with scrunched-up tissues. Emotionally exhausted, Elsie had cried herself to sleep. And she didn't want to ever wake up, not if the news that the body they'd found belonged to her darling husband. That news could wait, indefinitely.

In the kitchen, Mary saw her mum lying on the floor, her arms stretched out, an empty bottle resting by her side. She leant down and held her ear over her mum's mouth, feeling for her warm breath. Mary had watched her dad do this before, the feeling of relief only coming when Martha's breath escaped. She was alive.

Mary grabbed some keys and walked to the front door. 'Follow me,' she whispered to Einstein, making her way outside, locking the door and placing the keys in her pocket. The darkness made them invisible once the motion sensor light turned off. The air outside felt cool and Mary noticed her breath turning to mist every time it escaped past her lips. She fumbled to zip up her fleece before running through the woods, her small torch illuminating the way.

'Stay close, Einstein,' she ordered as his legs bounded through the darkness, navigating the concealed maze. Mary stopped to gaze beyond the trees in search of the flicker of light that she'd seen from her bedroom. 'I can't see the light.' Einstein's ears pricked at the sound of rustling in the nearby trees, causing him to respond with a low growl.

'Should we go over to his house instead?' Mary's heart galloped as the provoked wildlife released their nightly calls, the sounds echoing through their nocturnal patch of paradise, causing her to feel terrified. She continued to walk, the ground below remaining in darkness. Her legs broke out into a run, heading in the direction of Perry's ivy igloo.

I'm scared. Her kidneys worked hard to combat the sudden increase in blood pressure that had been brought about by her fear. She turned her head every few paces, the darkness stealing her sight. With her arms outstretched, scouring the way, she raided through the barrage of shadows being reflected off her torch. The wind cascaded through the trees, and the once silent, sleeping forest was now alive.

'Come on, Einstein,' she demanded. 'Are you still here?' Mary turned to ensure he obeyed and, as her body spun, she found herself becoming disorientated. Her eyes searched the woods, picking out nothing but tiny specks of light above, a sporadic stretch of stars breaking through the blackened barrier. 'Where are you, Einstein?' she asked, addressing the darkness whilst trying to figure out which direction she had travelled from. Standing still, Mary could hear nothing but her own frantic breath, the warm moisture releasing like smoke from a dragon.

A dog's bark in the distance acted like a beacon, encouraging her to follow the origin of the noise.

'Thank goodness,' she proclaimed, finally reaching the fence enclosing Perry's property, which also now housed Einstein. 'Do you think he's home?' she asked, 'It all looks dark, and there's no car,' she added whilst trying to look through the fence panel peep holes. 'I'm going to go and look,' she said, pushing a loose panel with her hands before crawling through. 'I've got to do it,' she mumbled to herself, unable to silence her doubts any longer, thinking of nothing but her grandad's jumper, her sister's doll, and how Perry had pulled at her hand in a way that made her want to cry and run away. Tears welled in her eyes, her hands were shaking and her heart pumped within her chest. Her eyes blinked in time with her heart, her pupils willing the sky to lose some of the darkness so that she wouldn't feel so afraid. The sense of fear filling her bones was greater than she'd ever imagined.

Einstein lay down, a low-level whimper of unease projecting into the night. He remained on guard.

Mary emerged from the bushes in Perry's garden, seeing nothing but a house in darkness, faintly illuminated by the lamp post on the main path. All of the back windows were closed apart from a small one on the ground floor. She stood deathly still, listening for any noises coming from the house. Previously, she thought she'd heard a girl screaming, but now there was nothing but silence. She caught sight of the shed, its outline coming into focus as her eyes adjusted to the darkness. She crouched down, arching her head so that her ears could hopefully detect any sound, no matter how faint. With the house silent and still, she made a run.

She darted across the lawn, her feet nearly tripping over a concealed object lurking in the long blades of grass. She yanked on the heavy, metal padlock bolted through the shed door, this one twice the size of the previous one in which she'd managed to break. Bending down with her eyes fixed on the house, her hands felt across the ground, searching for anything which could do damage. All the bricks and tools had been removed. Lowering her head, she flicked her torch on and shone it beneath the small gap under the door, her eyes searching the interior, but it was impossible to see anything.

'Lucy?' she whispered, her tears falling to the floor. There was no reply.

She scurried to the door at the side of the house, trying the locked handle. She heard voices, too faint to tell what they were saying, coming from inside. She turned off her torch and ducked, her heart jumping into her mouth. After a few seconds of crouching, she peered through the window in the door, spying a radio that was playing away to itself. She scanned the deserted hallway, thinking that she saw something moving, right at the end of the hallway. However, through the frosted glass and tear drenched eyes, it was impossible to tell.

The familiar feeling that her sister was somewhere close by tingled once again through Mary's body, making her stop, listen and look around.

Lucy, are you here? It's Mary.

If Lucy was close by, she wasn't making a noise.

The interior of the house remained still. Mary moved round to the kitchen window at the back. She shone her torch in to illuminate pots, pans, dirty cutlery and rubbish all lining the work surfaces. She pressed her hands against the window, peering into the room and searching once more for movement. 'Is anyone home?' she attempted to ask, her apprehension stealing her voice, only a whisper emerging. 'I'm scared, please come out.' She didn't really know who she was talking to, but wanted someone to appear, for the lights to be switched on, and to be told that everything would be alright. She hoped, prayed and willed for that somebody to be Lucy, safe and well, ready to come home.

Guided by the assumption that Perry wasn't home, her courage heightened. She grabbed a discarded, plastic garden chair and manoeuvred it beneath the kitchen window. She balanced herself on the flimsy seat whilst trying to reach up to the opening, pulling it as wide as it would go. She arched her head in and shouted.

'Lucy can you hear me?' She waited for a reply, listening for noises above the sound of the radio, but there was nothing to be heard. She stretched up onto her tiptoes and managed to pull herself up through the window, disturbing the cups and plates on the draining board as she landed inside Perry's kitchen. She illuminated the room with her torch.

Her heart pounded along to the frenzied beat of the song now playing. Her feet remained still amongst the clutter of dishes on the kitchen counter, almost cemented in place with the fear brewing in her bones.

What am I doing? She thought once her feet landed, but it was too late - she was inside now.

Her body remained frozen. Crouching on the counter top, her heart continued to thump and she couldn't keep her hands from quivering. She gripped the torch tightly, holding it aloft like a weapon, and climbed down, shining her light around the room. Evidence of the presence of young children lay everywhere. There were open boxes of Sugar Puffs and Coco Pops, Postman Pat cereal bowls and toy puppets resting on the table, along with abandoned, half-empty beakers of juice. Her cheeks became flushed in the darkness at the sight of the items, a sickening feeling flooding her stomach. Through Mary's eyes, the house didn't seem normal, something wasn't right, and she knew it. Deep down, she knew it.

She tiptoed further into the darkness of the house, through the kitchen door and out into the hallway, where all the downstairs rooms remained silent. She paused, listening for noises above the radio. Her heart threatened to rupture, the delicate organ pounding at capacity.

She edged forward. 'Lucy, are you here?' she dared to whisper, her sixth sense returning, making her want to shout out for her sister. She shone her torch around the empty space, pausing when she spotted a picture hanging on the wall. She scanned the photo of the girl, her face beaming brighter than the sun in the background, her strawberry blonde hair caught in mid-air just as it had been blown by the wind. Mary looked closely at the photo, trying to remember if she had played with the girl, or if she had crossed paths with her during her summer holiday visits to Finchley. The girl in the photo must've been about ten and her face was familiar, but Mary just couldn't place where she had seen her before.

'I'm scared, Lucy, are you here?' Mary paused in front of every room, her eyes scanning the quiet interiors through the open doors. She placed one foot on the bottom step, her head telling her not to venture any further, but her heart spurring her on. She made her way up the stairs, glancing up to the landing and shining her torch, illuminating what lay ahead before taking another step. She placed her other hand over her heart, trying to stop it from pounding.

'Lucy, are you here?' she whispered again. Mary approached the landing, a chill sweeping through the dark corridor, taking with it the ends of her hair and causing the loose strands to tickle her face. She felt frantically along the wall for a light switch. Her heart leapt as her fingers finally landed on it, but when she pressed it nothing happened. Using her torch, she could see that the doors to all three upstairs rooms remained closed. After pressing her ear to the first, she eased it open with her hand, pausing in the doorway as the wood creaked away from its snug frame.

'Perry, where are you?' She waved her torch into the open space, illuminating nothing but a bunch of tatty boxes, piles of rubbish and a battered bicycle. Her tears started to fall again. She began to walk back out to the hallway. *I want my Mum* she thought, terrified by the situation she had somehow gotten herself into. She regretted not telling the truth from the start. She wished she'd told her parents, everything, and let them deal with Perry whilst she was safe at home, with Grandma. She cried harder at what she knew now was a stupid thing to do.

Cobwebs dangled above her head, years' worth of dust and cigarette smoke lined the walls. A ceiling bulb hung from a tattered cord, no decorative shade to conceal the exposed, dangerous wires. The loft hatch looked recently used, a handprint still evident in the dirt where it had been pushed open. The landing floor was patched up with different scraps of carpet, all working together to try and conceal the loose floorboards below.

There were two indentations in the carpet where a ladder had been placed, right below the loft hatch.

Lucy's bright smile beamed from behind glass panes that lined the walls, but Mary's torchlight failed to land on them, so they remained in the darkness, hidden and unnoticed. It was a shrine. Each photo of Lucy taken close-up, her smile beaming in each. Had anyone set eyes on the wall, their heart would have fell to the floor in a second, imagining the worst. Also concealed by the darkness, at the far side of the hallway, was a high-performance telescope. Had Mary looked through, she would have seen her Grandma's house appear in the lens, its focus directed right onto her attic room.

She placed her hand on the second door, pushing hard on the wood until it opened up. She shone her torch inside, revealing a scantily decorated bathroom, the paint on the walls peeling off as a result of damp and mould. Dirty towels lay on the floor amongst piles of newspapers, some of the pages of which had been ripped. The doors of the cluttered cabinet above the basin had been left open, and Mary could see that it hosted a collection of toothbrushes, all of which looked to have been chewed. Mary picked up the smallest brush, her torch revealing a picture of a cartoon kitten on the pink handle. She felt the moist bristles with her fingers, the smell of toothpaste travelling up her nose. Her tears streamed at what she knew was a child's toothbrush, knowing that no child lived here. Perry Golifer didn't have children. He lived alone, that's what he'd said to her, and that's what people believed. Mary's head was shaking in protest at the thoughts running through her mind, the thought that people had been right all along; Perry Golifer was a bad man, and deep down, Mary knew it.

With the brush still in her hand, she turned and noticed an airing cupboard door. It looked similar to the one at Wisteria, a white door raised about a metre off the floor, with a silver handle. Mary experienced a sense of déjà vu, recalling that one of her sister's favourite hiding places at Grandma's had been the airing cupboard. You could climb up and hide behind the towels and, whilst you waited to be found, it was always cosy and warm. Lucy had once hidden in the airing cupboard for so long that she'd fallen asleep. Mary had given up looking that day and went to play elsewhere. Lucy remained in situ and took years off Henry's life hours later when he went to get a fresh towel, lifting the top one off the pile to reveal Lucy's sleeping body.

Mary placed her fingers on the handle and pressed her ear against the door, just as she always did as a child. Unlike the boiler at her grandma's house, this one wasn't making any sounds, and she couldn't hear Lucy's giggles coming from behind the door. She pulled on the handle and took a deep breath, closing her eyes and hoping that she would open them to see Lucy standing before her, laughing, ready to come home

Mary opened her eyes.

Inside the airing cupboard there was nothing but a load of dripping, wet clothes hanging from a makeshift drying rack. Her heart plummeted to the floor along with her tears. She closed the door, refusing to accept the fact that Lucy was not there, and wishing she could try again and receive a different outcome. With her sister by her side she wouldn't be so scared, and they would escape together, and tell their parents the truth, making sure Perry was taken away and never allowed to come home. Mary knew that Lucy was somewhere close, her prickling skin told her so. So, she once again clasped her fingers round the handle and pulled the cupboard door, opening her eyes at the same time. She held the torch up and shone it into the cupboard.

Mary staggered backwards as she was met with Lucy's smile, and the outline of her figure. She held out her hand, but the image had been projected by a tormenting figment of her imagination. She had wanted so badly for Lucy to appear in the cupboard that her brain had willed it so. Mary scrunched her face in a flood of emotion – anger, heartbreak, fear - and she closed the door before exiting the bathroom, slipping the child's toothbrush in her pocket.

Back in the hallway, there was only one door left to look behind; the door to Perry's master bedroom.

She tried to push her way inside, the knob twisting but refusing to release the catch. She pushed her shoulder against the wood, her mounting sense of panic producing a strength she didn't know she had.

'Just open,' she mumbled, plunging her whole body against the wood, her shoulder aching beneath the force as the door remained in its frame.

From outside, the sound of a dog barking travelled into the house, but Mary was slightly out of range to be able to pick out the sound of heavy footsteps approaching the house.

'Just open.' Mary slammed her body against the stubborn door in a last, desperate attempt to enter the final room. The door surrendered, flinging open. She stood still, panting for breath and clenching her right arm. The dim light from her torch made a weak attempt to break through the abyss. She forced herself to move forward, her eyes darting in all directions, trying to inspect the room. Einstein's growls were escalating into a full-blown bark outside, the sound penetrated the walls of the house and rang through to Mary's ears, making her head turn. As she did, she caught sight of the wall behind the double bed.

'Oh, God…' Shock induced Mary's stomach to produce an instant spew of vomit. She reached out with her right hand to steady herself against the wall, no longer able to feel her legs. She bent down to try to alleviate the pain stabbing her insides. She scrunched her eyes shut; a means of protection. Her body felt weak, riddled with fear.

With her body still arched, Mary cast her glance back towards the wall.

Images of both her and her sister were plastered over the entire wall. She stood up and shone her torch over the collage, the beam of light illuminating one photo and then another. Some of the photos were blurred, like they had been taken in haste, while others were clear and in focus, seemingly taken only a few feet away. There were also dozens of newspaper cuttings, bits of ripped fabrics, empty crisp packets, juice bottles, used tissues. An array of other random everyday items was littered amongst the paraphernalia.

Anything that Perry had been able to steal from the bins that he knew Lucy or Mary had touched was now displayed across his wall like some kind of sadistic shrine. One photo in particular stood out as it was picked up by Mary's torchlight. It was of her and Einstein sitting on the lawn at Wisteria, taken only days ago. The photo was in focus, and therefore must have been taken from close range. Perry must have been hidden only metres away. The ripped piece of Mary's lilac dress and hair accessory had been salvaged from the bin and were pinned to the photo.

Mary's bottom lip quivered, though strangely she didn't cry. Mary had known that her sister was close by; her instincts had told her as much. And, in a way, her intuition was right. Her sister, Lucy, was everywhere.

Mary wet herself, her fear taking control of her bladder, but she didn't notice.

She bent down and peered beneath the bed, before moving further into the room and standing in front of the double wardrobe. She held out her tingling arm and took hold of the handle of the wardrobe, listening for Lucy. She eased the door open, a river of objects falling out and cascading over the floor. She bent down to look at all the stuff, noticing things she recognised, like a comic she'd thrown in the bin a few days ago, an old swimming costume she recalled once wearing, plus a huge collection of yellow and lilac hair clips. Mary held the things in her hands, not knowing what to do, other than scream and pray that someone, anyone, would come and help. But her throat had been seized, the shock temporarily paralysing her vocal cords, rendering her mute.

She got up off the floor and tried to shout again, only a husky voice emerging. 'Lucy, are you here? Can you hear me?' She listened in the darkness, the dim glow from her torch hanging by the side of her body, shaking as it remained cradled in her hand. She ripped some of the photos off the wall and stuffed them in her backpack.

Outside, Perry had made his way down the main road and through his front gate. Locking it behind him, he listened for the barking dog that he'd heard only moments earlier. His eyes scanned his garden, his fingers bolting the lock on the gate. Perry was paranoid, and rightly so. Everyone in the village despised him. And, if given the chance, most would have wanted to deliver him the fruitiest of all punches, right between his eye sockets.

Outside, Perry had tripped over the step into his property, the contents of his pockets spilling over the stone drive, his lost coins and keys proving hard to locate in the darkness. Whilst mumbling to himself, he ran his hand across the ground, haphazardly searching for his valuables, before grabbing what he could and standing. After a handful of minutes, the sound of the gate's bolt sliding through the lock made Mary run back down the stairs. In the rush to escape, her feet became tangled and her body was toppled down a short flight of six steps. She pulled herself up and paused at the bottom. She could hear a man's voice outside, above the din of the radio which was still playing. A shadow appeared in the crack in the back door, an outside light flickering on.

Perry fumbled in his pocket, struggling to locate his door keys.

'Where the bloody hell are they?' he groaned, patting down every pocket before turning back to retrace his steps. When the shadow moved, Mary turned off her torch and scurried down the hallway, grabbing the photo of the other girl off the wall when she passed, stuffing it into her backpack.

'Help!' she shouted, yet only a whisper was produced. She panicked, becoming confused and disorientated. She tried to find her escape route, but all the doors now looked the same, and she couldn't remember which one led to the kitchen.

Outside, Perry's shadow reappeared at the back door, his face pressing against the glass. He struggled with the bunch of keys in his hands, having found it on the floor by his front gate. He peered through the glass like he was looking for someone; and, right in front of him, Mary stood still as a statue, her figure blending into the darkness of the hallway. Another song played on the radio, and Mary was able to trace the noise. When she saw him moving away from the door, she ran. She didn't know where he'd gone. She didn't know if he was coming back. She just ran.

She climbed up onto the kitchen work surface, pulling herself up to the window. She could hear a key turning in the side door, the handle being pressed. Missing the chair as she fell, her body landed on the ground outside just as the door swung open. Perry threw an empty brown paper bag on the kitchen floor, taking a deep swig straight from a bottle. The kitchen light switched on.

'Fuckin' stuff everywhere!' he shouted upon entering, tripping over the shoes scattering the floor and failing to notice the missing picture in the hallway. Mary remained ducked below the kitchen windowsill, her back pressed against the wall, waiting for an opportunity to run across the garden.

'Shut the hell up,' she heard Perry shouting inside. He grabbed the radio and flung it across the room. 'Giving me a bloody headache.' The clatter made Mary jump, and she remained crouched, the sound of things being kicked travelled through the open window before total silence fell. The kitchen window banged closed above her head, and she released a gasp.

'Who's there?' Perry whispered, leaning forward and peering out. He pressed his face against the glass, looking out over the garden, grabbing a knife off the draining board and clenching it in his hand.

Mary remained stooped, holding her breath so that it wouldn't be visible in the cold air. She scanned the periphery in search of Perry, unsure whether he was still inside the house. The silence was broken with the loud sounds of him crashing around in the kitchen before the light was turned out and, without a thought, Mary made a dash. She ran across the garden until she was submerged within the shrubbery, just as the lights in the upstairs rooms illuminated. Mary peered through the gaps in the branches, hearing Perry's anger erupt, his drunken arms thrashing and knocking anything in his path.

She watched him plunge his fist into the space where Mary had stolen the photos, his nerves temporarily numbed.

Back outside, Mary panicked, trying unsuccessfully to find the panel through which she'd entered.

'Help me...' She spoke to no one. Her hands reached to grab the top of a fence panel and she held on hard, trying with all her strength to clamber up. 'Let me out,' she cried. She looked back towards the house and noticed that the bedroom was now empty.

She scrambled again. 'I can't get out.' The sound of the door opening forced blood to pump rapidly around her body as her young arms tried again and again to hoist her weight over the fence.

'I know someone's out here,' announced Perry in a slur, still swigging from his near empty bottle. 'And I'm gonna get you.'

The sound of his footsteps neared Mary's hideaway. She fell back down, her hands losing their grip, her arms not strong enough to heave her weight. She stumbled over an old plastic box in the shrubbery. Standing on it, she reached up and pulled herself over the fence, her body making a thud when she crashed to the ground on the other side. Einstein's bark broke the silence, and they both ran like the wind.

'Mary?' Perry shouted.

Her legs charged through the forest.

'I'm coming for you.' His body made a thud sound as he, too, managed to clamber over the fence.

Mary looked back whilst running, her foot tripping over an outstretched branch, sending her crashing to the spikey forest floor. She released a scream. Einstein stood over her, his warm, panting breath in her face, his slobber falling onto her cheek.

'I think it's broken,' she said, grabbing her ankle, feeling her foot throb inside her trainer. 'I don't think I can get up.'

In the distance, Mary heard footsteps approaching, Perry's

mumbles travelling through the forest. He was getting closer. He could smell her.

'Mary? Is that you?' he shouted. His intoxicated mind struggled to point his body in the right direction, the blackness of the night sky hindering his vision whilst his ears picked up the sound of panting. 'Did you come over to see me? Come back. Don't run away.'

'Oh, God, he's coming.' Trying to get to her feet, her body fell back, her bruised ankle buckling beneath the weight.

'I knew I recognised that voice,' he said, stumbling through the woods. He watched whilst Mary lay on the ground, not too far in the distance. 'Why are you running away, Mary? I thought we were friends?' He strode forward, his arms outstretched, indicating for her not to move.

'Don't come any closer or I'll scream,' she threatened. Mary's bravery crumbled. She couldn't stop crying. She edged backwards across the ground, her legs trailing and her hands ploughing through the leaves.

'Mary, listen to me,' Perry began 'I found the man who took Lucy. I wasn't sure when we could next be together, so I went and looked for him by myself.'

Mary shook her head. 'You're a liar.'

'I'm not, Mary, I promise. All those photos I have were just to help me find her,' Perry continued working his performance, holding out his hand and encouraging her to take it. 'But, guess what, Mary? It worked, because I've found her! I've found Lucy. That man I told you about did have her, and I've brought her back. I made a special bedroom for her in the loft until I could come and get you. I bet you didn't go up there, did you?'

Mary looked at Perry. He was bent down, a strong smell of alcohol permeating the air each time he coughed. Einstein remained by her side, a continuous growl rumbling in his throat whenever Perry moved. He wasn't about to be fooled.

'I don't believe you.'

'I promise. I've found her, Mary. Had you waited for me to

come home, I could have taken you right to her. You could have seen Lucy for yourself. She looks just like you, Mary. She has longer hair now, like yours, and she remembers you, she knows your name. She's excited to see you.'

Mary shook her head. 'I shouted for her. She wasn't there.'

'She was probably asleep, and she wouldn't have heard you up in the loft. She was tired when I brought her home.'

'I shouted really loud. She didn't hear me. She didn't shout back. She wasn't there.' Mary's hysterics heightened and her strength was wavering. Yet, there was also a slight glimmer of hope welling in her chest.

'Why would you put her in the attic?'

'She wanted to be in the attic,' replied Perry. 'That's where all the toys are that I bought for her, for you.'

'Why didn't you bring her straight home to see Mum and Dad? Or why didn't you take her to the police? That's what you should have done.'

'Because your parents, and the police, would think that I was the one that took her away, and that I've been hiding her all this time. You need to come to my house, then *you* can take Lucy home. Isn't that what you wanted, Mary? Isn't that what we planned?'

Mary's mind attempted to process all of Perry's lies. Her skin felt warm despite the cool chill in the air. She didn't notice the strengthening wind. She just scrutinised his face, his sinister smirk no longer masked. His trembling hands couldn't be hidden. The thoughts running through his mind couldn't be tamed, nor could his hands. Perry lunged himself forward and grabbed Mary's leg. He wasn't going to let her go again, not tonight, not when there wasn't a single witness.

'You're coming with me.'

Her body jostled.

'If you don't come with me, I'll take your sister away, and she'll never be found again, ever,' he threatened. But Mary couldn't hear his words, her legs kicking like a bucking horse until Perry released his grip.

'I mean it, Mary,' he said. 'Tell anyone, and I'll kill Lucy, and it'll be all your fault.'

She scrambled to her feet and ran, dropping her torch, her injured ankle pounding. Einstein ran ahead, the chase now feeling like a game.

'Where are you, you little bitch?' Perry mumbled, his feet stumbling the faster he chased.

Mary navigated the dark contours of the woods surrounding her grandparents' house, her legs striding over outstretched, broken trunks, her body ducking beneath low-lying branches, and her internal compass successfully directing her home. Mary didn't stop. She didn't think about the pain. She just ran and ran.

'I'm coming for you, Mary,' Perry shouted, following her trail and listening to the sound of the disturbed branches creaking ahead. 'You'll never be able to escape, Mary. You're all mine now,' he laughed, the alcohol fuelling his ego. Mary and Einstein kept on running, hurling themselves further into the hollow of the woods.

'You're all alone, Mary, and I'm going to get you,' he called, just as she finally broke through the barrier of trees and out into the safety of her grandparents' lawn. Not far behind, Perry paused, watching her fumbling with the keys on the porch before vanishing inside, the lamps downstairs switching on. He could see her shadow hiding behind the floor-length curtain in the lounge. He fell to the floor, and watched.

Twenty-Eight

MARY STAYED HIDDEN BEHIND THE FLORAL LOUNGE curtains for at least twenty minutes. Her mum was still passed out on the kitchen floor, sleeping off the last deluge of alcohol. Wrapped within the embrace of the curtain, Mary felt safe, like nobody could harm her. She forced her eyes to close and pretended that she and Lucy were toddlers again. The more she forced herself to imagine the past, the less her mind was able to visualise the horrors she'd just uncovered. She didn't want to imagine that Lucy was in his attic. She didn't want to remember all the things that she'd seen, or the terrible things that she'd smelt, or how scared she felt standing in his bedroom, alone. She didn't want to think about anything, other than her and Lucy pretending to jump into the lake.

Tucked within the curtain's pleats, Mary felt she could hide from the world. But Perry remained outside, watching her every move. He was in no hurry, savouring the opportunity to admire the shadow of her shaking body. He watched each time she scratched her face, and he admired her silhouette whenever she moved her leg, transferring to a more comfortable position. He wasn't rushing home to move everything she'd seen just in case she went to the police, he thought he was smarter, cleverer.

Had Mary been able to stand on her tiring legs behind the curtain for longer, she'd have stayed there forever. The feeling that she'd experienced in Perry's house, of her sister being close by, was now gone. Her mind relaxed for a moment, permitting Perry's threat to seep into her thoughts. '*I'll kill Lucy if you tell anyone*' and '*I'm going to get you.*'

The thoughts running through her mind made her leave the safety of the curtain. She turned the lamps off, her shadow now engulfed by the surrounding darkness. She spied outside through one of the other windows and spotted Perry hiding behind some of the bushes near the woods. Her heart pumped. She looked to the front door, realising she hadn't locked it. 'He's coming for me, isn't he?' she mumbled.

I need to hide, she thought. The thought cartwheeled around in her mind, rolling over and eliminating every other thought.

In the kitchen, Martha was still lying on the floor, passed out, which meant that Elsie was probably upstairs in bed, and Hank hadn't returned from the morgue. She ran upstairs to her bedroom. Mary changed, leaving her dirty clothes on the floor, her top still stained with vomit. She pushed her feet into a different pair of tatty trainers, her sprained ankle throbbing, not that she noticed, or cared. She took off her glasses and threw them in the bin, and put her hair in a bobble.

Mary crouched to kiss Einstein. 'You stay here this time. I'll be back soon.' She held Einstein back, keeping him in her bedroom while she closed the door, trapping him inside. Elsie was still asleep on top of the covers, surrounded by tissues, the bedside photo of Henry resting by her side. She went into her parents' room. There was a collection of wine bottles on the bed, each drained of every last drop of liquid, plus an array of painkillers, paracetamols and sleeping pills. She shut the door and made her way back downstairs. Kneeling at her mum's side, she leant down and checked her breathing once again. Her mum's warm breath felt nice against her cheek, despite it wreaking of alcohol. Mary leant back, shaking her head.

'I'm scared and I need you,' she whispered. She looked at her mum, checking to see if there was any reaction. From her initial few words, Martha remained out for the count.

'I need you, Mum.' Mary shrugged her shoulders at the helplessness of the situation, not knowing what else to do.

If there was ever a time for Martha to wake up, it was now. Right at this very second.

Despite Perry's threat running through her mind, Mary wanted to tell her mum anyway, tell her everything. She pulled out the photos from her bag that she'd taken from Perry's, and placed them on the floor by the side of her mum.

'Perry Golifer said he knew who'd taken Lucy, and so he went to get her and now she's in his attic, waiting for me to go and bring her home. But I don't know if he's telling the truth, Mum.' Mary waited for the words to affect her mum in some way, but Martha remained unresponsive.

She lay down on the floor with Martha, their noses almost touching. 'I went to his house, all by myself. I looked in every room, and I shouted for Lucy, but she wasn't there, I promise she wasn't. If she was, she would have shouted back, I know she would. Even if she didn't recognise my voice, or remember who I was, she would've shouted for help because she wouldn't have wanted to stay there on her own, not with him. It's dark at his house, and scary.' Mary's tears flooded her face, her mum's body twitching as she fell into a deeper sleep.

'His house is horrible, Mum. There are loads of photos of Lucy and me on his walls. He isn't a nice man. You were right. I tried to be his friend, just to help bring Lucy home.' Mary closed her eyes, trying to escape from the image of Perry's wall. 'I'm scared to stay here. He said he's going to come and get me, and you'll be too drunk to stop him, and Dad will be out, and Grandma will be asleep. He said the next time he sees me he'll take me away. And then I'll vanish, too, just like Lucy. He's outside right now, waiting to take me away.' Mary sat up and slid herself away from her mum until her back was pressed against the fridge.

She wanted to leave behind the world which felt so terrifying. She wanted to go and hide until all this was over. She wanted to sleep, and never wake up. She didn't want to imagine that her sister was locked away in Perry Golifer's attic. And for the first time in years, Mary didn't feel haunted by the feeling that it could have been her, or her Grandparents, that had harmed Lucy, and as such, a weight had been lifted.

Mary crept over to the window in the lounge and peered through, spotting Perry still crouched outside. She carefully opened the back door, and slipped out the house. 'Bye, Mum,' she whispered, looking back one last time before leaving.

Martha would wake, eventually, at which point it would be too late. The damage would have been done. Mary would be gone.

****

CLAIRE SWIFT WAS sitting upright in bed. She was wide awake, and had been for hours. It was 4.30 am. Not even the birds were awake, and people somewhere were probably just returning from a night out on the town. Swift was staring at her alarm clock, waiting for the buzzer to signal that it was time to get up. She had another half an hour to wait. She thought that getting up any earlier would be crazy; not that she considered staring at the clock for hours to be sane behaviour, but at least she was still in bed. She had just another half hour to stew things over in her mind. Half an hour to wonder what the new day would bring, and if it would bring her any closer to finding Lucy Lane. Since discovering the note in Elsie's bin, she'd been on edge. She shouldn't have bothered trying to sleep; she'd seen each new hour announce itself on her clock.

Today was set to be a big day and, although she already felt ragged round the edges due to tiredness, Swift was ready. She'd already decided to forgo breakfast, and she couldn't be bothered to make a packed lunch. She was secretly hoping that she'd be too busy for lunch if the morning went as planned. Maybe later on in the day there'd be reason to celebrate, and all the office could have a trip to Tom's Teatime Treats. That was her goal for the day; to make such an incredible breakthrough that they'd end up at Tom's. All major case breakthroughs were celebrated in the same fashion; over a mug of tea and a plate of whatever Tom's daily special dish was. Swift hoped that today's special would be his minted lamb hotpot, with a side portion of red cabbage.

After contemplating the café menu in her mind, the half-hour had passed, and the alarm performed as expected with an annoying buzzing sound that made Swift want to lunge the clock against the wall. She silenced it instead, and began to prepare for the day.

Sergeant Swift led her team down to Finchley allotments on foot. There was no reason to make a big song and dance about their presence with police cars and vans lining the main road, or garish yellow and black incident tape cordoning off the area. Those extreme measures would only hinder their efforts. The allotment was suitably placed, off the beaten track where very few, if any, people would see. There may be a rogue passing dog walker, but, other than that, the operation could easily be carried out in a covert nature.

Despite her best attempts, Swift had failed to obtain the information she wanted from the council. They refused to release details of who owned which plot of land unless requested via the appropriate channels, a formality which would take longer than she was willing to wait. Effectively, this meant that Swift and her team were looking for a specific grain of sand in the Sahara. Unperturbed by the task, at 6 am the inspection commenced.

With their jackets zipped up to their chins, everyone gathered in a huddle. 'We're going to form a line, and we'll work from the far side, back,' Swift instructed, signalling with her hands exactly where she wanted to concentrate efforts. 'We're looking for anything that has recently been disturbed, freshly dug soil, newly planted flowers, footprints, absolutely anything.'

Swift hadn't told the team about Elsie's note, or about the bloody trowel, or even what they were looking for. Everyone in the Finchley force was emotionally invested in the case of Lucy Lane, and she didn't want to raise hopes unnecessarily. But the main reason she hadn't told the team was that she wanted to protect them. Having not sought the formal authorities to reopen the case, nobody was meant to be actively investigating the disappearance of Lucy Lane. It was still officially closed.

'There's something hidden here, and we're not leaving until we unearth it. Understood?' Her team of five nodded their heads. They knew she stood by her words. Unless they found what she was looking for, it was going to be a long shift, followed by mandatory overtime.

Formed in their instructed line, the officers waited for the signal to start.

'Should you spot something, raise your hand and shout up. Any questions before we get going?' Nobody replied to Swift's question. 'Right then, let's crack on.'

In an organised concentration, the officers began to creep forward, their trained eyes scanning the ground each time they took one step after another. They each donned a pair of gloves and carried a baton, swiping through the ground, moving aside any longer grass or objects causing an obstruction.

The sun rose behind their backs, their reflective gear shining when the sun crept higher into the sky, the warmth replacing the cool morning breath lingering amongst the wall of trees. The note that Swift had found in Elsie's lounge was still clear in her mind, along with her mantra, *Never give up until the case is solved.* Despite having advanced to the rank of sergeant, Swift was a mucker-inner. Eager to escape the confines of her desk and never-ending pile of paperwork, she loved nothing more than getting her hands dirty. The paperwork could wait until she was home and sitting in front of the television watching Corrie, with a brew and a brown banana.

On this occasion, Swift had drawn upon her strong connections within the community to try and ascertain which plot of allotment land the Lane family owned. Derek Farmer was the village know-it-all, and frequent visitor to the Black Fryer on a Friday night for his weekly pint and pack of salted peanuts.

Derek had lived in Finchley as long as any other resident, and took it upon himself to run the Neighbourhood Watch scheme. He was basically just a busybody, and busybodies tended to come in useful to the police.

Being no pushover, Swift knew she'd need to barter in order to strike a deal with Derek, and an underhand deal she was more than willing to shake on. Derek knew a good deal when it came his way, and when Sergeant Swift had offered to buy him a pint, plus offer extra help in tackling the antisocial behaviour occurring in his cul-de-sac, he wasn't about to turn it down. He offered up the required information and the two nodded, their silent form of handshake sealing their deal.

Swift positioned herself right on track for where Derek Farmer had confirmed that Henry Lane had once tended to his allotment, the patch of land now only a few paces away. She slowed her pace, scouring the shrubbery, being careful where to place her next step, not wanting to damage anything with her boots.

Then, she paused. 'Bingo,' she whispered. She leant down, ignoring her own specific instructions to raise a hand and shout. Amongst the neglected patch of land, Swift caught a glimpse of some freshly turned soil. She knelt down and put her baton in her kit belt, freeing up both hands. She held out her left arm, indicating for the team to stop. She took a photo before fanning away the soil.

Come on. Come on. Come on.

Her insides became knotted with adrenaline, an addictive part of the job she thrived on. With her hands soon covered in mud, she puffed away a stray hair from her eye, the irritation causing her lid to twitch.

Don't let me down now, not now, not on this one. She was talking to her own intuition, the main thing driving her intentions whilst all her colleagues looked on, bewildered by the whole secretive operation of which they knew little about. A mound appeared at the side of her, her hands scooping out a shallow hole. She heard a rustling noise. Her heart leapt from her chest, her hands shaking when they took hold of a plastic bag. She skipped a breath, not quite believing that she'd actually found something.

'What you found, Sarge?' asked one of her colleagues, but she didn't reply. In that precise moment, Swift could hear nothing, only her own stream of thoughts.

Is this the day I'll find her?

Swift untied the handles and opened the bag, peering in. The lilac socks within had retained their colour, having been protected for so many years.

Sonofabitch.

She held the bag close to her face, getting a better look at the socks without actually touching the material. Her eyes wanted to well up, her emotions flooding to the surface and threatening to taint her professional persona. She couldn't take her eyes off the lace frills at the top of the socks.

They're Lucy's, aren't they?

On the left sock, a line of blue cotton ran the length, the manufacturing imperfection she hoped to see, the same imperfection visible on the sock Lucy was wearing on the pictures plastered all over the station wall. The sock was definitely the one that Lucy had been wearing the day she vanished.

Swift announced her discovery for all to hear, her words almost choking up. 'They're Lucy Lane's socks. I know they are.'

And, of course, Sergeant Swift was right.

Twenty-Nine

B IRDS BROKE INTO MORNING SONG, AND IT WAS THE dawning of a new day. The prospect of a sticky, hot summer's day hung in the wings, and parents across the country prayed it would materialise, knowing that they could get away with a cheaper day by simply packing a picnic and spending the day in the park where children could entertain themselves. The scattering of remaining clouds dispersed, revealing the iridescent sky beneath.

The new day had begun.

Mary's body lay hidden in the shed at Wisteria. She'd snuck out of the house without Perry spotting her, his drunken eyes remaining firmly fixed on the front door, watching and waiting. From his hidden location, Perry could see Mary's bedroom, her light still switched on from when she'd returned. He knew she'd be in there; she had to be. 'I'm not leaving without her, not this time,' he mumbled to himself in a drunken daze, his body flooded with alcohol in an attempt to drown his sorrows. He'd waited for so many years to snatch Mary during the annual event at Crest Cove, and yet once again he'd failed. But this year, he'd come close than years gone by, and had actually held her hand. He'd felt Mary's skin. He'd already won her trust. He'd done all of the hard work, and yet he'd left emptyhanded. *Why didn't I just run with her, I could have had her away, I knew I could.* He couldn't bear the thought of waiting another year, he couldn't wait another year. He wanted Mary now, and no longer cared how and when he snatched her, just as long as he did.

Once in the relative safety of the shed, Mary grabbed as much junk as she could, and pushed it behind the door, trying to barricade herself in. Old bicycles, boxes filled with old tat plus an array of fishing tackle was piled up against the shabby door. The clutter wouldn't have stopped anyone who was desperate to enter, but it made her feel better; safer.

The interior of the shed was dark, only snippets of light seeping in through the many holes that Perry had created. Mary could hear her own breathing, fear causing her heart to pound like the thrashing of a drum. Her eyes blinked in quick succession. She stood as far away from the door as she could, listening for anyone who had followed. Noticing the dawning of a new day seeping through the holes, she repositioned herself. The main spy hole that was allowing in the majority of the light was strategically positioned, and when Mary looked through, her gaze ended at her attic window. No coincidence.

She pressed her face against one of the other many spy holes. She could see Perry's body still crouched, his head tilted upwards, looking towards her bedroom. She cried at the sight of him stalking her bedroom. She imagined how she had stood at the very same window whilst Perry had been staring at her. Her skin crawled, her hands itching her arms, then her body.

'He's waiting for me,' she sobbed, her body shaking with fear. She trembled at the thought of having once held his hand. She felt sick at the image of being in his house. She knew he was coming after her, and that no matter what, she wouldn't let him take her away. She moved away and sat huddled in the corner, her body shaking with shock and her mind reliving each terrifying moment she'd witnessed over at Ivy Dean.

'Please, some body help me.' She closed her eyes and pulled her knees into her chest. She lowered her head and repeated over and over *somebody help me.*

Then, she heard a noise outside.

She jumped up and pressed her face against the shed wall, her eye peering through a hole. 'Oh, God, he's coming.' Mary watched as Perry stumbled to his feet, his legs walking haphazardly across the garden. He looked in through the front door, noticing Martha collapsed on the floor. He disappeared behind the far saide of the house. He was no longer willing to sit back and waiting for an opportunity to present.

'Where's he going?' she cried, moving her body so that she could look through another hole. But she couldn't see where he'd gone. She cowered back into the corner, and crouched. Her heart felt like it was going to explode from her chest. Her sobs were now audible should anyone have been in close proximity to the shed, which they were. Perry was stood behind the shed, right at the corner spot where Mary was hiding within. He pressed his ear against the wood, listening. *She's in there.* He looked through one of the spy holes he'd created, his widened eye blocking a snippet of light. Mary heard his breathing, her eyes darting to the left where it suddenly went dark.

'I know you're in there, Mary,' he whispered. His eye blinked, the white part visible to Mary.

'Oh, God, please leave me alone,' she mumbled.

She heard the sound of footsteps approaching round to the front, followed by a man's cough. She placed her hands over her ears, trying to block out the noise terrifying her to the core. The footsteps stopped; Perry was now right outside the shed door. She removed her hands, and listened, her head looking up at the door upon sensing he was there.

Perry placed his hand on the shed door's handle, and pushed. The junk pressed behind gave resistance, and Mary could hear him muttering.

'Why's it not opening?'

Mary pushed herself back against the wall, trying to escape but with nowhere to go. She saw all the rubbish slowly sliding towards her the more Perry pushed from the other side. She shot up, and threw herself against the door.

'Leave me alone,' she cried, pushing all her weight against the wood, feeling Perry pushing from the other side.

'I knew I'd find you,' whispered Perry, his excitement peaking. 'It's time to come with me, Mary.'

'Leave me alone,' she cried, pushing with all her strength.

'Its no use, Mary. There's no escape now,' Perry whispered through the crack that'd appeared in the door, his foot ramming itself in the narrow gap. Mary cried, panic sabotaging her ability to prevent him from entering. Perry placed his hand through the gap, and grabbed hold of Mary's hair, her back pressed against the door. 'Gotcha now.'

The sound of a car came tearing up the drive, and Perry released his grip, the door banging shut as his foot moved. Mary scrambled to look through a hole, witnessing the police car now on the drive. She saw Hank get out and quickly walk up to the front door. The car then reversed back down the path until out of sight.

'Where's he gone?' Mary mumbled, her eyes scouring as much of the garden as she could see – but Perry was no longer there. She looked at the shed door, pressing more stuff against it, terrified he would come back for her. She then watched again as Hank opened the front door, leaving it ajar as he ventured inside. Mary could hear him shouting her name, his screams getting louder as the seconds passed. She could see him upstairs in her bedroom, and after only a couple of seconds, he was back outside shouting her name. Mary remained still. She wasn't about to move, too terrified that Perry would be waiting, and that this time she wouldn't be able to escape his clutches. Martha and Elsie soon joined Hank on the front porch, each one screaming Mary's name. The photo's Mary had left next to Martha in the kitchen were now clenched in her mum's hand, Martha's face more frightful than it'd ever looked before.

'Call the police,' Hank's voice bellowed in through the shed walls. Mary's breathing quickened, panic setting in and her mind not knowing what to do. She watched her frantic parents running in and out of the house, Hank's voice shouting the loudest. 'Check inside again, she must be here, she must be.' Mary had never seen her Dad's face look so pale, his dark eyes making him look like a ghost. She kept watching for Perry, wondering if it was finally safe for her to leave the shed, and make a dash over to her parents.

'MARY! MARY!' she heard her mum shouting, her harrowing voice making Mary cry harder, and all she wanted to do was hug her mum, and feel protected. She rummaged past all the clutter, rambling over the junk and pulled at the door, tugging to pull it free.

'I'm coming,' she shouted as loud as she could. The door finally gave way, and Mary stepped out onto the lawn, the bright sky making her squint and cover her eyes. Mary darted whilst looking behind her, expecting at any moment that Perry would reach out and grab her.

'Oh, God, Mary!' shouted Martha, who came running down the lawn, flinging her arms around her daughter.

'Where have you been? Oh, thank God you're okay.' Martha hugged Mary tight, refusing to let go. Mary plunged her face into her mum's shoulder, burying her face and hiding her tears. Hank and Elsie came running behind.

'Mary, where've you been? We've been going out of our mind with worry – we've called the police.' Hank also fell to his knees, hugging both his wife and daughter in one long embrace. 'Thank God you're okay.' He pulled himself away, looking at Mary in the eyes. 'Where have you been?'

'I was scared. I didn't feel safe,' was all she could muster.

'It doesn't matter where she was,' interrupted Martha, 'as long as she's alright.'

Elsie bent down, also taking her turn to hug Mary, relief pouring from her eyes. She whispered into Mary's ear, desperate to tell her the wonderful news. 'I was scared too,' she began, assuming Mary had been scared by what the police had told them about Henry and the body which had been found. 'The body they found wasn't your grandad's.'

Mary pulled away from Elsie so she could look her in the eyes.

'It wasn't Grandad. He's still out there somewhere, Mary, waiting to be found, waiting to come back. There's nothing to be scared of,' Mary hugged her grandma again. The sound of a car approaching interrupted the reunion. Hank left his family on the lawn and scurried over to greet Sergeant Swift. Mary saw her dad handing over the photos she'd found, his hands gesticulating. There were no more raised voices, no shouting, and no commotion. Wisteria fell quiet, and the world around it appeared to progress in slow motion the moment Swift took a first glance at the photos.

'These were in the house. They were next to Martha in the kitchen when she woke up. We've no idea where they've come from,' added Hank, witnessing the look of horror on Swift's face.

Perry was watching from afar, knowing full well what Hank was handing to the police. He watched Swift's reaction, witnessing in slow motion the look of horror taking over her face. In the next blink he'd vanished.

Having taken the phone call herself, Swift thought she was prepared for what was to come, but she wasn't. Her hands shook as she held the photos, and her heart raced when her eyes caught sight of the Lane girls, and then Katie Banks. She held back her tears and her eyes blinked in quick succession, trying to banish her emotions and digest every detail depicted in the pictures. Her mascara smudged, the moisture creating black streaks that ran from her eyes, tarnishing her flawless appearance. She swore beneath her breath, the words escaping through gritted teeth. Her jaw became tense, her teeth grinding beneath the pressure and anxiety filling her body. The invisible smell of Perry's house lingered on the paper, transferring to her hands. Swifts astute senses picked up on the strong aroma, her insides churning. She'd been to Perry's house before, she knew how it smelt, the stench was unmistakable; unforgettable. She pressed her finger on her radio before uttering the command.

'We need to find Perry Golifer, now.'

Thirty

AN ARMY OF OFFICERS HAD BEEN STALKING Ivy Dean from secret vantagepoints all day. Teams of officers were out searching the area, hunting down their target. Mary and her family remained locked behind the doors at Wisteria, Martha not letting Mary out of her sight until she put her to bed early evening, Mary's body unable to remain awake any longer. With her bedroom windows closed, and her bedroom door open, Martha sat on the landing and waited for news. The family didn't speak, not knowing what to say. They didn't eat and they were barely able to breathe. As the hours passed, and night time came without any update, Elsie, Martha and Hank had no choice but to go to bed. Who knew when they would get any news? They climbed the stairs to their bedrooms, and each sunk their bodies beneath the duvets. Unsure if they would get any sleep, they all lay awake, waiting and praying.

Then, after an agonising wait, it was time.

In an orchestrated manoeuvre conducted by Sergeant Swift, an army of police officers pounced from their hideaways at 1 o'clock in the morning, not long after the Lane family had fallen asleep. The officers surrounded their target, the target which they were now confident was back behind the doors at Ivy Dean. The clouds above parted to reveal a silver, shimmering full moon. The circling black dot created by the helicopter looked like a darting bat trying to escape the moon's reflection. Police cars and vans pulled up in front of the target, their flashing lights penetrating the closed curtains.

Swift got out of the leading car once her team on the ground and in the air were in situ, placing her hat on her head and adjusting it until it was set central. She needed a moment to compose herself, the images of Lucy's smile tormenting her mind. She took a deep breath and tried not to think beyond entering the ivy-covered house belonging to Perry Golifer. Anything could be waiting for her behind those doors, she knew that only too well. And she needed to be prepared. Her team of officers were counting on her. She was the leading force; they followed her command.

'Right, let's get this started.'

The Lane family all remained oblivious to the search being carried out. They were all sleeping, but not for much longer.

But thirty-five minutes later, Mary's eyes were the first to open.

'What is it?' she mumbled, fearful that the noise was Perry coming to take her away. There wasn't anybody in her room, and relief filled her body. She staggered across to the window. Her squinting eyes watched in the distance, witnessing beneath the glow of the street lamp the police swarming like a concentration of ants. Their reflective uniforms illuminated beneath the glare of search lights that were being erected high up on stands, adjacent to the four corners of Perry Golifer's property.

'They're back,' she announced, attempting to swallow, her barren throat acting as a blockade to her saliva. 'They're in his garden, aren't they?' she mumbled just as another light powered up, shining directly over Perry's back garden. Einstein remained hidden beneath the bed, only the tips of his outstretched paws visible.

Too scared to stay on her own, Mary ventured out from her bedroom, her bare feet feeling cold against the floor.

'Mum, what's happening?' she asked, her mum and dad emerging on the landing at the same time, wrapping their dressing gowns around their shivering bodies and squinting when Mary turned on a lamp. Hank bent down to look into Mary's eyes.

'I don't know, Mary, but I need you to go back to bed, okay?' Hank heard the commotion revving up outside, search helicopters, police cars and the slamming of doors all echoing through the woods, piercing the once virgin night.

'Do you think they're looking for Lucy somewhere?' Mary asked. She watched for Hank's reaction, her dad standing and taking a deep breath before replying. That said it all. Actions spoke louder than words, even Mary knew that, and she was only ten.

'I'm not sure, Mary,' he replied. 'Maybe.'

Martha began to cry, her body swaying. The shock of the situation crippled her already unstable body.

'Oh God, what's happening now?' she asked. She shielded her eyes. Her body stiffened with fear at the sight of the police approaching the house. 'They're coming here, aren't they? They've found her, haven't they? Why else would they be coming in the middle of the night?'

Hank peered out through the landing window. 'We don't know if they're coming about Lucy, Martha.' But then he gasped.

'What is it?' Martha asked, also trying to look out the window upon hearing her husband's reaction, his face falling at the realisation of the officer's exact location. 'Just tell me, what is it?' Martha demanded. She pushed Hank aside, placing her hands on the window ledge and standing on tiptoes.

'They're at Golifer's.' Hank's words ricocheted through every fragile bone in his wife's body, wounding each organ until her feeble frame crumbled.

Mary already knew where the police were, she had been able to tell as much from her bedroom window.

'Oh, God, no,' declared Martha, the colour vanishing from her face, her body lying in a heap on the floor like an abandoned rag doll.

Hank bent down. 'Stay strong,' he insisted, scooping Martha into his arms and rocking her fragile body like a baby. 'Don't think the worst. You have to stay positive, for Lucy's sake.' Mary also crouched. She held her mum's cold, limp hand.

'It'll be alright, Mum,' she whispered, acting like one of the grown-ups in the situation.

A sound coming from the kitchen took them all by surprise, and they moved in unison. Hank held on to both Martha and Mary's weary bodies, navigating his family down the stairs and into the heart of the lake house.

'Grandma, what are you doing?' asked Mary, witnessing Elsie kneading dough, flour scattered throughout her hair like fine flakes of dandruff.

'Mum, what's going on?' added Hank.

'I thought some fresh bread would be nice for breakfast,' said Elsie. 'I think we'll all be hungry by dawn, and I just couldn't sleep.' Her hands were working methodically to shape the loaves. 'Would you like it plain or with poppyseeds?' she asked, holding the bag of flour in her hand.

'Not the bloody bread, Mum,' said Hank. 'I mean, what's going on outside? Haven't you seen that there's police everywhere?' He flung his arms in frustration, his hand accidentally knocking the bag of flour from Elsie's hand, causing a fog to appear over the entire kitchen.

'They've not long since arrived,' she replied casually, whilst continuing with her baking. 'That Swift woman knocked a few minutes ago and said they're performing a search on a neighbouring house. They're only six years too bloody late, aren't they?' Elsie slammed the next batch of dough onto the work surface before scraping it off and repeating the process. 'Why didn't they just say they're at Golifer's? We can bloody see them with our own eyes, for crying out loud.'

Martha lost her balance again, a feeling of faintness threatening to dislodge her upright position. Hank grabbed hold, preventing her from falling.

'Here, sit down,' he suggested, assisting his wife to a chair and getting her a glass of water.

Martha rested her elbows on the table and steadied her throbbing head in the palms of her hands, her body still swaying.

All she could think about was Lucy, imagining what it'd feel like, knowing that her daughter had been over at Ivy Dean all this time, only yards from where they had stayed every single summer since her disappearance. She just wanted to run outside in her dressing gown, barefooted, and ask what the bloody hell was going on. What or who were they looking for? Was it Lucy? Did they think she was alive? She just wanted to know. She needed to know. A prolonged wait would kill her. Her rocketing blood pressure would cause her to die, and then she'd go to her grave never finding out what had happened to her daughter.

'Why didn't you wake me?' Hank whispered into Elsie's ear. 'At least I could have prepared myself.' The police search lights shone in through the kitchen window, the chopper flying over, shadows appearing in the garden the more the trees swayed beneath the pressure.

'Did she say anything about Lucy?' he whispered to Elsie with an air of hesitance, looking over at Mary, who was now sitting in the lounge and staring out at all the lights, Einstein lying by her side.

'No,' Elsie replied, finally turning to look at Hank, her eyes welling. 'But we all know, don't we?' Hank wrapped his arms round his mum, feeling her fragility when she pressed her head into his warm, waiting embrace.

'You need to prepare yourselves,' she added. 'They wouldn't be going to these lengths in the middle of the night if they didn't finally have some strong evidence.' Elsie pulled away, her moment of weakness passing, her resilience regaining control.

'Mum, please come and sit down,' Hank insisted, making Elsie release the dough before helping her to a chair. 'And neck a glass of this.' He poured out a tumbler of whiskey behind Martha's back. Elsie glugged the entire glass in one, the golden liquor burning her throat.

'We all just need to calm down,' he said. 'We don't know anything yet, so let's just wait and see, shall we?' He turned towards Mary. 'Should I try and put her back in bed?' he asked

Martha, just as the sound of footsteps could be heard crunching across the driveway pebbles, everybody's head turning in unison.

A few heartbeats later, there was a gentle tap. Einstein immediately growled, his ears pricking up from within the lounge. He plunged his body towards the door, the clatter of his sharp claws scraping across the floorboards. He stood on guard.

'Here we go,' mumbled Hank beneath his breath, seeing the two officers standing outside on the porch. His hand opened the door slowly, as if the delay would ease the words he anticipated were about to follow. A crack in the door emerged, permitting a bitter breeze to bite at his exposed skin.

'Sorry to disturb you, Mr Lane,' Sergeant Swift began, taking her hat off when he opened the door wider. 'But we're going to need you to remain indoors until further notice.' Hank scrutinised her glossy lips, anticipating what she was about to say. He turned to see who in the house could hear his words before asking his question.

'What's going on? Is it Lucy?'

Swift paused for a moment, diverting her stare before replying.

'I'm sorry, Mr Lane. We can't confirm anything at this stage.' Swift adjusted her radio attached to her jacket, turning the volume down when the sound of voices emerged. 'We need you all to remain inside.' Hank's heart raced. He wanted to grab Swift and shake the information out.

'Where the bloody hell do you think we'd be going in the middle of the night?' he said.

Swift didn't reply. She raised her eyebrows, which acted as a suitable response.

'Can't you just bloody tell us?' snapped Hank. 'Have you any idea what it's like to be on this side of the door?' He smashed his fist into the door frame, his bleeding knuckles throbbing. Mary looked on from the lounge, cowering behind a cushion.

Martha lunged herself at the front door. 'Just bloody well tell us. Have you found our daughter?' Her words exploded, her body landing in Swift's personal space. Their noses weren't far off touching, and yet Swift didn't step back, or flinch. Her colleague swooped to her defence.

'It's alright,' Swift whispered, instructing the other officer to step down. She looked into Martha's eyes. 'We do understand, Mrs Lane.' She placed her hand on Martha's arm before moving her away. 'As soon as our investigation concludes, you'll be informed. But, until then, we do need you, and your family, to stay inside.'

Martha stepped back. She slumped herself on the bottom step of the stairs, cradling her head in her hands.

'How long will it take?' asked Hank.

'We can't say at the moment, but we'll keep you informed,' replied Swift. 'The best thing to do is for you and your family to go back to bed and get some rest.'

Hank closed the door, noticing another officer standing on guard outside the house. He went and sat next to Martha on the stairs, her head leaning on his shoulder when he kissed her hair.

'Is it her?' she asked quietly. 'I need to know. I can't take it anymore. I feel like I'm dying.'

Hank put his arm round her, trying to shield her from the news that he anticipated. 'I don't know. We'll just have to wait, and pray.' He felt helpless. 'Remember what they said at the hospital,' he said. 'One breath at a time, until the pain passes, okay?'

Mary appeared in the hallway, waiting for someone, anyone, to offer her some means of comfort.

Hank ushered Mary to move closer to him, allowing him to kiss her forehead. 'Why don't you go back upstairs and get back into bed? I'll be up in a second to tuck you in,' he insisted, wiping away Mary's tears with his handkerchief.

'Do you promise to come up?' Mary asked as she began to skulk upstairs. When she looked back to acknowledge his response, the bottom step was empty and her parents had already disappeared.

'He'll come, I know he will,' she said to herself.

Mary entered her bedroom and knelt on her toy box, looking over towards Perry's house. The stars above twinkled with innocence. Mary had once relished looking up at the stars, watching how they sparkled like her mum's diamond earrings.

But now she hated them. Watching the stars reminded her of being awake in the middle of the night, scared. If she had the ability, Mary often thought that she would reach a ladder all the way up to the stars, and turn each of them off. Her mum had once sung 'Twinkle, Twinkle, Little Star' to her and Lucy at night until they both closed their eyes and fell asleep. Martha hadn't sung the nursery rhyme in years, and never would again.

Mary closed her eyes, pressing her eyelids tight so that nothing could penetrate. *Please, please, please bring her home*, she prayed, pressing her palms together, her fingers interlinking whilst she said her prayer. *Please bring Lucy back home. Please let her be alright. Please let her remember that I'm her sister. Please don't let her be frightened. Tell her that I'm here, waiting for her. I promise to always be good from now on, and I'll never fight with her if she comes home, I promise I won't.*

Mary didn't really know who she was saying the prayer to. She didn't really believe in God, or understand the concept. Neither had she ever attended church. Her parents had never introduced religion into their daily life, and faith hadn't played a part of her upbringing. But, over the recent years, she had secretly watched her mum doing exactly what she was doing, each night before she got into bed. Mary had watched Martha kneeling on the floor, her elbows resting against the bed. She would whisper, whilst her eyes were closed, talking to someone, this person called God, asking him to bring Lucy home. And so, Mary imitated.

With her prayer for Lucy delivered, she crawled back beneath her duvet, pulling it up to her neck. She listened for her dad's footsteps. He'd be up soon, right? Isn't that what he'd said? Another handful of minutes passed. And then another handful of minutes passed.

'Where is he?' Mary lay on her side looking at the door, the police lights outside still shining onto her bed. Her eyes began to feel heavy, the minutes turning into hours. Before too much longer, she had cried herself to sleep, the darkness of the night-time transforming into the dawning of another new day.

Thirty-One

THE EARLY MORNING SKY BLUSHED, AN ARRAY OF PASTEL pinks shining over Wisteria. Venturing from their nests, the awakening birds warmed their feathers beneath the rising sun, fluttering across the lake in search of a snippet. Leaves fell from trees in sporadic flurries, the surface of the lake soon scattered with a foliage collage. Across the other side of town, the Finchley milkman continued to make his rounds, the glass bottles ratting on the back of his van every time his wheel found a divot. Gwen from Finchley's Fine Cuts was brewing up and plugging in all the hairdryers, ready for a busy day of perms. The neighbourhood chief nosey parker, Mr Derek Farmer, was busy inspecting his cul-de-sac, noting any rubbish that'd been abandoned the night before, along with any incidents of dog fouling.

Having stayed up all night waiting for the police to come knocking, Elsie lingered in the kitchen, slicing her freshly-baked poppyseed bread with a serrated knife. The mouth-watering aroma drifted through the house, yet failed to persuade even the emptiest of stomachs to sample the doughy delight. Martha and Hank remained slumped on the sofa, their darkened eyes heavy, the weight of the night haunting their drawn features. They looked like they had a hangover; however, for once, they were simply exhausted.

Upstairs, Mary awoke.

As soon as she opened her eyes, a feeling of disappointment washed over her.

'Dad never came up, did he?' she said upon stirring. 'I knew he wouldn't.' She looked out towards Perry's. Police were still surrounding the property.

Mary got out of bed and looked through her binoculars. 'I thought they'd be finished by now.' She tossed the binoculars to the floor and walked away from the window, sitting back on her bed.

'Maybe they've found her, and now they're just telling her about us, and what she's missed in the past six years. Maybe that's why it's taking so long.'

She jumped up. 'I should get some things out ready, shouldn't I? Just in case she's home today?' A little spark ignited life back into her bones. 'When she comes home, she'll be so excited if the first thing she sees is Penelope Pickles, won't she?' Mary rummaged under her bed, pulling out her secret box before emptying the contents onto the floor. Along with her bear Mr Twitch, she'd forgotten all about hiding the bones that Einstein had found in her tin, each one falling to the floor. Amongst with the bones, Lucy's old cuddly toy along with Mary's precious photo of her and Lucy also fell out. Mary placed Penelope Pickles and Lucy's other cuddly toy together so that they were lying side by side on the floor.

'Lucy will love having Penelope Pickles back,' she said whilst admiring the toys. Einstein's head raised and he looked at the door, a grumble rumbling in his throat without producing an actual bark.

'What can you hear?' Mary got up and opened her door, listening to the conversation occurring at the front door, edging down a bit further but staying out of sight.

'Mr Lane, can we come in?' Mary heard Sergeant Swift ask in a soft voice when Hank opened the door.

Martha appeared in the hallway. 'Oh, God,' she began. 'Just tell me. I need to know.'

'It's alright,' said Hank, wrapping his arms around Martha,

allowing his wife to bury her head into his neck, his hands applying pressure to her back. 'We need to hear this, don't we?' he said, looking into Martha's eyes and taking hold of her hand.

There were a few moments of silence before Mary heard more voices, her eyes blinking to the rhythm of her heartbeat.

Swift took off her hat, her auburn hair remaining perfectly in place. She didn't ask to go into the lounge. She didn't engage in any light-hearted formalities. She didn't ask how they were. She just delivered the news like a bullet, the only way she could deliver the words.

'A child's body has been found, Mr and Mrs Lane. I'm so sorry.' Her words hung like death in the air. The world fell silent, like time had stopped still, prolonging the suffering. No birds could be heard. The wind didn't blow. No cars on the main road whizzed past. No ambient noise of any kind dared to be the first to break the silence. Even the grandfather clock didn't seem to tick on to the next second. Just silence.

Swift hated with a passion the first few moments immediately after bad news had been delivered, because she never really knew how things were going to pan out. Would the person hearing the news break down? Would the person get angry, or act out in violence? Would the person suffer from some kind of fatal attack?

Upstairs, Mary's heart was the one in jeopardy. It skipped a few beats, her delicate organ feeling the brunt of her shock. Swift's words didn't fully register, but the look on each of her parents' face did as she peered down from the landing. Hank and Martha's simultaneous looks of horror scared Mary. It was like they had seen a ghost, or that they had been told they were dying – which, inside, they were. She bit down on her lip, her senses failing to register the pain and subsequent trickle of blood.

The extended silence continued for a lifetime. Martha and Hank waited to be told that the body wasn't that of their daughter, that the child's body wasn't Lucy's. But that confirmation didn't materialise. It was the rustle of Swift's coat that finally broke the silence, her arm extending.

'I'm so sorry,' she consoled.

Martha's initial scream travelled far beyond the perimeters of the house, the piercing noise forcing its way out, scaring anyone who may have heard it in the vicinity. They may have mistaken it for a woman in the throes of childbirth, or for someone having just had a limb amputated in an horrific accident.

Swift attempted to sympathise, not that she or anybody else could. 'I'm so sorry, Martha.'

'I don't want you to be sorry,' Martha shrieked, her words rattling through the window. 'I want you to tell me that it's not my daughter lying dead over there in that bastard's house!'

'We don't know the identity at this stage,' replied Swift. 'All we do know is that the body *is* a child's.'

Swift drew upon all her training, knowing that it was far worse to try and sugar-coat anything. Tell it to them straight, right? That's the job. That's what police officers are paid to do. They're the bad guys. They find out the truth, and then they tell people what they don't want to hear. But that's exactly what people need to hear, the truth, whether they want to or not. Any attempt at lessening the impact of the news wasn't going to help anyone, not in the long run.

On the landing, Mary placed her hands over her ears. 'Make it stop,' she whispered, attempting to block out the harrowing words, now full of meaning from rattling through her brain.

She ran back upstairs and closed her door, standing with her back pressed against it. She recited Swift's words, 'A child's body has been found.' She hadn't said that a *child* had been found, but a *child's body*. Mary wondered if just finding a body always meant that it was dead. If the body was alive, would Swift have said 'We've found a girl' or 'We've found a child'? Mary didn't know the answers to her questions, and there was nobody to ask.

She slumped herself up against the door, covering her eyes. *They've found Lucy, haven't they? She was over there in the loft and I left her there, alone. I couldn't find her, and now it's all my fault she's dead. I could have stopped him from hurting her. I could have tried harder to be his friend, then maybe Lucy could've come home. But now she's gone, and it's all my fault.*

Einstein remained by her side, his head tilting when he heard someone approaching. Mary also heard footsteps climbing the stairs, so she quickly scurried to throw a blanket over the items that lay exposed in the middle of her room.

Swift stood behind her door, and knocked. Hank was with her.

'Mum, why are you knocking?' asked Mary, assuming that it'd be Martha coming to tell her the news she already knew. Mary was sitting on the floor, protecting the things beneath the blanket, when the door opened.

'Mary, this police officer would like to have a talk with you, would that be okay?' her dad asked, Swift standing by his side.

'Hi, Mary, my name is Claire,' said Swift. 'Would it be okay if I came in and talked to you for a while? Do you remember me from before?' She walked over to where Mary was sitting, bending down to her level. 'Dad can stay and chat, too, if that would be better?'

I know who you are, thought Mary. *You're the lady that tells people bad news.*

Mary didn't answer; instead, she just shrugged, giving the merest of nods. 'You can't look under here,' she announced as an afterthought, ensuring the blanket was covering all the items.

'That's okay, I won't look, I promise,' Swift replied whilst turning, subtly nodding at Hank before she sat down. Hank closed the door and left.

Swift felt a strange feeling seeping into her bloodstream upon stepping into what had been Lucy's room. Over the years, she'd looked at Lucy more than she'd looked at some of her own family members. To Swift, Lucy felt like part of her own family. Sometimes, when alone in the station after everyone had clocked off for the day, she had spoken to Lucy aloud, standing right in front of her picture. *Where are you? Why can't I find you? What have I missed?*

Swift sat on the floor. Mary liked her perfume, the sweet

aroma drowning out the stale smell of alcohol now permanently ingrained up her nostrils. Mary glanced down at Swift's nails, her hand propping her body up, a manicure making the nails shimmer each time the sun caught the glittery polish. Swift's uniform looked bulky over her slim frame, and Mary noticed her slender wrists and striking cheek bones when she walked into the room. The radio clipped on to her jacket made Mary feel uneasy, intermittent noises channelling via the secure frequency. Swift noticed Mary eyeing up the radio, and so she switched it off, and also took off her weapons belt, the cumbersome strap clattering against the floor.

'You're here to tell me that you've found my sister, aren't you?' said Mary without looking up. 'I know you've found a body; a small one, just like mine.' Swift didn't react to the question, and instead stroked Einstein, who was lying sandwiched between them on the floor.

'He's a lovely dog. Is he yours?'

Answer my question. Don't make me ask again.

Mary gave Swift every opportunity to reply before forcing the issue.

'Have you found my sister?' Through the silence that clung to the air, Mary heard Swift take a sharp intake of breath. 'I know you're here because you've found a body, so you can tell me the truth. I'm not a baby. I'm ten. I'm starting secondary school in September.'

'I know you're not a baby, Mary, and I'm sorry for not answering your question,' Swift replied. Mary looked up, scrutinising Swift's green eyes. Although Swift wasn't crying, her eyes looked glazed, her face hiding an underlying unhappiness.

'Your mum and dad have asked me to talk to you about what's been happening. It's part of my job to talk to families during investigations.' Mary looked away, no longer wanting to look at Swift's sad expression.

'You're right, Mary,' continued Swift. 'We've found a child's body, but we're not sure if it is your sister, Lucy. We won't know that for at least a few more hours.'

Mary fidgeted with Einstein's fur. 'Is the body dead?' This time, after asking her question, there was no pause.

'Yes, Mary. The body we've found is dead,' Swift replied with an air of unwavering certainty. No sugar-coating. No dodging the answer. Just the truth.

Mary frowned, her nose scrunched a bit. 'Why don't you know if it's Lucy?'

She thought about the clothes she knew Lucy was dressed in the day she went missing; the lilac dress, the bow. She also thought about the other clothes Lucy might be wearing that would make her identifiable. She thought about the way Lucy's hair would have been styled, and which toys she could have had in her hand.

'Lucy was wearing a lilac dress when she went missing, and she had a lilac bow in her hair,' said Mary. 'So that will make it easier to know if it's her.' A frown line took up residency in the middle of her forehead. 'She wouldn't have been wearing anything brown or green, she didn't like those colours, and she would've had a doll her in her hand. Lucy always liked to hold a toy in her hand, even in the bath.'

Swift thought for a moment before answering.

'Well, Mary. Sometimes, when someone has been missing for a long time, we can't always tell exactly what they look like because their appearance will have changed. So, we do tests to make sure we've got the correct identity. Does that make sense?'

No. Not really.

Mary was still dumbfounded. 'Lucy will look like me, won't she?' she questioned.

'I know she will, Mary, and there are officers right now who are working hard so that we can be sure.'

'You could just let me go and look at Lucy, or let Mum and Dad. We'll be able to tell you straight away.' Swift fell silent for a few seconds, stricken by the innocence. Her nervous hand continued to stroke Einstein.

'I need you to stay here and look after Einstein,' she said. 'I think he'd be lonely without you.'

Mary heard her mum going into the bathroom, her stream of cries failing to subside despite the door shutting.

'Can I ask a question?' asked Swift. Mary nodded, her eyes continuing to look to the floor. 'We found some things that helped us to find the body. Mary, did you leave those photos of Lucy downstairs?' Mary thought for a moment, distracted by the sound of her mum still crying in the bathroom.

'Please, will you tell my mum as soon as you can, about the body I mean? She misses Lucy and she won't be able to sleep until you tell her. And when she gets too tired, she goes to a special hospital, and I don't like it there. It scares me. I like it better when Mum is here with me, at Grandma's house.'

Swift reached out her hand and took hold of Mary's, resting it on the floor and squeezing ever so slightly whilst they continued to talk.

'I promise I'll tell your mum as soon as I can, Mary,' she replied. 'You must miss your sister too.' Mary looked down at Swift's hand stroking hers, liking the warmth and comfort her soft skin provided.

'I do miss her. I think about her all the time.'

So do I, thought Swift.

'I've got Lucy's dolls ready for when she comes home,' said Mary. 'And a few other things I've kept hidden.' She showed Swift her empty box. Mary placed her hand over the blanket, the hard bone beneath making an ambiguous shape, the material draping over the contours.

'Can I have a look? I'd love to see what you've got for her.' She placed her hand on the blanket.

'No. It's a secret. Only Lucy can see,' snapped Mary before walking over and sitting on her bed, swinging her legs whilst folding her arms. She didn't want anybody to see the bone, and she wanted Lucy to be the first person to see her old teddies.

'Lucy is really lucky to have a sister that's so good at keeping secrets,' said Swift. 'When I was your age, I would tell my big brother all my secrets, and he promised not to tell anyone. But, one day, I found out that he'd told everyone in school. I always wanted a sister just like you.' Swift rarely spoke about her personal life on the job, but today it just felt appropriate. 'You know, Mary, I'm really good at keeping secrets, too.' Swift also stood and walked over to Mary's bed, sitting beside her. 'Did you find those photographs, Mary? It's really important that we know.'

Mary started to cry, wiping her nose on her sleeve.

'If I tell you, you have to promise to keep it a secret,' she began. 'I wanted to tell Mum and Dad, but they don't listen. They're always drunk or shouting, and I was too scared.'

'I'll keep it a secret from your mum and dad, Mary. And you won't be in trouble, I promise.'

Mary took a deep breath. 'I found the photos in Perry Golifer's house.' All colour drained from Swift in a second. The thought of Mary being in his house made her want to vomit. Her body shivered all over, and she instantly took hold of Mary's hand, wanting instantly to protect, knowing how much danger she had placed herself in. 'I found some of the photos upstairs in his bedroom, and one was in the hallway.'

Swift's shock was hard to disguise. It wasn't the answer she was expecting to hear, and shivers continued to prickle over her entire body at the thought of that bastard befriending yet another young girl in Finchley.

Mary continued. 'I thought he was a bad person, and I wanted to find out the truth. I shouted for Lucy when I was in there, but she didn't answer. He told me that she was in his attic. But I didn't believe him. He said that Lucy would be staying at his house until I went over to bring her home. That's what he said.'

Mary paused, her hands fiddling with loose strands of hair, all her trapped feelings releasing in one long breath. 'His house was dark and dirty, and I don't think Lucy would have liked it there. She would've been scared, like I was, and so she would have shouted back when she heard my voice. But she didn't.'

Swift wanted to burst out crying. How unprofessional! But even police officers had feelings. She wanted to run and wrap her perfectly manicured nails round that bastard's neck. She wanted to see fear in his eyes right before she killed him. She then wanted to beat the living daylights out of Martha and Hank. How could they possibly lose sight of their daughter for so long that she had time to search Perry Golifer's house? For crying out loud, they'd already lost one daughter, and now they'd come close to losing a second. Had it been up to her, she would have had social services over in a flash. But she knew how the system worked, and it didn't always work very well, or at least not how she expected.

'I found Lucy's doll, Penelope Pickles, outside, in his shed,' continued Mary. 'I told my mum it was in Grandma's basement because I was scared at what she would do, but it wasn't.' Swift used all her professional prowess not to grab hold of Mary and never let her go. She wanted to take her home, keep her safe and tell her that, no matter how bad things were right now, they would get better, and that she would smile again, and feel loved by another human being.

Mary shook her head, trying to release her pain. 'I wanted to know what had happened to Lucy. I thought that *I* might have been the one who did something to make Lucy go away. I was with her at Grandma's house the day she went missing. I should have been with her. I should have kept her safe. I was in charge. And I don't like it when people say horrible things about my Grandma and Grandad. I wanted to know that they didn't do anything bad either. That's why I went to his house. I knew he was bad, and I wanted to find out the truth.' Mary's tears dripped onto her leg. Her hand gripped Swift's as she spoke, relishing the feeling of finally being safe. 'He told me he was coming for me, he wanted to take me away too. He chased me, he grabbed hold of me and was pulling me away.' Mary flung her arms around Swift, every single one of her fears finally releasing in one long breath.

Swift finally took a deep inhalation of breath once Mary's words stopped flowing.

'You are so brave, Mary. Thank you for telling me everything,' she began, holding her tight, waiting for Mary to release. 'I promise, I won't tell your mum and dad. But, for me to not tell them, you have to promise to do something for me in return. Do you think that sounds fair?' Swift stood up and crouched on the floor, looking up to try and encourage Mary to look directly into her eyes. 'It's really important, Mary, so I need you to listen to me carefully.' Mary reluctantly looked up, inspecting Swift's hair, before diverting her eyes again.

'You must promise *never* to do anything like that again. You must *never* go into a stranger's house. And, if someone you don't know asks to be your friend, you should tell your parents and make them listen – shout if you have to. You've done a brilliant job in trying to find Lucy, but now you need to let us do the rest. Going into someone else's house is against the law, Mary, and we put people in jail who get caught.' Mary's big, brown eyes looked up, her hand trembling.

Am I going to jail?

'But, because this is our secret, just yours and mine, nobody else needs to know, just as long as you promise me that you'll never do anything like that again. Will you promise me, Mary?' Swift asked, ducking her head low to try and keep a hold of Mary's gaze. 'Do you promise?' Mary nodded and Swift held her hand.

'That's a deal then. We've shaken on it.' Swift released Mary's hand and gave her another prolonged hug, an embrace that felt so good that Mary clung on for a few seconds longer, which was fine by Swift. 'And, if your parents won't listen, you can call me and I'll make them listen. How about that?' Mary nodded, a glimmer of a smile emerging.

'I was scared in his house,' she mumbled, keeping hold of Swift's hand once the hug concluded. 'Do you think the body *is* my sister?' The room fell quiet and Swift got up, sitting back next to Mary on the bed.

'I don't know, Mary,' she replied, moving Mary's hair away from her face, placing it carefully behind her ear. 'But I hope not.' Mary got up and went to sit back on the floor, wanting to show Swift the stuff from her secret box.

Claire's radio vibrated. Swift got straight up to leave.

'I'm sorry, Mary. I've got to go. I'll come back and talk to you soon, okay?' Swift opened the door. 'I promise I will,' she concluded before disappearing.

Mary followed her out, watching her scurry down the stairs whilst talking into her radio, her other hand getting something out of her pocket. By the time Sergeant Swift reached the bottom of the stairs, there was already a large gathering of officers at the front door.

'What's happening?' asked Hank, he and Martha emerging from the lounge. There were too many people talking at once for Mary to pick up on the conversation, until her mum's words were projected above everyone's, silencing all other voices.

'Oh, thank goodness!' announced Martha whilst sobbing, throwing her arms around Swift, her cries continuing to pour. 'Thank you so much,' she repeated as Swift helped her to sit on the bottom of the stairs.

'You must understand, Martha, it's not over yet,' said Swift. 'There could be more.'

The child's body uncovered in Perry Golifer's attic was that of missing schoolgirl, Katie Banks. Her small, fractured skull was uncovered in his shed. Items of Katie's clothing lay scattered on the floor, marking the spot where she'd been hung, the rope still attached to the bolt. Just when the police thought they could find nothing more upsetting, the team on the ground revealed a second bolt nailed to the shed rafters.

Thirty-Two

FOOTSTEPS MARCHED TOWARDS THE CELL LOCATED AT THE far end of the corridor at Shelton Police Station. Huddled on the floor, with his back leaning against the wall and his knees pressed against his chest, Perry Golifer opened his eyes. Even after the body of Katie Banks had been unearthed from his property, her skull found separately beneath his shed, along with a few final pieces of her skeleton, he had shaken his head and denied the charge of murder. Whilst an excavation of his property continued, he maintained his muted mantra whilst being questioned.

Perry hadn't had any visitors, and yet the person approaching his cell was set to be his penultimate. Since being arrested a few hours previous, he hadn't spoken a word. He had nothing to say, apart from the obligatory confirmation of his full name, plus the acceptance to having a lawyer present. But even the best lawyer in the world wouldn't be able to perform a miracle great enough to see a happy ending. Perry Golifer needed more than a miracle. His trademark smirk was still slapped across his face. But it wouldn't last long.

Sergeant Swift had made the trip up to Shelton specifically. She hadn't trusted herself to detain Golifer at the holding cell in her own station. She had strong, unyielding urges to throttle him to death, as did most of the Finchley residents, if not all. No doubt any one of them would have volunteered to do the throttling on her behalf. But Swift couldn't have that, could she? Any sign of wrongdoing on such a high-profile case would cause suspicion and attract scrutiny. Neither she, nor the village, could cope with any more unwanted attention.

So, Golifer was safer staying in Shelton, away from the vultures that circled, ready to eat him alive. And that's how Swift justified Perry's move to her boss, after which a mutual nod of agreement was exchanged. In return for the favour of housing her detainee, she had agreed to cover a graveyard shift over at Shelton station, helping them out with a paperwork backlog. Off the record.

Swift was the person marching towards Perry's cell. But she wasn't alone. Standing next to her was a stocky, bald man with tattoos covering his entire face. The man stood a good foot clear of Swift, the unsightly scar sprawling the length of his cheek was still visible beneath the heavy layer of black ink. Swift turned the key to open the steel-barred door containing Perry. Once the new offender stepped into the cell and the bars were bolted, Perry spoke his first words.

'You can't do this.' The cell was snug, really only fit for one person for any length of time. Keeping two people in the same cell wasn't ideal, but, on this occasion, it happened to be the only cell available.

'Do you know my name?' asked the man now approaching Golifer, bending down and whispering so that Swift couldn't hear. Perry knew exactly who he was. 'My name is Mr Sidney Banks.' The man stood up, looking down on Perry, who still remained stooped on the floor. 'You of all people should remember my name. After all, I am Katie Banks' uncle.' Sidney smiled.

On the outside, Swift remained poker-faced. Of course, she knew who he was, and who he was related to, but she'd had no choice but to lock him up for the crime he had just been caught committing. She was simply doing her job.

'I've just done something very silly so that I can be thrown in here and keep you company,' Sid added, laughing. 'And I'm

probably never going to be let out again, but it'll all be worth it!'
He sniggered, his facial expression taking on a true representation
of the devil.

Fear filled Perry's eyes and he felt Sid's warm breath brush
over his face. 'I know who you are, and what you did to my niece,
you bastard,' he said, looking back at Swift.

The sound of the cell being locked induced a look of fear
on Perry's face that Swift would never forget. She'd earned the
right to witness that look of fright. Now, every time Swift saw
a photo of Katie, or recalled her memory, she could draw upon
the image of Perry's harrowing expression, and be comforted in
the knowledge that the world had been put to rights.

'Behave yourselves,' she shouted whilst walking away,
dimming down the lights, the windowless corridor becoming
drenched in darkness.

'Bitch! You can't do this. Let me out, I'll tell you everything,'
shouted Golifer, who had suddenly found his voice. 'Don't leave
me here,' he begged.

Within seconds, Sid had taken hold of him by the neck,
ramming his fist into his mouth. Swift didn't negotiate with
murderers.

'It's no use shouting, she's not coming back,' said Sid, his nose
touching Perry's. 'Not until I've finished with you, anyway. And
then they'll be scraping parts of you off these walls for weeks.'
Perry soiled himself, the stench of urine making Sid snigger.

'Scared, are we?' No answer came forth. 'Did my Katie look
scared when you were about to kill her?' Sid asked. Perry heard
the question, but found himself unable to reply, a collection
of smashed teeth filling his mouth, blood pouring down his
injured gullet.

'How did you kill her? Did you touch her? I want to know
everything, and I'll keep you alive until I do.' Sid plunged his
heavy boot into Perry's abdomen, again and again, until his leg
tired and no sound of pain could be heard. 'This is what happens
when bastards like you touch innocent children like my niece,' he

said, spraying spit over Perry and delivering one last blow to his head. Perry's skull smashed against the wall, the cracking sound signalling what was to be the end.

'You'll be sorry for ever laying even a finger on her,' Sid added. He sought pleasure from watching the life drain from Perry, his features unrecognisable, blood staining every inch of skin. 'You've touched Lucy Lane, too, haven't you?' But, at this point, Perry was incapable of answering, his soul now clinging to life. His internal organs and battered body held together only by threads.

Please let me die, prayed Perry, his laboured breathing barely able to draw enough oxygen into his punctured lungs, and he gasped for each breath. Sid gripped his neck, releasing just before strangulation. Perry's suffering was silenced some three hours later, when he begged for mercy, and when mercy wasn't granted, he pleaded to die.

*****

A NEW DAY dawned and, whilst Martha Lane sat peering out of the window at Wisteria, a team of police experts continued with the delicate excavation of Perry's house and back garden, sifting through every grain of earth scattered across what was now already known to be a child's graveyard. Elsie and Hank were also seated in the lounge, neither one of them talking. They scrutinised the walls, now familiar with every crack and flaw after hours of staring at the same square foot. Nobody spoke; what was there to say? There were no words that seemed appropriate. Usually, during trying times, someone would offer to make everyone a cup of tea, like that would somehow make everything better. Today, nobody wanted tea.

Please don't let her be there. Please don't let her be there, prayed Martha at the very same time that Perry Golifer was praying to die. Her body rocked within the confinements of the chair propped up against the window.

'Please don't let her be there,' she whispered aloud. Her body finally stopped rocking, her head slumping to one side and her eyes continuing to stare into the distance.

Martha wanted a drink, but she didn't have the energy to beg someone to give her one. Like Perry, she too wanted to die. Life was too painful, the not knowing felt too painful. She was expecting the worst, and the worst wasn't worth living for. She wasn't sure that she could live if Lucy's body was exhumed. Lucy would've been there the whole time. Each summer, when Martha had returned, she would have only been metres away from her daughter, doing nothing as Lucy was being tormented, butchered or molested. Martha couldn't live with those thoughts. Few parents could.

Her body jolted. 'Oh God, they're coming,' she shouted, her head lifting.

She watched officers approaching the house, her body trembling at the sight. Martha wanted to run. She didn't want to hear the news, not now. She wasn't prepared to be told that her daughter was dead. She thought about running upstairs, or opening the front door and bolting like a bull out of a cage. She wanted to be anywhere else and doing anything other than watching the police approach. Hank stood up and walked over to the door, ready to take the bullet for the family.

Outside, Swift cleared her voice, witnessing Hank's approach. 'Still nothing,' she announced when Hank opened the door. 'But I don't think it'll be too much longer now. They've nearly finished.'

Martha jumped out of her chair. 'I can't take this anymore. I just need to know. I need to know if my daughter's in that bastard's house,' she shouted, knocking over the small side table, the lamp smashing to the floor. 'I want to kill him. I just want to kill him!'

Martha began grabbing pictures off the wall and throwing them against the floor. Her body crumbled to the floor, her arms sprawled amid shards of broken glass. Her hair covered her face and only the sound of her sobs could be heard.

'I can't cope anymore,' she continued. 'I just want to sleep.

Please, let me sleep.' Then Martha fell silent. Swift wanted to tell her about what was happening to Perry, but she knew she couldn't. She'd never be able to speak about it.

Swift heard a noise. 'Hi, Mary. Why don't you go and take Einstein for a walk? I think he'd like that after being cooped up for so long in here.' She watched Mary walk down the stairs. Mary took a long glance at her mum.

'Am I allowed now?' she asked, having obeyed the previous order to remain inside. Swift held out her hand to aid Mary over the glass.

'Yes, Mary, you're allowed. Just don't go too far. Stay near the house, okay?' Swift took it upon herself to dish up a bit of positive parenting, given that nobody else seemed capable of playing the role. She bent down so that she was at Mary's level. 'Are you okay? Is there anything you want to ask me before you go?'

'Is it safe now?' asked Mary, looking directly into Swift's eyes. Swift knew what Mary was asking, and nodded whilst bending down and whispering. 'Yes, Mary, Its safe now.'

'Come on, Einstein.' Mary swung her backpack over her shoulder and plunged her feet into her usual pair of tatty trainers. 'Will Mum be alright?' She watched her dad and Officer Swift dragging Martha off the floor, her mum's head hanging forwards so that her face was concealed. Mary had witnessed her mum in some shocking states before, but right now, in Mary's eyes, her mum looked broken. She wanted to cry, but she didn't have any tears left.

'She'll be just fine, Mary,' said Swift. 'Now, remember what I said. Stay close to the house and don't be too long, otherwise your dad will be out to check on you.' Mary grabbed hold of Einstein's squeaky rubber ball and headed outside.

Swift and Hank dragged Martha's dead weight onto the sofa.

'A coffee would be nice, if you don't mind. Milk and one sugar?' Swift asked, taking a seat next to Martha once she was seated. Hank didn't really want to make her a drink, but reluctantly obliged.

'Sure, give me two minutes,' he said. Elsie got up and followed, not wanting to spend any more time in Swift's company than was completely necessary.

Swift sat upright, pressing her shoulders back and clearing her throat. She meant business. Martha remained slouched, the vacant expression on her face proving that, although she was present in body, her mind had temporarily departed.

'Martha, can you hear me?' There was no response. Swift grabbed hold of Martha's shoulders and shook, forcing her to take notice and drag herself out from wherever it was she was hiding. Martha turned to acknowledge the heavy-handed, unorthodox approach.

'You need to pull yourself together,' Swift began, checking that Hank was still occupied with making drinks. 'You're acting like you're the only one affected by all this, but you're not, Martha. Mary needs you. She's just a child.' Martha didn't react; she just sat fumbling with the tissue in her hands, her head lowered.

Not tough enough? We'll see, thought Swift.

'Mary needs a mother. A mother that isn't a pathetic drunk.' Martha's face portrayed a look that all alcoholics who are still in denial relay. *I don't know what you're talking about.*

Martha took the bait and retaliated. 'Does it look like I'm drinking? Can you see a drink in my hand? Can you?'

'I know it's hard,' said Swift, 'and I know you want to give up, but you can't. Mary needs you to be her mum. She's scared, and alone.' Martha sniggered, making Swift shake her head, knowing her words still weren't getting through. 'You'll regret it for the rest of your life if you don't start being a mother. She'll grow up to hate you.' Swift placed her hand on Martha's, showing a sign of solidarity. 'I can get you all the help you need, but you have to be willing to accept it.'

Martha pulled her hand away. 'I don't need your bloody help, and I don't need your advice. I need you to do your job and find my daughter. There's nothing wrong with me other than the fact that Lucy is still missing. Surely to God I'm allowed to be upset?'

Swift got up, bending down and looking Martha directly in the eyes.

'Stop fucking drinking, Martha! Otherwise, I'll make a call to social services and they'll take Mary away from you, and then you'll have nothing. How do you think you'd feel then? I'm pretty sure you'd want that drink, wouldn't you?'

Martha digested the threat before looking up at Swift, ready to deliver a smack to her cheek, wiping the perfectly applied blusher off her face.

Hank entered, two steaming mugs in his hands.

'Everything okay in here?'

'Absolutely,' said Swift, standing up. 'We were just having a little chat, weren't we, Martha?' Hank sensed an atmosphere and looked at his wife, making a face to silently ask if she was okay.

'Is your mum free for a quick chat, too?'

Swift was on a roll.

'Well, I don't think this is a good—'

'It's important. I'll only take two minutes of her time, then I'll be on my way.' Elsie appeared in the doorway.

'I'm free,' she began. 'But you'll have to follow me outside. I'm just about to hang some washing out.' Elsie stood with the basket in her hands, pegs piled into the pocket of her pinafore.

'Hello, Mrs Lane. That would be great, thank you.' Elsie and Swift walked through the house and out into the back garden.

'What can I do for you?' Elsie asked, pulling out a pair of Mary's trousers from the basket and pegging them to the line.

Swift came straight out with it. She didn't have time to beat around the bush, and her patience was wearing thin. 'Tell me about the things you buried at the allotments.' Elsie dropped the pegs.

'How do you know about that?'

'I'm a police officer, Mrs Lane. It's my job to know everything that goes on in this village.' Elsie scooped up the pegs and continued to hang the damp clothes.

'Those things are precious, that's why I hid them. I didn't

want to lose them, or for anyone else to find them.'

'Well, I did,' said Swift. 'So, unless you want me to take you down to the station for formal questioning, I suggest you answer my questions. Why did you hide those things?' Elsie flicked her head to look at Swift.

'Have you come here to charge me with something?'

Swift took out some clothes from the basket and began to hang them on the line.

'Not unless I have to. Just tell me about the socks and knife, Elsie, that's all I'm asking. I'm not charging you, not yet. I'm not bothered about anything else that's going on. But those socks you hid were the ones that Lucy was wearing the day she vanished, weren't they? She has them on in the photo. And why was there a knife? Was that found the day that Lucy went missing? That was never disclosed in the original statement you supplied.'

For Elsie, the events of that horrific morning came flooding back, like the event had only happened yesterday.

'She was wearing those lilac socks when I left to go and buy the milk. And when I got home, Henry was in the bathroom alone, the knife and socks by his side. Lucy had vanished.' Elsie shrugged at the simplicity of the story, and the helplessness of the situation. 'I don't know what happened that day. Don't you think I'd tell you if I did? Henry doesn't know, either. All I do know is that he would've tried his best to protect her from whoever it was that took her away from us.'

Swift had based her career on intuition and instincts. And, for some reason, her instincts were telling her that Elsie was telling the truth. It was the tone of Elsie's voice; she didn't sound like someone trying to hide something. She sounded like a defeated woman; a woman giving up.

'Henry's statement at the time, and yours, stated that he was sleeping upstairs, and heard nothing, and saw nothing. And now, all of a sudden, he was downstairs in the bathroom with a knife and Lucy's socks? I find it terribly worrying that you lied to the police. That's an offence in itself.'

Elsie took a deep breath. 'I didn't want Martha knowing that her daughter had gone missing, possibly being injured and without wearing any socks, so I hid them. As for Henry, he was having one of his turns, and had used the knife to protect Lucy. He cut his own hand. He hadn't used it to hurt Lucy, he was trying to protect her. I just don't know who he was protecting her from, and neither does he.' Elsie wiped away a tear from her cheek. 'Even now, he still doesn't know. Henry's been poorly for a long time, longer than anyone really knows.'

She paused and composed herself. 'In his mind that day, without question, he thought that someone was coming for Lucy, and he had tried to protect her. He doesn't know who it was. He doesn't know what he or she looked like. He doesn't know anything. Some days, he doesn't even know his own name.' Elsie held her face in her hands. 'That's why I hid the socks and the knife. It didn't make any difference to the investigation. I wasn't hiding something that was going to make Lucy come back.'

'But you don't know that. That was for the police to decide,' Swift corrected. 'Why take the time and effort to hide those things down at the allotment? It makes you look suspicious, underhand.'

Elsie dropped the clothes that were draped over her arm. 'I forget where I've put things.' Finally admitting her fears out loud meant that a weight was lifted from her burdened shoulders. 'I'm struggling to remember things,' she confessed. 'It's the way Henry started, I know it is.'

Elsie just wanted to be able to take out all the precious memories she'd accumulated over the years, and place them in a box, somewhere safe and protected. She didn't ever want to forget the day she had first met Henry at Finchley outdoor market, their hands both reaching for the same punnet of strawberries. She didn't want to forget how happy she had felt on her wedding day, or the way the first kiss as being Mrs Henry Lane had felt. Elsie didn't want to forget all the wonderful feelings she'd experienced the day that Hank was born, or the way her newborn baby smelt whilst cradled in her arms for the first time. And she didn't want to forget about her grandchildren, who meant everything to her. Swift could see the fear in Elsie's eyes, a look that couldn't be faked.

'I didn't want to leave those things in the house, only to forget and then for Martha or Hank to stumble across them.' Elsie pictured Martha finding the socks and knife, and the look of devastation that would spread across her face. 'There would be shouting, and there would be rows, and there would be tears, and for what? Nothing. Because Lucy would still be missing, wouldn't she?' added Elsie.

'If you want to arrest me, then go ahead,' she added. 'Otherwise, there's nothing else I can say.'

Swift felt little compassion; she only cared about Lucy. 'You left the trowel and photo of Lucy in the church, didn't you? You were the person reported that morning looking dishevelled.'

Elsie nodded. 'Lucy needs all the prayers she can get, and I pray for her every day, Sergeant Swift. I'm not sorry for what I did, or how I acted. I'm only sorry that I went to buy milk that day. That's the crime that I should be charged with, and would be guilty of.'

'When we find Henry, I'll have no choice but to take him in for formal questioning after what you've told me,' said Swift. 'You do understand that, don't you?' Elsie understood, but remained silent. 'And the knife and socks will be put through forensic analysis. Even after all these years, there may be clues that can tell us things that you and Henry can't, or won't.'

Elsie turned to walk away. She'd heard the comment, and wanted to shield her reaction, taking a few seconds to compose herself.

'Can we keep this from Hank and Martha?' she asked. 'At least until we find Henry, or the search of Golifer's house is finished. They don't need to know, not yet.'

Swift ignored the comment and followed Elsie into the house. She paused at the front door, picking up her hat.

'I'll leave the drink,' she said to Hank, 'but thanks anyway.

I'll be going, but I'll be back when I have any more news. It shouldn't be long.' She didn't wait for a reply before continuing, turning to open the front door. 'And don't forget, I told Mary you'd check on her.'

She slammed the door and drove off down the drive, dust lingering in the air for minutes after she'd left, her eyes watching in the rear-view mirror, witnessing Mary playing ball with Einstein on the lawn.

The chopper above also vacated the vicinity and, after a few moments, the birds could be heard singing once again. A flock of ducks glided down beneath the climbing wisteria trees and took their rightful positions on the lake, now that the perturbing noise had left their vicinity. Wisteria petals fell like snow onto the lake. The church bells rang in the distance. The sound of cars travelling up and down the main road could be heard. Finchley village was returning to normality.

Swift's eyes peered out through the top of her windscreen, watching the helicopter fly off into the distance. She drove past Perry's, the blockade of police now gone, only a few stationed officers remaining, keeping guard on the property.

She leant over and grabbed the radio which she'd purposefully left in the car. She knew her team would have reached the end of the excavation; only a small area had been left to search when she visited the family. And yet, she didn't want to hear the final verdict. She, like Martha, wanted to delay the news. She wasn't ready to learn that Lucy's body had been hidden, down the road from her station, for all these years. She wanted to continue to live in a world where there was hope; hope of still finding Lucy alive.

Swift pressed the side button on her radio whilst speaking. 'Did we find any others?'

Nobody replied, so she asked again.

'I said, did we find any other bodies? Somebody answer me.'

Thirty-Three

To any outsiders looking in, Wisteria appeared deserted; an abandoned ship. All the curtains were drawn, both upstairs and downstairs. No steam could be witnessed seeping through the air from the boiler, and there were no ambient noises being produced by either a kettle, the washing machine, or the radio. The post on the other side of the front door lay strewn over the floor, and two milk bottles were still sitting on the porch, the birds having pecked holes through the flimsy foil. The blossom decorating the lawn remained undisturbed, a fine blanket of lilac petals concealing the green blades of grass below. But the house wasn't abandoned; there were still heartbeats to be heard within.

Journalist Chester Harrington, who had remained perched high up in one of the trees out front, could have testified that the house had been deserted for a number of hours. He'd been watching for signs of life, his camera at the ready; and yet, despite his patience, he'd failed to witness any movement. He didn't care that he was trespassing, or infringing on a family's privacy; the risk of being arrested was worth it for the killer shot.

Chester was desperate to know if any other bodies had been found at Perry Golifer's, and knew that the Lane family would be the first to find out. And he wanted to capture the first image of the family after they were informed of the news, the image would translate what had or hadn't been found. *Genius*, thought

Chester. Heartless, but genius. That first photo of the family would be the money shot.

Chester Harrington was hungry for another scoop. The paper with a picture of Martha collapsed on the beach at Crest Cove, a bottle of vodka in her hand, had been a bestselling issue. Although people didn't like to admit it, there was something intrinsically appealing about The Lane family, and the mystery that surrounded them. No news thus far had been leaked about the excavation at Perry Golifer's house, and Harrington wanted the scoop; it would cement his career.

But Wisteria wasn't abandoned; the family inside had deliberately chosen to hide themselves away from the world. They were still waiting on pins, desperate for confirmation to come through about what else, if anything, had been uncovered. Martha had finally fallen asleep in the lounge whilst waiting for the phone to ring, exhaustion having taken control of her body. She hadn't had a wash in days, she hadn't eaten more than a morsel, and she hadn't spoken in hours, not to anyone; all she wanted to do was sleep, and wait for the news to be delivered. The phone rested on her lap, her hand on the receiver, ready.

The delicate heat of warm, summer sun encouraged Mary to wake some time close to five in the morning. Along with Martha, Hank and Elsie were out for the count, having only fallen asleep a few hours previous. The only person awake was Mary. Had Chester Harrington not been desperate for the toilet and something to eat, and stayed perched in his lookout for twenty minutes longer, he'd have got the scoop of his career.

Mary felt unable to sit and wait for the phone to ring or the door to knock any longer, and she needed to escape what had become an excruciating wait. She'd bitten all her nails, and had started to pull out strands of hair, her scalp now sore in patches. So, she grabbed her backpack, Penelope Pickles and made her way downstairs with Einstein. She wasn't particularly trying to be quiet, or not wake anyone up; it was just that everyone else couldn't be woken, at least not yet. But they would soon wake;

it wouldn't be long now.

She went out into the garden; the stark brightness of the sky startled her eyes and the smell of flora awoke her senses. She'd started to feel like a prisoner, an innocent one at that. She took in deep breaths, the fresh air replacing the stagnant oxygen that'd taken up residence in her lungs these past few days whilst she had been kept hostage for most of the time. Her eyes immediately gravitated upwards, checking for the helicopter. It was nowhere to be seen. *Thank God.*

Mary and Einstein meandered down into the woods, their legs desperate to stretch. Einstein's tail wagged merrily at the prospect of a long walk, his paws immediately bounding off into the distance. Mary didn't try to keep up; she was too busy kicking leaves and relishing looking at something other than the walls of her bedroom. Just like the room her mum had stayed in at Herons Hook, Mary knew every detail of her attic room at Wisteria. She'd come to memorise the pattern of the garish wallpaper that Elsie had chosen just a few years before the twins were born. She knew which floorboards creaked, and which didn't. She knew the location of each dangling thread of dust, and how many cracks were scattered across the ceiling.

'Einstein, stop,' she shouted, noticing that he'd run so far away that he was almost out of sight, disappearing amongst the myriad of trees. She chased, the sticks and leaves crunching beneath her feet each time she trampled over the uneven terrain.

Beneath the shelter of the trees, the blue sky above became disguised by shades of lilac and green, a canvas scene in the offering. Mary ventured further into the thick undergrowth upon hearing Einstein barking in the distance. Breathless by the time she reached him, she rested her hands on her knees.

'What is it?' She walked towards where Einstein was lying in his favourite shaded patch, beneath the cluster of three smaller trees. He, too, was panting.

'Did you just want me to chase after you?' Mary sat on the floor, trying to catch her breath, before lying flat out on the ground. She watched the sun breaking through the protective umbrella, warming her face whilst she gazed at the mass of wispy clouds tumbling through the sky with a sense of purpose and poise. 'It feels nice to be outside, doesn't it?'

She closed her eyes, her hands sprawled out by the side of her body, her arms and legs stretching to make a circle in the forest floor foliage. She tried not to think about what else had been found at Ivy Dean. She tried her best not to think about anything.

'Are you still there?' she asked, looking over towards him. 'What're you doing?' Mary got up and stumbled over to where Einstein was lying, enclosed within the safety provided by the three tree trunks.

The ground was disturbed from where he'd been digging. 'What've you found now?' she asked. She crouched, her knees pressing into the forest carpet, splinters from twigs piercing her trousers and stabbing her soft skin beneath. 'I hope it's not more scrap bones.'

Her eyes gravitated towards a flicker of something bright poking out of the ground, the object shining from beneath a bundle of leaves. 'Grandma promised me she'd moved all the bin bags so that you couldn't reach them anymore, and I don't want to be going out on the lake again to hide them.' Mary watched Einstein's paws digging.

'What is it?' She looked closer, a flicker of colour reflecting when the sun caught the shimmering object, making the surface sparkle as it lay amongst the dirt. When she scooped the item up in her hands, the flushed colour that had been decorating her face drained. She sat back whilst holding her right hand aloft, the missing sequined hat from her sister's doll lying cupped in her hand.

Mary stared at the hat for a few seconds in confusion, recalling it from all the photos she'd seen in her mum's albums of Lucy. The hat was forever being lost and Lucy never felt settled unless Penelope Pickles was wearing the accessory.

She shot up like a jack-in-a-box.

'Lucy? Where are you?' she shouted in a sudden flood of panic, her eyes scanning the vicinity, assuming her sister must've just dropped it. 'Lucy?' Her hysterics heightened and her hair stuck to her face, her head flinging from one side to another. 'Lucy, shout if you can hear me.' Mary looked up into the web of tree branches towering her petite frame, thinking her sister could be hiding in the trees.

She must be here. She must've dropped it.

'I'm here, Lucy. I'm coming to find you,' she shouted whilst running, gripping the hat, her body darting to every secluded nook, expecting her sister to suddenly appear. Her breathing became erratic. Her eyes welled. She didn't know what to do, where to look, or who to shout to for help. After a few moments of fraught searching, the scenery before Mary merged into one distorted image, her body spinning on the spot, her head dizzy from haphazardly darting in every direction.

In between panting for gulps of breath, she attempted one last plead. 'Lucy, where are you? Can you hear me?'

The woods maintained its silent stance, only the intermittent sound of leaves rustling could be heard. The faint sound of faraway birds travelled in once the wind altered course and swept through the forest.

'Please come out, Lucy. I know you're here.'

Mary was right. Lucy was close by.

Einstein barked in the distance, pulling Mary out from her panicked world, his familiar high-pitched, unhappy tone travelling through the forest like a poisoned dart. She ran back to where he was still standing, his paws digging in the same spot of mud, his snout sniffing, his two front paws ferreting deeper down into the exposed cavity.

'Is there something else of Lucy's?' she mumbled. Einstein barked louder, making Mary fall to her knees alongside him, her hands helping to scoop out some of the packed soil. Einstein's warm breath infused the air and his tongue dangled. *What have you found?* Mary's hands were blackened with mud, reminiscent of grave diggers of old.

A flicker of gold shone, the sun catching the surface of the metal. The buried item beamed through the soil like a diamond on the verge of discovery. 'What is it?' Mary reached in to scoop out more earth, bringing with it the shiny gold ring. Henry Lane's heavy wedding band rested in Mary's palm, the inscription on the inside becoming legible once the mud was wiped away, the letters revealing the inscription *For My Love, Henry.*

Grandad's ring? With her heart still racing, and her eyes constantly searching over her shoulder for Lucy, she rubbed the gold harder against her trouser leg, looking again at the words she'd read so many times before.

'What's it doing here?' Mary placed the ring over her index finger, trying to recall the last time that she'd seen her grandad out in the woods.

Henry hadn't gardened for years.

Einstein stopped rummaging and he lay down, whimpering incessantly. His tongue remained flopped to one side and he panted from the rising heat of the morning. With the ring still over her finger, Mary looked back to the ground, her legs becoming covered in dirt the more they embedded into the disrupted earth. She wanted to leave the hole that Einstein had begun to dig, and run and call Sergeant Swift to tell her all about finding the hat, and Henry's ring, both of which could help the police to find her missing family. That's what Swift had instructed her to do; leave it up to them. But the hole drew her in, her hands reaching down.

Mary's skin began to tingle, though the sensation didn't register amid her panic.

As the scoop of soil that Mary had in her hands trickled through her fingers, she expected to find a pair of Henry's glasses, an old trowel, or maybe his handkerchief. Henry was always losing his handkerchiefs, and they would turn up in the most peculiar of places, like in a kitchen drawer along with the cutlery, on top of the television set, or in the abandoned bucket on the porch that was typically used for housing wet umbrellas.

A frown appeared across Mary's face; a deep indentation visible in the centre of her forehead. She held her left hand aloft, parting her fingers to allow the remaining soil to fall. Once all the dirt had drained through her fingers, a tiny silver bracelet lay entwined between her fingers, engraved into the silver bar was the name *Lucy*.

Thirty-Four

ESPITE A SUMMER SWELL SCATTERING ITS WARM, JULY heat over Finchley, a spine-chilling cold snap hung over Wisteria. A blanket of low-lying mist clung to the air just above the lake. Dew-covered spider's webs hung like decorations from tree branches and flowers, the tiny threads glistening with early morning moisture. Below the tree-top canopy deep in the woods, animal inhabitants were bearing witness to the events occurring below; events that would leave scars on the land for decades.

Mary flung her hands in the air, her fingers releasing the bracelet, allowing the delicate chain to tumble through the air. The snippets of sun breaking through the trees reflected off the bracelet, the shiny metal having its first airing in years. The fine dusting of soil and forest debris from Mary's hands tumbled through the air too, and the silver bracelet landed back on the ground. Wrenched from the pit of her stomach, she released a scream so haunting that the echo etched itself into the surrounding bark, leaving its mark forever. The barrier of woodlands swallowed the harrowing noise before it could reach the main house, her sleeping family unaware of what was occurring right outside.

Mary's child-like features fell from her face, replaced by a look of despair that, no matter how hard she tried to hide, would never be removed. She leaned over and stretched out her shaking hand, carefully taking hold of the bracelet, conscious of how delicate it may be. Through her tears, she examined the silver bar, wiping her eyes with the back of her hand. She held the bracelet right up to her eyes, squinting to see past her tears. She rubbed the bracelet on her sleeve, removing the layers of dirt engrained into the intricate design. Once again, she saw the name *Lucy*, the scroll letters clear to see. She knew the bracelet belonged to her sister because it was identical to one that she had as a child, only hers had *Mary* engraved into the metal.

She looked around in every direction, expecting to see her sister, a look of confusion spreading across her face when the woods remained deserted. She looked closely at the bracelet, holding it with a delicate touch.

'Lucy?' she called out, and when there was no reply, she shouted again 'Lucy?'

She flinched at every noise, expecting someone to be there; expecting to see her sister.

'I don't understand,' she whispered, confusion clouding her mind the more she tried to understand how the items had ended up buried in the soil. She looked around, searching for her sister and grandad, hoping that they had been playing in the woods somewhere and that's how they must have lost their things. Her heart galloped at the thought, her hopes raised at the possibility, and she remained crouched on the ground, waiting for her lost family members to come running over. The woods teased and heightened Mary's anticipation, her heart leaping into her mouth each time a noise resonated in the distance, the wind causing the leaves and branches to rustle. When there was no sign of life, she hung her head and cried even harder, scared by what she had found, and what it meant.

With her knees still pressed into the soil, she forced herself to take a breath and regain a regular breathing pattern, a feeling of lightheadedness threatening to make her pass out. Her chest finally stopped juddering. She blinked a few times to encourage her tears to fall, and she listened, panic causing her eyes to dart in every direction. Her mind conjured up another possibility, that it was all just a game, and that her Grandad and sister were leaving clues and they were just hiding from her.

'Please come out, I'm scared,' she whispered. Her eyes searched the woods, trying to spot any signs of movement.

Where are you both?

Mary clasped her fingers together, like she was praying, and closed her eyes. Every memory of her sister flooded to the forefront of her mind. She thought back to the day that her sister had gone missing and tried desperately to remember if she'd seen Lucy in the woods, having thought all this time that she was in the house. Mary cried harder at the image that maybe her sister had been kicking and shouting when someone removed her bracelet. She searched her mind, trying to think if she'd heard her sister screaming the day she went missing, thinking she could now hear the sound of a child's scream ringing in her ear.

The cruel, fictitious noise in her mind set about another wave of panic. Urged to search for more clues, Mary plunged her shaking hands back into the earth, rummaging through the soil. She finally felt something in her hands, something soft to the touch. She pulled her hands out and shook away the mud, leaving behind Lucy's lilac hair bow. Mary's heart skipped. She shook her head in disbelief and her face scrunched. Her head flung round upon hearing something in the distance, anticipating seeing her sister.

'Lucy, where are you?' she shouted.

She scrambled back, her feet acting as a propeller, reversing her body. She only came to a stop when she collided with a tree, and she tried to hide, fearful that someone was watching. Her eyes darted between the bow in her hand and her surroundings. Her ghostly complexion ingrained itself into her pores. Her dry lips cracked and the shadows under her eyes deepened. The dark bags would never be removed, instead they would become ingrained in the pigment of her skin, forever serving as a reminder of this very day.

Where are you, Lucy? Somebody, help me, she shouted internally, but no sound emerged from her mouth, the fright having now stolen her voice, as well as her innocence. *I need help. Please, somebody come and help me.*

With her sister's bow and bracelet in her hand, Mary could now feel her skin tingling, the sensation spreading across her entire body like a disease. If her sister wasn't stood right in front of her having retuned home, then she didn't want to feel Lucy's presence. The sensation felt too upsetting, fooling her to feel something that wasn't real.

Come home, Lucy.

Mary's tears fell like a torrent. She held the bow close to her eyes so that she could see it through her flooded vision, making sure it was the same one; the one that she remembered so well. The size was the same, the metal clasp on the back was the same; and, although dirty and deteriorated in places, she could see the familiar lilac material beneath. She held the bow to her nose, inhaling what she knew had once been her sister's smell. She pressed it to her face, relishing a moment of once again feeling close to Lucy. She closed her eyes and remembered how Lucy looked with the bow in her hair, and the bracelet wrapped around her tiny wrist. She could see the image of Lucy perfectly in her mind, and she didn't want to open her eyes, knowing that the image would vanish, just like her sister. The tree continued to support Mary's frame, encouraging her body to remain upright.

For the next half an hour, all Mary was able to do was sit. She stared at the location where she'd found her sister's items, half expecting Lucy to suddenly jump out from behind a tree and appear right before her eyes. She didn't blink. Anticipation held her breath captive. She wanted to run, but she didn't know where to go. She wanted to shout, but she didn't know what to say. She felt terrified, and yet she couldn't move. She kept questioning in her mind how the items had become lost, or if someone had taken them away from Lucy on purpose.

A meek whisper emerged after sitting in silence for so long.

'Lucy? It's me, Mary. Where are you?' She knew now that her sister wasn't going to appear, but it didn't make her stop wanting to talk to her. 'I'm sorry I didn't look after you. I'm sorry I wasn't a better sister. I'm sorry—'

A great sense of sadness encouraged Mary to cry like she'd never cried before. Her whole body juddered, and she held on to her sister's bow and bracelet like she was holding Lucy's hand, never wanting to let it go. Her torso fell to the floor, her body naturally curling into the foetal position. She cast her eyes over towards where Einstein was now lying fast asleep beneath the apple trees.

The woods remained quiet, keeping its secrets close to its heart.

The wind ceased and the birds no longer felt the need to announce their presence. Mary thought about what it would be like to tell her parents about what she had found. But, each time she did, she cried harder, covering her face and shaking her head. She knew her mum's hopes would be raised, only to be shattered when she learned that Lucy hadn't also been found. She pictured how her mum had reacted to seeing Penelope Pickles. Martha hadn't been pleased to find the doll after so many years, she'd been distraught at the finding. Mary imagined her mum grabbing the things from her hands before running straight outside, screaming Lucy's name and searching the woods until her body became so tired that she fell to the floor. In Mary's mind, that's when Martha would be taken back to Herons Hook.

I can't do it. I can't. I don't know how.

In her mind, Mary practised over and over what she was going to say when she got back to the house, trying not to let her fears get in the way

Mum, I have something important to show you.

Mum, I've found something in the woods.

Mum, look at these, at which point, Mary would open up her palm to reveal her sister's jewellery and lilac hair bow.

No matter how Mary practiced telling her mum in her mind,

it never sounded right, and obviously, it never would.

How had Grandma or Grandad not seen someone hide Lucy's things in the woods? thought Mary. And then her long-held fears returned, her mind plagued by the thought that it could've been her grandparents all along. *Why was grandad's ring there too?* Mary placed Henry's wedding band over her thumb, the ring feeling heavy on her hand. Over the years when nobody was listening, Mary had asked her grandad dozens of times what had happened to Lucy, each time getting the same reply, "I don't know, Mary, I was in bed, asleep." She had always believed her grandad, but now, with his ring on her finger, her churning insides told her otherwise.

Mary looked over towards the house, terrified to return, thinking in her mind that her own grandma could have been the one who made her sister, and now her grandad, disappear. She hung her head, her tears falling to the ground before soaking into the disturbed earth. She felt cold, the shock sabotaging her body's ability to regulate. Einstein came and sat by her side, the warmth from his body feeling comforting against her skin.

I'll tell them another day. By then, I'll have thought of what to say.

Mary took off her backpack, placing the silver bracelet, the lilac bow and her grandad's gold ring inside. She then took hold of Penelope Pickles, placing the hat in its rightful position.

She filled in the hole where Einstein had been digging, and then covered the ground with twigs and leaves so that it didn't look disturbed. Mary stood and took hold of a rock, placing it next to where she'd found everything. She wouldn't forget the location, the apple trees serving as a reference, but she just wanted to make sure.

On the walk back from the woods, she had thought of a way to tell her parents about Lucy's things. She'd turned it over and over in her mind, practicing saying the words aloud. The sentence began 'There's something important I need to tell you both.' Despite knowing what her Mum's reaction would be, Mary just hoped that she would survive hearing the news. In Mary's eyes, her mum always looked so fragile, like words alone could have the ability to make her drop to the floor. Walking across the lawn, Mary imagined hugging her mum after showing her Lucy's bracelet, and wiping away her mum's tears. Mary always liked it when her mum used to sweep a soft tissue across her cheeks any time that she had been upset, the delicate touch magically making her feel better.

Mary wiped her eyes and continued to take deep breaths, trying to gather courage through the oxygen that filled her lungs, and whatever else she needed to make it through the next ten minutes. And although there wasn't a drop of colour in her face, with her hair straightened out and her cheeks dry, her features were almost able to carry off a look that told the world everything was okay. She just looked like a child who had been playing outside; tired and dirty.

Her legs continued to walk, robotically, without her having to think about which direction was the way home. She wasn't scared that anyone was following her anymore, and had someone taken her away, she wouldn't have minded; anything would be better than going home and speaking her practiced words aloud. She had hoped that the walk back to the house would take forever, that maybe she would never find her way home. But soon enough, she broke out from the woods, Wisteria coming into view across the garden. She gulped. She held back the tears brimming behind her eyes. Her dry throat felt sore, and she practiced her words again and again, making sure they would get past the lump lodged in her throat.

Her limbs felt heavy as she neared the front door, and it took all her courage to take each additional step. She paused on the porch, listening. She wasn't really sure what she was listening for, anything which could act as an excuse not to talk to her parents. Yet the house was silent. She placed her hand on the doorknob, slowly twisting. She eased the wood from the frame and hovered in the doorway.

Two minutes earlier, inside the house the phone had rang.

The receiver had rattled in its cradle, vibrating on Martha's lap. It was fast approaching 7 am, too early for anyone to be calling. Upon hearing the incessant ring, Martha's eyes opened wide and her body jumped. Her hand was shaking. She urged her fingers to lift the handset off its cradle, but her hand froze. Martha knew what the call was. She knew whose voice would be greeting her on the other end.

But no matter how much Martha ignored it, the phone was never going to stop ringing until someone answered.

Martha finally lifted the receiver.

'Hello,' said the person on the other end.

Martha didn't move. She sat still, floods of tears rolling off her cheeks, the phone still clenched in her hand.

Sergeant Swift's voice echoed through the receiver.

'Martha? Are you there?'

'Just tell me,' she whispered, her head shaking in anticipation of the reply. Martha closed her eyes, bracing herself for the news. In her mind, she repeated the words she wanted to hear, urging them to materialise. At the other end of the phone, Swift looked across her office towards the evidence wall, the photo of Lucy coming into view. Swift could almost see Lucy's body swinging through the air, her legs encouraging the swing to go higher. In her mind, Swift could hear Lucy's voice, laughing and telling her mum to push her again, the powerful image producing a swath of goosepimples to cover her skin. Swift also closed her eyes, tears trickling down her cheeks.

'Martha, we didn't find Lucy.'

Martha's eyes released an immediate flood of tears, the overwhelming amount of stress resting on her shoulders lifting as soon as the statement was spoken.

'Are you sure?' muttered Martha.

'We searched everywhere, Martha, she isn't there, I promise you, she isn't there.'

She had received confirmation only moments before that the search of Perry Golifer's property had been completed. No grain of earth, no brick, and no floorboard had been left untouched during the search.

Moments after hearing the news, Martha dropped the handset to the floor, the receiver dangling upside down by its cord. She couldn't stop crying, or smiling. Hank appeared in the lounge, looking at his wife and waiting for verbal confirmation of the news.

'They didn't find her.' Hank fell to the floor next to his wife, the pair hugging and holding one another tight.

'Oh, thank God.' He released a breath that sounded like it had been held captive for hours, if not days, or years. 'Oh, thank God.'

It was at that moment that Mary and Einstein walked in through the front door, Mary's hands black with dirt, her knees sodden where they'd been scrambling in the moist ground.

Mum. Dad. There's something important I need to tell you.

Mary stepped inside, took a breath, and began her sentence. 'Mum-,' but the following string of words vanished once she saw her parents on the floor, both of them crying and hugging. Her insides tumbled. If only Swift had called five minutes later, after Mary had walked through the door.

What's happened?

'What's happened to you, Mary? Why are you so muddy? Have you been crying? Your eyes look puffy,' asked Martha, noticing her daughter's appearance before walking over towards the door. Mary quickly ran through her sentence in her head having been distracted by the crying, ready to show them what she'd found.

'I fell in some mud, but I'm okay,' she replied, replacing her anticipated sentence.

'They've finished the search, Mary,' said Martha. Mary remained near the doorway.

'They didn't find Lucy,' declared Hank, he too walking over towards Mary.

Mary didn't react to the news in the same emotional manner as her parents. She remained still. She didn't smile. She didn't jump up and down. She didn't run to hug someone. She didn't utter a single word.

Martha waited a few seconds longer, waiting for a reaction that was never going to come.

'Did you hear what Dad said, Mary? They didn't find Lucy at Perry Golifer's house. It's wonderful news, Mary,' added Hank, a perplexed expression on his face. Mary still hovered in the doorway.

'But I thought we *wanted* them to find Lucy, and now you're happy that they haven't?' asked Mary. 'I don't understand.' She didn't move, but remained within the safety of the doorway, confusion filling her mind the more she witnessed her parent's happy faces.

'Of course we wanted to find Lucy, Mary, we still do,' began Martha, a smile also shining from her face. It had been so long since Martha had released a genuine, happy expression that her face struggled to perform the required look. 'But we didn't want them to find her at Perry Golifer's house.'

Martha stood and walked over to Mary, taking hold of her daughter like she was seeing her for the first time. 'We knew that, if she was found in his house, then she wouldn't ever be coming home. Do you understand that, Mary? Perry Golifer is a bad man. He's done some terrible things to other children, things that he's now in jail for, and will be staying in jail for for a long, long time.'

Mary wriggled free from her mum's suffocating embrace. 'So, you're happy now? Now that you don't know where Lucy is, you're happy?' Mary shook her head. She tried to make sense of the situation, she tried not to forget her practiced words, but all she was able to do was become lost in her mum's look of happiness, a look she couldn't ever remember seeing on her mum's face.

'I'm happy now that we know that Lucy isn't over there,' replied Martha. 'I'm happy that we have hope again, Mary. All I ever wanted them to do was search that awful house, and now they finally have. I now know that, one day, we'll be able to find your sister and bring her back home.' Martha took hold of Mary once again, wrapping her arms around her and drawing her closer. 'We have *hope* now, Mary. And as long as we have hope, everything will be alright.'

Mary pulled away from her mother's embrace, looking into her eyes. Her practiced words had been erased from her memory, and would never return. It was like the words, and their meaning, had never existed.

Over the years, Mary had forgotten how it felt to be hugged, especially by her mum. But, once wrapped in Martha's maternal love, the embrace felt so warm, so comforting, and so reassuring, that Mary didn't want her mum to ever let her go.

'I'm sorry I've been so horrible recently, a terrible mum. But I promise that everything will change now, okay?' Martha reassured, whispering in Mary's ear whilst stroking the back of her head. 'I'm going to go back to Herons Hook. I'll be staying there for a few weeks, but it'll be for the very last time, I promise you, Mary. Nobody will be forcing me to go. I want to go this time. Then, when I come home, there will be no more drinking and no more arguing. How does that sound?' Mary shrugged her shoulders; she'd heard it all before.

Hank took hold of Mary's hand. 'Come on, why don't we get you cleaned up and then go and get some ice cream.' He kissed her soft skin, waiting for a reply.

An unusual expression appeared across Mary's face. She might not have been able to vocalise what she'd found in the woods, but she felt sure that her parents would be able to tell something was the matter, just by looking at her face, spotting the sadness welling behind her eyes. So, she stood still for a few seconds, permitting her parents to see the truth for themselves.

'What do you think?' he asked Mary. 'At last we have something to cling onto. The police have finally done something that we've been asking them to do for years, and now at least we all know that Lucy isn't being kept over there,' Hank pointed in the direction of Perry's house. 'I know we still haven't found your sister, I know that, but it's a tiny glimmer of hope and we have to hold on to that Mary. Everyone can now focus all their attention on finding who took Lucy, and help us bring her home.' For so many years, Hank hadn't been able to ignore a sinking feeling in the pit of his stomach that Perry had taken his daughter, and even though she was still missing, he felt relieved; at least his daughter wasn't buried beneath Ivy Dean. He bent down, looking Mary right in the eyes. At that exact moment over at Shelton police station, a paramedic lifted Perry's Golifer's eye lids and shone a torch into his pupils. Perry Golifer was dead, and Sidney Banks was charged with first degree murder.

Thirty-Five

A CHORUS OF GRANDFATHER CLOCKS IN A NEARBY ANTIQUE shop simultaneously announced the arrival of midnight. At the strike of twelve, Henry Lane's body filled with life, like it had been charged with a defibrillator. A nightmare had shocked his brain into awakening, and pangs of adrenaline flooded his flatlining veins. Rising like Frankenstein's monster, Henry's torso lifted off the ground; each vertebra in his twisted spine creaked and he released a moan of discomfort once his back straightened. His legs reluctantly took the weight of his body and, although a good few pounds lighter than when he had left home, initially his limbs struggled to keep his unsteady stature aloft. Henry wasn't making a miraculous recovery. His body was tricking him into a false sense of security, offering him one final burst of life, before his time was set to end. With vigour back in his veins, Henry knew where he wanted to go, and who he needed to see.

His hand pushed on the broken plank of wood he'd placed over the entrance of the cow shed, the makeshift door falling to the floor and permitting a breeze to enter. A collection of lingering spiders and woodlice that had been sharing the secret hideaway scurried back into concealed crevices, themselves unwilling to brave the new world. The breeze swept across Henry's face, and his wispy hair danced on top of his head.

Once out in the wide-open space, Henry looked around,

searching for elements of familiarity.

'Mary?' he announced, his eyes trying to adjust and his body sweating, despite the cool temperature of the late summer air. In the darkness, he tried to scan his unfamiliar location, nothing but shadows from the surrounding cluster of trees visible. There were no streetlamps, and no lights shone from nearby houses; the field was flooded by the gloom that accompanied midnight.

'Where are you?' he shouted.

He took a few tentative steps further away from the safety of his hideaway.

'Where am I?' He looked back at the place where he'd been hiding, and knew, somewhere in the back of his mind, that it wasn't where he belonged. He needed to find his granddaughter. He needed to save her from the voices in his mind which were now telling him they were coming back, and this time, they wanted Mary.

Henry began to make his way across Finchley, like a zombie risen from the dead. He didn't stick to the pavement, but instead wandered like a drunk into the road, then across people's gardens, before finding himself staggering up a main road, Wisteria now only a stone's throw away behind the woods. The village lay dormant while he aimlessly trawled the deserted streets, and in his state of confusion, his mumbles became audible.

'Please don't take her,' he repeated. *We're coming to take her away, Henry,* was all he could hear, the voice in his mind refusing to silence.

If only someone had driven past and spotted his unkempt state. If only the milkman had started his rounds earlier. If only the last bus of the night had been delayed by ten minutes. If only Mr Derek Farmer had been prowling the streets checking for unruly kids. If only Hank and Martha had been on their way home from the pub. If only Sergeant Swift had taken a left turn at the end of Hobbs Street, then maybe the events that were set to occur could have been avoided.

But, it turns out that nobody spotted Henry that night, other than darting bats and curious cats. After hours of wandering the streets and side alleys, he finally stumbled upon Wisteria. The drifting perfumery of the lake infused his senses and, somehow, guided him home. His heavy footsteps crunched across the driveway and his eyes scanned the house, searching for the invasion of people that he could hear in his mind. The voices were now screaming at him, *I'm going to take her away, Henry, unless you stop me. I'm at the house right now, and I can see Mary from where I'm standing. You'll never see her again, Henry, ever.* Terrified by the voices, Henry covered his ears with his hands in a vain attempt to silence the threats. Standing at the front of his home, he shook his head, trying to make his enemies disappear.

'Please don't take her,' he replied, stepping forwards and instinctively scraping his shoes across the porch doormat before taking out the single key from his pocket and opening the door. His weary frame stumbled into the hallway. He closed the door behind him and peered back through the net curtain, the shadows of the night taunting his already fragile mind, his starved frame trembling. To Henry, the bad men in his mind were outside the door, banging on the glass and threatening to come in.

I'm taking her away, Henry. I've come to get her and there's nothing you can do to stop me.

'Mary?' he whispered, putting his key in his pocket before climbing the stairs.

Upstairs in the attic, Mary lay fast asleep, cocooned in the duvet with Penelope Pickles and Mr Twitch by her side.

Navigating the dark interior of his home, Henry's hand slid up the banister, his damp, cold socks slipping across the landing, the wooden floorboards creaking under his weight. *I'm taking her away, Henry, unless you come and stop me.*

Einstein crawled out from under Mary's bed and sat on guard. Outside, the ostentatious owl nesting in the trees was performing its secret serenade.

'I'm coming, Mary, don't worry,' Henry mumbled. Walking up the second set of stairs, he made it to Mary's bedroom door, twisting the knob until the wood eased out of its snug frame. As the door opened, Einstein jumped up, placing his paws on Henry.

Taken aback, Henry crouched, stroking Einstein.

'Who are you? Are you with them?' he whispered, rubbing behind Einstein's ears. Einstein's tail wagged in appreciation of the affection, and Henry tried to recall if he knew the dog's name. 'Where's Mary? Have they already taken her?' He tiptoed over to Mary's bed, kissing his granddaughter on the cheek with such a great sense of relief that tears welled behind his glasses.

Mary sat bolt upright in a startle. She thrashed her arms and kicked, thinking it was Perry that had come to take her away. Her heart raced and she released a gasp. 'Grandad?'

She rubbed her eyes and drank in the distinctive smell caressing the inside of her nostrils, the comforting aroma of her grandad still lingering on his dirty clothes. The smell of Old Spice produced an invisible smile that broke through the darkness, spreading across Mary's face.

'You frightened me. Is it really you?' She held out her hands in the darkness to feel Henry's freezing face, her fingers recognising every frown line and dimple.

Henry pressed Mary's hands to his face, feeling her warmth on his skin. 'Oh, Mary. Thank goodness you're okay. They were coming to take you away, just like they did with your sister,' he rambled, hugging Mary with a protective force. He closed his eyes and relished the physical feeling of knowing that his granddaughter was alright, pressing her slight frame close to his chest.

Muddled images from July 17th, 1982 flashed in a constant cycle through his mind.

'I heard the same voices again, Mary, saying that they were going to take *you* away this time. Are you sure you're okay?' Mary felt her grandad's tears trickle onto her cheek. Their faces remained touching, the warmth from Mary permeating her grandad's skin during the prolonged reunion.

'Grandad, I'm alright. I'm not hurt. Nobody has taken me away.'

Henry didn't hear his granddaughter's words. His mind was too distracted by a stream of chaotic thoughts, unable to process anything concrete.

Mary caught sight of Henry once the clouds parted and the moon shone in through her bedroom window. 'We've been so worried about you, Grandad. Where've you been? Everyone's been looking for you, even the police.'

Henry examined her arms, touching her head and feeling her face.

'Thank goodness I got here in time, Mary, before they could hurt you too,' he said. 'I heard them. They were already here, at the house, surrounding us, and all I wanted to do was grab you and hold you as tight as I could, just like I did the day they came for Lucy. I was too late to save her, but thank goodness I made it in time for you. I won't let them hurt you, Mary, I promise I won't.' The images of Lucy's body cradled in his arms, lifeless, flashed through his mind like bolts from the Blitz, before quickly disappearing, leaving behind only fragments of memories in the wreckage. Mary pulled her face away from Henry, frown lines scattering her forehead.

'Who came for Lucy, Granddad?' she asked, confused by his stream of muddled mumbles.

'The bad men. They had the house surrounded. We couldn't escape. I heard them in the house, in her bedroom. They were everywhere, even on the roof. And now they've come back for you.' Henry looked to the ceiling. 'I can hear them. They have us trapped.' Mary traced her Grandad's line of vision, hearing nothing but his laboured breathing. She listened again, just to make sure, her ears working hard to seek out any external, ambient noises. The moment Mary understood that there was nobody there, that nobody had come to take her away, her heart performed a series of tumbles and her face flushed with fear. Terrified, her body froze, rigid with fright. Her eyes watched Henry, witnessing the angry expression on his face the moment he thought he heard another threatening voice. Henry moved closer to Mary, her body flinching when he pulled her close.

'I got to Lucy too late, Mary, but I'm here to save you,' he continued wrapping his arms around her body. 'I held Lucy's body just like this. She wasn't breathing and I didn't know what to do, so I just held her so they couldn't take her body.'

After years of trying, Henry was finally recalling his version of events, speaking aloud exactly what he thought had happened the day that Lucy disappeared. But his version wasn't accurate. There were no voices. There were no threats of an abduction. The house hadn't been surrounded. Nobody came and took Lucy away. There was still life in Lucy's lungs when Henry had taken her into his arms, trying in vain to protect.

'When they left last time, I wrapped Lucy in a blanket and ran outside.' Henry looked towards the window, cowering at the thought of carrying his granddaughter's dead body out into the darkness. Henry was acting like he was reliving the horrifying moment, his speech rambling, like he was once again running scared into the night.

'I knew they'd come back for her, so I lay Lucy under the apple trees in the woods, hiding her body as best as I could. I knew they wouldn't find her there; nobody would ever find her there. I knew she'd be safe, Mary, and that I'd always be able to protect her when they did come back.' Henry's body shuddered, his eyes darting this way and that, his paranoia reaching a pinnacle. 'And now they've come back, but this time they want you, Mary, and I won't let them hurt you. Thank goodness I got to you first.' Henry wrapped his arms around Mary so tightly that he threatened to crush her delicate bones, the air within her body struggling to pass freely, her internal organs compressing.

'You're hurting me,' she said, trying to wriggle free from the suffocating embrace, urging his arms to set her free. Henry held her captive, the stream of hallucinations preventing him from ever wanting to let her go. Her ribs ached, her grandad's arms leaving indentations on her delicate skin, bruises beneath the surface swelling.

Lucy's spirit screamed; it, too, reliving the moment that she had lost her life in the same vain, cradled in her grandad's arms six years previous when he was trying to protect her from the fictitious voices haunting his mind.

Mary held her ribcage. 'You've hurt me.' Fear filled her lungs, her entire body shaking. She wanted to run away. She wanted to scream, yet all she could do was look at her grandad, fright making her tears stream down her face. He no longer looked like her grandad, he looked like a stranger and someone to be scared of. Within the darkness of her Wisteria bedroom, Mary Lane now understood what had happened to her sister on that July morning, and it felt like her heart was slowly dying. She now understood why Lucy's bracelet and her grandad's ring were buried in the soil. She knew that had she dug her hands deeper into the earth, that she would have uncovered her sister's body. Mary didn't yet understand that the bones Einstein had found were actually part of Lucy's skeleton, but she would, in time.

Mary now knew exactly how her sister had died, and understood that she would never be coming home. Mary was the first to learn that it had been her own grandad who had killed her twin sister. Henry Lane had squeezed the life from Lucy, albeit innocently, trying to offer protection. And now, Mary was in exactly the same situation as her sister; under the threat of being killed.

If only Mary hadn't spilt the milk that July morning. If only she and Lucy hadn't demanded strawberry milkshakes. If only there had been another pint of milk in the fridge. If only Elsie hadn't gone to the shop. If only she hadn't been delayed getting home. If only Henry had remained asleep for another hour. If only Martha and Hank had cancelled their day trip. If only the car tyre had suffered a puncture. If only Henry had experienced his hallucination a week later, when the family had finished their holiday and already returned home.

If only.

Thirty-Six

TERRIFIED OF HER GRANDAD, MARY'S INSTINCTS TOLD her to run away. To Mary, Henry no longer felt like the same person; to her, he was now the person who had killed her sister. She wanted to hit him until her arms fell off, and make him take back the terrible thing that he'd done. She wanted to go back in time and place herself right next to Lucy to protect her. She wanted to be able to stop their grandad from hurting her sister, and make him release her before he crushed her to death. She wanted to go back in time and grab hold of Lucy's hand and make her escape, running as far away from her grandad as they possibly could, hiding until their grandma returned. After all these years, Mary now knew that she hadn't been the one who had hurt her sister, but the revelation didn't make her pain go away. Instead, a feeling of guilt flooded her mind because she now knew that she could've done something that day to save her sister. *Why didn't I stay inside? Why did I leave her alone? Why didn't I stay and play with her? Why didn't I stop him?*

Sitting on her bed, Mary couldn't see past the confusion in Henry's words or actions. To her, there was no explanation for what he had done. He had killed her sister, and she didn't care about the reasons why. The reasons weren't going to bring Lucy back, and that's all Mary wanted; to have her sister back home.

She swung her legs round, ready to get out of bed. 'I'm going to go and get Mum.' Henry's arms opened up and scooped her body back.

'You can't leave, not yet, Mary. You've got to stay with me.' Mary flinched when her grandad touched her, her body cowering against the wall, trying to escape his grip. But it was no use; Henry grabbed hold of her as if she was a rag doll.

Please don't hurt me, Grandad.

'What's going on, Mary? Who you talking to?' asked Hank, her door swinging open. He'd heard Mary's voice from the hallway whilst on his way to the bathroom. 'Why are you awake?' he asked before switching on the light and squinting. 'Dad? Oh, thank goodness you're home.'

Henry jumped, grabbing Mary, holding her tight and preventing her from escaping.

'Don't come any closer!' He held out his free hand, demanding for Hank to stop. Mary began to cry, Henry's restraints threatening her ability to breathe, her already delicate ribs suffering another bout of bruising. Hanks initial relief at seeing his Dad safe and well back home was short lived.

Hank held out his hands, signalling for Henry to calm down. 'Dad, it's just me, Hank.' He spoke in a soft voice, attempting to defuse the situation. 'Let Mary go, Dad. You're hurting her.'

'You're with them, aren't you?' said Henry. 'Where are the rest of them? You've come to take her away, haven't you? Well, I won't let you.' He tightened his already deadly grip, his eyes checking the ceiling and each window.

'Dad, I'm your son. Please, listen to me,' begged Hank. 'You're confused. Let Mary go and I'll prove that there's nobody else here.' He took a small step closer. Henry thrashed his head with frustration.

'No, you're lying. You've come to hurt her, and I won't let you. I won't let you take her away.' Mary's body weakened, her grandad restricting the amount of air getting to her lungs, starving her body of oxygen.

Hank began to talk with urgency. 'You like lots of butter on your toast, Dad. You like sleeping with the window open, even when there's frost on the lake. You take two teaspoons of sugar in your tea, but really, you'd prefer three. You hate your bath too warm. Your favourite subject at school was woodwork.' Hank scoured his memory for information that would restore his dad's flailing faith. Henry shook his head profusely, listening to the voices that remained dominant in his head.

He's lying to you, Henry. He's with us. He wants to take Mary. Don't let him trick you.

'No! I don't believe you. You've been watching me, haven't you? You're spying on me.'

He moved with Mary off the bed and over towards the window. 'Come any closer, and we'll both jump,' he insisted, his hand opening the window, a gust of wind surging through the house, causing internal doors to simultaneously slam and the curtains to flutter. Mary remained silent, her tears cascading, her grandad pulling her closer. She heard someone in the hallway.

Please let it be the police. Where's Sergeant Swift? She said I'd be safe, so, where is she?

'What's all the—' began Martha, who walked in upon hearing the kerfuffle. 'Oh, Henry!' she said, tears chasing her words. 'Where've you been? We've been going out of our minds with worry. Are you okay? Are you hurt?' Martha innocently moved further into the room, unawares.

'Don't come any closer!'

'What's going on?' she asked, looking at Hank's worried expression.

'Dad's confused. He thinks we're out to harm Mary.'

'Henry, it's me, Martha. Please let her go. You're frightening her.'

'You're with them too, aren't you? They've sent *you* this time to try and trick me. Well, it won't work. I'm not letting you take her away.' Henry tried to shield Mary's body away from her parents. 'You came last time and hurt Lucy, I was too late, but I won't let you hurt Mary, not this time.' A look of confusion spread across Martha's face.

'What do you mean, Henry, that we hurt Lucy? Lucy's our

daughter, Henry, we would never hurt her. Lucy's missing, don't you remember?' Martha didn't take her eyes off Henry. 'Do *you* know what happened to Lucy? Do you know who took her?' All Martha's questions blurred into one muddled question in Henry's mind.

'I can hear their voices, the same ones that hurt Lucy, and now they've come back to take Mary,' Henry looked up at the ceiling, thinking he could hear footsteps. 'But I won't let them. I know Lucy's body is safe in the woods, so all I need to do now is protect Mary.' Henry's muddled stream of thoughts fought their way to the surface, elements of truth being spoken for the first time in years.

Martha began to cry and her hands were shaking, the words *Lucy's body* running through her mind. Her jaw quivered, along with every other nerve in her body. She immediately felt physically sick and all colour in her face drained in a second.

'Lucy's body? What do you mean Lucy's body? Oh God, is she dead? Where is she, Henry? Tell me, where's Lucy? I'm begging you, tell me where my daughter is.' Martha's entire body continued to tremble as she attempted to coax out the truth. She barely permitted time for Henry to speak before she pleaded again. 'Please, Henry, just tell me, is Lucy okay?' Martha couldn't breathe, a mixture of hope and fear working to steal her breath. Panicked and wanting to try and shake the information out of Henry, she attempted to move closer.

'Stay there,' he threatened, moving himself and Mary further towards the window. Martha froze like a deer in the headlights, obeying orders.

'For God's sake, Henry, just let her go. Look, she's frightened and you're hurting her.' Martha witnessed the look of fright on her daughter's face, her body becoming limp. Mary looked at her mum, the internal pain making her cry harder.

'You're scaring her, not me. I'm trying to protect her, don't you understand?'

'I'm her mother, Henry. She doesn't need protecting from

me.' Martha wiped her eyes before placing her hands over her heart. 'I beg of you Henry, just let Mary go.'

'You're trying to take her away, just like you tried with Lucy. But I didn't let you then, and I won't let you now.' Martha cried harder. She wanted to scream at Henry to let Mary go, she wanted to scream at him to tell her everything he now seemed to know about Lucy's disappearance.

'Oh God, Henry. What've you done?' cried Martha, shaking her head in disbelief.

Thinking he could hear more people approaching the house, Henry repositioned his arm around Mary, making sure his grip felt secure. He looked through the window, peering down to see how far he would fall. 'She's safe with me. I'll protect her.'

Hank stepped closer, his paternal instinct overriding all other emotions.

'Dad, you're hurting her. Look,' he said, witnessing the despair on his daughter's face, piercing pain stabbing Mary's insides. 'Please, just let her go, then we can talk.'

'She's crying because of you,' shouted Henry. 'You're both scaring her, sneaking up on us like this and trying to take her away. Well, I won't let you.' He kissed Mary on the head, failing to see her pool of tears on the floor.

'Just let Mary go, Dad,' Hank demanded, risking taking another step closer, his arms outstretched to try to squash any sense of threat.

'Don't come *any* nearer!' Henry shouted. 'I want you both to sit on the bed, *now*.' All Martha and Hank could do was obey, perching themselves on Mary's bed next to the wall.

The bedroom door opened.

'Henry?' said Elsie, who was now standing in the doorway. 'Oh God, Henry. Is it really you? Oh, thank goodness you're safe. I've been so worried, I've been going out of my mind,' she whispered, her tears running down her cheeks, her shaking hands trying to put on her glasses. 'Thank God you're home safe.' Elsie took a step towards Henry, wanting to wrap her arms around her husband, and never let go.

'Sit over there, next to them,' Henry ordered, looking at Elsie like she was a complete stranger.

'Henry, it's me, Elsie.' Elsie spoke softly, like she always had done whenever she knew that her husband was experiencing an hallucination. 'You remember me, don't you?'

Henry paused for a moment, frowning, scrutinising his wife's face for traces of familiarity.

'They've sent you too, haven't they? You want to take her away. How many more are there?' Henry looked out through the window and down on to the garden, certain he could hear more people on the roof each time the wind knocked the tree branches against the side of the house, the falling foliage clattering down the slates like footsteps. 'Close the door and lock it, then go and sit on the bed next to them,' he ordered.

Elsie turned the key in the lock, then took a place next to Martha, playing along, just like she had always done. 'There's nobody else here, darling, just us. We're on your side, Henry. So why don't we all hide under the bed until the bad men have gone? Because remember, they do go away, eventually, don't they?'

'He's said that Lucy's body is safe in the woods,' rambled Martha, her sense of helplessness causing her face to become saturated with tears. A pang of fear ripped its way through Elsie's body. Flashbacks to the day Lucy vanished coursed through her mind.

'Henry, when the men came before, did they hurt Lucy? Did they take her away?' Elsie too began to cry, her tears falling onto her lap, her shaking hands clasped together, praying. Elsie asked the question she'd already asked her husband a hundred times. 'Do you know where Lucy is, Henry?' Henry looked through the window and down to the woods.

'I did my best but they'd already hurt her when I found her. I was too late. I wrapped her body in a blanket so she wouldn't get cold, and hid her beneath the trees in the woods. I knew she'd be safe there. I didn't want them to take her away.' Martha's heart fell to her feet. An outpour of emotions broke through the surface, her harrowing cries ricocheting off the bedroom walls. Six years' worth of fear released from the depths of her stomach, the nesting birds outside fluttering away at the piercing noise.

'Oh, God, please don't let it be true.' Martha's body fell off the bed and crumbled to the floor. Hank jumped to his wife's aid, all colour drained from his face, his rocketing heartrate threatening a black-out. The sudden movement scared Henry. 'Get under the bed, all of you. Now!' Martha couldn't move, she felt paralysed. Hank reached out his arms and helped her to move, pulling her body across the floor and underneath the bed, a trail of tears scattered on the wooden floor. Hank could feel the fragility of his wife, her entire body trembling. Her head continued to shake in protest at the news she'd just heard, and her heart wavered.

Henry pulled a chest of drawers in front of them, dragging the cumbersome piece of furniture across the floor, blocking them in so that an escape wouldn't be quick or easy. Seeing the opportunity, Mary ran across the room, but Henry followed, turning the key in the lock and ushering her out of the door.

'Come on, Mary.' He kept a firm hold of her waist, slamming the door behind them and locking it.

Hank immediately pushed the drawers aside and scrambled out. 'Dad, let us out!' he shouted as he desperately tried to open the door. Martha got up and banged her fists against the thick panes of wood.

'Henry, let us out!' she screamed, pulling frantically on the handle. 'Help us, somebody help.' Martha fell to the floor. 'Oh God, please let her be okay, please let her be alright,' she cried, her body slumping up against the door.

Hank suddenly stopped struggling. 'He's taking her outside,' he announced, hearing the front door swing open and then slam shut. 'Move out the way,' he ordered, grabbing a chair and plunging it towards the bedroom door, the chair legs shattering beneath the force. He threw the chair to one side before thrusting his shoulder into the wood. Martha and Elsie gravitated to the window, now innocent spectators.

OUT BY THE lake, little could be seen beneath the reflection of the moon, the glimmer of electric light seeping down from the house offering limited advantage. Henry made his way to the dinghy, forcing Mary into the shabby boat before pushing it out onto the water.

'Hold on, Mary,' he instructed, his legs wading into the icy lake, his mind failing to register the freezing water despite it stinging his skin, sending his already weakened internal organs into the preliminary stages of shock and hypothermia. 'We'll be safe here, you and me together.'

Ambling into the boat, his hands plunged through the water, guiding it towards the far side of the lake. 'Let me know if you see anyone coming!' he instructed, his eyes scouring the surrounding wisteria, the foliage rustling in the breeze. 'I can hear them all, Mary, they're shouting your name. They're hiding in the woods, I know they are,' he announced, panic making his hands wade faster. Mary cast her eyes out over the surrounding woods, scouring for signs of the apparent invasion. But she couldn't hear anyone shouting her name, and she couldn't see a single person, let alone a group.

'Look, over there,' shouted Henry, pointing to some trees behind them when he heard a noise. 'They're surrounding us, they're everywhere.' Mary looked in the same direction, hearing the trees rustling beneath the breeze, but seeing nothing. She knew there was nobody there. The lake wasn't surrounded. There was only Mary and Henry present at the lake, nobody else.

Mary turned back and watched her grandad. She saw how scared he was, the terrified look on his face that wasn't going away. She began to understand that he was only trying to help; that's all he was doing. Her Grandad was trying to protect her from harm. This wasn't his fault. None of this was really his fault.

'It's just the trees making that noise, Grandad,' she replied. 'There's no one out there, I promise.' She played along with the hallucination. 'But, just in case there's someone hiding somewhere, we'll see them coming from here, won't we?'

After a few moments, Henry's frantic breathing began to slow to a more normal pace. But each time the breeze picked up, the noises echoing from the woods made him flinch and jump, his head spinning round, certain he was going to catch sight of his enemies once again.

'It's just the trees, Grandad,' Mary reassured, taking hold of his hands and stroking his skin, trying to ease the shakes taking control of his fragile body. To Mary, his skin felt soft, just like it had always done. His hands were giant in comparison to hers, just like they'd always been. When he spoke, his voice sounded familiar, like the Grandad she knew and loved. When she leant in close to his body, his clothes smelt just like they'd always done. Although Henry had accidentally hurt Mary back in the attic, whilst they were sat huddled together in the boat, he went back to just being Grandad.

'I'm glad you're home now, Grandad, to protect me from the bad men,' she whispered, recalling her grandma's instruction last summer of playing along with Henry's game whenever he was experiencing one of his 'funny turns', as Elsie would put it.

'They're hiding, Mary,' said Henry, 'but if we stay here, we'll be able to see them coming from all directions, won't we?' His eyes continued to dart to the left upon hearing an animal manoeuvre from its nocturnal nest.

The chill in the air made Mary shiver, the cool temperature helping to numb the sore parts of her body where her grandad had held on too tight. Her teeth chattered and even though she tried, she was unable to stop her jaw from jittering. Her heart raced as she sat beneath the darkness, seeing only her bedroom window illuminated in the distance, the shadowy figures of her mum and grandma loitering helplessly in the background. Mary didn't like being on the lake anymore, especially at night. Having already fallen in not so long ago, she now felt scared that it could happen again. She peered overboard and remembered how it had felt the time she had fallen into the dark, deep abyss. Her breathing raced, and it was like she was experiencing a panic attack. She imagined the water surrounding her, and how it had felt not to be able to breathe or see. She felt trapped. She wanted to jump and swim to the surface, anything to get out of the boat, but she was too scared. *What if the same thing happens again? What if I can't swim?* She kept on looking over at her mum standing in the attic window, wishing that she would come and get her. She willed her Grandad's funny turn to pass, so that they could paddle to the water's edge and all go inside and get warm.

'Grandad, I think the bad men must've gone by now. I think we'll be safe to go back to the house. What do you think?' Mary looked at Henry, his mind failing to register her words, too busy processing his thoughts of paranoia.

'Keep down, Mary, so they can't see you!' he instructed. Henry pushed Mary back onto the deck. 'They'll come for you; I know they will. They want to take you away, but I won't let them. I'll keep you safe, I promise.' He continued to use his arms as paddles, the boat navigating further across the lake, away from the house.

All of a sudden, Henry looked round. 'Did you hear that? They're coming, aren't they, Mary? I won't let them hurt you, I won't let them hurt you like they did to Lucy.'

'They're not coming, Grandad,' she declared aloud, sobbing harder than she'd ever done before. She led down on her stomach next to Henry, wrapping her arm over his torso, his arms still in the water.

'Grandad,' she began, her sobs and speech uncontrollable. 'I know what happened. I know what happened to Lucy. I know what you did. You were just trying to keep Lucy safe from the bad men, weren't you? You held her tight so they couldn't take her away. You waited until they'd gone, and then you took Lucy into the woods and hid her, didn't you Grandad? But there wasn't anybody coming,' Mary looked down and paused, shaking her head and crying so hard that her vision blurred. 'There wasn't anybody trying to take her away. You just thought there was. You held on to her too tight, like you did with me. You held her tight and now she's dead. Lucy is dead, isn't she Grandad? She's never coming back. Isn't that right?' her hysterics fell on deaf ears.

Henry made a sudden move, pulling Mary's body closer.

'I won't let them take you, Mary,' he whispered, hearing a banging coming from the house.

BACK INSIDE, HANK finally managed to break down the door. 'Thank God,' he shouted, the broken wood panel smashing to the floor beneath the force of his foot.

'Quickly! Run, Hank,' urged Elsie, who was still standing at the window, watching her husband holding onto Mary out on the lake. 'Before there's an accident.'

Martha chased after Hank. 'Call the police, Elsie,' she screamed. 'Now!' The pair flung themselves out through the front door. Wearing only their pyjamas, they scurried across the grass and down to the lakeside.

'Mary!' shouted Martha, running towards the lake, her voice echoing through the surrounding woods. Panic caused her to trip and fall flat on the ground, her front teeth puncturing her lip and impaling into the soft skin. 'Keep going,' she insisted when Hank stopped to help, witnessing the blood pouring from his wife's mouth. 'Go!'

In the boat, Mary stood up and waved her arms upon hearing the scream, watching Hank hurtle down the garden.

'Dad,' she shouted. The dinghy rocked off balance. Henry looked up before turning to grab Mary, the sudden shift in weight causing the boat to capsize.

Martha looked up. 'Oh God, Mary!' she shouted, wading into the freezing lake behind Hank, her mouth drinking in swathes of water. She spluttered to stay afloat in the perishing temperatures. 'Mary!'

Upon impact, Mary's shocked body tumbled down through the murky water, the freezing temperature attacking her core. Her limbs spun in a whirl, the ripples of water sending her plummeting. Henry tumbled in a faster cycle below his granddaughter, his weight dragging him deeper into the body of water. His mind suffered a seizure as soon as the bitter temperature penetrated. His delusional thoughts heightened, making him think the accident had been caused by his enemies.

His glasses fell from his face, the spectacles falling to the lake floor and embedding themselves into the soft silt. His fine, white hair swirled amid the undercurrent and his clothes drank in the water, the material becoming heavy, adding to the drag that was forcing his body further down. His limbs thrust in all directions, his hands reaching out, searching for Mary, still trying to protect her, right to the end.

His weakened lungs fought to conserve his breath, but his brain was too preoccupied by searching, so the inevitable happened.

'Mary,' he shouted through the darkness. And, as soon as his mouth opened, his body flooded with water. Both lungs filled to capacity, the drowning process depriving his brain of oxygen. 'Mary,' he mouthed one last time whilst taking his final breath, his arms remaining outstretched, his soul passing from one life to another. The water carried his body to the bottom of the lake, and Henry's limp, pale corpse nestled into the sandy bed, right next to his glasses.

Just above Henry's resting body, Mary fought to save her own life. She attempted to swim, her arms plunging through the water, trying to find a way to break through to the surface. Recent experience had taught her to never give up, and to thrash her legs, and not to stop until the surface of the water broke.

ABOVE WATER, MARTHA and Hank continued to head towards the boat.

'Find her, Hank,' Martha spluttered, the sound of her arms frantically plunging into the water awakening the surrounding wildlife. The birds nesting in the treetops fluttered away in unison upon being roused by the calamity occurring below. 'Can you see her?'

Hank treaded water, searching the lake before his body

disappeared beneath the surface, only to reappear seconds later, breathless and spluttering, trying to catch his breath.

'I can't see her!'

Elsie appeared on the edge of the lake. 'Henry! Mary!' she shouted, her shaking hand shining a light over the lake, the torch illuminating Hank and Martha, both taking it in turns to dive beneath the surface. 'Oh God, Mary...'

The surface of the water remained still, only the rustling sound of the surrounding trees breaking the eerie silence.

Then a breakthrough.

The surface of the lake exploded like an underwater, volatile volcano.

'Over there,' beckoned Elsie, witnessing the surface of the water breaking in the distance. Martha kicked her legs, dragging herself over upon hearing her mother-in-law's declaration of hope. 'She's over there!'

No sooner had Elsie spotted her, than Mary's weary body disappeared again, her heavy limbs unable to keep her body afloat. 'Oh, God. Quickly, Hank! She's going back under.'

Hank followed the reflection of the torchlight shining across the lake, immersing himself below the surface and scooping Mary's body into his arms, thrusting her head above the surface.

Martha reached the scene. 'Oh, God, is she alright?' she shouted, moving the hair that was covering her daughter's face. Mary's eyes remained closed. 'Mary! Mary! Open your eyes,' she cried whilst attempting to open Mary's mouth. Hank flipped his daughter's delicate body over. Mary coughed, her lungs releasing a plume of water.

'Mum,' she spluttered. Mary began to cry and her body continued to cough up water. Her lungs took in large gasps of air, her body drinking in the oxygen, filtering it out to every corner of her deprived system.

'Take her, Martha,' instructed Hank, handing Mary over before diving back beneath the surface. Martha struggled to swim to shore with Mary's limp limbs resting on her torso. Mary's head hung back on her mum's shoulder, the perishing temperature making their teeth chatter. Her lips had turned pale blue, and the feeling in her fingers and toes had disappeared, the nerves shocked into a temporary coma.

'Hold on, Mary, we're nearly there,' said Martha, fighting for breath.

Mary started to come around, realising that she couldn't hear Henry's voice. *Where's Grandad?*

Martha heaved her daughter up onto the bank. 'Grab her,' she instructed Elsie. Mary's body slipped back into the water as Martha's strength gave way. Elsie dropped to her knees and gripped onto Mary's freezing hand, dragging her small body up onto the grass before turning back and helping Martha.

'Oh, thank God!' Once out of the water, Martha grabbed hold of Mary, holding her closer than a newborn baby. 'Mary, are you alright?' she whispered. Their sodden clothes clung to their shivering bodies, aiding the process of hyperthermia. 'I thought I'd lost you, Mary. I can't lose you too, you're my world. You're all I have left.' Martha continued to hold her daughter in a consuming embrace, looking to the dark sky with relief and releasing a silent prayer.

Back in the water, Hank shouted out. 'Can you see him?' By this stage, his legs were struggling to keep his weary body afloat. His arms clung onto the boat and he pulled himself aboard. 'Dad!' he shouted. 'Dad!'

Elsie continued to scan the lake with her torch, the surface of the water calm, the breeze of the night taking shelter elsewhere.

'Henry! Henry!' shouted Elsie, her words becoming more desperate as each one was released. The sound of police sirens rang in the distance, in answer to Elsie's earlier distress call, the noise getting louder, the cars careering up the drive. A surge of officers got out and ran the length of the lawn, Sergeant Swift leading the pack. The helicopter above ripped through the tranquil lake, the search light shining onto the surface. Three divers were lowered down before disappearing beneath the water.

In the dinghy, Hank shielded his face, the force from the helicopter threatening to throw debris into his eyes. 'Thank God...'

Back on the bank, an officer asked his initial question upon his approach to Elsie. Mary remained cocooned within her mum's arms, their bodies entwined in a ball on the ground.

'How long as he been down, Mrs Lane?'

Elsie wanted to lie and say only a couple of minutes, knowing that they might call off the search if she was truthful. 'I'm not sure. Five minutes, maybe more.' Elsie's feet teetered on the edge of the lake, and she continued to call out. 'Henry, where are you?'

Her peach nightdress became caught up in the gust from the chopper, and she couldn't hear her own voice, her words becoming swept away. The officer went and stood next to Elsie, trying to guide her back from the edge, escorting her away from what was now a crime scene.

Swift walked over and placed her hand on Martha's shoulder. 'Martha, I think it's best that you take Mary and Mrs Lane inside.' Martha stood up. She pressed Mary's head into her body, ensuring her ears were protected, though she needn't have bothered; Mary already knew everything. Through a tumble of tears, Martha recited the words.

'Henry told us that Lucy's body is in the woods.' The white parts of Swift and Martha's eyes locked, a mutual look of horror appearing. Swift slowly turned her head, her eyes scanning the surrounding woods.

'Go inside, Martha,' ordered Swift before taking out her radio and pressing the button. 'We need more officers on the ground, now.' Hearing the order, a wave of shivers soared through Martha's body. She knew, once again, that the police were out searching for her daughter's body. 'We need to search the woods for a child's body.' Swift took a breath, swallowing deeply, pushing back her fears.

'Take her inside, now,' ordered Swift, looking down at Mary. 'Let us do our job.'

'Let's go Mary,' suggested Martha, turning to walk towards the house.

Despite being unstable on her feet, Mary refused to move. 'No. I won't leave until they've found Grandad,' she cried. 'He was trying to save me.' Mary then wriggled free and ran to the edge of the lake, her mum chasing. 'I won't leave him,' she cried, her body collapsing on the side of the bank, drenched strands of hair blowing across her face, the helicopter hovering above. 'He'll be okay when they find him, won't he, Mum?' she whispered. Martha wrapped her arms around Mary's quivering body.

The surface of the water broke and a diver appeared.

'We've got a body.'

Thirty-Seven

ITHIN MINUTES, AN ARMY OF BACKUP OFFICERS arrived at Wisteria. The notorious lake house once again became surrounded. Residents of Finchley stopped upon hearing the commotion. Some people looked out of their windows, watching all the cars as they drove down the private path leading to Wisteria. Each witness to the police presence asked themselves, *what's happened this time?*

Beneath the darkened sky, Swift instructed her army of officers.

'We're searching the entire woods surrounding this house. We're leaving no leaf, no stone and no patch of earth unturned. She's out here somewhere, and this time, we will find her.' The officers knew who their boss was referring to, Swift just couldn't bring herself to say Lucy's name, not yet.

In groups, her team descended into the woods, dog handlers forming part of the search party. Swift wasn't standing back on this one, waiting for news to come back to base. This was her case, and she wanted, needed, to be in the thick of the action. She owed it to Lucy to do everything she could to find her, even if it meant searching under every tree in the entire area with her own bare hands.

The chill of the night bit at Swift's exposed skin, her left hand shining a torch methodically across the forest floor as she entered the woods, her right hand moving aside dangling, outstretched branches. With her heart racing, her feet crunched over the carpet of forest foliage. She couldn't stop her heart from racing, or her mind anticipating what she was about to uncover. A sinking feeling brewed in the pit of her stomach, a feeling she tried her best to ignore. Specs of light flashed all around when each officer shone his or her torch in a different direction. Apart from the sound of footsteps, nothing could be heard. Nobody dared to speak. Nobody coughed. Nobody asked a question. The congregation of officers simply searched with a dignified silence.

Internally, as the search progressed deeper into the woods, Swift continued to beat herself up. *How could we have missed something?* she thought, her feet striding further into the woods, getting closer to the location of Lucy's grave. *We've search here before, and couldn't find anything.* She allowed her heightened instincts to guide her feet, instincts that rarely failed. She could hear her own erratic breathing, and felt sure that her accompanying officers could sense her emotions. One pace at a time, Swift scoured the ground, her boots carefully treading over debris only when she felt comfortable that nothing was hidden below.

After about ten minutes, she stopped. She held her breath and bent down. The moment she paused, so did her team, everyone thinking *Is this it? What's she found?* Swift ran her torch just a few inches off the ground, slowly inspecting the earth for signs of disturbance. She held out her right arm, running her fingers across the disturbed, moist forest floor, moving leaves and debris aside. She was getting closer; she could feel it in her bones. Unbeknown to Swift, she'd found the place where Mary had sat, having just discovered her sister's grave. Swift felt the tingle of apprehension, a feeling that often came when she knew a breakthrough was beaconing.

Back at Wisteria, the family remained inside, their shivering bodies huddled on the sofa. A silent sense of grief hung in the air like a volatile, black cloud. Elsie was still crying; she hadn't stopped since the moment the police had confirmed that Henry had drowned. A scattering of tissues lined the floor next to her feet, each one drowned with a precious memory. Her head remained bowed, her eyes admiring her wedding ring. A look of grief clung to her face, yet she felt unable to express her sadness. She thought about who she would kiss at the stroke of midnight on New Years Eve. She thought about how she would feel getting into an empty bed each night. She thought about who she would share her cup of coffee with, a whole cup having always been too big just for her. She looked at Henry's slippers by the side of the couch, a sense of vulnerability rattling through her bones. Elsie had known Henry all of her adult life, and didn't know how life felt without him by her side, ensuring she didn't fall during tough times.

For the first time in her life, Elsie felt lonely. She couldn't bear the thought of life without her husband, her best friend, and soulmate. She knew she'd have to say goodbye, and let him go. But the thought made her heart shatter, and so for a precious few moments, she pretended he was still missing; he was still out there somewhere waiting to be found. Then, when the time was right, and she could muster the correct string of words, she'd let him go, and say goodbye.

Even though Elsie knew the terrible thing that Henry done, she still loved him, and she always would. The same couldn't be said for Martha, who was sitting in the same room. Her thoughts remained with her missing daughter. She couldn't think about Henry, not yet. She sat in silence at the other end of the sofa, trapped in her own world. She knew Elsie was crying, but she was unable to register the sound. All she could think about was Lucy, and if tonight was set to be the night that her daughter would be finally found. In Martha's opinion, there was no time to mourn for Henry, not yet. In her mind, she was about to be faced with having to mourn the loss of her baby girl.

At the other side of the room, Mary tucked her knees into her chest, her body cradled in the single seat by the arched window. A blanket covered her cold limbs, her bones beneath still trembling.

Her mind flickered between thoughts of losing her grandfather, and thoughts of the police outside who were about to find her sister's grave. She knew the discovery wouldn't take long. Even beneath the darkness of the night sky, the recently disturbed earth at the gravesite would be spotted. It was only a matter of time.

Martha was the first to break the silence. She had begun to question what she'd heard, wanting to believe that it couldn't be possible. She wanted to believe that Lucy wasn't hurt. She needed to believe that her daughter's body wasn't waiting to be found.

'I heard him right, didn't I?' muttered Martha to nobody in particular. 'He did say that Lucy's body is in the woods, didn't he? I'm not imagining it?' Martha questioned her own sanity, her delicate mind wavering beneath the weight of the world which rested upon it. 'He said he was hiding her from someone who'd come to take her away, that's what he said, wasn't it?' Martha stared at the wall directly before her, not turning to pose the question to anyone directly. Hank looked over at Mary, her mum's words making her cry. He stood up and nestled himself on the seat next to her, placing his arm round her frame, holding her just tight enough to offer comfort, and protection.

'Why don't I take you up to bed? I'll get you a hot water bottle and tuck you up nice and warm.' Mary shook her head.

'I want to be with you. I don't want to be on my own. I'm scared.' Mary pressed her face into Hank's chest, hiding her face and tears.

'Of course, you're scared. I'm scared too, Mary. We all are.' Hank kissed Mary's head, inhaling the scent of her shampoo.

'What's he done to my daughter?' muttered Martha, still staring at the wall.

Grappling with her own initial waves of grief, Elsie replied, wanting to defend her late husband's name.

'Henry loved Lucy, more than you will ever know,' she began, looking across the room to her favourite photo of Henry. The black and white photo had been taken on their wedding day; a secret moment captured when neither the bride nor groom knew they were being watched. Henry was looking into Elsie's eyes whilst removing a leaf that'd got caught in her ivory, lace veil. 'All he would have done was try and protect her. He would never have done anything to hurt Lucy intentionally, not ever.' Elsie shook her head. 'He wasn't well. He really wasn't well.' Elsie hung her head, deeply regretting having not done more to try and help her ailing husband before it was too late. *Why didn't I take him to the doctors? Why didn't I insist? Why did I leave him alone? Why did I leave them alone with him?*

Hank passed his mum more tissues. He had no words to offer. He'd lost his father, and with no time to grieve, he was now facing the prospect of learning that he'd lost his daughter too. Like Martha, he thought back to every word his father had said, wondering if they were all misinterpreting. *He was confused. Muddled. He could have meant anything. Stay strong. Keep it together. They're relying on me.*

Then, Martha noticed the sudden change in brightness outside. She rose off the sofa and walked towards the window. She moved the net curtain aside with her hand before pressing her face against the glass. 'I think they've found something. The lights have gone out. They must've stopped walking.' Hank let go of Mary and walked towards the window, placing his hands upon Martha's shoulders, his eye's peering out through the glass.

'We don't know that, Martha.'

Mary didn't move. She just sat and thought about Lucy. She thought about what life was going to be like without her sister by her side. She anticipated her mum's reaction when Swift knocked on the door, ready to deliver the devastating news she herself already knew. Mary's body continued to shake beneath the blanket, her fear unable to be restrained. She thought about standing up and telling her parents what she already knew, what she'd found in the woods, wondering if it would help. But she couldn't speak. There were no words willing to leave her mouth. She didn't want to be the one who made her mum cry.

'I do know, I can just feel it,' Martha replied, her eyes refusing to blink. She spotted the flicker of light from Swift's torch as it broke through the woods, the light forcing her eyes to blink. 'I just know they've found her.' Martha released the curtain and dashed to the downstairs bathroom, leaving Hank alone in front of the window.

Outside, the search continued. Swift was now only a few paces away from the grave. She held out her right arm, signalling for those around her to stop. She stood still, shining her torch across the ground, noticing the way the loose shrubbery looked freshly turned. *Is this it?* she thought to herself. A sudden swell of tears formed in her eyes, providing her with an answer to her question. She took a breath before moving one pace closer. Her insides tumbled and her mind raced. The world around her paused. She couldn't hear anything in her periphery. The ambient, background night-time noises fell silent. All Swift could hear was the sound of her own heart beating. It was as if she was alone in the world. Nothing else, and nobody else existed. Swift shone her torch upwards, the three apple trees becoming illuminated. The gentle night breeze rustled the collection of lush green leaves, finally breaking the silence in Swift's mind. The pale green apples hung heavy on the branches, threatening to fall if disturbed with a heavy hand.

Swift positioned herself beneath the apple trees, noticing what she thought resembled disturbed earth. 'Nobody move until I say so,' she ordered, her colleagues looking on from behind, their breaths held in unison. 'And turn off your torches.' Like a light switch had been turned off, the area became drenched in darkness. Swift took two more paces, then paused. Her feet stood right on the perimeter of the disturbed ground. She took out some gloves from her pocket, pulling them over her hands one by one. She kept her eyes focused on the ground, working robotically to prepare herself before investigating the area.

She knelt beneath the apple trees, her knees embedding into the ground. She clipped a torched onto her jacket, freeing up both hands. With careful, delicate movements, she brushed aside the collection of loose leaves. Noticing the rock that Mary had placed at the gravesite, Swift took hold of the stone, gently moving it aside. Swift's eyes welled with tears. She fought back her emotions, unwilling to accept her deepest fears. Her breathing galloped, warm mist releasing from her mouth as she exhaled. In the distance behind the Cumbrian hills, the new day was dawning, the middle-of-the-night darkness becoming replaced by a lighter shade of sky, the stars disappearing from sight. Swift scooped handfuls of earth, placing them to one side. She didn't stop digging, knowing deep down in the pit of her stomach that if she paused, even for a second, she wouldn't have enough courage to continue.

Then, she felt something hard against her hands.

As she dug a little deeper, her fingers glided across part of Lucy Lane's skull, a tiny part of the eye socket just coming into view. The sight of the exposed skull stole Swift's breath right from out of her lungs. 'Please God, no,' she cried, closing her eyes. All the colour in Swift's face fell off her now ghostly features. Her head shook before resting on her shoulder, trying to protect her eyes. She forced herself to open her eyes, needing to make sure that was she had found was correct. The small cranium was visible, even through her saddened eyes, Swift knew exactly what she'd found. A piercing pain stabbed through her heart, the part that had been clinging onto the hope of one day finding Lucy Lane, alive.

She didn't move her hands. Her body froze. She tried to recall all her training, drawing upon her experience and forcing herself to deal with the heartbreak. But her mind went blank. All she could see in her mind was the photo of Lucy playing on the swing. All she could hear was Lucy's childlike laugh. All Swift was able to do was shake her head, knowing in the pit of her stomach that the search had come to a devastating end. She retracted her hands, remnants of earth clinging to her gloves. She hung her head and closed her eyes. After saying a silent prayer, a ritual she religiously performed whenever she uncovered a body at a crime scene, Swift made the announcement.

'I've found a child's body.'

After a six-year investigation, the search for Lucy Catherine Lane was finally over.

Her body had always been buried beneath the fallen wisteria.

Thirty-Eight

AFTER WHAT HAD AMOUNTED TO A FIFTEEN YEAR WAIT, today was set to be the day.

A tall lady of about five foot six stood alone watching the final preparations. Her name was Lizzie, and she was the first to appear. Across the main road from where she was stood, a hive of activity was unfolding. Wearing nothing but a plain white t-shirt, denim jeans and navy pumps, Lizzie's long, wavy, auburn hair fell past her shoulders, delicate ribbons of curls hanging in the centre of her back. Her hair was parted to one side and scooped effortlessly behind her left ear. She wore glasses; the kind of frames that didn't draw attention, but which suited her youthful face perfectly, adding an element of sophistication to her effortless appearance. A splash of freckles dotted her nose, a fine layer of pale gloss decorated her lips, and her cheeks were accentuated by the slightest blush. Her natural beauty turned heads, just as it had always done.

After a few moments of standing, nerves soaring through her body, Lizzie glanced at her wristwatch. It was now only fifteen minutes until midday. That meant it was nearly time. *Not long to wait now*, Lizzie thought to herself, her lungs taking in a deep breath. Whilst she waited, she leant against the wall and held onto her umbrella, the material of which was decorated with an array of brightly coloured wellington boots. Grey clouds scattered the sky, the ones which looked a little unsightly on a summer's day, but not which were unlikely to produce an unwelcome downpour. Lizzie glanced up and down the pavement, her eyes inspecting the trees to determine the strength of the wind. It wasn't a particularly breezy day. The conditions for what was to come were perfect; Lizzie knew that there would be no need to delay or postpone.

The police arrived not too long after. As expected, they worked fast to cordon off the main road; no traffic would be passing until the deed was done. They set a safe perimeter so that nobody would accidentally get too close, police tape soon crisscrossing the entire area. Lizzie scrutinised each officer's face as they passed her, eager to spot the person she anticipated would be joining the crowd of spectators. Summersaults swirled in Lizzies stomach the moment someone tapped her on the shoulder.

'What's going on over there?' the young chap asked as he walked past, spotting the heavy police presence. Lizzie didn't really want to talk, but she suspected that a suitable reply would get rid of the person quicker than if she simply shrugged her shoulders.

'The house is being demolished,' Lizzie took a glance at her wrist, 'in about 7 minutes.' The guy raised his eyes.

'Oh, I see,' he replied, before carrying on up the road. His nonchalant response made Lizzie conclude that the chap must've been new to the village.

Once the road was closed, the lack of traffic meant an unusual quietness descended over the typically busy stretch of A-road. Instead of hearing car radios blaring, screeching brakes and the impatient hooting of horns, an unfamiliar quietness hung in the air. But the peace didn't last for long because within a few minutes, Lizzie had company. To her left, a small gathering of onlookers appeared; some had come alone, whilst others were congregated in what appeared to be family structures; a mixture of generations huddled and chatting amongst themselves.

To her right, there was a bigger crowd forming, maybe twenty-plus people appearing at once. None of the faces that Lizzie spotted were familiar. Although time had moved on, and the faces of people will have inevitably changed, Lizzie felt certain that the person she was looking out for would be instantly recognisable to her. In Lizzie's opinion, this person had saved her life. Of course she would recognise her, she could never forget.

And then, after what life like a lifetime of waiting, it was time for the demolition to start.

The crane driver across the road adjusted his white safety helmet before inserting the key into the ignition. He waited for the signal which would tell him that he could begin.

'Let's get this started,' a voice announced through the driver's radio. The site manager standing on the ground looked up once he'd given his command, a show of thumbs up also acting as confirmation. A long-standing resident of Finchely, the driver of the crane didn't need to be asked twice - this was set to be his most enjoyable assignment to date. He manoeuvred his hands into the correct position, swinging round the demolition ball and taking an initial, devastating strike against the property that once belonged to Mr Perry Golifer. The sound of smashing glass and tumbling rubble could be heard across the length of the village, and beyond. If some people close by hadn't heard what was happening, they soon would.

Lizzie's body flinched when the pendulum struck for the first time, the brutality of the force striking a nerve that, despite having healed over time, would always, in part, remain raw. Her eyes welled at the sight of the first segment of bricks toppling, her hand plunging into her pocket for one of the many tissues she had placed there in anticipation. Her eyes followed the mighty steel ball, watching as it swung round ready to take another strike only moments later, this time crumbling the distinctive features that were once synonymous with the house. Her body trembled as she watched the building begin to crumble, the ghosts once trapped inside the house finally set free. She thought she could hear screams, but of course it was just her mind playing tricks. Spine chilling screams had once broken through the walls, but had long since been silenced.

Those onlookers standing alongside Lizzie released a simultaneous cheer when the last strike demolished every last brick of the property. Lizzie could hear some spectators crying, sobbing even, whilst others clapped. Out of the corner of her eye, she could see some people had their heads bowed, as if they were saying a silent prayer. Lizzie remained poker faced. She didn't cheer, nor did she heckle. But had someone been watching her closely, they would have noticed her prolonged intakes of breath, and her saturated, saddened eyes.

An invisible mixture of feelings swept through Lizzie's body. She felt elated that the house of horrors had finally been destroyed, knowing that she'd never again have to look at the house known to locals as Ivy Dean. But at the same time, whilst she watched the bricks tumble, her heart shattered into a million pieces. Memories that had haunted her for so many years, had once again been released. She lowered her head and closed her eyes, but the memories were still there, clearer than ever before. Lizzie could see the wall; the shrine. She could see the pictures of her and her sister everywhere. She could feel the warmth of Perry's skin. She could smell his tobacco breath, and hear his whispers. Her body flinched, the way it would whilst experiencing a nightmare.

'Do you know who bought it?' asked the lady now standing next to Lizzie. Still lost in her inner tangle of torment, the question fell on deaf ears, so it was repeated. 'Are you aware of who the property had been bought by?'

Without looking round, this time Lizzie replied. 'I don't, no,' she muttered without looking up.

'I have my suspicions,' the lady added, at which point Lizzie turned to look at the stranger who was engaging in conversation. Immediately, she knew the person's identity. The voice, although not at first, was now familiar. Her eyes hadn't changed. And although her hair was shorter, flecked with grey strands, her facial features hadn't altered greatly; life, it appears, had treated her well. Lizzie felt her heart pumping. She'd wanted to meet this very person for some many years, and now they were stood side by side. In Lizzie's opinion, the pair had so much to talk about. Lizzie felt overcome, and wanted to wrap her arms around the lady, whispering in her ear *thank you for saving my life*. Lizzie felt like she owed the lady so much, yet had never had the opportunity to express her gratitude.

Just like it had done with her, Lizzie waited for the moment of familiarity to announce itself to the stranger, and then maybe a reciprocated embrace would be forthcoming.

'I don't suppose we'll ever find out, and it doesn't really matter,' added Claire Swift, dressed in civilian clothing and accompanied by a shaggy looking dog. 'For all I care, they should've done it years ago,' she added, looking directly at Lizzie. Swift no longer lived in Finchely, and now worked for a different police force. After she uncovered the body of Lucy Lane, she had requested a transfer. She needed to escape all the ghosts that continued to haunt her in Finchley, and despite moving on with her life, after nearly twenty years she still couldn't help but take a second look at every child who she passed, an ingrained habit that would stay with her forever.

Sergeant Claire Swift often thought about the Lane family, wondering how they had dealt with the tragic death of Lucy. But she mainly thought about Mary, imagining in her mind how she would look as an adult. She had often thought about pulling a few strings, and finding out where Lucy was living, but had never picked up the phone and made the call. Had Claire realised the person's identity that she was now talking to, she would have flung her arms around Lizzie. Claire would have prolonged the long-awaited embrace, savouring every second. She would have offered to buy Lizzie a coffee. She would have asked her a hundred questions, and memorised each answer to recall at a later date. She would have held Lizzie's hand, and savoured the feeling of her warm skin. But above anything else, Claire would have been savouring a secret smile within, relishing how wonderful Lizzie looked.

'I agree,' replied Lizzie, still waiting for the stranger to acknowledge who she was. But Swift just shrugged her shoulders and then walked off up the road, soon out of sight. Lizzie's face remained flushed; a secret moment of excitement ignited within. She had passed her own secret test. For the first time in her life, she had gone unrecognised in Finchley; now just another face amongst a crowd. In Lizzie's mind, the reunion wasn't meant to be, and maybe it was for the best anyway, for everyone.

With a cloud of grey smog rising from the wreckage, the minimal breeze doing its best to encourage the dust to disperse, Lizzie crossed the road and made her way up the private path that led to Wisteria.

In the few months following her death, Elsie Lane's lake house had remained empty. After the tragic death of both her husband and granddaughter, Elsie had chosen to carry on living a shielded existence at her lake house. She was never seen in the village, and very few people dared to venture up the private track. With all the tragedies that had happened at Wisteria, people felt too intimidated to approach the now infamous house, a place where two people had been tragically killed.

Local residents speculated what would become of the property now that Elsie had passed away, knowing that nobody would ever want to live there. But the residents were wrong.

A new owner was about to move into Wisteria.

Lizzie emerged at the other end of the private track. She had commissioned a swarm of builders, roofers, painters, joiners and electricians to transform the entire property, and after weeks of renovations, the day for her to move in had come.

'Are we all done?' she asked the gardener, the only workman remaining on site.

'Yes. Everything has been completed that you requested. Here's the keys.' She held out her hand and took back the keys to the property which she now owned.

Lizzie took a moment to look up at the house. 'Many thanks,' she replied before watching the last van depart. She stood before the impressive four-story house, inspecting the frontage and taking a moment to admire her new home. It was still recognisable, but now, instead of the house hiding behind the mass of climbing wisteria, it had become accentuated by the pale lilac foliage.

Every one of the rotten window frames had been replaced, the disintegrating net curtains that had once covered the dirty glass now joining the mass of rubble that had been taken away in a skip. The new cream front door and matching guttering, garden lighting and an external *Welcome Home* door mat all served to bring the once crumbling house back to life. On the porch there were plant pots brimming with colourful, summer treats, and a collection of wicker chairs, perfect for admiring the evening sunsets.

Lizzie remained in the same spot out front, readying herself for taking that first step through the door. She took a few steps closer, half expecting her grandma to appear with a glass of lemonade in hand. The sound Lizzie's feet made as her shoes crunched over the stones stirred buried emotions, and for a brief moment she looked around. There was nobody there, just ghosts of old that would eventually find peace.

Lizzie placed the key in the front door and twisted, easing the tight-fitted wooden door from its frame. The waft of paint fumes was the first thing Lizzie's senses noticed. It felt emotional to be back, but a smile spread across her face as soon as she walked over the threshold. Once inside, she closed the door and pressed her back against it, allowing herself to become acquainted.

'I'm home,' she whispered to herself, placing the keys in her jeans pocket. The bright magnolia walls and polished wooden floorboards enticed her to venture further into the heart of her new home. She meandered to the left, the kitchen having been ripped out and now, instead of a single small window overlooking the spectacular lake, new double doors had been fitted which opened out onto the lawn and lake beyond. She ran her fingers across the new kitchen worktop before opening up the doors to the garden, a flurry of leaves and petals scattering around her feet as they were carried in by the breeze. The lake shimmered in the distance, the summer sun reflecting off the water and creating a mirage. A bunch of pale pink and white roses sat on the counter top, a card from her parents simply stating *We Love You xx*. Her parents didn't understand the new move, but knew to be supportive, life had taught them as much.

Lizzie sauntered from one room to another, the outdated

wallpaper once peeling off every wall had been replaced by pastel shades of paint. New furniture filled the empty spaces and vases of freshly-cut flowers sat decorating every windowsill. Soft furnishing throughout the house added a cosy feel to the interior; floral cushions, patchwork quilts and traditional bell-style lampshades made the house feel like a home. Sporadic family portraits could be found in every room, Lizzie's subtle way of acknowledging the heritage she never wanted to forget. Her favourite family photo hung in the lounge; a picture of Lizzie alongside her sister when they were younger. The photo was taken when the twin sisters had just turned four. They were sat in the bath tub together, probably on a Sunday night when it was known to be 'bath day.' A swath of bubbles covered their bodies, and bubble hats sat on top of their heads. Both girls were laughing, the kind of laugh that was infectious. Lizzie had strategically placed the photo so she would look at it every day, recalling nothing but happy memories of her and her twin sister.

Barefooted, Lizzie climbed the stairs, the new banister rail feeling soft beneath her hand, and the stairs no longer creaked beneath her slight frame. At the pinnacle of the house, the attic now boasted a spectacular view, the demolition of Ivy Dean meaning you could now see far and wide across the village, giving those who would be fortunate enough to stay at Wisteria the best view in the whole of Finchley. Lizzie had no plans of building a new house on the neighbouring land she had bought, land once belonging to Perry Golifer. All she wanted to do with her remaining inheritance was demolish the eyesore so that it could no longer be visible from Wisteria.

Outside the property, the transformation continued. Lizzie walked along one of the new stepping-stone paths that acted to connect the house with the garden, the woods, and also the lake. One step at a time, she snaked her way from the front door, all the way through to a newly constructed patio area in the private woods. The landscaped trees at either side of the path guided the way, and at night, below the glimmer of the moonlight, the path would become illuminated by dotted lanterns.

Flashbacks raced through Lizzie's mind as soon as the mature apple trees at the end of the path came into full view. The trees in question were now mighty, but their formation hadn't altered since the day that they were planted, decades ago. Lizzie delved her hand into her pocket, pulling out the silver bracelet that had belonged to her sister, plus her Grandad's gold wedding band. She had kept the jewellery a secret ever since the day that she had found them buried in the exact location that she now found herself standing as an adult.

Lizzie bent down, crouching next to the three small wooden plaques, the area where her sister's and grandparents' ashes had been scattered. She ran her hand over the surface of the wooden tributes, her fingers following the curvature of the words, the names Lucy, Henry and Elsie engraved into each. She could hear her sister's laugh, the infectious giggle that Lucy had never been able to control. Lizzie could picture Lucy skipping through the woods, kicking the wisteria petals until it rained lilac confetti. Lizzie could hear her grandad's voice and smell the distinctive fragrance of his cologne. She could taste her grandma's sweet, blackberry jam and homemade bread, a smile spreading across her face.

Mary Elizabeth Lane, or Lizzie as she was now better known, had inherited Wisteria. In the years before Elsie died, Lizzie had spent every single summer returning to Wisteria to stay with her ageing, fragile grandma. She and Elsie had passed the long, lazy summer days sitting next to the lakeside, sipping on homemade, fresh lemonade and eating heaping bowls of fruit crumbles. They would reminisce, revelling in some of the fond memories that Lizzie could recall from her childhood. They talked about Henry with frequency, and Elsie would share some of the funny stories she had from the time when they were courting.

Despite all the tragedies that had happened at Wisteria, Elsie witnessed for herself the connection her granddaughter had formed with the lake house, and knew that one day, it would be hers to keep as she wished. Lizzie never once blamed either of her grandparents for what had happened to her sister the day she died. How could she when she herself had experienced Henry's hallucination. She had witnessed how terrifying it was to believe that someone was trying to hurt the people you love. In Lizzie's mind, all Henry had done was try to save her sister. It had been a tragic accident. It had all just been a tragic accident.

Martha and Hank, both now in their early sixties, fifteen years sober and still married, had never once returned to Wisteria. Martha couldn't forget what had happened there, and neither could she forgive. In Martha's eyes, although Henry had been the one who killed her daughter, Elsie was just as much to blame. She had known how poorly Henry was, and yet kept the secret hidden. In Martha's eyes, if Elsie hadn't left her daughters alone with Henry that fateful day, Lucy would still be alive. And because of that, Martha and Elsie hadn't exchanged a single word since the day Lucy's body had been found. Hank had spoken to his mum over the phone during the years, but like his wife, he couldn't face ever returning to Wisteria. The image of his dad's body being hauled out of the lake, and the sight of the three apple trees where his daughter had been buried remained his constant shadow. There was nothing Hank feared more than ever having to return to his childhood home.

Upon reading Elsie's will, both Hank and Martha assumed that Mary, as they still insisted on calling her, would be desperate to sell the house. They felt certain that their daughter would want to free herself of all the haunting memories which, in their opinion, clung to Wisteria like disease. They thought that Mary would want to finally free herself of the burden of ever having to return to the secluded, tragic lake house.

But after fifteen years of searching, Mary Elizabeth Lane had finally found the place that she loved, and which she could call home.

The End